the
HONEYTRAP

Louise Lee was once a Geography teacher. When oxbow lakes no longer floated her boat, she took the next, natural step in her career progression and became a Private Investigator. Memorable cases include a high-functioning bigamist with three wives and six children, who was set to marry a fourth; and losing a target because George Clooney started chatting her up in a bar.

Louise undertook a MA in Creative Writing at Birkbeck, and has had work commissioned by and broadcasted on BBC Radio Four. Her debut novel, *The Last Honeytrap*, is the first in a series following the cases of Florence Love, a PI who specialises in entrapment.

If Louise's mum is reading this, the books are in no way based on her true experiences.

Honest.

LOUISE LEE

the Last
HONEYTRAP

headline

Copyright © 2015 Louise Lee

The right of Louise Lee to be identified as the Author of
the Work has been asserted by her in accordance with the
Copyright, Designs and Patents Act 1988.

First published in Great Britain in 2015 by
HEADLINE PUBLISHING GROUP

First published in paperback in 2015 by
HEADLINE PUBLISHING GROUP

1

Cataloguing in Publication Data is available from the British Library

ISBN 978 1 4722 2442 2

Typeset in Garamond MT Std by Palimpsest Book Production Ltd,
Falkirk, Stirlingshire

Printed and bound in Great Britain by Clays Ltd, St Ives plc

Headline's policy is to use papers that are natural, renewable and recyclable products and
made from wood grown in well-managed forests and other controlled sources. The
logging and manufacturing processes are expected to conform to the environmental
regulations of the country of origin.

For Callum and Lyra

Entrapment 101 Tip #1: Never be yourself

Be this woman instead, the one with a fabulous name – you choose, have fun with it.

Affect a show-stopping walk. Glide as though your head is being pulled up and away from your shoulders by an invisible rope. The postural device elongates the neck, flattens the stomach and makes saggy babaloos pert.

Pretend you're French. Acting French is the best entrapment tip ever. Yes, they can be flat-chested, with alarming teeth (see Vanessa Paradis). But by God, they can exude the most breathtaking allure (see Vanessa Paradis).

A rough guide to being Vanessa Paradis: put your copy of *Feminist Literary Theory* in the shredder. Your new bible is *Fatale: How French Women Do It.* Now ooze attainability and elusiveness in equal amounts, using only your eyes.

Practise on homely strangers. Oh, men aren't stupid, they'll see straight through it, but it's too tantalising a game – like football, or doctors and nurses, or punters and lap-dancers. Evolution has programmed them to play it, even when they shouldn't.

Always have a golden rule. This is mine: one kiss, with tongues, five seconds, case closed.

Finally, find your motivation. My suggestion: nobody should be duped into living a lie – whatever that lie may be.

The Human Zoo

The tongue in my ear belongs to the Dutch Minister for Security and Justice.

We are huddled in a dimly lit corner of the 101, an exclusive members' club in London's Mayfair. A popular haunt for the rich and famous, the bar has a discreet, almost diaphanous waiter service. Dark oak panels, cubbyholes, anonymous jazz – it's the perfect place in which to disappear.

Minister de Groot was hoping for such a night – quiet, uninterrupted, with just an indiscreetly plopped bodyguard for company.

The bullet-stopper is three tables behind us. I spotted him as soon as I walked in; talking to his wrist, feigning nonchalance. Gustav is his name, and although I can't see him at the moment, I can feel his eyes. They bore into my back like a wolf watching a cocky caribou, because quite uninvited, I sashayed directly to the bar and sat beside his boss.

He has no need to fret. Minister de Groot is the biggest fish I've ever had to sear; cocky I'm not.

Indeed, the minister took a while to bite, given his distinguished job, one in which he helps run the entire world. Yes, he humoured me, agreed to buy me a drink, but his chest remained pointed ahead, both hands defending a tumbler of Glendronach.

I put the minister's mind at rest. Played silently with my wedding ring. I have as much to lose as you, the gold band whispered up at him.

His eyes flicked north to my chest . . .

With the right posture and bra, I have an impeccable décolletage. A physically unappealing teenager, I deserved a little aesthetic luck. It arrived five years ago, when, without warning, my face and body fell into place. I was twenty-seven. For a year I watched myself blossom. To cement the good work, I studied the Alexander Technique and bought a biofit uplift bra.

Voluptuous yet chaste, that's what a guy said at the time. He worked at the post office, at the counter next to mine. *You're the type of bird men want to deflower; until you open your mouth*, he said. I've never been so happy – attractive at last. Alternative life choices cascaded like ticker tape.

Next Minister de Groot studied my face . . .

I would like to think it conveys intelligence. Not too much – my IQ would frighten them off – just a soupçon. Enough to reassure them: women like me don't end up in an underwear-clad kiss and tell.

They're right, I don't. That's not my style.

I doubt very much that the minister wondered about my current job, which is a shame. It could have saved him a whole world of shit. Plus from a personal point of view it's ever so nice when the target shows an interest in you. They rarely do. And that disappoints me, because I always show an interest in them.

Tonight, for example.

I asked about his accent, the purpose of his visit, his tie – Aspinal of London; he'd smoothed it flat, all proud like a tourist. This, an extraordinarily bright man who makes decisions on behalf of a nation, gooey at the groin because I complimented his neckwear – ugly neckwear with no practical purpose other than to point directions to his beef bayonet.

Yet as he stroked the paisley sliver of silk, he repositioned his knees to face me, a manoeuvre that speaks volumes – he was inviting his groin to join in the conversation.

4

Tonight was a goer.

Kinesics fact: human communication consists of ninety-three per cent body language and paralinguistic cues. That leaves just seven per cent for actual words, which are very easily manipulated; whereas body language is subliminal and extremely hard to fake, unless you're a Royal Marine or a psychopath.

The silent language, they call it, and I'm fluent.

I'd never visited Holland, I told the minister, not properly. The culture nevertheless fascinated me . . .

This gave him the floor – a luxury wives tend not to bestow – and throughout his soliloquy I giggled, asked pertinent questions and placed flirtatious fingers on his arm, each time counting to three in my head.

Touch test fact: if a date returns your touch within ten minutes, there is sexual chemistry. On a successful first date, there will be three sets of touching, three seconds apiece.

Tonight there were eight.

By 9.53 p.m. the minister had slow-danced me away from the bar and into a booth. Here he ordered champagne, homed in on my neck and wheedled a route to my ear.

That's where we're at now.

And although I'm satisfied with my success so far, I've had quite enough of my ear being licked. Women like me, however, have a game to play. We titter inanely. We stroke the pride of unprincipled men. We remind ourselves constantly that this job is a worthy way to make a pound.

Or in tonight's case, thousands of the little buggers.

The minister had assumed we'd be making our way to the Mayfair Hotel. The Schiaparelli Suite, to be precise – that's where he generally takes his conquests. It's a shame really. According to the literature, the suite is named after the designer who first unleashed fuchsia on a glamour-starved world. Antique Chinese art, pink pony-skin bed dressing, I'm sorely tempted to pop along just to have a peek.

Trouble is, I have a very strict rule. Never go back to theirs on a first date.

There's a further rule too. Don't shit on your own doorstep.

Here my brother helps me out. Lets me shit on his. Though I'm mindful not to put him in danger. Michael and I are professional partners, yes; but first and foremost I'm his big sister – it's my duty to look after him.

My brother's only rule: *never* touch his stuff.

He has a touch of the OCD.

Yet the look I'm going for is *sinuous* and *alluring*; it's imperative I finger ornaments and stroke the frames of black and white photos.

One of the frames contains a photograph of our mother.

Bambi, everyone called her. Because the world left her simultaneously startled and astonished? No. I caress her frame a little longer than the others. Because she was Italian and that was her name.

Women like me usually hide evidence of their identity. Especially photos of their mums. But mine's in no danger. It's been twenty-five years since we saw her last – if I can't find her, nobody can.

'Minister de Groot,' I swivel Bambi so she's facing the wall, 'a sensible offer, please.'

The minister is animated. His original assumptions about me were wrong.

'A woman of the night,' he is saying. 'I had no idea.'

I am not.

'I'd have got down to business sooner . . .' looking through his wallet, pulling out one card after another, plumping finally for an Amex, which he proceeds to glide up and down my arm as if icing my bicep.

How many working girls back in Holland have credit-card machines? I wonder.

'Five hundred,' he says.

'Excuse me?'

'For the night. Five hundred pounds.'

I scoff.

Were I to sleep with a man for money – which incidentally hasn't happened and never will – it would be for a good deal more than five hundred quid.

'Six hundred, then?'

That doesn't warrant a response. I know the minister's paid five times that in the past. He tells people he was Maurice of Nassau, Prince of Orange, in a previous incarnation – throwing money at sexually charged serfs plays to his megalomaniacal streak. Though I'm informed that he errs towards the high-class hooker, it being safer. In a fortnight they make the same as your average tabloid exposé, so selling a story makes no business sense. Sometimes, too, prostitutes are rather nice to talk to. Unlike his wife they simply listen and nod and groan as if he's the most desirable man they've ever had to fellate.

Yes, a good old-fashioned, no-strings business arrangement suits the minister right down to the ground.

Look at him now, I smile despite myself. He thinks he's at a charity auction.

'Seven hundred!'

Pushing my chest against him, I half-whisper, 'You get what you pay for, Minister de Groot.'

I'm rather pleased with how that comes out. Counterfeit sexiness can sometimes fall flat on its face, the naff words left hanging in the air like a ring of Stilton. In this instance, however, my timing and tone are consummate.

Even the minister does a half-clap. 'You drive a hard bargain. I like it. I like you, Isabella.'

My name is not Isabella.

I use it because it conjures images of ball-tingling eroticism and Latin fire. I stole it from a girl I went to school with. Isabella Purdy-Valentine. Her parents had really given that thought – the boys got erections just hearing it read out at registration.

Minister de Groot has an erection – it follows me around the room like a dowsing rod.

'Nine hundred? Come on, Isabella, that's an awful lot of money.'

I wholeheartedly agree. It remains, however, some way off Robert Redford's very decent proposal of one million dollars.

My eyes twinkle as I smooth imaginary creases from my hips. 'A lot of woman, Pieter, requires an awful lot of money.'

Momentarily I forget to slink as I move back to the shelving unit and reposition a hefty book: *Family: Nature's Masterpiece* by Dr Dan Halliday.

Were the minister to peruse this hardback, he'd see that on the front cover it says: *The nuclear family – a definitive guide to happiness.*

That's quite a promise.

He won't pick this book up, however. Men never pick up self-help manuals once their brains have slithered south.

My first husband, now he did a lot of thinking with his genitals. Eureka moments, if you like, and they struck in the most unexpected of places, my best friend being one of them. I actually caught them at it, yet still they maintained an indignant astonishment, as if I'd accused them of something implausible, like ram-raiding or starting forest fires.

He admitted his infidelity finally, though put the blame squarely in my court – I had become complacent, he told everybody; let the sexual fervour dwindle. Oh, I fought my corner. *I'm just a bit shy.* But guys kept their distance for a while after that, the least attractive trait in a woman being sexual sloth.

Tonight my smile promises filth.

'Isabella, Isabella. You're bleeding me dry.'

I certainly am not.

'Fifteen hundred?'

'Better.' Secretly I look up his nose. The man's face is fleshy and wrinkled as a Shar Pei puppy, yet he has not one strand of nasal hair – for all his faults, I like that in a man, bald sinuses.

Husband Number Two was extremely hirsute. In the nude he looked like he was wearing a gorilla suit without the head. I married him on the rebound. He felt such a safe bet. Friendship surely had to be the most sensible basis for an enduring marriage? Turns out that obsessive animal passion that refuses to dissipate is the more effective ingredient.

Three years of marriage and still it remained awkward in the bedroom – we went at different tempos: slow rumba and disco beat.

My second husband held me a little responsible. Men don't want to marry their sister or best friend, he told the marriage counsellor. And he was right. They'd rather opt for eternity with a domesticated whore.

Bent over, checking the contents of my handbag, my face is flush with my knees. This position is called a Standing Forward Bend, or Uttanasana for the purists. My life coach taught it to me. It is supposed to evoke mental calmness, stress reduction and body awareness. Today it provides Minister de Groot with an opportunity to leer at my arse.

I give him a better view; lean against the windowsill, look out on to Greek Street below, its pavement a twinkling strip of eateries, its hum as magnetic as an electric fly trap. Leaving life above ground level to dissipate clandestinely into the night – which is why so many of the top flats in this street are walk-ins, the walk-in being a provider of legal prostitution. There's one just across the road, nesting above the seductive rouge of a Lebanese restaurant.

I look back down at the street – holding gently on to the sill because I suffer a smidge of vertigo – and peruse bald patches, ponytails, the roof of a black Bentley Continental Flying Spur, the minister's bullet-saver leaning against the driver's door.

Unblinking, he stares back up at me. His look is one of repugnance.

Total fact: it should be one of marvel, because I know an awful lot about him . . .

His full name is Gustav Aart Nijstad, and he is one of perhaps twelve people in Holland who cannot speak English better than the English. Maybe his non-bilingualism is a deliberate show of patriotism – he is an extraordinarily dedicated employee of the Netherlands government, and particularly of Minister de Groot. His job is to accompany and guard his protectee to the death (his own), which he'd do in a heartbeat if only someone would just launch an attack. When not waiting for assassins, however, Gustav can find himself sitting outside hotel rooms and walk-ins. Naturally he is bound by a contract that ensures the minister's frolics remain top secret. The contract is, however, unnecessary. He'd triple-jump into hot oil rather than compromise Pieter de Groot. In fact if Gustav had any friends, they'd take the piss, say he had a crush on his blubbery boss; and he'd shoot them in the head because Gustav's so far in the closet, he's emigrated to Narnia.

I am well apprised. Then again, my contact is excellent.

Look at him – I give the bullet-saver a finger wave. His chin strains up at me, at his beloved boss somewhere in the room behind me; he reminds me of a lovelorn meerkat.

Spinning back around, I sit on the sill, my back against

cold glass, and issue the minister with a thin, honest smile – because Pieter de Groot is living on the edge. Unlike Gustav, I have not signed a contract. Well, I did once, when I started at the post office, but that was ten years ago and unless Minister de Groot was mentioned in the small print, I'm pretty sure I can say what I like to whomever I like.

Silly man.

Minister de Groot moves at me, grabs my waist, manoeuvres me towards the hall as if I'm a delightfully petulant child.

'Fifteen hundred it is then,' he says, no-nonsense. 'Let's take this to the bedroom.'

There is one bedroom in the apartment – my brother's room, a no-go area, always. As a matter of damage limitation I pull the minister on to the sofa. The weight of his stomach drives every drop of air from the scatter cushions beneath me, scatter cushions I should *always* place in a tidy stack against the wall – extremely important rule.

Now the minister rediscovers my ear.

'Two thousand.' I push him out of my neck. 'But you can't stay the night,'

'Done.' His smile is triumphant. 'I'd have given you five.'

I maintain my cool. Not one penny will change hands this evening, yet I feel duped, totally duped – the minister now considers me a bargain.

'So, Minister. Have you done this kind of thing before? You know . . .' I spell it out, 'paid women to sleep with you?'

He is thoroughly amused. Rearranges himself. My internal organs sigh with relief.

'And why, Isabella, do you ask?'

'Because I've met many men like you, Pieter. Rich men. Powerful men. Extremely famous men. And it never fails to fascinate me – the indiscretions of such *commanding* individuals as yourself.'

I slap his bottom hard and summon a look that says: Tell me how despicable you are, because, by God, I fucking love it.

That look has taken some work.

His shrug is indulgent, unrepentant. 'I'm a very bad man. I have an uncontrollable penchant for working girls. And you, Isabella, are one in a rather long line.'

'You disgust me.' My smile is genuine. 'Tell me more.'

His confession is elaborate and depraved. Now and then he dry-humps my thigh, but mainly he concentrates on telling me filthy secrets. I can see he's enjoying this bit the best. And as his admission gathers momentum, it dawns on me. How remarkable that it took me two failed marriages to work out a simple universal truth – that strange is erotic.

Once aware of this truth, other truths became apparent. Like, the institution of marriage is flawed, as is monogamy, as is truth and respect and honour, because at some point a less attractive person, dim-witted, maybe unkind, will turn your partner's head. In the black of night he'll be pretending your shoulder blades, the small of your back, your buttocks are hers. And it will be for one reason only. She is *not you*. Anything that is *not you* will be sexier. Because strange is so bloody erotic, it makes a mockery of love, leaving marriage as the cruellest joke ever.

The minister's confession over, I watch him fumble with his belt – he is ready to seal the deal.

Hurry up, I beg of my brother, because he's cutting it fine.

And when, at last, I see him come into the room, I scream; not too loudly – the neighbours might knock – just loud enough for Minister de Groot to stop unbuckling and look up from the sofa.

'Fuck,' he shrieks, because a man of baby-giraffe proportions looks down on us.

My brother's name is Michael, after St Michael the

Archangel. Six feet two, twenty-eight years old, lateral muscles like folded-up wings. Erudite-looking, singularly benevolent, a total mix between Noël Coward and Lennie Small (the mentally impaired lovable murderer in *Of Mice and Men*) – only my brother is strawberry blond, with a beautiful West Country lilt, its undulating song as familiar as the Purbeck Hills, if you're from Dorset.

He's also a very mediocre actor, so even I'm surprised at the menace with which he says, 'You are squashing my fucking cushions.'

Bewildered, the minister flies to his feet, half holds out a hand.

Formalities don't interest Michael. He's in character – the aggrieved husband. Revolted, he glares at the stranger in his living room whilst pointing a rigid finger in my direction.

'She's a married woman,' he spits.

Technically this is true. Though I haven't seen Husband Number Two in years, he's no doubt looking for me. Eager to untie the knot and retie it with some domesticated whore he picked up in Poole. Well, he can look for me all he likes. I intend on doing her a favour.

'You're married?' The minister looks at me, sickened, like he didn't notice the ring; and I in turn shrug at the unfaithful father of four, because mine is a very long story.

Not that he's interested. They never are.

He simply holds his hands aloft as if Michael is pointing a gun and gestures desperately at the door with his chin.

Let me live, the minister's eyes beg.

But Michael has first to sob at me, 'How could you do this?'

My heart sinks for him. He's never landed an acting gig. Years of drama school and Michael still struggles with angst.

The minister doesn't notice – he's too intent on squeezing

a route past him and out of the front door, back to his trusted Gustav.

There is no backward glance from Pieter de Groot. No request for my telephone number. No plan ever to meet in the future. Categorically I will never see the Dutch Minister for Security and Justice ever again.

In the silence of the living room, my brother and I look at one another and sigh.

He picks up a scatter cushion as though it's a dead dog.

Quickly I fetch my purse. 'Buy yourself some more.' It's time to spend a little time chivvying him along, because although Michael's been bursting in on me for a year now, he remains his own harshest critic.

Sitting on the sofa, I tap the space beside me.

'Brilliant timing, partner,' I nod.

He brushes fresh air from the coffee table. 'I was total litter. A chimp could do better.'

'A chimp couldn't bring the performance element, though, could it? *How could you do this?* You've been practising, right?'

He straightens his smoking jacket. 'I'm trying to use my own emotions and memories.' He squints, tries to recall what it said in the textbook. 'I'm developing my internal sensory abilities.'

'Sounds hard.'

'It is hard.'

'It's paying off, though.'

'Yes, it is,' he says without modesty. 'It's important to consider the character's motives; to identify with them. That's what Christian Bale does, and Dustin Hoffman.'

'And the smoking jacket?' I neaten up its velvet lapels, like a mum.

'I'm using the Method,' he explains. Then his eyes become wide. 'Do you fancy sushi?'

I punch his thigh. 'Totally.'

14

The ephemeral nature of his thoughts.

Michael can feel a moment so passionately, only to discard it one second later in favour of a new, more intriguing one. He's always been like that. The teachers at school were disconcerted by him – Sister Angela, whose nerves he frazzled regularly, once told him that his educational needs were special. He had been extremely sorry about the fact; had shaken the nun's hand. Thirty-nine on the autistic spectrum sounded woefully low – he'd try harder next time.

Mum called him special too, because the fleeting heartfelt moments were the very best of all, she told him earnestly. Certainly they're the most truthful – they've had no time to tarnish. Asperger's, my elbow, she said. Michael was just extraordinarily unique.

I smooth the hair from his forehead. 'Sushi it is. But first I've got to do my stuff. You hoover. Then we'll eat and close this case.'

We're too old to high-five really, but we perform one with gusto.

Midnight.

The vacuum cleaner roars into action and I move to the bookshelf, carefully pulling free the self-help book, *Family: Nature's Masterpiece*.

Its author, Dr Dan, was the relationship expert on a morning programme. The picture on the front cover shows a congenial and wise man – bald as a bowling ball, a moustache like a yard broom – who has changed the lives of a million Britons.

I open the hardback.

There are no pages inside. The book's not worth the paper it's written on. Dr Dan was later outed as an unethical businessman who abused his wife. I didn't feel so bad then about cutting up his life's work, replacing the sanctimonious pages with a wireless unit the size of a deck of cards.

The camera's a great bit of kit – sixty-two-degree view, three-eighty TV line quality, powerful built-in microphone, the lens peeping through an imperceptibly small hole in the book's spine.

There are also pinhole cameras in my handbag and the smoke detector above the sofa.

In the wrong hands, the DVD of tonight's proceedings could destroy the minister professionally. Political ruin, however, is not my client's intention.

I'm not hungry, but I eat – Michael loves watching me gorge on makizushi whilst congratulating him on his culinary skills. Afterwards I download the DVD of tonight's proceedings, though not before turning the photograph on the shelf back around.

I look into my mother's eyes – they're wide as coat buttons – and I wonder if the world remains a riddle to her. Assuming, of course, that Bambi Love still inhabits it.

Two a.m.

My client waits for us in the lobby of the Knightsbridge Hotel in Chelsea.

Michael and I sit at the lights on the King's Road; me in the passenger seat, Michael at the wheel tapping imprecisely to the radio – it's free jazz, the genre of music that accompanied late-night US shows back in the seventies. The ones about talk-show radio DJs who worked on the suicide shift; and the cop shows; and the shows about serial killers with telescopes who lived opposite women who perpetually undressed for bed. Their soundtracks were always a funky fusion of lonely and sinister jazz. Like the music out of *Dirty Harry* – Lalo Schifrin was the composer who wrote that score.

I look out of the car window.

Soundtrack fact: one day, Lalo Schifrin will write the music to my life too – something experimental and timeless, fifteen or so tracks, the dominant theme a driving percussion and restless electric bass. Assuming, of course, he's not dead by then.

To stop Lalo Schifrin from being dead by then, I do a secret sign of the cross – scratch my temple, fiddle with a button on my jacket, pick dust from the left shoulder, straighten the right sleeve. I have to perform it secretly because I don't *do* God. Plus Michael would join in because he does do God, religion being a far comfier option than scientific truth.

I am saying Amen with my eyes when I spot the Jiffy bag in the footwell – inside is tonight's ensemble of video footage and still shots.

It'll be a simple handover. Nonetheless, I dread this bit. I imagine the client's face – the nausea as she flicks through her husband's holiday snaps – and my stomach slumps.

Noticing I've gone quiet, Michael gives me a dead leg.

'It's your birthday next week,' he tells me, all mature.

I rub my thigh and stare at a teenage couple frantically kissing against a street light.

'Bet they're French.' I point.

'Flo, you have to celebrate. We could go to a club or a bar.'

'Sounds like a busman's holiday.'

'Good,' he says, satisfied. 'I'll invite Sébastien.'

'Yay,' I mumble. 'I'll spend my birthday playing gooseberry at PDA Central.'

But public displays of affection are Michael's speciality. He's too faithful to the moment, *way* too unconcerned with diplomatic social etiquette – just like the French teenagers, who are currently kissing like it's a life-or-death situation.

'Do you think he's trying to get gum out of her gullet?'

Michael becomes concerned. 'Shout out of the window, Flo. Tell him to use his fingers.'

'I am actually doing a sympathy heave.'

'Me too,' says Michael, even though he's not.

Flopping exhausted back into my seat, I explain birthday facts.

'A quiet night in on my own is just the job – when you get to twenty-nine, it's rude to keep counting.'

'You'll be thirty-three.'

'It is *infinitely* more rude for you to keep counting. Let me just be on my own. I'll watch a film or something – *Sleepless in Seattle, Gone with the Wind*.' I mouth at the French lovers, 'Something romantic.'

'*PS I Love you*.' He makes this suggestion because he once bought me this book. I've not read it, though he doesn't know that. As far as he's concerned, I thought it a corker of a read.

The light turns green.

I continue to spy on the French lovers in the wing mirror until their pumping heads shrink from view.

The reflection doesn't stay empty for long.

A black Triumph Scrambler trails ten metres behind. I squint into the side mirror, then turn around. Through the rear window I see only black leathers and a loud pelmet of white-blond hair; his tresses sprout from the helmet's sides and back like a wacky hi-vis accessory.

Scientific blondness fact: gentlemen might prefer them, but blonds have nothing whatsoever to be proud of. They suffer a deficiency of eumelanin, the dark pigment in hair. And on the Fischer-Saller scale of blondness, the motor-cyclist behind would be ranked a paltry B.

That's virtually albino.

I, on the other hand, am full of eumelanin. Like Pocahontas. That's what a homeless drunk called me when I first arrived in London, three years ago now. A rucksack on my back, a rolled-up private investigations diploma in its side pocket – an online course for which I achieved a hundred per cent.

I was a wide-eyed newbie to the Big Smoke.

The tramp was sitting on the steps at Paddington train station. *Oi, Pocahontas!* He shouted it with considerable venom. White spit coagulated like spunk in the corners of his mouth. Yet I smiled and waved back as if I were indeed she, because Pocahontas was very beautiful in the cartoon. In real life, not so much. I looked her up on Wikipedia.

The Triumph Scrambler behind us growls, speeds up, overtakes slowly. I watch it, watch the motorcyclist pass Michael's window. Instinctively I pick up the Jiffy bag, put it inside my jacket, under my armpit.

There's no need.

The flaxen-haired rider doesn't glance in at us, at me, at it – he seems aware only of the road ahead.

The Naked Woman

We lie on our tummies watching *Charlie's Angels*. Bambi and me. She feeds me frittata with her fingers, which is called 'damage limitation'. Damage limitation is when my mum watches TV and uses the tips of her long nails to move food from plate to tongue, direct.

No crumbs.

Very important rule.

Mum nods at *Charlie's Angels*.

'They're even sexier in Italy,' she whispers, like we're at the cinema.

We're not at the cinema. It's just her and me in the living room watching repeats. And if Dad were here, he'd be telling her off.

'Sexier' is not age-appropriate, he'd say.

But I'm growing up too fast for Dad. He forgets I'm seven and a half now. So when my mum says *sexier*, I make sure I giggle with gusto.

But she shushes me sharply. 'Florence, you'll wake him.'

Him.

Michael is asleep upstairs.

Three and a *total* pain, my brother is always good and always quiet and always not wanting for much.

The trouble is I was here first.

'Did every country have their own *Charlie's Angels*?' I ask my mum.

She shakes her head as if I'm mad. 'Same women, different voices.'

'I knew that.' I nod maturely.

'It's called dubbing,' she says.

'I knew that too.'

'*Bugiardo*,' she smiles, without taking her eyes from Farrah Fawcett, her pointy talons still pushing eggy potato at the back of my throat.

Different language fact: *bugiardo* means liar in Italian.

I laugh, with gusto, very quietly.

The jokiness between me and my mum is our secret thing. Dad works at the post office so doesn't have much time to be funny. Michael's three, so hasn't grown a sense of humour yet. But my mother is *hysterical*. Not with anyone else. Just with me. With everybody else she's totally shy.

She is also very beautiful. Exactly like the olden-day TV detective programmes she loves to watch.

I spy on her face now.

Her eyelashes, hair and eyes are the colour of dark chocolate. Her skin is pale – the exact shade Mediterranean people would go if they'd been kept in a cellar. Mum hasn't been kept in a cellar. She just keeps herself to herself.

Especially she loves these shows because she watched them back in Monte San Savino, which is in Italy, which is where she's from. She dreamed of becoming a policewoman when she was a little girl. Her grandpa had been one. Not a policewoman, but a *poliziotto* which is policeman in Italian. But he got killed on the job, and future relatives were banned from following in his footsteps because Italian mothers are terrible worriers when it comes to getting murdered.

So Bambi was waiting for Michael to grow up. Then she'd go out to work – secretly – as a private detective, and only I would know about her double life.

Bambi had told me her crime-fighting plans in full.

'I'll wear such stylish cords, Piccolina. Flared at the hem, fitted around the backside, with a tight polo neck that makes your boobies look like upside-down Cornettos.' More than anything Mum wanted a pointy pair of boobies.

The frittata finished, she now uses her nails to tickle my arm. It makes me do a love sigh – that's what you call them, those big, contented sighs that arrive very suddenly.

'When I'm old, I'm going to have nails exactly the same longness as yours,' I tell my mum.

'Not a little longer?'

'No, I like your longness.'

'And I like your style.' She nods at the television. 'Now watch while we can.'

Other repeats Bambi loves to watch:

Cagney and Lacey.

Magnum PI. (He's sexier in Italy too.)

Hill Street Blues.

Chips.

Thanks to Mum, I'm learning a lot about murder. In America, gun crime is through the roof. *DOA* means dead on arrival. *Perp* means the bad guy, and so does *psycho,* and *mutt,* and *mope.* An ambulance is called a *bus.*

Michael stirs upstairs. Mum does a pretend groan. Mine is totally real. But for a minute or two Bambi pulls me into her chest and we pretend we didn't hear a thing.

We pretend it's just us.

I finger her necklace – a little golden chilli. It hangs from a yellow chain that's as thin as a thread of silk. But it's not an actual chilli, it's a *cornicello*, which is an Italian lucky horn that scares off the Evil Eye. I'm not sure who the Evil Eye is, but he harms mothers and their babies, according to Italy.

Michael's gurgles continue, because he's inconsiderate like that. And I know it's wrong, but sometimes I wish it was just me again, just for a few weeks here and there, without all those cute noises – they're totally distracting.

'It's Saturday tomorrow, Piccolina.' Mum cups my ears and makes promises. 'We'll watch *The A-Team*.'

My mum is a mum of her word. But I don't say anything back, because I'm deliberately punishing her. This is what grown-ups do when they feel hard done by. (I've watched them do it hundreds of hundreds of times. I've written the technique down in my secret detective notebook.)

'Mr T is *much* funnier in Italian.' She flicks my nose. 'That's a fact.'

But I'm fantastic at the silent treatment, so I stomp furiously into the garden. Only when I'm sure she's not looking any more do I skip excitedly towards the Yellow House.

The Yellow House is a cabin in a patch of woodland at the back of our garden. It has a ladder with thirteen wooden steps – which is quite a climb when you're seven and a half, and a girl, and you suffer from vertigo, which is a phobia. But luckily I'm brilliant at it. I pretend I'm in a film and getting to the top is a matter of life and death.

The Book of British Birds sits on the wooden-slatted floor. Bravely I kick it away, because there's a lot of fly corpses on the cover and they're crunchy like Coco Pops. Then I slap my thigh like a proper cop and sit open-legged on an upturned bucket.

There's a notepad hidden inside a crisp packet in the corner. My red plastic binoculars are on the windowsill. I clean their lenses with my sleeve.

Binoculars fact: you have to look through the right end, otherwise everything looks really small.

Binoculars pushed tight into my eye sockets, I twizzle the focus, squint through the lenses. I look into our cottage, in through the kitchen window.

Deep inside my tummy I feel a happy tickle. Michael is sitting on the kitchen worktop, a flowery tea towel across his chest, its edges tucked tightly into the neck of his jumper

23

as if Mum's going to give him a haircut. She's not: she's protecting his clothes from being *up and about*, because stains and mess give her a bout of 'Latin temperament'.

Mum feeds him frittata in between telling him a story that makes him chuckle. Only she can make him chuckle. Normally Michael doesn't chuckle that much.

Then I see Dad. He's home early from work. And like every day, he hugs Mum hard, cradling her face like he hasn't seen her for months. He has. He saw her at breakfast this morning – I was there, I wrote it down.

Very neatly, I do a spying report in my secret detective notebook:

The time is 16:36. It's just Mum, Dad, Michael and me. All is quite quiet in the hood. Over and out.

They can't see me, because I'm in the Yellow House and on a mission, but I mouth secret codes to them.

'Elephant juice,' I whisper through the dirty window, pretending they're watching me – because saying *elephant juice* looks like you're saying *I love you*, but only when you're miming it. Then I do another love sigh, which is very greedy for one day.

Last night I took a sleeping tablet.

Suddenly it's morning, some bastard having whipped up the volume on London.

I hear traffic – a symphony of black cabs, bendy buses, Smart cars carving a route through students, joggers, cycles sponsored by Barclays. Hooters, bike bells, congenial shouting, less congenial shouting. A reggae bass, morning radio, *Madame Butterfly*, the soundtrack of cars rising and falling away again, fleeting as an orgasm.

With no memory of sleep, I stare bleary-eyed at a window from which I can see only silent sky.

This is London.

My secret studio flat is on Torrington Place, just off Tottenham Court Road. A spit from London's West End, I'm seven floors up, on the top floor of a red-brick mansion block, which is quite a feat for a girl with a splash of vertigo. Yet I'm up in the gods, facing my demons, because I'm pig-headed like that. Though I do have my books, towers of them; they reinforce my walls, truths and thoughts recorded indelibly.

Essential life tool: always barricade yourself in by certainties.

This flat is the perfect PI base camp.

They don't know at pavement level that I exist – the gossiping students, time-pressed cyclists, joggers with backpacks of neatly rolled work clothes – not unless they push their chins up and back as far as they'll go. I can see them, though. I have a Spy Scope, which I keep on the windowsill. Now and then I'm in the mood to people-watch.

Not today.

I re-count my earnings from the de Groot entrapment case, seven days ago now. Three grand. Some might say: *Not bad for a night's work.* But they don't get the bigger picture. Entrapment is like demolishing an industrial chimney stack – ten seconds of implosion follows weeks and weeks of the most meticulous prep.

The money pushed back into my pillowcase, I immediately feel uneasy. It's the normal thing, remembering the men – wrathful, many with the wherewithal to find me.

I pull the pepper spray from my handbag. Tuck it under the pillow next to mine; the side usually reserved for a husband.

Ayurveda fact: meditation quietens mental chatter, cleanses the consciousness and enables a state of transcendence.

For ten whole seconds I deep-breathe and think of nothing at all. By twelve seconds in, I'm looking at the clothes-strewn floor, noticing a dress. The one I wore last week on the night I seduced the Dutch Minister for Security and Justice. If anyone has the resources to find me, it's him.

Momentarily I recall the client . . .

Her face, when we met her in the lobby of the Knightsbridge Hotel. Actually I remember her chin mostly. Because when I handed her the Jiffy bag containing video evidence of Minister de Groot's extramarital antics, she stretched her neck three inches and lifted her jaw in a manner unusual in this game. The chin jut said simply, *Thank you, I have my honour back.* I felt like a member of the emergency services.

The client: Lidia de Groot. She was married to the minister for twenty-seven years. Now divorced, she still wears her husband's surname like a vintage football shirt.

He's exceptional at his job, she was keen to tell me during our first meeting. *It would be selfish to deprive the Dutch people of him.*

For this reason, she had no intention of going public with the findings of this case. Extraordinary considering that three years ago she walked into their en suite to find Minister de Groot sitting on the loo. No big deal, had he not been straddled by Edith Lammers, Minister for Education.

Lidia had wept during our initial meeting, *Nobody, nobody should witness such a thing.*

She was preaching to the converted. Yet her bone was not with Pieter, who might as well have suffered from a bothersome genetic condition; it was entirely with the mistress, Edith Lammers – now Mrs Edith de Groot, the minister's current wife.

Lidia's brief was crystal: *I want the bitch to know how it feels.*

Hate and revenge are as insidious as cancer, I warned her – but the clients are usually too ruined to care.

The first wife has all the ammunition she needs.

The second wife has it coming, both barrels and a Kalashnikov.

As for me: case closed.

And so, with little else to do, I slip a hand between my legs. It's my birthday after all. But whilst so doing, I check the door.

Rim-latched, deadlocked, barrel bolts and tower bolts: nobody can enter my bedsit without a battering ram, yet I keep an eye on it. It's a leftover from pubescence, in case my dad walked in. Thinking about God, that's another left-over too – though I try, these days, to be less specific with regard to denomination.

I'll rephrase: thinking about God or Allah or Shiva or any theistic deity whatsoever whilst polishing the pearl can be an especially annoying relic from one's youth.

Let's face it, their title is irrelevant. Ultimately they're united in one creepy detail:

We know what you're doing.

That's the fallout of a convent school education. Injected with Catholicism every day for fourteen years, the habit can take a while to kick. You do in the end. But God (or what-ever you wish to call Him) will keep turning up, wafting Christianity (or some other ecclesiastical tipple) under your nose, making you woozy with guilt. Always when you're least expecting it, usually when you're having a wank.

My child, I'm watching you.

Other things I try not to think about when masturbating: dead people.

Here I can see I've made a rod for my own back. At the hospice, I asked my grandmother to watch over me. Specifically I wailed: *Don't ever leave me, be with me for ever and ever and ever. Swear it, Granny, swear it!* To which she grasped my hand so hard her eternity ring left a dent in my thumb. In the earnest way only a dying Irishwoman can, she vowed,

My spirit will hover at yer shoulder, sweet child, day and night, for ever and ever, as the good Lord Jesus is my witness and so help me God.

Using my free hand, I yank the duvet over my shoulders. I hope she's turned her back. Puts my behaviour down to a birthday treat. Most probably she's busy complaining about the pillars of dusty books and periodicals, the filthy picture rails, the fact that this place hasn't seen a cloth in over a year.

I focus.

Try hard not to imagine her sitting disapproving on my shoulder, warbling 'What a Friend We Have in Jesus', ignoring her granddaughter self-polluting beneath the chewing-gum-grey duvet that, Jesus, Mary and Joseph, seriously needs a wash.

For fuck's sake, I give up.

God dances a victory conga out of my head.

Spotting the cord of my laptop, I pull it towards me and yank the computer angrily on to my lap.

My inbox is never full, but today I find there are two enquiry emails. In this profession, that constitutes a better day than most.

My freind missing
Wednesday 25/6/14 02.23 a.m.
From: tarikma68@yahoo.co.uk
To: info@londonpiservices.uk.net

Dear Sir,
I wonder about servise to find person that is missing. It is old freind who I like to see again. We were freinds that were very close then he move away and I am sad. I not see him in twelf years and wonder if you

28

deel in case like mine. I think he move back to Libya. Please tell me how much this cost but please I have very littil money.

Yours sincerly,

Tarik Mohammad Amazigh

Let's get this straight. I steer clear of countries prone to civil war and religious unrest. I also avoid clients who tell me they're skint. Invariably they're not. They're just not tormented enough to splash the requisite cash. And successful private investigation requires commitment on both sides. Like my second enquirer:

Please help!
Wednesday 25/6/14 03.39 a.m.
From: steveloveskatie@gmail.com
To: info@londonpiservices.uk.net

Hi there,

I'm searching for an ex-girlfriend, Katie Helen Knight (date of birth: 13.06.1985; National Insurance number: JL 56 78 00 B; old mobile phone numbers: 08750 567329, 08750 333901, 07739 324578, 07654 900051, 07739 566773, 08756 892486, 07871 677811, 07899 545452).

We split up approximately 38 months and 3 days ago and she left the area soon after. Although I monitored her movements successfully for a long time, I lost track of her at 13.34 p.m. on 06.06.14. My intentions are honourable and once I find her I'm going to propose again. The problem is, her husband feels threatened by our connection and is trying to cut me out of the loop. He's brainwashed her, her family and friends. They ignore my calls, letters and visits, which is a shame but I guess they're in the middle.

Can you help? A dossier is attached (past addresses, employers, education, family details, vehicles owned, hobbies, etc.). Please get back to me with your rates.

Best,
Steve

The dossier is twenty-three pages long. I'd bet the cash content of my pillowcase he has a restraining order. Stalkers, however, are excellent business. The romantic in me respects their resolve – relentless, devoted to their intended partner, and ready to put their cash ISA where their mouth is. Unlike others I could mention.

My freind missing
Wednesday 25/6/14 04.44 a.m.
From: tarikma68@yahoo.co.uk
To: info@londonpiservices.uk.net

Dear Sir,
Or he in Maghreb.
Yours sincerly,
Tarik Mohammad Amazigh

Were I a normal PI, Tarik Mohammad Amazigh would not receive a reply. But I like to thank these people for their interest – it takes guts and a little madness to email a private detective. When I can't help, I'll guide them in the right direction.

Re: My freind missing
Wednesday 25/6/14 11.02 a.m.
From: info@londonpiservices.uk.net
To: tarikma68@yahoo.co.uk

Dear Tarik,
I am afraid our contacts in Libya, indeed the whole
Maghreb region, are limited. I would also warn that international searches are expensive. If you wish to proceed,
you could approach an agency with specific interests in
that geographical area. Alternatively you might like to
refer to the World Association of Private Investigators.
   Good luck.
   The London PI Services Team

Notice I call myself London PI Services. There's safety
in numbers. Look at my website and you'll see I've invented
an entire office of consultants:

Keith is our surveillance specialist – he spent fifteen years
working for Special Branch.

Maureen's expertise lies in computer forensics – her past
clients include the Mongolian computer giant Bull-Tech.

Ken loves nothing more than a corporate background
check – a residue of his days spent providing employee
screening services for the Rhodesian militia.

PI fact: this level of fabrication is essential.

As is the 0800 number displayed flashily across the website
– it bolsters the corporate illusion. Look at us, so busy and
profitable we have to employ sales operatives and qualified
specialists. So utterly first-rate and minted, we'll even pay
for your call.

In reality your phone call will go straight to a mobile
phone; the single phone belonging to the only employee;

his office the back of a Renault Kangoo. And when he needs extra manpower, he'll rope in an eager dad or best mate. *Wanna help me on a stakeout?* he'll ask, frowning a little because he can't pay them or anything. No matter; said dad or best mate will still do that overexcited palm-pump, like they've won all-inclusive tickets to the Maldives.

Other things my website will tell you:

Private investigators provide many investigative services. Most people think all we do is follow cheating spouses! Matrimonial infidelity investigations actually represent a tiny segment of our cases.

There follows an extensive list – paternity tests, lie detection, child recovery, corporate espionage, bounty-hunting to name a few. But this list is quoted in the safest knowledge: nobody will ever request any of it.

Fundamentally PIs have one major role – to follow cheating spouses. And one lesser role – to find missing people. But mainly to follow cheating spouses.

Of course there's the corporate work, newspapers mostly, and in these cases a PI's role is largely one-fold – to follow cheating celebrities.

I'm halfway through responding to Steve the Stalker when a chirpy trill tells me I have new mail. That's three enquiries in one day. Pleased, I read it, then frown – I don't know *Alice*, yet she addresses me by name.

An elementary PI rule: *never, ever* tell them your name.

Marital case
Wednesday 25/6/14 11.04 a.m.
From: asc345@hotmail.com
To: info@londonpiservices.uk.net

Dear Ms Love,
    Your details were forwarded to me by a friend. She

will remain anonymous, as will I, initially. She was, however, extremely complimentary regarding your service. Importantly, I have been assured of your discretion, this being particularly vital in my case.

I wonder if we might arrange a meeting, Ms Love? Do name a time and any place that is convenient to you.

During this interview, I will require a full and frank rundown of your fees. The services in which I am interested are surveillance and ultimately entrapment. Some background information may also need to be collected. The acquisition of photographs and video footage is paramount.

To reiterate, the sensitivity of my personal situation requires complete discretion. That said, I am eager that this job should not be rushed, but planned and executed meticulously. Assuming your diary permits, I would require your services to start as soon as possible. This is naturally dependent upon our meeting, during which I shall be assessing whether you're a viable candidate, physically, for the job.

I very much look forward to hearing from you.

Kind regards,

Alice

She wants to assess whether I'm physically up to it? Cheeky bitch. Yet it sets an old ball rolling: *am* I physically up to it?

There's a cloudy mirror in my bathroom, a fluorescent light above. Pull its dirty cord and the white bar hems and haws before emitting a pale and unflattering light. I push my face at the mirror beneath.

Last night's mascara stains my face. Sushi seaweed nestles

between my teeth. Yes, I should be worrying about how Alice got my name, but for the moment I fret that my nose is too long, that I'm too old for her specific requirements.

The shower spits hot pellets at my face and, eyes firmly shut, I plan ahead.

I'll wear Karen Millen, studs by Tiffany, Chanel No. 5. Subtle make-up, expertly applied. A sleek chignon – no, too Princess Anne. I'll wear it free, ruffled like Beyoncé's, show this Alice that I'm an extremely viable candidate for the job, physically.

First, however, I rescue a stale towel from the kitchenette floor, wrap it around my head and ring Michael.

It's barely midday; he's still in bed, so I leave him a message.

'Oi, lazybones. Fancy earning a few quid? About to arrange a meeting for later today. Prospective client.'

I spot my unlucky coin on the floor. It must have fallen out of my pocket. Scooping it up, I place it precisely on my bedside crate.

'Normal thing, Michael. Just need you in the shadows to watch my back. Let's say five p.m., usual place.'

Entrapment 101 Tip #2: Don't tell a soul

A perk of the job. It's super-glamorous. When you tell people, they'll beam and do a fast palm-clap. So will you, because being enthralling never wears thin. Particularly you'll find their facial expression a joy. For one uninhibited, bunkum-free moment, they want to be *you.*

Reality check. A platoon of retribution-hungry targets will be baying for your blood – if only they can find you. It's best, therefore, never to tell a soul what you do.

Safety tips:
i. *Sideline unessential family and friends.* It means not as much palm-clapping as you'd hope, but helps ensure your anonymity.
ii. *Consider a weapon.* Firearms are extremely illegal. I use pepper spray, also prohibited, but less likely to result in a murder charge. An effective alternative: salt water marinated in ground chilli decanted into a water pistol. Use sparingly; it stings like fuck.
iii. *A professional partner.* Get one of these. They have your back. Your surveillance success rate will increase exponentially. Choose very wisely indeed, mind. Living in the shadows is a brutally lonely job. The only true witness to your life, they can become your everything.

The Prey

Five p.m. Charing Cross Hotel.

Michael's already there. Far side of the bar, dressed as a country gent, pretending to read a copy of *Variety*, nonchalantly sucking at a mojito. Inwardly I sigh. His disguises never fail to solicit attention.

Looking ahead now, I see the client, Alice.

She has followed my instructions precisely. She sits in an ivory lounge chair in the bay window. Her seat faces the door. A pot of tea is on the table and a copy of the *Independent* is on the chair opposite.

She spots me as I approach and I soften my eyes, smile warmly.

It's an effective look and one I rehearse lots. First impressions count. I have three seconds tops to secure the job, so I utilise every one of them fully.

Along with the smile, I give her a snapshot of my repertoire – slink a little, shake my hair back and away from my face, creating the fleeting illusion that I'm walking into a wind machine. I finish it off with an empathetic cock of the head. *I'm on your side*, it says.

Alice does not smile back.

I remove the newspaper and sit in the chair. Her nod of acknowledgement is barely perceptible.

Unusually for this game, Alice is neither middle-aged nor expensively groomed. She's late twenties, early thirties. Her clothes are high street, high-end to be fair, but not cutting edge – more Roedean head girl than Kate Moss. Aesthetically, on a scale of one to ten, I'd put her at a seven. Pretty, but not beautiful. Wife material for a doctor or a polo player, perhaps. Nowhere near mistress material like me.

I feel vindicated.

Then she opens her mouth and I reassess. An eight is within her sights because immediately I'm mesmerised. Such a hypnotic voice; it's like she's caressing my neck with long fingernails.

'Forgive me, Ms Love, I'm extremely nervous. I never envisaged doing anything like this . . .'

Melodious, precise, a little childlike, her soft Irish lilt makes me want to shoo her away – run, run, pure one, before it's too late. In twenty minutes' time I'll have talked you into an immoral plan. A plan that will end in heartache, even though I'm very likely to say: *Ideally we'll discover what an admirable and faithful man you've bagged.*

'Alice, relax. You're in extremely safe hands.' I touch the table gently. 'Tell me your situation and let's see if I can help. Rest assured, anything you say will be treated in the strictest confidence.'

Inwardly I cringe. I spoke too posh, tried in vain to match a woman who's in a superior vocal league. I'm like Eliza Doolittle doing 'The Rain in Spain'. Yet to suddenly change voices would raise questions about my sanity. I'll tone it down by increments.

'Everybody's the same, Alice – they're all as anxious as you. It would be rather strange if you weren't.' *Rather* strange. Urgh.

'Thank you, yes, I'm sure everyone is terribly nervous.'

Yep – nervous, then exhilarated, then sickened, then vengeful.

'You know my name,' I tell her.

'As you know mine.'

I check out the other patrons. Two men, sitting separately, one reading a newspaper, the other buttering a scone. An elderly woman attempting to text. Michael at the bar, on his second mojito at eight quid a pop.

'I don't give my name to clients.' I glare at my brother. 'My anonymity is essential for all concerned. I'd like to know your contact.'

'I've been asked not to say.'

'By whom?'

She smoothes her skirt flat. 'The person who recommended you.'

'Who is . . .?'

'This is especially sensitive, Ms Love. This person used you for their own specific purposes . . .' She talks to her knees. 'I don't see the need.'

Standing up, I slip my bag on to a shoulder. 'I'm sorry, Alice. The problem we have here is honesty. It's key.'

She whispers up at me. 'My partner is very much in the public eye.'

'My speciality,' I lie.

'This could prove very, *very* tricky indeed, Ms Love.'

'Par for the course.'

'I suggest trickier for you than normal.'

Intrigued and a little impatient, I sit back down. 'How about you start at the beginning?'

Slowly she pours two cups of Earl Grey.

'My partner and I have known each other for a very long time. We were at secondary school together. We dated on and off. It was quite innocent really, but we always held a torch for one another.' She crinkles her nose, looks suddenly vulnerable. 'Unfortunately he was destined for a different path to mine.'

I lean forward. 'Who is he, your boyfriend?'

She pulls a large brown envelope from her bag, places it on the table between us.

'We met up again six months ago. He was on a trip back

home – to Cork; that's where he's from, where we're from.' She allows herself a smile. 'It was as though no time had passed at all. No entourage, just him and me, childhood sweethearts. He said I felt like home.'

Earnestly she looks me square in the eyes. 'Do you believe in soulmates?'

I don't even have to think about: 'The more interesting question is whether you become soulmates over time, or whether it's an instinctive, immediate thing.'

She says it without prevarication. 'Ours was immediate.'

I nod. 'The best kind.'

'Then again, we were children the first time round.' She makes excuses, but soulmate fact: celestial age is beside the point.

'I've had boyfriends over the years, Ms Love. He's had a lot of girls, I'm sure. That's his business. Irrelevant. His management liked to keep them out of the public eye anyway – it doesn't fit his image.' She takes a sip of tea. 'Over the last few months we've become close again. We're each other's delicious secret.'

Who wouldn't feel a little envious? 'Who is he?' I ask again.

'An exceptionally talented man, but I'm not silly: with talent comes opportunity.'

I look at the envelope. *Florence Love* is written on the front. My whole name.

My eyes taper. 'So your man has an eye for the ladies?'

'No more than normal.'

'Alcohol? Drugs?'

She shakes her head impatiently. 'He's body-conscious.'

I sit back. 'So why am I here?'

She leans forwards. 'I worry I'm missing something. That over the years he's become someone else. That he's less . . .' she offers a word, but she's unsure herself, '*honourable*.'

'And entrapment's the answer?'

'I don't expect you to understand.' She shuffles in her seat.

'Then make me,' I tell her straight.

It's almost imperceptible, but I see her nostrils flare. She certainly doesn't want to have this conversation; nonetheless, she relents, provides me with some tangible facts.

'When I was two, my mother left us for another man. Just like that. Without a backward glance. Oh, my dad muddled along, but he was never the same again. He'd thought they were soulmates. Nobody else came close. Not even me. He passed away last year.'

I put a hand to my chest.

This is *exactly* why I couldn't do counselling. Because when I say, 'I'm so sorry for your loss,' I instinctively want to have a little cry for/with her. But that's called sympathy, not empathy, and sympathy is of no practical use to anyone whatsoever, according to my life coach.

Scrutinising her knee, Alice continues.

'Dad had a heart attack. I'm not sure my heart could cope either. Knowing that the happiest moment of my life had been and gone, and it wasn't even real, because the person I thought was my soulmate was a figment of my romantic imagination.'

That kills me.

Grudgingly, I like this Alice. Especially when she rubs her face roughly and whispers: 'I'm being totally irrational.'

I put a firm hand on hers. 'You're being prudent.'

She squeezes back. For a split second, I feel like her friend.

'If I've misjudged him and he's not who I remember him to be, our relationship will be played out in the newspapers, Ms Love.'

The newspapers?

'If he's unfaithful, the world will watch my devastation.

40

That's cruel.' Armour dissolved, Alice now speaks plainly. 'He's approached his management and told them we're coming clean, that he wants to tell the world he has a significant other.' She pauses. 'The truth of the matter? I'm scared.'

The world?

'People won't expect him to remain a bachelor for ever,' I tell her.

'Yoko Ono, Linda McCartney, Priscilla Presley, Mary Magdalene – each one received death threats. The consequence of becoming his girlfriend isn't all photo shoots and show-biz parties. Plus my partner's at odds with his management. They want the slow reveal method. He prefers the whirlwind romance tack. It's more romantic,' she tells me, bemused, and finally gets to the point. 'He is going to present me to the world. I'm accompanying him to a red-carpet event.'

'Really?' I nod, because that's very exciting.

Alice doesn't think so. 'An awards ceremony. Two weeks from today. That's a Thursday. People are apparently in a good mood on a Thursday – the weekend's approaching. They will be more forgiving that their idol is no longer on the market.'

'Fascinating.'

'I'm very sure we *are* soulmates,' she tells me earnestly. 'And more than anything I want us to be *normal* – to take the dog for a walk, go to the theatre, start a family. I want to do all the things regular couples do – the things you've been able to do without a second thought. But first, Ms Love, I have to be certain – before I put myself out there.'

'Out where?'

She looks at me, irritated – haven't I been listening?

'Those flashing bulbs, the media intrusion, the *Daily Mail* commenting on my waistline, my wardrobe malfunctions, whether or not I'm pregnant. The photos of him talking to a girl – *any* girl – the ensuing media twist. I need to be so very sure. I'm not a WAG or a wannabe. I'm a primary school teacher from Cork.'

'That's a nice job,' I tell her.

She nods, because it is. 'His world is new to me. Do you know, he has this entire *machine* around him, ensuring he stays squeaky clean. It helps record sales. They'll do anything to maintain that image, even if it involves deceiving me. I want to know who to trust, Ms Love. I *have* to know who to trust.'

Alice's next statement sums up the crux:

'I won't end up like Dad.'

Accidentally I glance at Michael.

My brother has forgotten we exist, a straw coquettishly at his lips, whispering with the bartender. My heart throbs in my throat. Were Michael sitting with us, his heart would be hammering too. Only difference, he'd have flung his lengthy arms in the air and told her he knows how she feels.

That we – he and I – both know how it feels to lose a parent.

A truth I would never tell Michael: it was worse for me. He was too little. Grief is not a competition – still, I'm the one who remembers best. So yes, unlike Michael, I'm in Alice's camp – maybe it would have been better all round if Mum and Dad had never got together, if we'd never been born at all.

'Plan a week away.' My own voice is back. 'Not Cork, somewhere else. Somewhere he knows you can't pop back from unexpectedly. Tell him as soon as possible – he must have notice so he can make plans; so he knows he has the house to himself.'

'Not in his home.' She looks aghast. 'That's just wrong.'

If that's how she wants it, but she's going to have to dish way more dirt.

'I need to know everything, Alice – where he drinks, his place of work, his daily routine.'

Alice is shaking her head. 'It's not as easy as that. He doesn't go to pubs. Half the time he doesn't know his own agenda. His PA turns up of a morning, ushers him off. The rest of the time, he stays in.'

'Addresses, property interests, personal details, hobbies, sexual penchants. And photos, lots of photos.' Inadvertently I wink. 'I'd hate to jump the wrong man.'

I regret the flippancy, but for the first time, Alice smiles. An eight, definitely an eight.

'Oh, I suggest one photo will be enough,' she says, pushing the brown envelope across the table towards me.

There's a magazine inside – *Time Out New York*. I pull it free and shake my head, because despite all the clues, I still don't understand.

She leans across, strokes the front cover. 'My partner is Scott Delaney, Ms Love.'

Scott Delaney.

He smiles out at me from the page, microphone in hand, his band in the background. He is looking right at me, into me. I quickly put the magazine down. Targets are rarely as in the public eye as he. Who am I kidding? They're *never* this good-looking. I'm touching my hair.

'Your fees?' she asks.

'It won't be cheap.'

She lifts her chin defensively. 'Dad left me solvent. What's your success rate?'

I lift my chin too. 'Excellent.'

'Good. Your fees, please?'

'Fifty pounds an hour per operative for background investigations, preparatory surveillance and reports. On top will be expenses and bribes. Video footage and photographs are inclusive. The night itself will cost one thousand pounds all in. After four hours, if he hasn't bitten, I'll give you a detached opinion, but ultimately it's for you to judge his behaviour and whether you want me to continue pursuing him. Where feasible, all conversations will be taped.'

I want to laugh out loud.

And there I spot it in her face too, a flicker of excitement. See! This game can ruin the purest mind.

Alice shakes her head a little absurdly. 'I don't know how you're even going to get close.'

I haven't a clue either. 'Leave that to me. But be aware, I have an important rule – I never, ever sleep with a target.'

Her face drops a little. Perhaps the magnitude of her plan is hitting home. Or is it the tiniest twang of disappointment? What a fuck-up my world is.

'There's no need for sex, Alice. Not when I can do better than that – solicit a larger confession.'

'You kiss, though?'

'I do – with tongues for five seconds, at which point the intention to philander has been realised. Case closed.'

Now she fumbles with a purse the size of a plum. 'Payment?'

'One thousand upfront, cash, non-refundable. I'll email you updates daily.'

Plans fly through my head. I have just fourteen days to ascertain a beautiful, globally celebrated man's routine, to wheedle my way into his life and seduce him.

She's still digging at that miniature purse. 'I need to go to the cashpoint.'

'No you don't,' I say firmly. 'You need to go home. Think hard as to whether this is the right road for you.'

'Right, yes.' She looks a little lost, gathers her coat, picks up the paper.

'Email me if you want to proceed.'

'Thank you. Yes. Thank you.'

'Oh, and include the name of your contact. I'm afraid that bit's non-negotiable.' And because last impressions count, I hold her hand as she passes. 'Chances are we'll discover what an admirable and faithful man you've bagged.'

I can't shut up. Inwardly I verge on hysteria.

In return, she bends down and gives me such a grateful hug, one that lasts a little too long. 'And that, Ms Love, is a special platform on which to build a future together.'

I pat her back warmly and wonder who's convincing whom.

Scott fucking Delaney.

As she leaves, I notice Michael. He's being a goon, looking at me boss-eyed from behind his magazine. Now he's doing a comedy thumbs-up – the underwater thumbs-up we used to do as children: me with goggles on, Michael pulling silly faces, both thumbs by his cheeks, flying to the water's surface before we drowned laughing, Michael forgetting to smile as he often does but ecstatic inside.

Suddenly I want to throw myself at his neck, squeeze him hard, apologise because, more than anything, I'm glad our mother had him.

'You're a twat.' I tut at him as I pass. 'Now let's go celebrate. I've got myself a job.'

Toxic 8as

Scott *Scat* Delaney
From Wikipedia, the free encyclopedia
Scott Delaney aka *Scat* **Delaney** (born 13 September 1980) is a jazz singer of Irish origin. He is the recipient of many awards, including two Grammy Awards[1][2] and a Brit Award.[3] His first album reached the top ten in the UK. He found commercial success with his 2011 album So What. His 2013 album *Scat and Django* was an even bigger success, reaching number one on the US Billboard 200 chart, the Australian ARIA albums chart and the European charts. Delaney is more commonly found performing intimate sets at jazz venues such as Birdland, Le Caveau de la Huchette and Ronnie Scott's. Despite his reclusive nature, he has sold more than 20 million albums worldwide.

Michael squints at the downloaded page on his iPhone, a palm at his chest.

'He's nicknamed Scat because he does that jazz singing thingy.' He reads out loud: 'The singing of improvised melodies and rhythms using the voice as an instrument rather than a speaking medium.'

I neaten Michael's cravat. It's true: Scott Delaney is sooo cool, his contemporaries have named him after a non-lexical vocables musical technique.

'Ella Fitzgerald was the best at scat,' I tell him.

'Can we see her live?' Michael begs.

'She's with Jesus, sweetheart.' He's not entirely clear who

Ella Fitzgerald was, but his world looks ready to implode. Quickly I placate him. 'Scott Delaney, however, is a total possibility. Assuming we play our cards right.'

But my wink is insincere, my confidence in a sudden catastrophic nosedive. Who am I trying to kid?

I am not a viable candidate, physically. Alice's concerns are entirely justified.

He is too handsome, too talented. Scott Delaney needs to be seduced by a woman in his own league. Angelina Jolie, perhaps. Elizabeth Taylor as Cleopatra. Helen of Troy if she weren't a myth.

But Alice isn't in his league. She's a primary school teacher from Cork.

The pub my brother has chosen is called the Perseverance. We're barely through the door when he starts clapping at the barman and failing to reach for his wallet. 'Champagne for the birthday girl!'

Wearily I pull out my purse, hand the barman a fifty; he takes it without requesting proof of age.

I still feel sixteen.

But he's just doing his job and is under no illusions regarding my demographic niche: *You are a woman now.* He simply mouths above the din, 'One glass or two?'

Two, I tell him via a V-sign.

'Flo, listen to this.' Michael neatens his cravat, clears his throat dramatically. 'Scott Delaney was first introduced to jazz music by his grandfather, who later offered his gardening services for free to musicians who let Scott scat with them on stage.'

'That's sweet,' I agree.

'That's family,' he nods sagely.

'Thursday week. There's an awards ceremony in London. What is it?'

Michael looks it up. 'The Urban Music Awards. Can we go?'

'Nope.'

'Why not?'

'The job will be over by then.'

The likeliest outcome: abysmal failure.

I look around the bar. Friends chat, laugh and shout good-naturedly. Couples sit in complete silence. How depressing. I sigh and wonder why they bothered to leave the house.

'Michael, maybe we should be realistic here. I'm probably not his type.'

'Shut up. You're everybody's type. I would.'

'That'd be incest.'

Michael pulls his tweed jacket around him. 'You know what I mean.'

I do, and I reward his flattery by pointing decisively at his phone.

'Find me skeletons. He must have done something wrong over the last ten years. S and M, cheap blondes, groupies?'

Michael searches for mud and I notice a man in the corner with shoulder-length blond hair. I'm suddenly reminded of an otherwise lost memory: the motorcyclist who overtook us the night we finished the de Groot case. It's not him, of course. This guy's a D on the Fischer-Saller scale of blondness. Nonetheless I pretend it's the leather-clad rider and squint as if I'm an actress playing a part in a film – in this scene I've clocked my menacing but strangely enchanting stalker hiding in the corner. I do that often: pretend I'm the star of my own production.

It's only been a minute, yet Michael says categorically:

'Scott Delaney is squeaky clean.'

I nod at his phone like he hasn't brushed his teeth for long enough. 'Look again, properly this time. Nobody's squeaky clean.'

And that's the truth. Everyone has an Achilles heel. Michael's is small, narcissistic men who know their Dyson from their

Electrolux. Mine is obsession. Someone who leaves thirty-six messages on your answer phone, watches you over fences, hacks your emails. There's nothing more romantic. Teasingly I smile at the blond-haired guy as if he's eyeing me up in return. He isn't. He's reading a copy of the *TV Times*.

I find myself remembering Wedding Number One. I'm embarrassed looking back.

The reading was Corinthians 13:4–7. I chose it especially. What a joke. Love isn't patient and kind. It's envious, boastful, proud and self-seeking. It keeps a record of wrongs, and it certainly doesn't always trust or hope – but isn't that the bloody beauty of it? How wonderful to think there's someone out there, just one person, who makes you behave very badly indeed because they – nobody else, just them – tinker dangerously with your moral compass.

'Know what you should do? Play hard to get with Scott.' Michael points his phone gravely. 'That's called reverse psychology.'

I laugh and ruffle his hair. 'Write a book, seriously.'

'About what?'

'The art of seduction.'

'Why?'

Sanskrit, Swahili, sarcasm, all indecipherable to Michael. I turn my attention back to the *TV Times* guy. Yes, there's something safe about an obsessive man. You simply have never to buckle, to remain elusive and act the bitch, then you have him for life. Husband Number One followed me everywhere, made sure I wasn't wearing a short skirt or too much make-up. It cheapened me, he said. And I played along because, back then, I was all about compromise.

A case in point: my ex-best friend, the one he's with now, slavers it on with a trowel. And although I wish her dead, she taught me a valuable lesson. Subservience is as erotic as tinnitus.

'Got it!' Michael screeches, staring at his phone.

'Go on?'

'No, I got it. The job!' He lifts his chin and speaks author-itatively in a non-West Country accent. 'Consolidate your debts into affordable monthly instalments, leaving *you* . . .' he points, pauses for dramatic effect, 'free to live life to the full.'

'No way! The commercial? That's great!'

I'm screeching because, really, it is. He's not had one acting job ever. In fact, other than the work I pass him, and the brief stint holding a 'Discount Leather Goods This Way' sign on Tottenham Court Road, he's done nothing.

'I'm going to be on the telly, Flo.' Intently he drums the bar with flat hands, and I do too – until he says, 'I'll phone Sébastien.'

Mobile to his ear, he paces backwards and forwards.

'Seb! It's Michael. You are never going to guess what.'

I look around the bar, watch the boyfriends and husbands who ignore the women they once chased, wooed and wanked over.

The *TV Times* guy I gaze at especially quizzically, as if he fascinates me, as if the director is zooming in on my face.

Nowadays I'm more of a Song of Solomon girl. I even provide a secret voiceover in my head. *Love is as strong as death, its jealousy unyielding as the grave. It burns like blazing fire, like a mighty flame.*

And . . . cut.

Scott Delaney would never look at me like that. And in this job, confidence is key. I decide, therefore, that it's prudent to avoid targets who mess with your self-belief.

Michael claps and holds his hands open. 'Seb's on his way.'

He mistakes me for someone who gives a shit.

It was best I leave the pub. Sébastien wears a lot of make-up – foundation, face powder, mascara, lip balm – all terribly natural, but I end up staring perplexed. He's too flawless. His hair and sideburns look painted on. Arms, chest and chin so bald he has to have had full-body electrolysis. The torpid, Botoxed smile of a Thunderbirds puppet. Eyes that can be operated via a swivel switch on his neck. OK, no switch, but his eyes are super-shifty. It's no wonder I frown whenever he's around.

Sébastien also has a pinch of dwarfism. Without the Cuban heels, he is definitely no taller than five foot two. His eyes are level with my brother's nipples.

I'm flummoxed as to why Michael fawns over him.

Tonight you might have thought Sébastien was the one with the TV job, or that it was Sébastien's thirty-third birthday. Like Sébastien is even his real name.

The tube home is rammed.

Seated but hemmed in by suits and zesty tourists, I think about Scott Delaney. Think of ways to entrap a famous man. Rub my face because it's preposterous, utterly hopeless. Remember Alice's father, a man who died because his heart was unable to cope with losing his soulmate.

Coronary blockage fact: in medical circles, a catastrophic cardiac event is called a widow maker.

The saddest thing here: Alice's dad's death made no one a widow. His destiny was to be completely dispensable.

My dad says that Mum was his soulmate. But how can that be? He carries on as if nothing happened. On a Tuesday morning he puts the rubbish out. He grows globe artichokes, parsley and verbena in a patch out back. He records nature programmes, reconciles the post office books, cleans his teeth and laughs at jokes.

I was eight when they found our mother's Datsun. A stranger was dead in the passenger seat. Bambi, however, was nowhere to be found.

The consensus is that she had second thoughts, vacated

the driver's seat at the last minute, leaving her suicide buddy behind. Large home-made stickers had been affixed to the windows: *Toxic gas – dangerous. Do not open car door.*

For some reason I remember those stickers. Did I see them in the papers? Maybe the police brought Dad photographs for identification purposes. Whatever, it was her writing. Her g's looked like 8's.

Toxic 8as – dan8erous.

For twenty-five years I've wondered why she didn't come back. Only one reason presents itself: dead or alive, her incentive to live wasn't us.

Dad is sitting on the edge of my single bed. He keeps pushing at my shoulder. My eyelashes are crusty with sleep. Fed up, I rub away grit and squint at the red electric numbers of my radio alarm clock: 05:06.

It's dark out. But there are people downstairs. I can hear them mumbling. It's like they're in the interval at a concert. When I look properly at Dad, it makes me stop breathing. His face looks as old as God's.

Slowly I pull the duvet up to my neck and whisper, 'What's the matter, Daddy?'

For a long time he stares at me, but his eyes are blurry like they don't see me properly. There's a worse thing too. His eyebrows are making the saddest shape – I've never seen them do this shape before. Now he's touching my cheek, but there's far too much love in his eyes, and when he speaks it sounds all wrong – high-pitched like a girl.

'I have terrible, terrible news, Florrie.'

The tear that runs down his cheek is fat and dead.

Straight away my heart starts to scream. I push at his hand and shout, 'No!' Because whatever the bad thing is that's happened, I'm not ready for it. Dad's voice, the tear, no *Rise and shine, sleepyhead*, no sausages popping in the frying pan downstairs, no Michael babbling. I'm not stupid. Something far worse than *bad* has happened.

Somebody is dead.

'Florrie, come here, darling.'

He holds his arms out to me. To comfort him? To comfort me? I'm not sure what his face is asking. Either way I'm having none of it. Until he says different, my life is exactly the same as when I went to bed last night.

But Dad's not getting it.

'Come here, please, sweetheart . . .'

Angrily I punch him in the chest, which is a *terrible* sin – but I don't feel guilty, because he didn't even notice. He just keeps looking at me with those eyebrows.

'Don't,' I tell him firmly. 'Don't bloody say it.'

This is the first time I've *ever* sworn out loud. Dad doesn't smack my hand, though, which proves my worst fear.

Three dreadful words arrive in my head: *Michael is dead.*

I hold my tummy tight, rock back and forth.

Michael is dead.

Michael is dead.

And it's all *my* fault.

I have a secret I can't ever tell anybody: a few times, when he went to bed and it was just Mum, Dad and me, I imagined what it would be like if he hadn't been born.

Be careful what you wish for, Dad said once about something different, but that saying stayed in my head.

What have I done?

Dad tries again to hold me, but I make a noise, a groan, like a mooing cow.

Because that's not all the truth.

Sometimes I left Michael out of my prayers altogether.

God bless Mummy, Daddy, the goats, a rabbit I saw skipping across the lane, the milkman. God bless Granny Love and Grandad Love . . .

I never even saw Grandad Love – not since I was the size of his forearm – yet I probably prayed for him more than I ever did my brother. Little St Michael didn't need God's help. Mum and Dad gave him all the attention a small boy needs.

I *swear* I was only being sulky. Now and then I just missed being as little as him. But I'm eight, all bloody grown up; there's nothing cute about eight.

I clasp my hands into a tight ball under the covers and pray like I've never prayed before.

Let it be Grandad Love, let it be him who's dead. I haven't even met him, not really. He's had a good life – I don't know this for sure, but I tell it to Jesus anyway – *and if Michael's not dead, I'll become a nun and pray for poor people every day for ever. And Michael. I'll especially make up for all the times I didn't pray enough for Michael.*

It's not Jesus who answers me back, it's the argumentative bit of my brain.

Let's face it, Florence, Michael did have a disorder. He was never going to last long. There have been plenty of clues he would die. He didn't laugh in the right places. He got upset if the different foods on his plate got mixed together . . .

Suddenly I'm wailing.

Dad won't take no for an answer. He pulls me angrily in to his shirt and I give in, flop on to his chest. But he smells of boiled vegetables, and the smell of broccoli, mashed potatoes, any food seems wrong; the thought of ever eating again is unbearable and cruel.

My stomach does a big jump. I'm sick into Dad's lap.

Now we rock together, my head floppy against his chest. He's trying his best to soothe me, but I need her.

'Mummy,' I tell him. 'I want Mummy.'

He starts trying to hold me too tightly again. I push him off, but he won't let me go.

'She loved you so much.' It's like he's done something wrong. 'Know this. She would never hurt you if she thought there was another way . . .'

She?

I stare at him for a long time, because it's like I'm looking through my binoculars the wrong way round. I'm in a tunnel and a mile in front is my dad. He's too far away, I can't see his face properly, but I can see the rough outline of him. My chin drops into my chest, because my neck can't take the weight of my concrete head.

Dad said: *She loved you so much*.

'We need to be strong for Michael, Piccolina.' He's saying that from a long way away. I look at him in the distance. His little head nods at the door . . . at the landing, at Michael's bedroom . . . Suddenly his massive hands are holding my limp head up. I look into his large wet eyes. 'For each other, too.'

It's like I actually feel her flutter away.

Furious with life, I elbow a girl standing immediately in front of me on the tube. I'm sitting, she's standing; her bottom keeps knocking my head.

She swings round and glares down at me in my seat. 'Did you do that deliberately?'

'Yes,' I tell an elderly guy beside me. 'Her arse is giving me a headache.'

'My fist'll give you a fucking headache in a moment.'

'Do you kiss your girlfriend with that mouth?'

'You calling me a dyke?'

Her insinuation is outrageous. I have nothing against lesbians. I had sex with one once. I stand up. The train is rammed, so I'm way too close to her. Our lady gardens are indignantly flush.

Clasping my palms I say flatly, 'Shorinji Kempo is a martial art. Have you heard of it?'

Her eye contact remains belligerent, I'll give her that.

'I'll take that as a no. It hurts – a lot. Want a demonstration, then by all means attack. Be warned, I *will* elbow-strike you to death.'

The carriage is mausoleum-quiet. Me and the homophobic dyke stare at one another for a while. Then I hold karate hands aloft, though I look more like a doctor awaiting surgical gloves, elbow room being at a premium.

She gets the drift; squints, then mumbles something about me being mad and a bitch, looks away first, manoeuvres her butt to the left.

'*Domo arigato gozaimashita.*' I thank her in Japanese and sit back down, sigh at the old man beside me. *Society today*, I'd say to him, to anyone, were the whole carriage not so doggedly avoiding eye contact with me.

Secret fact: a little bit of me had hoped for a splatter of applause.

But there's a good reason why people don't play themselves in the biopic of their lives. Without a Hollywood glow, the offbeat is uncomfortable viewing. Not kooky, certainly not endearing.

My cheeks turn a hot pink. I look at people's shoes and face facts. A woman like me would have no hope with a man like Scott Delaney.

Outside Goodge Street tube station, I receive a call from my dad. He reminds me that I haven't seen him in four months.

'I'll visit as soon as I can, Dad. I promise.'

And I do want to. It's just whenever I get on that coach at Victoria, it feels like somebody's plinking stones in my heart. By the time we pull into Christchurch, I can barely lift myself out of the seat. It's like returning to the scene of an accident.

'So how's the birthday girl?' he says in a sing-songy voice.

'Great!' I fumble for my keys.

'The computer course?'

'Oh, now that's really great.'

'Good,' he says, entirely satisfied.

My dad doesn't see the point in me going overboard qualification-wise. A levels, university, my first in evolutionary biology, they were charming whims. Ultimately, however, I needed a job for life; something from which I could pop off to get married and have children, then pop back to again. To this end he purchased the village post office for me.

And to my brother he would one day bequeath the rest of his retail empire – a grocery stall. Michael, a man as unlikely as Elvis to don a money-apron.

As a result, we are bound to him for ever. The post office, that stall, tied to our wrists like carbonic thread, the type clipped to astronauts when they climb into space. Dad has made sure his children don't disappear into the ether, unlike their mum.

He loves us too much: I get it. It makes me feel sorry for him.

Still, he's treating our time in London as a super idea. You're never too old for a sabbatical, he tells the customers in our absence. It goes without saying he's expecting us back. Especially Michael – Dad was very reluctant to let him join me in London. But I talked him to death; he lost the will to live and let Michael come. It's a girl thing, being unbeatable at arguing. I promised solemnly to look after my little brother.

'What have you learnt this week?' Dad asks.

'Thadodastic hardware systems.'

'That'll be useful for the post office. Keep us moving with the times.'

Sometimes I wish he weren't so accepting. That he had put his foot down, given me a hiding now and then, forbidden me from fulfilling my dreams and following my heart. All this trusting my judgement implicitly, loving me so blindly, it makes me feel a failure.

'So how's that brother of yours?' Dad is asking.

I frown, because my keys are not in my pocket. Nor are they in my bag. I had them when I left the flat this afternoon.

'He's fine, really great . . .'

I forget to tell him about Michael's TV gig, buzzing my neighbour Zanna instead – she keeps a spare key.

Dad chats enthusiastically about the extension to the post office's storeroom, while I take the stairs two at a time, stopping dead at the top step of the seventh floor.

The door to my flat is directly ahead. An inch of dusty daylight escapes its perimeter.

'Listen, Dad, I have the girls coming over tonight.' Tentatively I approach the door. I use a firm foot to push it wide open. I poke my head inside. Nobody's there. 'I need to get on with the nibbles.'

'The girls, eh? Good for you. Well, I'll leave you to it. Happy birthday, my lovely.'

I blow him some quick kisses and hang up, then negotiate towels, clothes, hardbacks, paperbacks, microwave cartons to arrive at my mattress. Here I sit and survey the room. To the untrained eye it looks exactly as I left it.

It is not.

Look at my laptop. See how it emerges from the papers on the floor.

A fundamental PI rule: when popping out, always submerge your computer fully under paperwork. In addition, position it at an angle (say, 135 degrees) from a chosen focal point. Intruders don't bring protractors. By the time they've been through your history, files and emails, installed spyware and browsed your holiday snaps, they'll have forgotten exact angles and submergence levels. No matter, they'll think: the owner of this shit pit couldn't find the bathroom, let alone notice that their laptop has moved a centimetre to the right. Foolishly, they will err on the side of complacency.

Be clear, I don't live in this mess through choice; not entirely.

The packet of sleeping tablets, for example. Last night I threw them on the floor. They landed eight inches NNW of *Intimate Behaviour: A Zoologist's Classic Study of Human Intimacy*. The chance that they'd end up back on the upturned crate beside me (in this universe, at least) is nil – trajectory fact.

The dread arrives to saturate my stomach.

Told you it was only a matter of time – somebody's gone and found you.

Entrapment is not like other PI work. You reveal your identity. Laugh bare-faced at men with vast fortunes and swollen egos. Of course many will pledge vengeance. A few will see it through. I know what I'd do to a woman like me – I've spent seven hundred and twelve nights thinking about it.

Pulling the pepper spray from under the pillow, I extend my arm fully and pigeon-step to the bathroom. I look behind its door, inside the shower cubicle; at the window I punch the flimsy curtain and rattle the wooden sash.

The girl on the tube – all that butt-butting: she was doing it deliberately, to encourage an altercation, to take my keys on behalf of a vengeful ex-client.

Don't be ridiculous. I rub my face. They'd have had to get here bloody fast.

I lock myself in – rim latch, deadlock, barrel bolt and tower bolt. Then I count the money in my pillowcase. It's all there.

A rowdy clatter in the hall outside momentarily closes my windpipe.

There are two other flats off this landing – one to my right and one to my left. On the right live a professional couple. I hear them fucking through the wall. She fakes it. He makes a little scream like a strangled chinchilla. On the left lives Zanna, an elderly woman whom I adore. Whenever I see her, I have to refrain from tapping her on the top of her head, because she's as small as a concrete bollard, with soft white curls like a Lagotto puppy.

She thinks I'm fab. I've helped investigate her family tree, thus imbuing her life with reason. In return she gives me crocheted things. A toilet-roll warmer, for example. And a little drawstring thingy, useful for storing a piccolo or a courgette. I keep my pepper spray in it – though I haven't told her this: I'm not sure where she stands on chemical weapons.

Zanna has a spare key and buzzes me in when I forget mine. The professional couple don't even say hello. Not when they're together, anyhow – on his own, Chinchilla Guy's all smiles.

Beethoven's Moonlight Sonata seeps through the wall.

Zanna's presence makes me feel safer. And today it sounds as though she has a visitor. I listen to them totter back and forth along the floorboards next door. They dance a waltz and my heartbeat steadies.

I adore old people, and although I wouldn't want to be one, I find their world refreshing. So black-and-white. I gate-crash it whenever I can. Why should they care if they offend you; they'll be necromass soon. I get it. I love it. An absence of bullshit is as refreshing as a power shower.

I put the pepper spray back under the pillow and remind myself: I am living the dream. Bambi would have been so proud.

But dream jobs have their down side too – something my mother never got to understand first-hand. Then I see it.

My unlucky twopence. Knocked off the crate and back on the floor. And quite suddenly the truth hits me like a bucket of piss.

I'm fed up of being scared.

I did it, fulfilled the fantasy.

People have palm-clapped and coveted my existence.

I have seduced rich men and found bad people.

I have worn the disguises, said *Follow that car*, peed in coffee cups, installed bugging equipment and rummaged through bins.

I have bribed, blagged, tracked and hacked.

Boxes ticked. Excitement banked. Congratulations me!

Now I want out.

I *need* out.

Throwing on a baseball cap, I decide to pay an old friend a visit. An ex-lover. The one who came after Husband Number Two.

Entrapment 101 Tip #3: Keep your assets close

You have ditched your friends and loved ones. Welcome to your new tribe – your contacts, also known as assets.

Top tip. Choose assets with a smidge of *je ne sais quoi*.

Who makes the best assets? Embittered administrators. One hundred per cent. The only requirement: they must have access to a database and a password. Get one from each of the following sectors: the tax office, prison service, DVLA, NHS and Barclays Bank. In the trade it's known as a right royal flush.

Can you ever be friends with an asset? Not on your nelly.

Can you make love to them? Yes. You live in an emotionless hinterland; it's prudent to keep a toe in the real world.

What happens if you fall in love with one? The relationship is doomed, the fallout will be inconvenient, but mostly it's *ever so* sad. Your tribe is quite small enough already.

It's best all round if you *never* love them back.

Psychosis

Back in the seventeenth century, nostalgia was considered a clinical illness. More specifically, one that could be suffered only by the Swiss, doctors believing that its symptoms were triggered exclusively by the racket of Alpine cowbells. In which case, I have a very generous splodge of the Swiss.

Maeve Rivers, on the other hand, has not one fucking smidge.

'Are you going to let me in?' I whisper at my ex.

Maeve pulls her dressing gown tightly around her chest and prevents the front door from opening further with a slippered foot.

'What the bloody hell are you doing here?'

'I was just passing.' I can't help but smile; she always makes me want to giggle childishly.

Today, however, she snarls back, 'I was asleep.'

The husband must be in.

'It's my birthday.' I clap a little, but her stare remains cold. I look past her into the hall. 'I could shout from the street if you prefer.'

Reluctantly she steps to one side and whispers, 'Shoes off.'

Now I make a big show of tiptoeing into the living room, though Maeve refuses to join in the joke. I feel ridiculous.

She used to like the offbeat, saw the comedy in everything I did. Now she finds my wit odd and uncomfortable. I wonder which is truer: the past, which has happened and is unequivocal; or the present, where – without the luxury of hindsight – the jury's out.

Maeve's apartment overlooks Hyde Park.

Tonight I ignore the view to sit in an Arne Jacobsen Egg Chair and stare at a canvas the size of a rug. Banksy. Holy shit, money really is no object to Maeve. *After all, what else is there?* she once said. I suggested, *Love?* Then pushed a tight curl from her eye, kissed her naked shoulder. I was just giving her an answer; I hadn't meant to play with her head.

Maeve comes into the living room with two mugs, but fails to hand me mine. Plonks it on the table instead.

She is not a classically beautiful woman. Tall, voluptuous in all the wrong places, her neck a little too elongated, an eruption of canary-yellow hair – in photographs she can look a bit odd. In the flesh, however, she is spellbinding. Animation suits her. It sends charisma charging around her face, along with wit and intelligence and ruthlessness. Employees, friends, loved ones, they're besotted and afraid of her in equal measure.

Not me, though. At least I never let on. In bed, I used to call her *Boudicca, queen of the bloody Iceni*. She liked the fact I didn't suck up.

'I read your paper on Sundays.'

That was supposed to be a conversation opener. I hadn't meant it to sound like I deserved a round of applause, but Maeve Rivers – editor of the *Daily News*, the biggest-selling tabloid in the world – gives me a very slow one.

For the second time that day, my face burns red.

We met through her paper. I sold Maeve gossip – juicy seeds from which her journalists grew almighty sweet chestnuts for headlines. A minister's penchant for S&M orgies – the germ for that scoop came from a drunken night out with his PA's cousin. Or the footballer and his fling with an underage girl – I listened to her voicemail: not ethical, but de rigueur back then.

Then the work dried up. Court cases, select committees, public outcry at invasions of privacy: nowadays the media have distanced themselves from the likes of me. It still goes on, of course, all of it. The journalists just do it themselves and avoid paper trails at all costs.

Maeve sits on the other side of the room as if I'm contagious.

'What do you want, Florence?'

I'm aware I sound a little wounded. 'You said if I ever needed anything . . .'

'That was ten months ago.'

'A promise is a promise.'

'Back on the wacky baccy?'

'Someone broke into my apartment.'

'I'm sorry to hear that.'

'Any ideas?'

'Why would I?'

My half-grin is supposed to be flirty. 'We annoyed a lot of people.'

'*I* annoyed a lot of people.' Maeve sounds bored. 'Trust me, you're safe.'

'Nobody's been asking questions about me?'

'The paper's not used you in a year. You're ancient history.'

I'm confused by her iciness. Instinctively I walk to her, kneel down and place my hand softly on hers.

'Maeve, I wouldn't be here if I weren't desperate. I need your help.'

For a while she stares back at me like a prizefighter at a weigh-in, then suddenly she exhales, drops her chin, looks at me with exhausted eyes. I find myself tracing the outline of her jaw with a finger.

I take a deep breath. 'I need you to get me a proper job, Maeve.'

'You're fucking incorrigible.' She flies to her feet.

But I don't see why. When I put a stop to our fling, she said, and I quote: *If you ever need anything, anything at all, you ask me. Day or night, I'll be at the end of a phone.*

She wouldn't let go of my arm as I tried to leave the restaurant. To be honest, she made a bit of a scene. I didn't judge her – I'd been exactly the same when I was with Husband Number One, but I didn't make him promises I'd no intention of keeping. Not like Maeve. Look at me now. Ten months down the line, I'm here in her pad, looking like a fool.

'What did he take – your intruder?' she asks, walking to another chair, putting space between us.

'A look around mostly.'

'No harm done, then.'

I frown. 'So I'll just change the locks?'

'Good idea.' She flicks a look at the door. Yep, Harry the Husband's asleep in the bedroom down the hall.

Doggedly I stay put. 'I cashed your cheque.'

'I saw.'

'I'll pay it all back. Bit of an emergency. Michael's college fees, his bar tab, mobile phone bill – pay-as-you-go from now on, that's what I told him.' I'm not sure she's even listening.

'I don't want the money.'

'You can't suddenly change the goalposts,' I tell her.

Our very last evening together was spent going over and over and over why I couldn't see her any more. I was not a lesbian, I told her; not in the committed and commendable way she was. In a final desperate move she scribbled me a cheque for £5,000. To help out a friend with an irregular income? To tempt me back? To ensure I remained forever indebted to her? I wasn't offended. Love that makes us behave that badly is the very best sort. I agreed only to hold on to the cheque in case of an emergency. Should I ever cash it,

I would pay every penny back – that was the condition of me accepting it. We sealed the deal with goodbye cunnilingus in the back of her V12 Zagato.

She can't renege on that now. It's making me feel stupid, like I'm the one chasing her.

'I will pay it back, Maeve.'

'Are we done here yet?'

I try and regain control, sound upbeat. 'So, I was thinking about a fresh start, you know, professionally. I could write my own column.'

She laughs like I'm Tommy Cooper. 'Your journalistic experience being . . .?'

'Irrelevant. I'll be anonymous. It'll be like a blog sort of thing. Reminiscences of my life in entrapment.'

She gets up and opens the door to the hall, but I'm not finished yet – I've been preparing this pitch since I left the flat.

'It's very of the moment, Maeve – blogging, saucy secrets, Belle de Jour type stuff.'

Suddenly she's talking through her teeth. 'Want to make some readies, Florence? Find a big name – married, of course. Sleep with him, take a shedload of VT while you're at it. Give a publicist a call, then sit back and enjoy your brand-new career as a Z-list celebrity.'

The venom.

For a moment I don't know what to say.

I thought Maeve was infatuated with me. Rather cosily, I'd been living with that perception for nigh on a year. 'I have *never* . . . would *never* sink that . . .' Disappointment, outrage, sadness makes me inarticulate.

Things I want to say: I provide a professional and sensitive private investigatory service. My anonymity is paramount. A strict code of ethics is key. I do not and will not do anything that compromises myself or the client. If there was a point in my getting top-notch references, I could, hundreds of them. For Christ's sake, I let you love me.

'I'm not a fucking prostitute, Maeve. I have a golden rule. One kiss, with tongues, five seconds: case closed.'

Maeve's face is Easter Island stony.

'It's a good rule,' I mumble, because she wants me gone, I can tell. Rowdily I stomp to the front door, shouting, 'See ya, Harry, wouldn't want to be ya,' because she cannot take away my pride.

The front door slams behind me.

Is it wrong that I assumed I might remain Maeve's Achilles heel for the rest of her broken existence?

Dispirited, I unlock the door to my apartment, re-inspect potential hiding places, assess angles and submergence levels, check rim-latch, deadlock, barrel bolt and tower bolt, sit on the mattress, put the duvet over my head and create an impenetrable duck-down tipi.

Single people feel a lot less lonely believing somebody pines for us.

Especially on our birthdays.

The girls are not coming over this evening. No prosecco, painting each other's toenails, dancing, pillow fights or rom-coms. In truth, it has never happened like that for me, all that girlie friendship stuff. Well, it did once with Olivia, my best friend at university. Look where that ended up – she and my first husband, procreating biannually in the idyllic Spanish mountain city of Toledo.

I pat my knees proactively.

It will have to be without Maeve's help that I magic up a new career path.

'What jobs, other than entrapment, make people clap?' I ask out loud, but a gaggle of girlfriends don't brainstorm ideas with me – neither do they moan about boys, plan shopping trips, pour sticky shots of sambuca and sing *For she's a bloody good bestie* . . .

Alone, I consider my options.

Apart from journalism; apparently you need experience for that.

I manoeuvre my laptop into the duvet tipi. Then I google 'the best jobs ever'. The article's been written by a man – professional prostitute tester, professional resort waterslide tester, professional World of Warcraft tester, *Top Gear* presenter . . . I end up checking my emails instead.

I've received one. The one I don't want.

Re: Marital case
Thursday 26/6/14 23.59 p.m.
From: asc345@hotmail.com
To: info@londonpiservices.uk.net

Hello Florence,
   Please accept this email as instruction to proceed at your earliest convenience. My contact is your ex-partner.
   Love,
   Alice

Colin? He was the first PI I ever worked with when I arrived in London. Just thinking of him makes my blood bubble and spit. Yet I forgive her for having anything to do with him. She wouldn't know what a prat he is. More importantly, she trusts me now. She signed the letter off with *Love*, which is really nice.

A word about me.

I am not like other PIs. They would jump all over this job, make a wedge in the preliminary enquiries then, when it came

69

to the crunch – in this case, an utterly impossible crunch – disappear like a will-o'-the-wisp. Sincerely I wish I had their gall. Trouble is, my ego's the size of South America. It allows me to do nothing other than my absolute best. Maeve reckoned my conscientiousness verged on pathological.

An excessive, unhealthy drive is key for professional and personal success. Just look at me, she said.

Yeah, right. In my book, Ms Rivers was not nearly pathological enough. I pick at rough skin on the ball of my foot and think about mental illnesses. The most brilliant people have them. Scientists suffer from autism. Creatives display bipolar tendencies. Politicians suffer from sex addiction. Serial killers have psychosis.

Psychosis, now that fascinates me.

I google 'forensic psychiatry' and wonder why I haven't thought of this before. Offender profiling, like off the television – that would solicit a palm-clap definitely. I'm doing a quiet one under the duvet now. But the air becomes thin and I shut the laptop to assume the foetal position, conserve oxygen and think about normal things – psychology conversion courses, universities, good cities in which to study and live and become a criminal psychiatrist.

Manchester. Cracker lived there – the ultimate anti-hero, yet a cerebral and gifted criminal profiler. I'll buy the box set tomorrow. Criminal psychologist, it feels so *me*.

Now I try and remember serial killers, because I've got all the books. Charles Manson. The Birnies. Dennis Nilsen. Richard Ramirez, aka the Night Stalker – he snuck into bedrooms in the early hours, stabbed and battered and murdered, then raped and mutilated, then raped again. Ted Bundy – educated, charismatic, handsome, he was also a sociopathic rapist, kidnapper and necrophile, who mutilated and defiled women who looked like his ex, because the bitch had made a fool of him.

I am a bitch.

I have made fools out of an awful lot of men. Lidia de Groot would vouch for that.

Suddenly I'm breathing too quickly.

Keep me safe. I make truces with God. *I'll go to church every Sunday for the rest of my life.*

Yet God is as flaky as Maeve. He fails to materialise in effulgent light under the covers beside me, to whisper tender reassurances, to wrap me in ethereal warmth. Which is the fundamental problem with God: he does nothing to help His own cause.

I throw off the duvet and whip on the light.

The sleepers are still placed neatly on the unit beside me. I force one down, then throw the packet like a frisbee. It lands six inches SSE of a pink envelope that's been slipped under the door. When? I have no idea.

I frown, because I hate birthdays, my own especially – they leave me wondering: is a child partly responsible for its mother's dogged absence?

Gingerly I crawl towards the envelope, pick it up, remove a birthday card.

Inside it simply says: *Thinking of you today X*

There is no name. There is no need. I concentrate on one word only.

Thinking . . .

Over and over and over I reread that word, and eventually I start to groan. A strange, deep whimper that comes from somewhere in my chest – my lungs maybe. No, my heart. I've never made this noise before.

Thinking.
Thinking.
Thinkin8.

I suppress an urge to vomit.

Thinkin8.

71

The pink envelope says nothing, not even my name. The card has balloons on the front, which is unbelievably poignant because I quite liked balloons when I was small. I inhale the flap, but I can't smell her spit.

I move to the window and stare ahead.

Can it really be her? Has Mum found me?

Something moves on the rooftop opposite – a cat, a stalker, a superhero; yes, the jagged assault course across the way is perfect for superheroes. They can run and soar and tumble for practice, a crew of costume-clad mutants protecting the ramparts. Maybe my mother's a member of this group, flipping acrobatically across rooftops, transmogrifying into gas and wafting in through windows, her mutant powers a result of the chemical concoction she inhaled before escaping the gas-filled car.

I know, I know, but for one beautiful moment anything feels possible.

Like it was *she* who found a way into my bedsit.

I try Michael's number again – no answer. So I rush into the hall, rap quickly on Zanna's door.

She takes an eternity to open it.

'It's my birthday today,' I tell her quickly. 'Well, yesterday.'

Zanna looks up at me – creamy blue eyes, the soft, sparse hair of a toddler – and makes a delighted sound, like I've detonated a firework. Pulling her child-sized dressing gown around her flat chest, she engages in polite chit-chat.

'What did you get from your mum and dad?'

'Dad gave me a post office when I was twenty-one.' I wave a dismissive hand. 'It's a joint birthday and Christmas present for the rest of my entire life.' I can see she's unsure what to do with this information. 'I didn't want it,' I clarify.

I notice Zanna has not moved to one side and ushered me in. Usually it's a matter of seconds before I'm inside drinking tea, listening to her latest genealogical discovery and receiving crocheted gifts.

Tonight she's intent on doorstep conversation only.

'And your mum?' she asks.

'No precise location on her just now.' I lay my cheek against her door frame.

Zanna shakes her head, maybe a little at me – normally mothers love their children too much to up and leave without trace. I steal a look over her head. An elderly gentleman sits on the sofa in his pyjamas, flicking through her LPs.

'I'm sorry.' I take a step back. 'I didn't realise you had visitors.'

A second look at the man and I realise it's Norm from the public records library.

'Wow.' I pat her shoulder, though struggle to congratulate her – the last time I heard, Norm was married. 'That's very modern of you,' I say.

In truth, when I visit the public records library I avoid Norm at all costs. Give him more than a minute and he'll tell you how he twice escaped the Gestapo – once with a severed leg and once with a bullet in the head; how he planted bombs for the French Resistance; slept in his own faeces in a coffin under the floorboards of a French farm; wooed the farmer's daughter, brought her back to England and impregnated her within twelve minutes of tying the knot . . .

He's annoying like that, can top-trump all my PI stories what with having lived through a proper world war. Before I go, however, I double-check with Zanna.

'You didn't send me a birthday card, did you?'

'No.' She shakes her head without embarrassment or regret.

'Good.' I point emphatically. 'Very good indeed.'

Back in my flat.

To celebrate, I rub my tired eyes until spangled nebulae

whirl across their lids. The possibilities are suddenly infinite. Christ, I feel alive. How can I move out of London now, away from this flat? If the birthday card is from Mum, she might lose me again.

I remember her pallid olive skin; her accent – half Italian, half West Country. Her scent, musky and sweet – some budget perfume. Charlie, it was called. She bought it from the local chemist – the place from which she also got Elnett hairspray and Mogadons. And lollipops for us, with their faded price stickers and no sell-by date.

Old hypotheses regarding her disappearance flood back. Some seem more plausible than ever. The one, for example, where I imagined that she had been kidnapped by a crazed stalker who was determined that they should die together. At the last second, she escaped from the car, but the chemicals had messed with her head, inducing a terrible amnesia that allowed her past to reveal itself only sparingly, one disparate moment at a time. She has probably put her recollections together as best she can, but it's difficult, her history like a jigsaw puzzle with no box and most of the pieces missing. And so for twenty years she's wandered from town to town, like David Banner did in the TV version of *The Incredible Hulk*. Christ, its theme tune played cat's cradle with my heart strings. Even Dad used to turn it off.

Yes, yes, yes, tonight that story works.

For a split second I think about ringing Dad. But he'll speak to me in that pitying, resigned tone; his children now and then are bound to clutch at straws.

The phone vibrates. Michael's number flashes up. I'm greeted by a cheerful racket – music, laughter, high spirits. Some gay bar, no doubt. Michael over-grateful that Sébastien's there. Sébastien. With his stock-still face and eagle eyes. I can't even see the man and I'm frowning.

'I've been calling all night,' I tell him crossly.

'I'm celebrating. I'm going to be on the telly!' Michael says again.

'And I am bloody proud of you. But before you get too famous, pop back down to earth for a bit and help me on a final job?'

'Doing what?' The attention span of a fruit fly.

'Err, the Scott Delaney case.'

He shrieks. I imagine he's fast palm-clapping at Sébastien. 'I thought you didn't want to do it?'

'Change of heart. I have decided, Michael, that anything is possible.'

I have also decided not to tell Michael about Mum. Not yet. My evidence is not watertight and Michael favours watertight – certainly I can't answer the questions he'll surely ask. Like, why the hell hasn't she been sending *him* anonymous cards or breaking into his pad? I can guess the reason, of course. She knows her disappearance was worse for me. Certain truths are best kept under your hat.

I will find something concrete.

'What if you're too old?' my brother says out of the blue.

'For what?'

'For Scott?'

'We're the same age, almost. Earlier you said I could have anybody.'

'You can, but what if you're not pretty enough?'

He does this when he wants to impress his friends – tries to sound concerned, adopts the voice of reason. As if, out of the two of us, he's the sagacious protector. Trouble is, the sentences sometimes fail to complement his intention. Usually I'd stifle a smile and play along, because assimilation is important for people like Michael. Tonight, however, Sébastien's there.

'Stop showing off.'

'Well, you can only do your best,' he says like he's the Dalai Lama, then squeaks, 'Sébastien's met Cher.'

I yawn, pretend the telephone line keeps cutting out, then hang up.

One last job. Just to give Bambi enough time to get in touch properly. I can pay off Maeve, then make my way to Manchester to study serial killers. But *only* once I am able to give my mother a forwarding address.

For once I wish I could stay awake. I want to think about her all night. Thinking time runs short, however. An hour has passed since I took my sleeper and it's doing its job. My blinking becomes relentless, like I'm on fast-forward.

When oblivion rushes me, I give in to it, secure in the knowledge that a brand-new dawn is just a finger-snap away.

Michael is right about one thing, though. The Scott Delaney case – I can only do my best.

Oh, and I will.

Watch and learn.

In London for just five weeks and already I've bagged myself a partner. That is *excellent* going for a wannabe PI from an unknown village north-west of Poole with no experience whatsoever.

Niente.

My partner is called Colin and is a proper private detective. He looks just like one too – a Colin, that is. His day job is as a London taxi driver, and he could tell you a few stories, which he will (at length) if you ever meet him. When he's not working as a cabbie, Colin moonlights as a private investigator and he's happy to talk about that too, which is very bad form. Nevertheless, he offered me a trial (though he couldn't pay me or anything). We're to call it work experience, which in this game is as rare as a white peacock. Of course I grabbed the opportunity with both hands.

Two heads are better than one, he said, waiting for his tip. *Especially when one of you is a bird, 'cause nobody suspects a bird of being a dick.*

Here we are tonight, three nights into my first case ever, and if I'm being totally honest, I am not enjoying it at all. Because this is a honeytrap. Or a *hiney*trap, as Colin calls it, because hiney is American for arse and my PI partner is turning out to be a huge one.

I'm not a prostitute, I clarified.

Too right, he replied. *Prossies don't kiss. Not unless you're stinking rich; then the brass wants to marry your ugly butt.*

PI fact: entrapment specialists do kiss, very much so.

Trouble is, the target is not my type at all. He is the deputy manager of the Kentucky Fried Chicken in Lewisham.

Barry. Fifty-eight. Long mid-grey hair. Greasy dark-grey lowlights. Worn in a neatly combed man-ponytail. Beard. Aviator-style reading glasses. Marillion fan.

Nonetheless, I'm a professional, and to this end have shown great willing. I've even had a tattoo on my forearm – an evil jester: it's a concurrent theme for Marillion and associated merchandise (see LP/EP covers for *Garden Party*, *Fugazi* and *He Knows You Know*, etc.).

The tat's a fake, naturally, but it's important to show initiative.

When Colin saw it, he laughed his head off.

It'll be a talking point, I told him defensively, because it is a brilliant idea.

If you say so. He nodded at my chest. *Pull your top down a bit, so he can see your tits.*

The Brockley Jack pub is Barry's local. He comes here for a snakebite before his shift. And after, depending on what time he finishes. His wife is convinced he's carrying on with his female staff. He's not. This is the third night I've sat three stools down from him, and he prefers not to look up from his pint.

Mrs Barry is delusional.

She's also running out of spondoolies, so tonight we'll be going gung-ho for the money shot, Colin has informed me.

The money shot is disgusting. It's where I make a pass at Barry.

Let's get this straight.

Apart from Husbands Number One and Two, and a few carefully chosen dalliances in between, I'm not hugely into kissing. Kissing is very intimate. Way more intimate than sex. Call me old-fashioned, but if I'm going to put out, kissing-wise, it has to mean something.

This presents a dilemma I am going to have to get my head around. The nature of private investigation means operating via a debatable moral code. You're dealing with shitty personal issues – adultery being the cruellest thing *ever*, because messing with somebody else's heart is unforgivable. I am, therefore, doing a worthy thing, I remind myself. To appease my conscience, I create some ground rules.

Kissing ground rules: I will try hard to kiss the target on the mouth for five seconds *only* if their mouth smells totally fresh and there's no food in their teeth. But definitely never, ever with tongues. Not unless they're super-hot.

That sits more palatably.

Feeling bilious to the core, I enter the pub. Sit at my normal stool. Order half a snakebite and pretend to read a copy of *Metal Hammer* magazine. Colin follows me in ten minutes later, orders a Coke, sits at a table in the corner and reads the *Sun*. A covert video camera watches the pair of us.

I tease my sleeve up so the tattoo's on full show; reluctantly I pull my top down a tiny bit. After ten minutes of nothing, I shuffle two seats along. Turn towards Barry's profile.

He has a *lot* of nostril hair. It's so dense, in fact, that his breathing will be impeded if we kiss, and yes, I'm clutching at straws, but on health and safety grounds I decide it's too risky to snog. Like I need an excuse. Nobody would ever snog him. His wife has shit in her eyes.

'Hi there.' I pretend he's just somebody safe for a girl to talk to. Like when you find yourself alone in any pub in east Dorset – there you can talk to anybody in the safest knowledge that they won't think there's a single ulterior motive. Dorsetians are simply thrilled to chat. They're clinically friendly.

For a painful moment I miss my own kind.

Londoners are hopeless at pleasantries. Should you instigate a conversation, they think you're unhinged, desperate, a chancer. I get it. Communication here is impeded by population density; it's oppressive. You scowl when there's *always* someone invading your space, as is exemplified by Barry's facial expression now.

'You've been here every evening this week,' I tell him, cheerfully.

'I've been here every evening for eight years. What are you, the alcohol police?'

'No, just new in town.'

This is an awful start. I don't want Barry to fancy me. But I really do need him to. Because if I can't pull him, then I'm going to be hopeless at this job. I'm infinitely prettier than him, but I start to worry that I'm deluded, like the tone-deaf person who hogs the karaoke.

Non-negotiable entrapment specialist fact: you should be body-confident and never exude vulnerability.

But I leak it in spades. What was I thinking? I pick up my bag and magazine, get ready to leave, because I'm not cut out for this.

'Sorry, I didn't mean to disturb you,' I say.

When Barry spots my tattoo, his smile becomes wide. I

see the inside of his mouth: blotchy gums, long-standing gingivitis, the beginnings of periodontal disease.

Urgently I glance at Colin. My eyes explain the whole situation in great detail:

Periodontal disease is not contagious, Colin, but it's absolutely disgusting. Kissing is one trillion per cent out of the question. Abort mission! Abort mission!

But Colin doesn't give a monkey's. He responds by issuing a *don't fuckin' look over 'ere* face.

I pat the tattoo. 'From my younger years.' Then change the conversation fast, because my head has emptied. Last night I researched Marillion in great depth; today I can't recall a single 1980s neo-progressive-rock fact.

I nod quickly at his hand. 'You're wearing a wedding ring?'

He taps the offending finger jewellery absent-mindedly on the bar. 'I was very bad in a previous life. Where you from?'

He's noticed the accent. I determine to lose it as quickly as possible. *The* most pleasant people in the world, inhabitants of the West Country get piss-poor press.

Total dialectal fact: the West Country accent is not lazy, but derives directly from the court of King Alfred. *We* are the ones who pronounce things correctly. But try telling a Londoner that.

'Gloucester,' I fib. 'Just arrived in London. New job. Feeling a bit lonely.'

And that's the truth.

Barry gets a little friendlier, offers me a drink. I accept but immediately make it clear our friendship can only ever be platonic.

'Missing the hubby, the kids, you know,' I say.

He takes the fact that I have a pretend family well, waves at the bartender. 'Blink of an eye and they'll have flown the nest.'

'You've got kids too?'

'Yup. Old ones. Long gone.'

'Must feel like you're waking up next to a stranger some-times, now they've left?'

He's switching off. Barry clearly tries not to feel too much. 'Suppose.'

'It's understandable. You spend years concentrating on the family's needs, which doesn't leave much space for you and her, as a couple.' I pick at the corner of my tattoo. 'Excuse the marriage guidance. I've been there, you know.'

This is a ridiculous thing to say – I'm twenty-eight and clearly have never been there. But I *am* perceptive; I can imagine.

Taking a large gulp of his pint, he passes me a half. 'Bugger-all in common any more.'

That's when it comes to me.

Maybe, just maybe, I can redeem this situation. Fix Barry and his marriage a little. Marriage guidance is quite a USP for an entrapment specialist. I grin, excited at the cool irony of that.

'It's called empty nest syndrome,' I tell him.

And it is. I know this because I researched it before leaving my dad and Michael back in Laurelbridge. I wanted to be sure they could cope without me.

'It's a phase. Most couples can rediscover a life together, just a different one from before, maybe even better.'

Dad and Michael waved me goodbye at Christchurch railway station. Dad trying to be excited for me, but mostly for Michael, who was struggling to cope with the thought of me leaving for London. My brother held on to my shoul-ders a lot, told me I wasn't allowed to go; that he wanted to come too.

I did a brave thing coming here to start afresh.

My confidence grows a smidge. 'Speak to her,' I tell him.

'Who?'

'Your wife.'

'About what?'

'How you feel.'

'Why?'

'Because it matters.'

I never spoke enough to my dad. We were too busy concentrating on our personal psychological mountains. Unfortunately our survival techniques were mutually exclusive.

I think of questions I've never asked my dad.

'Ask her what music you'd take to a desert island and why? Or if you could learn a new talent, what would it be? Come up with something you'd like to do together.'

'Scuba diving,' he tells the barman loudly. 'Can't do it, though: she's scared of sharks, even in swimming pools. Eh, Terry?'

Terry, the barman, laughs.

'That's called galeophobia,' I tell them.

Phobias are my thing – I'm a complete anorak.

A fear of death is called thanatophobia; a fear of atomic explosions is atomosophobia; a fear of the colour purple is porphyrophobia.

'One in three people suffer from a phobia,' I tell them.

Barry points his glass at me. 'Dogs make me jittery.'

'That's cynophobia.'

He laughs out loud. 'Are you going to tell me your name?'

Never, ever tell them your name. Colin has made this very clear. Unstable clients, livid targets, they come back to haunt you. *Especially if you're a bird.*

'My name is irrelevant,' I tell Barry. 'Concentrate on your wife. A little time and effort and you'll reconnect.'

Barry is thoroughly amused and sarcastic. 'Righty-oh, Doc. I'll just call you Marie Curie, shall I?'

I look at him straight on and tell him with my eyes: *Marie Curie was a pioneer in the field of radioactivity, wanker. My counselling skills are way off curing death.*

Admittedly my eye contact is possibly too sultry. It certainly provides a cue for him to sneak his palm inside my jacket and cup a breast.

We sit there motionless for a few screamingly silent seconds; him looking around in the hope that no one's watching, or maybe in the hope that everybody's watching.

The reason I don't move a muscle is because I'm stuck somewhere between unbridled personal outrage and an innate sense of professionalism. Whilst oscillating between the two, I watch – in slow, painful motion – Barry's face moving in towards mine.

Further fact about Barry: he has the tongue of a salamander – its attempts to bore a passage into my mouth and towards my gag reflex are formidable. Luckily I am absolutely furious, so keep my lips as pursed as an anus.

Barry makes no inroads.

Five, four, three, two, one.

Just enough time for Colin to get the money shot and clinch a bonus from Barry's soon-to-be heartbroken sharkphobic wife.

Poor, poor woman.

I issue Barry with a Budokan elbow strike to the bridge of his nose that snaps his nasal bone in two.

No, I don't.

But I *totally* intend taking a course in killing, should I ever do another entrapment, which I certainly won't be doing, because I feel like a disgusting hunk of meat.

On the way back to his taxi, Colin pats his duffle bag excitedly. He's got the footage and is elated. Everyone at his upcoming BBQ will be hearing the details in full, because apparently it was comedy gold.

'Next time, though, put a bit of effort in,' he tells me, like he's directing a porn shoot. 'Pretend like you're enjoying it.'

'OK,' I say, spitting into a tissue, scrubbing my tongue with a Femfresh.

Colin drops me back to my bedsit in Torrington Place. I thank him for the opportunity. Wish him good night, because Dorsetians are polite like that. Though I don't tell him I've changed my mind. About him. About private investigation. About London.

Operation Delaney

Preparation is vital to a successful entrapment. Take a leaf out of Abraham Lincoln's book; he said: *Give me six hours to chop down a tree and I will spend the first four sharpening the axe.*

Trouble is, I've been unable to delve as much as I'd like. Scott Delaney is a closed book; his marketing machine is consummate.

My regular checks are out of the question too – he's not a British citizen. I could outsource the work to a guy I know in Dublin, but what would that achieve? Scott is rich, famous, has properties, no county court judgments, no misdemeanours – none of this is of any use to me, not when my job is onefold: to seduce him.

Monday. Day One: Operation Delaney.

I'm currently watching Scott's London home. It's one of four. His other pads are in Cork, Tuscany and Bel Air. This particular property is a seventeenth-century white stucco mansion situated in the Little Venice region of Maida Vale, west London.

Just ten minutes in, and already I need the toilet.

It does that to me, surveillance. The naughtiness of it. My bowel flutters excitedly, like it's being tickled with a tiny rectal quill. I'm exactly the same when I go to the library or wait for public transport at night.

To occupy my mind, I pull a magazine article from my rucksack – just one page torn from *Architectural Digest.*

This is the gen: the previous owner of Delaney's house was an American record producer who, prior to putting it on the market, invited the glossy monthly to feature the property – crucial when you have a home as exquisite as this: it drums up interest amongst the loaded.

Indeed Delaney went on to buy it for eight million smackers.

According to the feature, the house has a recording studio, cinema and wet rooms the size of my bedsit.

I sigh. This ripped-out page is as close as I'm going to get to its interior. Alice was unequivocal: *Do what you must, just not in there.*

I've been barred. It means I can't plant recording devices or bug the landline, which would have helped enormously. But the client is king and this one was particularly adamant: his home should not be violated.

I am allowed, however, to mooch outside. Which is just as well. Alice provided me with a lot of information – by and large useless but interesting for, say, members of the public nonetheless.

Alice's top ten facts about internationally renowned jazz musician and boyfriend Scott Scat Delaney:

1. Car registration number: TB64 MDP.

2. Mobile telephone number: 07883 284812.

3. Dietary regime: Atkins.

4. Favourite Xbox game: Red Dead Redemption.

5. Pastimes: Staying in.

6. Target's current routine: in London for next three weeks, resting between tour dates. Some publicity obligations for a forthcoming album. *A compilation of duets with jazz greats and pop giants.* Alice was very precise, as

if she was reading from the back of the CD box. And of course the Urban Music Awards in just eleven days' time.

7. Work days: organised by his PA, Harvey Cadwalader.

8. Harvey Cadwalader: thirty-nine, Cambridge graduate. First-class degree in condescension. Acts like no-nonsense governess. *He'd spoon-feed Scott if it were socially acceptable.* Photograph: large as a bouncer, half something, Caribbean at a guess; looks like a trumpeter.

9. Scott's relatives in London: one younger sister called Elle. Twenty-four. Loves to visit Scott for days on end. *A hanger-on and sponge.* Photograph: long caramel-coloured hair, legs up to her cheekbones. An unequivocal ten out of ten.

10. Scott's close friends in London: none.

Alice was particularly disdainful about the hanger-on sister, which is fair enough – wives don't appreciate being physically top-trumped by a close relative. Even I gasped when I saw Elle's snapshot. The woman was born a Bond girl.

Last night I did a little research of my own.

I typed 'Scott Delaney' into Google. A name that pulls up reams of results: fan sites, social networking sites, his Wikipedia page, a Twitter account, online stores selling his music. Most reaffirmed hackneyed hoopla. His upcoming album – *a compilation of duets with jazz greats and pop giants.* His favourite colour. The green-fingered grandfather who kick-started his career.

So I narrowed it down and typed 'Scott Scat Delaney girlfriend'.

There've been a few dalliances with famous girl-next-door-types. Nothing confirmed. No conclusive photo evidence. No admissions from either party. Just enough gossip to create the desired message for his fans – Scott Delaney is straight and attainable.

I don't have my client's surname, common in my business, so I gave Google a little more to go on: 'Scott Scat Delaney girlfriend ALICE'.

One solitary snippet popped up. It was from a blogging site renowned for scandal-mongering – a site that outs the famous, shares their drug habits, then reveals their deaths before the tabloids. The reveal about Scott was hardly earth-shattering. Still, it's more than any reporter has ever got on him before. The one solitary snippet on Scott Delaney being this:

Over drinks at a show-biz party, the blogger had asked Scott who his first love had been.

Alice St Croix, Scott had responded unequivocally. *We first sat next to each other in geography. The most beautiful girl I ever laid eyes on.*

And that's it: the sum total of info on Alice.

Following this slip-up, Scott's junta had done a consummate job. No doubt banned him from drinking in public. Reminded him that his job was simple – to play God in a theocracy directed entirely by other people. No wonder the man's a hermit. He's scared stiff to open his mouth.

But at least I've discovered my client's full name.

Being of French lineage is extraordinarily sophisticated. It certainly explains something of his attraction to her. French women are the most desirable in the world – even the seven/eight-out-of-tens like Alice.

Finally I put 'Alice St Croix' into the internet.

Bingo.

She's on the staff list at a primary school in County Cork.

It's called Scoil Mhuire agus Maomh Treasa: quite a mouthful, but us Catholics love a bit of pomp. I also discovered that Alice is a special educational needs teacher, which is really nice.

In another life, I'd tell her all about Michael.

In this one, she will know *nothing* about me or my family.

SEN teachers don't get many internet hits, so beyond this school website, I found bugger-all else on my client.

Alice St Croix is now in Italy with a teacher friend. They're holidaying at Scott's pad in Siena – a centuries-old chestnut-drying barn that Scott has had renovated, extended, pimped up. Alice sent me a photo. It looks sublime.

She'll stay there for ten nights, providing ample space for Scott to stray. Her return date is one week on Wednesday.

The following day, a Thursday, Scott will be taking her as his plus-one to a globally televised awards ceremony.

Assuming, of course, that Scott Delaney is a faithful and admirable man . . .

The baton is now with me. I, a physically and profession-ally inferior person, must orchestrate a liaison with an anti-social jazz singer whose ideal night involves a slab of tuna and his games console.

Just ten days.

The clock ticks loud as a cartoon bomb.

I lean against the trunk of a tree and scratch my head. This wig is the itchiest I own. It remains, however, a surveillance must.

PI fact: men don't notice women with a mousy bob. Team it with a cagoule and some M&S slacks and you're as incon-spicuous as knotweed.

Between you and me, this degree of invisibility doesn't sit comfortably.

Nonetheless, I'm a professional, and central to the success

of any surveillance operation is unattractiveness. No one looks at plain people. They're atmosphere – that's what American TV people call extras.

Today I am an extra.

And this is one of the handiest locations I've come across surveillance-wise. I can amble past Scott's house, sit on one of many benches, read a tourist information board, study its woefully inadequate map, queue for a canal tour on the opposite bank. In fact I can pretty much watch Scott's house from all angles, thanks to Regent's Canal. Just twenty steps from fortified driveways, its vibrant houseboats, with names like *Coeur de Lion* and *Serendipity*, hug the canal's sides like multicoloured algae, bobbing all homey as tourist barges glide through the centre of them. Joggers pad the towpaths either side. Cyclists get on everybody's nerves. Sightseers wander enchanted through the quirkiness of it all, stopping to peek inside a floating home, queuing for an audio walk, admiring the bankside shrubbery.

The big houses either side of the canal might as well be a delightful folly.

Stucco mansion fact: you've see one, you've seen them all. People stop looking. Leaving the famous to hide in plain sight.

Clever.

Because some of the most famous people in the world live here, yet their majestic houses are, by and large, quite *samey*. It provides inconspicuousness, even when the area in question is Maida Vale, a total honeypot for the eulogised.

Residents past and present: Sigmund Freud, Robert Browning, Annie Lennox, Kate Moss, the guy out of Pink Floyd.

Scott bloody Delaney.

I still can't believe it.

I'll describe his stucco mansion.

It consists of three grand storeys, plus a grand converted basement. The electric gates are eight feet tall. Thick net curtains – the type you get in foreign embassies and posh hotels – veil all signs of life within. To the side of the house, however, there is a peep of garden. If you stop and stare for longer than you should, you'll spot a corner of the detached sun room, suggestions of a Japanese rock garden and the edge of an arboretum. There's an eco-pool too, though I can't see that, but it's definitely somewhere out back – *Architectural Digest* said so.

I phone Michael to hurry him along – the rectal quill is in overdrive.

Finally he rocks up wearing tracksuit bottoms (too short), hoodie (too short) and snapback cap. In addition he assumes the accent of a Dickensian street urchin.

''Ow goes it?' he asks.

I stare up at him. 'You're an hour late.'

He does surreptitious jazz hands – I'm to guess what he's come as.

'A burglar?'

'A local,' he corrects me.

'From where? Maida Vale is one of the most affluent districts of the modern world.'

'I do know.'

I want to reach up and tweak his cheeks too hard, because he did not know.

'Perhaps we should decide on your characters beforehand.' I put the surveillance rucksack on his back. 'Tomorrow you come as someone with neurotic timekeeping skills, got it?' I nod at Delaney's house opposite. 'Nice pad. Whilst I'm gone, don't take your eye off it. Not for one solitary second.'

A five-minute walk away, at the corner of the Edgware Road and Aberdeen Place, is Café Laville, a glass-fronted bistro straddling the canal. Its underbelly forms the start of a tunnel beneath which narrowboats float towards Camden Lock and back again.

Before I sit down, I use the facilities, learn five new words on my Oxford Dictionary phone app, then wash my hands with soap that gives me an instant dose of eczema.

I find a seat on the terrace outside, order a latte, and rest my arms and chin on the railings that overlook the waterway beneath.

There's nothing very romantic about Regent's Canal. It's gun-metal grey, always, like a puddle; psychedelically cheery boats can never change that.

Thirty metres ahead, a tourist boat drifts towards the café's terrace, which gives me an excellent idea. Tomorrow Michael will come as a sightseer – a Norwegian one, Norwegians being tall, nice and punctilious. Then I look at the boat more closely, because suddenly I remember: it's feasible that Bambi is amongst the tourists; just as it's feasible that Bambi is anywhere, doing anything at all.

On the roadside, for instance, taking her dog for a walk.

It's ridiculous, but I consider quite seriously what type of dog my mother would have. One of those gerbil-like creatures definitely. A very cute, fun-sized canine that produces small, manageable turds – my mother would panic at anything larger than an aniseed twist.

Aniseed-twist poo is a good analogy – Mum would have roared – but I don't giggle to myself, because a warring couple to my left are messing with my mirth. The female is hunched over the bistro table in tears; the guy looks bored stiff.

Seven billion people to choose from, yet we elect just *one* to spend eternity with.

The irony?

It doesn't matter who we pick or how many; eventually they morph into a cruel individual for whom our pain grates.

Anybody else would pat your hand or stroke your hair at the sign of a tear. At the very least, they'd feign concern. Even other species manage empathy: I bet those gerbil-dogs scurry all panicked when their owners weep.

But not *the One*.

Husband Numero Uno, for example. He stopped hiding the fact that my anguish had worn thin, that half the time he thought I was putting it on, that my tears did little more than make him twitchy and jaded and a little bit furious. Correct me if I'm wrong, but such a lack of compassion is indicative of someone with a personality disorder.

My phone rings.

It's Michael. 'The target has emerged.'

On any other occasion I'd throw a fiver on the table and shoot from the café. But I've spotted someone on the narrowboat below that glides towards us, destined for the tunnel beneath our feet.

A man. He's not like the other passengers, who are all inside, sitting on red leatherette seats, staring through glass. He stands at the stern, though he's not the captain.

Thirty-five tops, a rigid gaze; he stares at the canal's water as if drowning in the cacophony of his own brilliant mind. And his blond hair leaps Medusa-like in the wind. White-blond hair, its hue a definite B on the Fischer-Saller scale. Precisely the same shade as the motorcyclist's.

As the boat gets closer, I can better make out his face – the long, pinched nose, pretty as a girl's. Pillowy earlobes, the type you want to roll between finger and thumb. No ring or jewellery, though not necessarily single. Out of habit I give my make-believe stalker a backstory, massage his cartoon outline into life.

My prowler, I conclude, is most likely a poet.

And while I give him a profession, the blond man pays me not one crumb of attention.

Jeans, T-shirt and Ray-Bans, a fleece tied around his waist, he gazes into the water and past it – unlike the rest of the tourists, who stare delighted up at us, the patrons of Café Laville. A child waves from the front of the boat, her mother taking a photo of us with her smartphone, me mouthing, 'London Zoo is that way,' because I *hate* having my photo taken.

My stalker ignores us all to pull a book from his back pocket.

Told you! A poetry book, I bet.

Look up! I try and communicate with him telepathically. Then I change my mind. *Do not, under any circumstances, look at me.* Because I'm wearing the mousy bob and cagoule of a trainspotter.

He doesn't look anywhere. He's too immersed in literature.

And now a young woman appears. Petite, barely reaching his shoulder, she comes on to the deck, puts an arm in his, snuggles the crook between his forearm and bicep. At first disappointment prickles at my chest, but it doesn't take long to see the truth. He doesn't love her. There's no cursory head tilt in her direction. The Poet fails entirely to notice this woman suckered to his arm.

Their relationship is fucked.

The boat is soon to vanish into the tunnel beneath us, so I lean over the railings to watch them more closely.

Sod's law: the Poet glances up.

Instinctively I look away. Well, I try to at least. But my eyes have become cemented to his; and his to mine. I watch him begin to frown, a sudden breeze from the tunnel sending his hair absolutely livid; it jumps up at me like white snakes.

Look away! my head screams.

But we maintain eye contact as his chin tilts back further and further, until finally he vanishes into the tunnel beneath us.

When I sit back down, it's with a dead thud. Dread scratches at the nape of my neck.

Because the Poet has the most furious eyes I've ever seen – furious, and vaguely familiar.

'Versace jeans – straight leg, stonewash black denim, thirty-two-inch waist, thirty-two-inch leg. Paul Smith slim-fit black chambray shirt – medium. Armani striped trilby – blue and white. That only comes in one size, but if I had to guess, I'd say his hat size was a seven and a quarter. That's a circumference of twenty-two and three-quarter inches.'

I shake my head.

Ask Michael the capital of the Federated States of Micronesia and he wouldn't have a scooby. Then again, people like him are often frighteningly good at just one thing. Computers is a common one; or they're comic-book aficionados; or they can tell the exact day of the week by its date, even if the date is ages ago, like 29 December 104 BC.

Michael's secret talent is guessing people's vital statistics. He's never worn a bra or had a girlfriend, yet he'll tell you your cup size within nanoseconds of meeting you. It's quite the party piece.

I lack my usual enthusiasm. The Poet has left me unsettled. 'What about his shoes?'

'Daps.'

'Make?'

'Adidas Vintage Turf.'

'Size?'

Michael looks furious with himself.

'You weird nerd, I'm joking. He was gorgeous, right?'

'Totally,' says Michael, still concerned with the length of Scott's feet.

'Footage?'

He taps the rucksack – it contains a pinhole camera, the

lens of which peeks from the teensiest hole in the shoulder strap. So teensy that if you put your index finger and thumb as close together as possible without touching skin, the gap between them is still larger than the size of the lens. Genius. Compare this to a Canon 1D Mark III, the camera traditionally used by the paparazzi and old-school detectives, which is the size of a four-barrel carburettor. Plus it costs four grand and you totally stick out.

Digital video is way more discreet – it has great visual clarity, provides an accurate representation of events and is much easier to smuggle into the Chiltern Firehouse or the House of Lords. You can hide the tiny recording device in bags, lapels, caps, sunglasses, pens, alarm clocks, anything. It's all very 007, but these gadgets do an excellent job.

'OK, give me a rundown of what you saw,' I say.

Pulling a notebook from his hoodie pocket, Michael applies an incongruous tenor, like he's doing the promotional voiceover for a horror film.

'Scott Delaney was dropped off in a car. It had a chauffeur. The registration number was HG59 NHK. The time was forty-six minutes past three. The date was today.'

'Make of the car?'

Michael shakes his head – cars aren't his thing.

'Was he alone?'

'Yes. Apart from the driver, who dropped him off and left immediately.'

'And Delaney went straight inside?'

'Yes.'

'Carrying anything?'

'His phone.'

'An iPhone or BlackBerry?'

'Yes.'

I laugh. Michael does not. My brother is a slave to pedantry. Intently he waits for the next question.

'And he let himself into the house?'

'Yes.'

'Using his own keys?'

'I cannot swear they were his.'

'But he got them out of his own pocket?'

'Yes.'

'OK.' I sit on a bench. 'I guess we now wait. See what Scott Delaney gets up to when wifey's away. Then you get to see me in professional action.'

Michael has seen me in professional action plenty of times. Still, it's ever so nice having a witness to your life. Especially one for whom you've never worn thin.

I initiate a covert low-five.

It's only Day One, yet I sense already we are in for a Delaney treat. My synapses are on fire.

NB: it is very annoying when people declare how terribly intuitive they are. It smacks of self-indulgent pseudoscience. But the truth is, I am. *Terribly* intuitive. Rest assured, it's nothing paranormal. For instance, I'm not psychic. I certainly have never communicated with the dead. Most days I don't read my stars in the newspaper (or my ex-husbands'). But I do get a sense of stuff before it happens. Darwin might argue I'm at an evolutionary advantage. Like people with good spatial awareness, or brilliant swimmers. Or men so mesmeric they become the polygamous leaders of religious cults. Whatever, mark my words, today something monumental is on the horizon.

Case 0135/Operation Delaney

Monday 30 June

7.00 a.m. Surveillance commenced.

3.46 p.m. Target was dropped off at his property on Blomfield Road, W2. He alighted from a chauffeur-driven car, registration number HG59 NHK. Mr

Delaney wore Versace jeans, straight leg, stonewash black denim, distressed edges and hems (32-inch waist, 32-inch leg), Paul Smith slim-fit black chambray shirt (medium), Armani blue and white striped trilby (one size). His head circumference is 22¾ inches. Adidas Vintage Turf trainers (size unknown). He carried a phone and let himself into his house using keys.

8.51 p.m. Light in the front reception room came on.
10.55 p.m. Light in the front reception room went off.
10.56 p.m. Light in the upstairs hall came on.
10.59 p.m. Light in the upstairs hall went off.
11.30 p.m. Surveillance terminated.

Today I muddled intuition with a whole host of other feelings.

I saw the Poet, who had identical hair to the motorcyclist, and we sustained eye contact, leading me to a disquieting conclusion – he didn't like me one bit.

Maybe he thought I was someone else? I was, after all, disguised as atmosphere.

Equally as possible – he's the crazed henchman of an ex-target.

Today I also realised that my mother could be anywhere, doing anything – and that is a *beautiful* thing. So you can see that on many levels my adrenal glands got overexcited, the waters became muddied. It happens; ask Darwin. If nothing else, it goes to prove an important scientific truth: happiness is a crock of shit, little more than a biochemical figment of our imagination.

At 11.30 p.m. on the first day of surveillance, my brother and I, bored and cold, call it a night.

First, however, I make him jump the electronic gates and crawl the circumference of the target's gravelled drive, careful to avoid the security lighting. Arriving on all fours at the

Mercedes SLK, Michael then places a twopenny piece – my unlucky coin – very precisely on Delaney's rear left tyre.

Harassed, my dad stirs the sausage casserole, because I'm fourteen and every question I ask is completely exhausting.

'If she's dead, where's her body?' I demand.

'We don't know, Florrie. She doesn't want us to find her.'

'*Doesn't?*' I gasp.

'Didn't.'

Plus all my questions without fail lead to another, more exhausting one.

'Where are her clothes?'

'What?'

'The clothes she was wearing. And her chilli necklace.' I caress my naked throat. 'She'd have left it to me if she planned to die.'

'We don't know she *planned* to die.' As usual, Dad becomes quickly tetchy. To be fair, he has told me this a lot of times before. 'Florence, she suffered from terribly low moods.'

But I never saw any sign of it. Surely I'd have sensed her unhappiness. I was a child. Children are able to detect the smallest change in their emotional environment. She wasn't depressed; I would have felt it.

'She had a Latin temperament,' I remind him.

He shakes his head. 'It was post-natal depression.'

I look at my dad suspiciously. I'm playing games with him, I know, but it's the only way I can break through the armour, weaken him: by bombarding him with questions.

'Was it Michael's fault, then? Did he cause her depression?'

'No!' His eyes get really angry, and it's horrible to admit, but I'm glad of it. He exists well enough as long as we pretend everything's perfectly fine. 'Your mother was devoted to that boy.'

He puts the wooden spoon down, turns to face me, leans

99

on the kitchen table. This is apparently a very important point – a new important point that will definitely infiltrate my angry pubescent brain.

Please God, let this sink in with her. His face looks full of hope.

He points. 'That's why she had the *cornichello* – to protect Michael. It protects mothers and their babies.'

I'm ashamed, but I didn't want to hear that; that her pretty golden chilli was all about her hopes for Michael.

I was her baby too.

I burst into tears. My father takes a step back. I'm not a crier, but since I started having periods, it's becoming a more common thing, usually when we're all least expecting it. He shuffles awkwardly, picks up the wooden spoon. He becomes totally useless whenever I get an attack of the hormones.

Today, however, he has a brilliant idea.

He suddenly waves the spoon at me: I'm not to move a muscle. Cleaning his hands on a tea towel, he digs in a pocket. Then in kitchen drawers – all nine of them. Then through the hall drawers. Screwdrivers, batteries, junk mail, buttons are tossed aside.

Finally he swings around.

Between a reverent finger and thumb he has a dirty coin. Like a priest proffering communion bread, he holds it aloft.

For the tiniest moment I wonder if saying *Amen* and sticking out my tongue is the correct response.

In a voice deserving of choral accompaniment, Dad now explains:

'This is an extremely rare coin, Florrie. A collector's item. Like a four-leaf clover. Or a Kabbalistic amulet.'

I frown. 'It's a two pee.'

He pushes the coin at me. I take it gingerly, because I don't like the smell of old coins.

'Between 1971 and 1981, the number two on a twopenny

piece was written below the plume of feathers. This was followed by the words "NEW PENCE". Then it all changed!'

I sniff and smile despite myself. 'All right, Gandalf.'

He ramps up the drama.

'From 1982, the Royal Mint wrote "TWO PENCE" instead of "NEW PENCE". And here's the strange part . . .'

He holds my arm, as if I'm about to run away. I'm not. I want to hear the strange part.

'Mysteriously, in 1983 a tiny number of "NEW PENCE" coins emerged.'

'Why?'

'Nobody knows.'

And that's it.

My dad just nods with the biggest eyes for quite a long time.

It's a rubbish story. I hold the smelly coin away from me and try to get this straight.

Michael has the (non) memory of a golden amulet worn about his dead mother's neck. I'm given a coin so immaterial, it lives with the spare buttons nobody will ever sew back on.

Dad goes back to cooking the casserole, as if everything is better.

And I slump in a kitchen chair – the pongy coin between my fingertips. I must come across as a very shallow girl, I conclude. It's really depressing when your dad really hasn't the foggiest idea who you really are.

It's two in the morning; nonetheless, I need to focus on the job in hand: Scott Delaney.

To help, I sit cross-legged on my mattress and build a spliff. Light it. Ensure its rim is an unremitting circle of fire.

Inhale the smoke. Admire all sides of its shaft as though it's an exquisite cigar. A Cohiba Espléndido, perhaps – that cigar was conceived by Che Guevara, who only let Fidel Castro and his Marxist cronies smoke them.

I have Husband Number One to blame for this habit. His medicine became mine.

I'm blinder than usual in this case, and my notes on Scott Delaney are sparse. I google him a little more . . .

His date of birth, for example.

Scott's a Pisces – a brilliant fact what with me being a Cancerian.

Piscean men and Cancerian women are a textbook match. They don't need words, their connection operating at a purely subconscious level. This is because Pisceans and Cancerians are neurochemically wired to experience the most scientific type of love there is – love at first sight.

FYI: astrology is the only subject upon which Richard Dawkins and I disagree. It isn't mumbo-jumbo. It's science that doesn't behave like modern science. And although we are yet to fathom the geometric correlations between planets, it does not mean we should pooh-pooh their influence on neurochemistry and/or the mystic spinning of threads.

On every other level Richard and I are on the same page.

Pisceans, a downside: they are neurotically loyal. Once they've identified the One (correctly or incorrectly), their faithfulness borders on obsequiousness. Rarely do they stray.

I examine the photograph of Scott on the front of *Time Out New York*, the publication that Alice gave me in the hotel bar. He's singing to the camera. One hand cradles a microphone. The other is aloft, as if he's holding a perfectly creamy note.

I study the shape of Scott's raised hand.

His palm is oval, his fingers more or less equal in height – I measure the dimensions roughly with a matchstick. They're also long and flexible – look how his little finger bows ever so slightly upwards. Scott is not just a water sign; he has a water hand.

Doubly fortuitous.

Because water hands belong to people who are extremely artistic, and artistic people are overemotional, rubbish with stress and fuelled by their feelings. In other words, they are flaky – flaky men being the best targets ever.

I clap. Which is silly; I'm studying his palm. But you get your ups where you can.

Excited now, I apply a little metoposcopy, also known as Chinese face-reading.

The hairline is particularly telling. In China it's known as 'mother's influence'. A mother's most important gift is an understanding of the rules of society – always pleasing others, giving them a good impression of yourself. As an evolutionary biologist, I can vouch for this fact: mingling socially is a crucial survival tool.

Trouble is, a mother's influence should be gentle.

If she's dictatorial in her opinions, has specific ideas as to the exact type of person you should be, then it can take a long time to figure out who you really are. Her influence becomes too entrenched in your psyche, her dominance remaining with you long after you've flown the nest.

A person who's had an oppressive mother's influence will have a beautifully rounded hairline. No wispiness. No unevenness. Because they've not been allowed to deviate.

Scott Delaney's hairline forms as perfect an arc as I've ever seen. Its edge is as smooth as the moon's.

He started his career young, I remember. Plucked from obscurity in Ireland at fifteen. The junta took the place of his mother – maybe it was them who carved his flawless hairline.

Firmly I close my laptop, think about my disguise for tomorrow, smooth wispy hairs from my temples.

Betty Blue

Tuesday. Day Two: Operation Delaney.

6.00 a.m.

Michael is at Regent's Canal before me. He looks tired but exhilarated – I'm twenty feet away, but he's already shouting as quietly as possible:

'His daps – they were size ten.'

On arrival at my brother's chest, I give him a sleepy hug and attempt to nestle my head between his pecs. But it's like being sandwiched by house bricks. Still, I could nod off here, in the grouting between his sternal muscles, his heartbeat so sturdy and predictable.

'You've been thinking about Delaney's trainers all night?' I mumble into his T-shirt.

'A lot of the night,' he admits, hands dangling at his sides.

I wish he'd hug me back. But if he did, it wouldn't be him, not really. Foisting social etiquette on the mentally left-of-field is not fair. So I eavesdrop on his heart instead and pretend it's singing my name.

Michael digs at his pocket and pulls out the coin.

'It was still on the back wheel,' he states.

'The target's been nowhere. Good.' I punch him in the appendix. 'Punctual and super-organised – I knew you'd be a great Norwegian.'

It's a classic investigative method, the coin-on-the-tyre trick. I use it often during infidelity cases. Local authorities use it too, though their goals are different to mine. They aim to decimate single-parent families mostly. A typical case:

A lover drives to said single parent's house. An investigator puts a coin on the lover's tyre at midnight. He then returns at six o'clock the following morning. If the coin's still there, legally speaking the lover has overstayed his welcome. If the lover repeats this routine three nights out of seven, then bingo. The local authority can take away the single parent's benefits, send them to prison and put their children in care. Benefit fraud fact: making love too often is technically cohabitation, and cohabitation makes you financially responsible for another man's progeny.

Taking my 2p, I poke it deep into the pocket of my jeans. The coin represents abject misery and symbolises everything I want to forget. I've been trying to lose it for years – accidentally, because I'd never forgive myself if I mislaid it deliberately. Yet today things feel a little different. I'm not so keen for the coin to ping back to the Royal Mint Twilight Zone whence it came. Maybe it's because everything's changed – what with my mum stalking me.

'Let's just hope we have more luck today, eh?' I say while Michael readjusts my beret so its piped edge is equidistant with my eyebrows. 'It's supposed to be crooked,' I tell him. 'I'm French.'

'I do know.'

Now he spends time straightening the auburn wig beneath my hat, because this boy loves things in their place, just like our mother.

I point at his jeans. 'Are they Dad's?'

'Yes.'

Michael's T-shirt, a maroon Fruit of the Loom affair, definitely belongs to Dad. And on my brother's nose sits a pair of square rimless glasses.

'*Bravo, très norvégien.*'

'I was going for asexual Scandinavian.' He has an actual twinkle in his eye, and real, proper twinkles are so rare; it feels for a split second like he's coming out of a coma. In these moments I think I see my brother – the one who might have been had his potential not been foiled by a neurodevelopmental blip.

I beam. 'Where did you get the specs?'

He beams too. 'Sébastien.'

'They're filthy,' I say flatly.

Then I shiver. It's my synapses; they're fizzing again. Yesterday's burst of intuition might not have been misplaced after all – just a little premature, which makes perfect sense. I'm a Cancerian – the impatient type. Plus Desmond Morris would tell you how the underuse of our sixth sense means that now and then it's a little off-piste.

For lunch I go straight to the Café Laville to sip a latte and look at Maida Vale. Mostly to look out for the Poet, because stalkers are unbelievably romantic *only* when they remain a figment of your imagination. The only exception to this: if the stalker is definitely your soulmate.

My stalker isn't. He looked at me with Robert Mugabe Eyes. I'm extremely pleased to see that he's nowhere in sight.

Twenty minutes into my countersurveillance, I get a phone call from Michael.

Case 0135/Operation Delaney
Tuesday 1 July
6.00 a.m. Surveillance commenced.
4.01 p.m. Target exited property in Blomfield Road, W2. He walked to his car and opened the passenger door. He pulled a CD from the glove compartment. He wore a dove-grey Nike fleece tracksuit, large. Adidas Vintage Turf trainers, size 10. A 59Fifty LA baseball cap, one size. He then returned inside the house.
8.23 p.m. Light in the front reception room came on.
10.55 p.m. Light in the front reception room went off.
10.56 p.m. Light in the upstairs hall came on.

10.59 p.m. Light in the upstairs hall went off.

11.30 p.m. Surveillance terminated.

A summary of day number two, then:

No Poet. No information on Scott Delaney that will facilitate my wheedling a route into his life. I arrive home at 11.58 p.m. to find my bedsit exactly as I left it. No enigmatic correspondence has been slipped under the door. My mother appears not to have transmogrified into gas and seeped in through the sash. Nothing in my flat has been moved, not even slightly. My internet history has not been deleted. My photos have not been accessed – especially not the photo of Michael, Dad and me holidaying in Bideford when I was twelve.

When I open my emails, I find no discount vouchers for Pizza Express. No Nigerian prince needs my help to free his millions from a British bank account. Cancer Research don't tell me they've raised four hundred million pounds thanks to women like me, and that I'm ethically obliged to walk, jog or run one of their events to ensure the survival of womankind. Just five tiny kilometres to help beat cancer – the equivalent of once up and down Oxford Street.

OK. Can I be honest?

I would flatly refuse to sponsor anyone who was doing the equivalent of an hour's stroll around the shops. Learn to run the distance, I'd tell them; it's hardly a marathon. Personally, I'd train to win it. Walking any distance for charity is a terrible cop-out. It makes a farce of the whole endeavour. It's like paying people to breathe or watch morning TV, or to exist in four-dimensional space–time.

I consider a consolatory flick of the bean, then remember I have life coaching at ten thirty the following morning. This is generally how it goes: I offload; in return, he tells me how to live my life. It's much the same as a normal relationship, only I pay a fee. During our last session we spoke about *Mastermind* and what my specialist subject would be. Men, I said, because they were by far the simplest of all topics. Dr Malik begged to differ: if I were such an expert, I wouldn't be thirty-three and twice divorced with not even the mirage of a boyfriend on the horizon.

I don't pay Dr Malik to coat it in sugar.

I send him an email to cancel and, while at the computer, forward today's surveillance report to Alice, along with a request for the transfer of more funds.

Immediately a new email pings into my inbox; my chin flops into my chest.

I am very professional indeed, yet I don't want an email from Alice, who is teetering on an appalling emotional precipice, watching her inbox all day, a surveillance report finally arriving, her heart pounding like a death drum; until she discovers that, for today at least, her boyfriend has remained faithful.

She should be relieved. But she won't be. The report is embarrassingly sparse. For the cash she's spending, she'll wants photos of drug-fuelled orgies. Well, she doesn't *want* drug-fuelled orgies per se; she just wants her money's worth. And so she'll email me a million pointless questions: were the blinds pulled halfway down or three quarters of the way down? Did the postman come once or twice? How's the rhododendron doing, the one left of the porch?

Thankfully the email is not from Alice.

Re: My freind missing
Tuesday 1/7/14 23.38 p.m.
From: tarikma68@yahoo.co.uk
To: info@londonpiservices.uk.net

Dear Sir,
    My freind no longer in Libya. Sauces tell me he
move to Brazil.
    Yours sincerely,
    Tarik Mohammad Amazigh

I shake my head at Tarik Mohammad Amazigh. He's quite
a character. I write back, decline again politely, point him in
the right direction one last time, because I know what it's like
to be on the lookout for a friend. Proper friends, true love,
all that TV-happy-ending shit doesn't come along too often.

It feels like a film.

Luke Birmingham is in my campus room at university.

I sit on the single bed. He sits opposite me on a desk
chair, smoking a joint. Blu-tacked to the breeze-block wall
behind his head is a film poster. *Betty Blue*.

The poignancy is breathtaking.

I draw positive vibes from Beatrice Dalle, from that entire
film, because possibly the most attractive boy that ever lived
is currently sitting opposite me.

Betty in *Betty Blue* was mentally unbalanced and sexually
aggressive, but boy, she did it with aplomb. If I'm *ever* to get
past third base, I have to start taking a leaf out of her book.

'It's a sub-field of biology,' I'm telling Luke Birmingham.

And he is saying, 'That's fascinating, Flo,' and is really
meaning it. I know this because I am brilliant at body language
and his lean is very enthusiastic.

'Basically I study the evolutionary processes that produced
the diversity of life on earth. The descent and origin of
species. I'm especially interested in human evolution, you
know, that socio-cultural stuff.'

I've never smoked drugs before, but when he offers me the

joint, I take it and puff on it once, far too quickly, like it's toxic.

I'm not the most experienced with boys, but even I know this topic's getting old. It's time to stop talking. Yet the last two months have been a revelation. Evolutionary science can answer almost every question in the emotional world, which is really exciting shit. It's psychotherapy for the scientist – of course I can't stop talking about it, because that is super-interesting. Plus there's nothing more aphrodisiacal than having a guy hang off your every word; which is exactly what Luke Birmingham has been doing all night.

Luke Birmingham.

At school, back in Laurelbridge, he was at the top of every girl's things-to-do list. He still is. Tonight, however, he's here with me, in my room at uni, asking a lot of questions, nodding slowly at my every utterance.

He's also smoking a joint in my room, which makes me feel totally cool.

It's as though he's seeing me for the first time. And that's the best feeling ever, when you fall into place for someone.

'You were always brainy at school,' Luke nods.

And so do I, because I was. 'I have an insatiable need to know everything.'

When he chuckles and claps on his knee like a saxophonist might, I feel so alive.

Luke Birmingham fact: he didn't know I existed at school, let alone the state of my academic progress. I was an extra in his school days. Why would he notice me? There were always girls with fatter, more delicious plaits. Girls who wore perennially washed and ironed school skirts rolled up at the waist to expose tanned and shaven knees. Girls with breasts, in itself ticking the boxes for his primal pubescent urges – an evolutionary science fact I learnt early on in this very degree course.

I cock my head inquisitively. 'You're here a lot, more than some of the students.'

He throws the finished joint out of the window, and I don't even worry that the ground staff might think it's mine. 'Visiting my cousin,' he says. 'He's doing media studies.'

'And when you're not here?'

'A venture capitalist,' he says.

'Wow,' I say, because that's unexpected. 'How does a nineteen-year-old make enough capital to have an adventure with?'

Luke becomes thoughtful; his brow clenches into a sort of frown. Maybe it's his thinking face. Or maybe it was a rude question; I probably did come across a bit sceptical. I glance at Betty Blue. *Enough*, she says. *You're at university now*. She's right – I've left all that playground bullshit behind.

And if there's one thing I've learnt since leaving Dorset for the University of Winchester, it's that three things cannot be hidden for long – the sun, the moon and the truth. My best friend, Olivia, said that. Well, Buddha said it first, but Olivia was the one who told me, because she's all about Truth, which means *always* being yourself.

We became instant besties at Freshers' Week. Olivia's doing physics, so she just instinctively comes at things from a very cool perspective.

Life is good.

I have a friend, and now Luke Birmingham is sitting here – tonight, at this precise moment – in my bedroom, looking at me as though I'm riveting.

Well, he was until I questioned his job title.

'Interested parties donate money,' he tells me earnestly, deciding to roll another joint, slowly, as though the information he's about to share is *huge*. 'People who have faith in me,' he nods.

His seriousness makes me smile. 'Are you starting a cult?'

He looks up from his plastic bag of grass and smiles mischievously. 'Why, would you join?'

'Depends on your manifesto.' The way that comes out is just awesome. It's probably one of the coolest thing I have *ever* said in my life.

It obviously has clout with Luke too, because he instantly moves off his chair, holds his fingers out towards my face.

Aortic function goes into immediate overdrive. A sound boom could pick up my heartbeat. Instinctively I close my eyes. My lips, however, forget entirely to pucker up, which I intend thanking God for later, because Luke doesn't conclude his manoeuvre with a kiss.

He flicks a small something from my nose.

My shoulders rocket.

He's back in the chair, sprinkling marijuana into a cigarette paper, talking shop. 'I'm devising a new type of board game,' he's saying.

Cruel, contagious purple splodges appear on my cheek – I feel like I've been hot-branded.

Jesus, let it have been an eyelash.

'It's a mix between Trivial Pursuits and Name That Tune, only revolving around the media of film.'

Or a crisp crumb. Please let it have been a crumb of salt and vinegar crisp – not ideal, but infinitely preferable to the worst-case scenario.

'Name That Film, I could call it.' He waves a hand, expertly licking the edge of the cigarette paper. 'It's a working title. Basically you guess the film from the strapline. There's a lot of room to expand the concept. Sub-categories, specific years and genres, catch lines from TV programmes. The possibilities are endless, you know . . .'

'Did I have a bogey on my nose?' I ask straight out, because this is quite a moment for me and I can't concentrate properly until I know one way or the other.

He laughs loudly, like I'm one of the boys. Nodding at his faux pas. Inhaling deeply on the joint.

'That gesture was supposed to be intimate.' He pauses, holds my gaze effortlessly. 'I just wanted to touch you.'

My cheek patches burn – I'd bet my portable TV they're the colour of meningitis.

'Good.' I point at his nostril. 'Because you've got a massive pile-up.'

After a nanosecond of nothing, Luke begins to roar. Then I do too. Soon we are laughing like idiots, abandoned, the way you laugh with cousins even when you haven't seen them in years.

The laughter is interspersed only with Luke secretly wiping his nose every ten seconds – but I don't tell him he hasn't really got a pile-up, because the vulnerability it affords him is mesmerising.

Then I cut the jollities dead.

'In Vietnam the wind doesn't blow it sucks,' I say.

He passes me the joint. 'You what?'

'*Platoon*. That's the strapline.'

He touches his cheeks like I'm the first woman who ever really got him. Then he says: 'They grew up on the outside of society. They weren't looking for a fight. They were looking to belong.'

My puff on the joint is a little braver than before. I hold down a cough. Tap my forehead with a fast fingernail, because the name of that film's on the tip of my tongue.

'*The Outsiders*,' he shouts.

I stamp and cough. 'Why did you do that? I was almost there.'

Quickly I try to think of straplines, but only rookie suggestions come to mind – *Just when you thought it was safe to go back in the water. In space no one can hear you scream.*

I point, triumphant. 'One man's struggle to take it easy.'

Luke totally ignores me. Instead, he directs his own strapline histrionically to the wall behind me: 'They only met once but it changed their lives forever.' He doesn't give me a millisecond to hazard a guess before spurting out the answer: '*The Breakfast Club*!'

'I knew that. It's not much of a game if you're the only one allowed to play.'

'*Ferris Bueller's Day Off*,' he says, victorious. 'That was yours.'

I kick his knee. 'How did you get that?'

'You'll have to excuse me.' He kicks me back. 'I'm just like you.'

I put a hand on my hip, hold the joint aloft with the free hand, do a face like Beatrice Dalle, who's pouting on the wall behind his head. 'And how, Luke, is that?'

'*Weirdly* passionate about my subject.'

In retrospect I might put this moment down to the alignment of the stars. For the moment, all I know is that I currently inhabit one of the most romantic moments of my life.

His eyes gleam, – I mean, *gleeeeam*. Luminosity emanates from his whole face.

When he stands up, walks to me, pulls me to my feet, I think I see his aura. My legs become frail, they actually shake, yet he holds on to me with an expert grip. One hand cups my cheek, the other my waist; he nudges the hair from my eyes with his nose.

Close up he's achingly Matt Dillon.

I wonder if, deep down, he's as tortured as me.

I forget entirely to think about what percentage of tongue to use, or how many open-mouthed plunges should be completed before the interspersion of some playful pecks. I guess sometimes a moment is so idyllic, it feels scripted. And in this scene, *the* Luke Birmingham kisses *me*, Florence Love, the brainy extra. And it's so bloody perfect, we could be in a TV programme.

The one in which I'm about to lose my virginity.

The Incest Taboo

Wednesday. Day Three: Operation Delaney.

8.23 a.m.

'Know what, Michael? I'm going to tackle Scott Delaney in the same way I would a potential husband.'

My brother peers over the rim of Sébastien's glasses. 'Ten minutes ago you said: *This, Michael, is the shite-ist stakeout I have ever orchestrated.*'

It's a good impression, but I do not congratulate him.

'The man can't stay inside for ever. When he does come out, and we're able to establish some kind of routine, I'm going to be very elusive.'

'That doesn't make sense.'

'Elusiveness is a very attractive attitude, Michael. An excellent attitude if you want a relationship to work.' I put a precautionary finger in the air. 'Never be yourself.'

Michael looks genuinely disappointed.

I shrug. 'That's evolution, Michael. It's not cynicism; it's science.'

'What happened with Luke, then? You're the cynicism type, but he still divorced you.'

A rule that Michael is unable to get his head around: I don't use the Luke word. Nor the Birmingham word. And he didn't divorce me. He screwed my best friend. There's no way round that.

I take a deep breath. The mention of his name releases a flock of rabid crows that nip ferociously at my heart. Every time.

'Husband Number One is a case in point.' I make my

voice strong. 'I wasn't elusive back then, to my detriment.'

Michael does the bouncy nod of someone for whom everything has fallen into place. It hasn't. He's bored. He wants me to stop talking.

Sébastien's face pops into my head. Sébastien's not a she, but I'm not entirely sure he's a he either. Sébastien is a Ridley Scott prototype for a horror film about mannequins – walking ones who forgo elbow and knee joints in favour of the fully functioning eyes of a large mammal.

I shudder. 'It's interesting what we find attractive.'

'Yes,' says Michael. 'In the olden days, men went for women with big vaginas. That meant they could have lots of children safely, one after the other.' He rubs his stomach as if pregnant. 'I'd kill for a Gourmet Burger.'

I squash a Pavarotti in his hand (middle-class for a tenner) and stare at Delaney's front door.

'That's when society favoured fecundity and reproduction, Michael. Nowadays women are happy to rely on hip signals instead.' I give him a practical demonstration – remind him of my slink.

'Now, go eat!'

But Michael's already gone.

It's good that I teach him this stuff. Who else does he have to talk to? Not Sébastien. Sébastien hasn't the facial dexterity to form words. Plus properly intelligent people don't have electrolysis only to paint hair back on, just more neatly.

When Michael comes back, I give him a test.

Unfortunately his carbohydrate buzz is waning.

'I know it all already,' he sighs.

'Consider it a refresher course.' I clap my hands proactively. 'OK, the basic stages for successful entrapment are . . .?'

I give him clues – hold four fingers in the air.

Michael's response is lacklustre: 'Surveillance. Bump One. Bump Two. And the money shot.'

'Surveillance being key. We glean the target's routine, whilst never making eye contact, otherwise it's . . .'

'Game over.'

'Good. Now tell me about Bump One.'

Michael impersonates someone who's semiconscious. 'Accidentally bump into your target.'

'A *hypothetical* bump, though. Not a proper bump. Enough to render the target intrigued. Now, Bump Two?'

'Bump into your target again – hypothetically.'

'Time to flirt a little.'

Michael kicks an empty water bottle into the canal. Then cigarette stubs. Then stones.

Then air.

'The money shot?' I keep him focused.

'He contacts you. Blah blah blah. Turn up late. Look hot.'

'Sophisticated-hot. Concentrate, Michael.'

'I am. Do that symbolic striptease stuff. The touch test thingy. Kiss him. Only for five seconds.' His sigh is suddenly hopeless, his eyes puppy-dog sad. 'You know, I've tried all this with Sébastien – all the stages, all four of them, Flo.'

This is what I *should* tell Michael:

Stop kissing him for just five seconds, then maybe try ten seconds next time, then fifteen.

But I don't, because I feel a bit weirded-out.

'Mix it up a bit.' My advice is non-committal.

Quickly I change the subject, nod across the canal at the big white mansion.

'God help this one, eh?' I snort like it's a done deal. 'Scott Delaney's got it coming. The whole shebang – surveillance, two bumps and a snog.' I tap my nose as if that's where I hide all my intuition.

'I'm feeling good today. Yep, today is *the* day. Watch this space.'

Michael stares at me as if I'm the one with a borderline personality disorder.

Case 0135/Operation Delaney
Wednesday 2 July
6.00 a.m. Surveillance commenced.
9.12 a.m. The postman called.
8:34 p.m. Light in the front reception room came on.
10.55 p.m. Light in the front reception room went off.
10.56 p.m. Light in the upstairs hall came on.
10.59 p.m. Light in the upstairs hall went off.
11.30 p.m. Surveillance terminated.

My very final word on intuition, ever:
Scientifically speaking, intuition is where past experiences and external cues lead us to make decisions on a non-conscious level. The subsequent reaction is ridiculously quick. So quick we're unaware that it shoots from a supercharged burst of logical thinking.

I reiterate: a supercharged burst of logical thinking.

And logic is not one hundred per cent guaranteed to be right — it's just likely to be a sensible punt. And in the inimitable words of my uncle Fergus: *The world don't always roll how you hope, baby.*

Uncle Fergus.

Now he was a worldly-wise man. And a paedophile, I think.

I feel very guilty — not about Uncle Fergus kissing me on the mouth when I was six, but about Alice. It's the end of day three and I'm sitting on my mattress totting up how much this case has cost her so far. Three and a half grand. The reports I've emailed average out at £12.80 a word. There are dictators on less.

My only consolation is that it's entirely her own fault. Had she let me in the house, I could have bugged it, which would have been an enormous help. Assuming of course she is named on the utility bills.

Legal fact: when installing covert surveillance in somebody's home, always get the permission of the bill-payer first. Stealing electricity is a crime. Bugging a target's bedroom, not so much – just one of the ironies of this profession.

When I email today's non-findings to Alice, I tell her straight. The man doesn't leave the bloody house. Unless she can come up with a way of my accidentally bumping into a hermit, I'm destined to continue wasting her cash.

But Alice sends a quite beautiful email. It's heartfelt. She begs me to stay on the case. As I read, I imagine her gorgeous voice. Wish that I were as articulate as her. Remember her father's broken heart, damaged beyond repair by a flibber-tigibbet of a soulmate. In another life, I wonder, would Alice and I have been friends?

I check myself.

When the job's done, you're instantly dumped; the very last person a client wants to be having girlie nights in with. Clients *always* make you feel imperative at the beginning. They need you. It's flattering, that's all.

Uncle Fergus used to flatter me all the time . . .

I was the prettiest thing he'd ever seen, he said. I was not. I've seen the photographs – ninety per cent snot, ten per cent one oversized front tooth.

God, I haven't thought about him in years.

Pushing my laptop to one side, I cut my toenails with some kitchen scissors, and for the first time in a decade I think about my dad's creepy younger brother.

Uncle Fergus whooshed into our lives on birthdays and at Christmas like an unwelcome drugs baron. Everyone was polite to the point of obsequiousness. Outsiders wouldn't necessarily have sensed the underlying atmosphere, but I was a child, able only to experience the world in its purest form, one untainted by hormones and experience. Even when I picture his visits now, our living room looks different in my head – it's tinged grey like a neo-noir film and we're all bathed in a shadowy hue.

I'll conjure an image of him for you, though I admit the passing of time may have reduced him to a caricature: John Travolta out of *Saturday Night Fever*, only portly, with a fat black moustache, perma-tan and Ray-Bans.

Other things I remember.

His aftershave was strong, in those days a sign of upward mobility, especially when it was an expensive brand bought from a proper concession in a proper department store – Kouros or Aramis. He smoked cigars that looked like fat black fingers. His breath was whisky-sweet. Gold signet ring, gold belcher chain, gold identity bracelet; one of his back teeth was gold too. Even his Ford Capri 3000E was a mustardy yellow.

He'd never married, but was a self-confessed ladies' man – the florid stories of his conquests were delivered freely and without appropriate consideration for his audience. I'm not sure I understood most of them at the time, but his antics definitely involved air hostesses and Avon ladies.

Gran would shake her head as if his incorrigibility was delightful.

Mum hedged her bets and half laughed at everything.

Dad became uncharacteristically domesticated – he'd get up and do things like straighten the rug or fill up a bowl with cheesy footballs.

Then the kissing incident happened.

We didn't see much of Uncle Fergus after that.

Extraordinary really – I can't believe I haven't thought

about this more deeply before: the enormity of that moment, twenty-seven years ago. A fully grown blood relative duped me into lip-kissing when I was a child – that's some heavy shit.

I guess heavier shit usurped it, with what happened to Mum.

I still have his vanity case, which now feels totally weird. It's on top of the wardrobe. I keep my surveillance equipment in it. I decide firmly to buy a new one.

Surprisingly, however, my paedophilic uncle Fergus gives me a brilliant idea. Immediately I phone Michael.

'Do you remember Uncle Fergus?' I ask.

'No.'

'Dad's brother.'

'Oh, yes,' he says. 'But no.'

'You were too little.' It's lonely being the elder child. 'Well, he's given me a brainwave.'

'When?'

'Just now.'

'He's there?'

'No. I was thinking about him and the thought I was thinking gave me an idea.'

'Oh.' He is smiling, I can hear it. 'I thought you said Uncle Fergus gave you the idea.'

Sometimes it's best to ignore Michael. 'Surveillance tomorrow. We've been resting on our laurels. This case requires a change of tack, so you'll be on your own for a bit. I'll join you after lunch.'

He starts to complain, but I am not in the mood – Uncle Fergus kissed me when I was six and I feel violated. Plus I've committed to a job that's going as slowly as a job can. I look like a clown. I also want to get off the phone and wonder things. Like, did Dad ever tell Mum or Gran about Uncle Fergus's penchant for pre-pubescent girls? How might

Uncle Fergus's life have changed if he had? What would he have done to keep everyone quiet, to appease those around him?

This is what I would do in Fergus's position: whatever the hell I was bloody well told.

I speak too quickly:

'I know the last three days have been long and dull, Michael, but we have to tackle every day with a more determined cunning. No arguments, I need you there tomorrow, bright and early.'

'I need a day off, Flo.'

So I play my trump card. 'Michael Love, don't you fucking dare. You owe me.'

He doesn't ask what for. He knows I have an encyclopedic list ready for the day he does.

More fed up than I've ever heard him, he grunts, ''K.'

He's not to know that tomorrow he'll learn this valuable lesson: that occasionally bribery has a *very* important place.

Huge Miscalculation

Thursday. Day Four: Operation Delaney.

13.03 p.m.

Maeve's eyes plead with me.

She is in the middle of a business lunch at the Square in Mayfair. I have shimmied straight in, past security, past the maître d'. They assume from my arrogance that I dine here daily. Now I kneel beside her.

'Do excuse me, ladies and gentlemen.' The smile I give Maeve's guests revolves largely around the eyes. It's a flirty, mischievous look – not one you'd do at a gathering where it's important the wives like you.

I turn to Maeve. 'A little chat?'

Her business associates have stopped eating, talking, breathing. Maeve's reaction is not one they've seen her do before. Her customary fearlessness has dissipated. Bewilderment is all that remains. Silently she drops her napkin and walks obediently to the door. I follow her, slinking as I go, because I know they're watching my arse.

Infidelity fact: *only* when approached by illicit ex-lovers do millionaire businesswomen drop their napkin and walk obediently to a door.

Naturally Maeve's lunch guests are too professional to say anything whilst she's in earshot. This, however, is what they'll be whispering as soon as we've left the room:

Fuck me sideways, Maeve Rivers, chief editor of a tabloid newspaper famed for its toe-curling exposés and the decimation of celebrity lives, has had an extramarital affair . . . with another woman.

Or something along those lines.

They are likely also to whisper:

And the other woman: did you see her? She is fit.

I apologise: the truth sometimes sounds egotistical when said out loud. But on the looks front, Maeve Rivers found herself playing in the Premiership. Which I think is what secretly riles me most of all – she's never been nearly grateful enough.

If I bagged Scott Delaney, for example, I'd be *forever* appreciative.

'What the fuck are you playing at?' Maeve spits at me once we're outside the restaurant, lighting a cigarette, forgetting to offer me one.

'I need to speak to you.'

'Now?'

'Err, yes.'

'This isn't about the bloody money?'

I pull an envelope from my pocket and hold it out to her. 'There's two grand in there.'

'I've told you, I don't want it.'

'And I've told you, a deal is a deal.'

'Keep it.'

'No.'

'Tell you what, Florence. Why don't you look at it as it was intended?' The flicker of a smile. 'A payment for services rendered.'

In the absence of hindsight, I still know this – Maeve Rivers has just shot herself in both feet with an Uzi semi-automatic machine gun. I'd simply hoped to ask for a little favour. A good turn between two friends once so close they played a game called Naked Superglue.

Slowly I growl, 'For services fucking rendered?'

In return, she rests a smug elbow in the palm of her free hand, holding her cigarette aloft as if she's Cruella fucking De Vil, or Greta fucking Garbo.

She thinks she's won.

I flick the cigarette out of her hand.

She laughs at me, so I put my nose too close to hers. 'I am not a prostitute, Maeve. Neither am I married or pretending to be anything I'm not.'

She doesn't take a step back. 'You're a private *dick*. Pretending to be anything other than yourself is compulsory.'

It is important I retain control.

'So this is the plan,' I tell her. 'I'm going to take your advice: sell a story. And I thought I'd give you first dibs. *Everybody* would be interested – those bigwigs in there, your readership, all eight million of them. Yep, a favour for a favour.'

Her eyes taper. 'What story?'

'Ours, Maeve. I will tell the world you're a two-timing lesbian. In return you can make me a Z-lister.'

'You're *bribing* me?'

'*Moi?* Come on. As if I'd ever keep the camera in my clutch bag turned on.'

'What?'

'When we were eating out.' I bump my nose against hers. 'When you were eating me out.'

Get this straight: I would *never* keep a camera in my clutch bag turned on during any coital encounter. Not unless it was part of a previously organised sex game between myself and a consenting adult.

'Unless of course I left it on by accident.'

'You filmed us?'

'Shedloads of VT – that's what you said the publicists like.'

'You disgusting bitch.'

'It was an accident, Maeve. Every time I filmed us – a total oversight. I swear on your mother's life.' I laugh and poke her in the clavicle. 'I met your mum once, remember?

Her homophobia made Hitler look half-hearted. Let's hope she'll be a little more accepting when it's one of her own.'

Maeve squints hatefully.

I get straight to the point.

'I need to bump into Scott Delaney. He'll be in somebody's contact book – yours, no doubt, or one of your journalist's. What about your show-biz correspondent? He's bound to be interviewing him. A new album's due out – it's a compilation of duets with jazz giants and pop greats. Delaney's in London to publicise it. Tell me your Sunday supplement isn't planning a feature on him?'

Finally she takes a step back, pulls another cigarette from her packet.

'And how, Florence, am I going to facilitate you *bumping* into Scott Delaney exactly?'

'Pathological. That's the word you used to blow smoke up your own arse. Women as *pathological* as you always find a way.' I slip the envelope of money under her arm. 'The briefest of bumps, that's all I need. I'll be in and out. It's nothing that can get you or him in trouble. All above board. I just need this favour. Afterwards, I might even leave London – a new job opportunity, criminal profiler. Your secret will be safe.'

She first needs to get something straight. 'Are you trying to entrap Scott Delaney?'

'I didn't say that.'

'What then?'

'I want free tickets.'

'Officially ridiculous.'

'As you will be, once I sell our sex tape. Think how interested the public will be in me and the work I did for your paper, the information you've slipped me over the years.'

That does it. The magnitude of my threat hits her frown

lines. Suddenly she's pushing the hair from her face, letting the tepid July breeze dry the sweat collecting in her temples and at the nape of her neck.

'I can't help you. He's a nice man.'

'You know him. Good.'

'You'll embarrass yourself.'

'You have my word, I won't. Not me or you. Was I ever anything other than discreet when I worked for you?'

She cannot argue with that. 'Your silence is guaranteed regardless of outcome?'

'That's the deal.'

Maeve Rivers is the coolest character I've ever met. Quick as that, her sweat dissolves. Because regardless of my threats, she knows as well as I do that the likelihood of my entrapping Scott Delaney is infinitesimally small. The ruination of her professional and personal reputation, however, is something I could arrange in a finger-snap.

'And I can trust you how?' she asks, businesslike. 'That you won't mention me to him? That once you've *bumped* into him, you'll fuck off forever?'

Now this I hiss: 'You will never see me again. I swear on *my* mother's life.'

Never, ever have I said that before. And she knows it. Her eyelids flicker.

When I walk away, I don't cry. Maeve's reaction hasn't filled me with confidence. She thinks I'm absurd. She also said, *for services rendered.*

I lift my chin and slink like my life depends upon it.

'And I need it to happen fast,' I shout without looking back at her. 'Like yesterday fast.'

Today Michael has come as a heterosexual.

Legs apart, he sits on a bench reading a copy of *FHM*. I park myself beside him. Neither of us looks at the other.

For surveillance purposes, and given my attire, we will behave like strangers.

I pull a cosmetics mirror from my bag.

It would now appear to an outsider that I am all-consumed in the application of Christian Dior lip gloss – Candy Apple, shade no. 178. In reality I am utilising an alternative optical function: peripheral vision.

Mine is consummate. The result of a higher than average number of receptor cells at the edge of my eyeballs. Unfortunately you'll have to take my word for it. The far peripheral system is notoriously difficult to study. Once you dissect an eyeball and examine it under a microscope, you've separated the eye's visual detection mechanism from the neural processing of the brain: a real bummer for ophthalmological research.

Watching me perched on that bench, touching up my make-up, an outsider might also assume I'm a lawyer of some sort, perhaps on a lunch break – the pinstripe pencil skirt, court shoes, nude tights, no wig, just my own hair: shiny and straight as a ribbon of black granite.

I've come from the Square and mustn't stay here too long. I'm not atmosphere. Men will look twice. The last thing I want is for Scott to finally emerge from his self-imposed house arrest and notice nothing else but the effulgent lawyer-looking type on the bench opposite.

I mumble at the cosmetics mirror.

'Surveillance phase is over, Michael. I have just sorted bump number one. You, my friend, are free to go home.'

My brother sighs, turns a page and says, 'Thanks.'

I wasn't expecting a Hawaiian garland or a commemorative plaque – just a teensy bit of appreciation.

'I'll pay you for the whole day,' I say.

Using the receptors at the edge of my eyes, I see him cross his legs and huffily reposition himself. His left buttock faces me – *talk to the arse*, it says, *'cause the face ain't listening.*

'You're sulking?'

'Not,' he tells his magazine.

'Seriously, Michael, you had better not be in a mood, because I ask for little from you, very little indeed.' He remains silent. 'You're tired and bored, get used to it. Fatigue, professional dissatisfaction, that's the way of the world. I can't mollycoddle you for ever.'

What I can do instead is reel off all the reasons why I am an excellent sister.

'Me and Dad, we pay the rent on your flat, your extortionate mobile bills, the Waitrose bills. I don't even tell you to shop at Asda like every other person who's not minted or got a regular income – have I *ever* told you to shop at Asda?'

Michael's silence is dogged.

I up the ante. 'When they tied you to the railings at school, who rescued you? Who? Who fought, *physically* fought people when they called you names?'

And by Christ, I did. Not in a cool way, either. I was a bashful and weedy assailant – the bullies only laughed harder. Still I pushed people shyly and yanked their hair hesitantly, because it broke my heart watching him try so hard to make them like him.

He gave them his pocket money; made glittery cards asking if they'd be his friend; he baked them sodding cakes. Still the children called him Chutney Farmer and Ginger Beer. They'd talk at him like their tongues were too big for their mouths. But he wasn't mental; he was unique. Things took a little longer to develop for him. Like understanding that cynicism and self-serving guile are more useful attributes than kindness and honesty – he never got his head around that.

I snap my mirror shut and turn and look directly at Michael. 'What about when you had your first wax?'

His chin begins to drop.

'No sister should have to see that. But I sat in the corner, didn't I?'

There it is! I see it wheedling a route into his face: remorse.

'Know why I did, Michael?'

Leaking into the capillaries of his face, like guilt-coloured dye.

'Because you *needed* me.'

Very quietly, he concedes, 'You had my back.'

'Your back, sack and crack.'

I'm wasted on him. He nods all mature, then turns his knees towards me, holds out a little finger and wiggles it. This is what we did when we were at primary school – I'd argue with him, he'd lose, then we'd connect pinkies and sing, *Make up, make up, never ever break up* . . .

Before I lock fingers with him now, however, I do a head shake. One that says: *I must be the biggest mug that ever lived.*

'Sorry.' His broad shoulders slump.

'Hey, you're all right.'

But he's not all right; his eyes are filling up, which makes me want to run in circles or call the police or put my fingers in my ears and sing *daa, dada, dadaah,* because it kills me when he cries.

'It's just I was really looking forward to it, you know?'

Urgently I pat at his tears. 'What were you looking forward to, sweetheart?'

He clears his throat, neatens his fair hair, points a stagy finger at me:

'Consolidate your debts into affordable monthly instalments, leaving *you* free to live life to the full.'

I whisper, 'That was today?'

'I've been practising a lot. But you're right.'

About what? I don't scream. *Tell me how I am possibly right about anything. Not today. Not when this was supposed to be your most special moment ever.*

'Can you do it another day?' It's a silly question.

'They got someone else.'

Michael Love, you owe me – that is what I said to a man who I've hard-wired to take everything that emanates from my mouth as sacrosanct.

Suddenly it is vital that I make this up to Michael, so vital I forget entirely the importance of forethought.

Very important note on forethought: when you feel bad – really, really bad – never speak. Speaking is a selfish biological mechanism undertaken simply to appease your own guilt. Speaking is as pointless as satisfying a nicotine craving. It is also infinitely more dangerous. In my defence, guilt often wrings the brain free of logic.

Bollocks, there is no defence for what I said next.

'You'll never guess what,' I half shout, because for one insane and misplaced second I think I can make him feel better. 'Mum's been in touch.'

Michael refuses to leave his flat.

His logic is simple: if she's stalking me, she'll be stalking him too. We are both her children, and parents love their offspring equally. It is natural, therefore, that at some point she will turn up at his place. I don't put him right.

When I first explained that Mum had sent me a birthday card and maybe taken a mosey around my bedsit, tidied up a little and looked for snapshots on my laptop, I'd had to put a hand over his mouth to stop him from wailing.

Because if Mum lived in paradise, how the hell was she arriving in my locked room unless she was an actual, proper ghost. And if the sleeping pills moved, truly moved, then she wasn't just a ghost, but a poltergeist.

The supernatural is Michael's horror – not because it's disturbing, but because it's unfathomable. He accepts God – a giant grandad in a cricket-white dress sitting on a cloud, a retired Jewish carpenter to his right, a spirit that is holy to his left – but ghosts, no way. In Michael's mind, they are a step too far.

Were it anybody else, I'd suggest reading materials. *The God Delusion*, for a starter. But Asperger's is not a social deficiency. It's quite the opposite. An acute hypersensitivity to experience, coupled with an all-consuming fear response. Which is why Michael prefers rules and absolutes, religion and cliché – it's his self-preservation mechanism and I've just robbed him of it.

Back at his flat, I pour him a brandy and try to explain things gently.

'I've always been a bit more open-minded about Mum's disappearance, I guess.'

'Dad said she was dead.'

With Michael, it's about pitching stuff at the right angle. 'You know my peripheral vision?' I say.

He nods and says a little childishly: 'It's as good as a fighter pilot's.'

'Or a falcon's.'

He hugs his chest tight. 'Or the girl in *The Exorcist*. She can turn her head all the way round.'

'That was special effects.' I've probably pitched this at the wrong angle. 'Well, where my peripheral vision is really good, normal people like you suffer from something called tunnel vision. Understand?'

'No,' he half shouts.

'It's not an illness.'

'I know what it is.'

'You don't, not really. It's part and parcel of being a human. Dad and the police, they have it too – tunnel vision. It's where you only see what's immediately in front of your nose.'

'I do know.'

'You plump for the most obvious answer.' I think of a parallel. 'Here you go – if it quacks like a duck, swims like a duck, looks like a duck, what is it?'

'A duck,' he cries.

I open my hands. Point proven. 'Unfortunately, Michael, it's not always that neat. The paradox of probability theory.'

His eyeballs tell me the scale of my mistake – I can see too much of them, top and sides. What was I thinking? Nonchalant as you like, *You'll never guess what. Mum's been in touch.* On the Richter scale of faux pas, this measures Fucking Cataclysmic.

My phone rings.

'I have to get this, Michael,' I tell him.

'Is it Mum?' he demands.

'No, no. A friend.'

I answer the phone: 'Maeve?'

Predictably, she has excelled herself. Maeve tells me the following facts:

I *will* bump into Scott Delaney. Details *will* follow in an email. As a consequence, she *will* keep her reputation intact. Assuming I'm true to my word, I *will* leave London in the very near future.

'Loud and clear,' I say, then hang up without a well-done or a thank-you.

Because I am not elated. How can I be? I surf on a tsunami of shit. I don't need a further depressing truth dumped on my shoulders – the one about Maeve Rivers knowing *nothing* about me at all. Never, ever would I go to the national papers, I am worth much more than that. I imagined she might have thought so too.

Plus where does she get off being so sure that I can't seduce Scott? Because she doesn't think I can. I could tell by her face.

134

'What friend was it?' Michael looks at my phone, his eyes pleading for boxes and neat bows.

'Maeve Rivers. Editor of the *Daily News*. The one who fell too deeply in love with me.'

That's neat enough for him.

Mum being alive, however, is not. 'If she's not dead, Flo, why did she leave us?'

And so it starts again.

This is the official police line:

Mum had second thoughts about killing herself. Yes, she got out of that car alive, only later to find another way of ending her life. They believe that her remains are long gone – washed down a river or buried by a tree.

'She's under a tree?'

Oh, I don't fucking know. 'Maybe she was ashamed of her suicide attempt, Michael. Maybe she was having a nervous breakdown. Maybe she lost her memory. I could come up with a thousand possibilities, but that's all they are, possibilities.' I put a hand on his large, soft face. 'There does, however, remain one undeniable fact . . .'

Michael leans forwards. Let this be my saving grace.

'One very neat, very concrete fact.'

Every sinew in his face says: this *so* wants to be your saving grace.

'Nobody, Michael, *nobody* has ever found a body.'

Silence.

I watch his brow slowly knit and his chest expand.

I'm not sure I've mentioned this before, but in addition to intuition and peripheral vision, I have the reflexes of a jellyfish. They have the capability to emit poison at velocities approaching the speed of light. See how quickly I move my hand. It's over Michael's mouth before he gets a chance to engage his voice box and wail.

*

Michael and I talked for many hours.

Gradually his fear began to dissolve. By mid-evening, we were hugging and yelping witlessly at the madness of it all. By late evening, even I'd forgotten that my theories, all one thousand of them, might be oceans south of the truth.

Then just when his face relaxes into something quite wonderful and I experience a stirring joy, he says resolutely:

'I want to be on my own now, Flo.'

I've not experienced this before, Michael telling me to go – like he can cope perfectly well without me.

'At least come get some food with me,' I tell him. 'You need to eat.'

'What if she comes here to see me?'

My heart sags. 'Well, if you won't come out, at least invite Sébastien over – a bit of company will do you good.' I find my purse, hand him some cash. 'Get yourselves a pizza.'

'No,' he says intently. 'Mum's a bit shy. She'll want to see me on my own.'

He's right – Bambi was often baffled around strangers. How on earth does he remember that? He was, what, three?

Upbeat, he looks around the pristine flat. 'I'll give the place a quick once-over, just in case.'

'Right. I'll go then. Organise some stuff.' I pick up my bag.

'I used to put my head on Mum's lap,' Michael is saying, straightening sofa cushions. 'She'd tell me stories about Jesus when he was a baby. He was a really good boy. He took after me, she said. Do you remember her fingernails? They were really long. She used to tickle the inside of our ears. That's true love, putting your fingertips inside someone else's ears.'

I walk home from Michael's and try to remember if she tickled my ears too. She tickled me all the time, but I can't remember a single, specific incident of her fingernails being in my ears.

It's midnight.

I should jump on the last tube. But I want bedlam – too much stimulus is an excellent antidote for guilt; it's therapeutic as whale song.

The reds and yellows of brake lights and street lamps. Neon blues above shop doorways. Traffic lights – scarlet, orange and teal. Theatres, their steps lit brightly, glittering with halogen promise like cubic zirconia in a jewellery shop window. Auditory disorder that batters the bejeebers out of your senses. Drunken laughter, exuberant screams, irritated hooting from the heart of a city where car, bus, cab, pedestrian and cyclist inhabit the same cage. Men, inebriated, lascivious, shouting things like *Oi, oi!* as I pass, an attempt at flirtatious banter. Not like the men on their own – they watch me surreptitiously. They might even follow me home.

I speed up.

Then force myself to slow down again – because although I'm over all that religious hooey, I deserve the unease. I was baptised a Catholic. Penance will always remain my birthright.

Entrapment 101 Tip #4: Be dangerously attractive

Common misconception: men prefer facial symmetry and femininity. Women are infinitely more cerebral, erring towards honesty, humour and benevolence.

Male or female, on a conscious level you won't have a clue what attracts you to another person. Speed-dating experiments have proven this. Women throw high-mindedness to the dogs when presented with just one extra variable – choice. In contrast, men are happy to bang whoever is game.

Scientific fact: men are not that picky.

Topic for discussion: how do you stand out when the choreography of courtship has myriad designs cut deep into the psyche, a result of time, selection and evolution?

Become dangerously attractive. There's no quick way around it. You'll need a degree.

The qualification boat has sailed? Read everything by Desmond Morris (*The Naked Woman* and *Intimate Behaviour* are corkers).

Not a reader? You're in the wrong game. Knowledge is your way in. Always.

Neotony

Saturday. Day Six: Operation Delaney.

> Re: Marital case
> Saturday 5/7/14 12.20 p.m.
> From: info@londonpiservices.uk.net
> To: asc345@hotmail.com
>
> Hello Alice,
>   I hope Tuscany treats you well.
>   I am pleased to inform you that a meeting with Scott has been arranged for this morning. Be assured the meeting will appear entirely natural and spontaneous; no suspicion will be aroused whatsoever.
>   I'm confident that swift progress can now be made.
>   In the meantime, do enjoy Tuscany's landscapes, artistic legacy and influence on high culture. The birthplace of the Italian Renaissance, it has been home to such people as Dante, Machiavelli and Puccini. I therefore encourage you to visit its museums and sample its wines. My suggestion would be Vino Nobile di Montepulciano, a red with aromas of dark cherry and rich plum.
>   Love,
>   London PI Services

And now I prepare for our first date: mine and Scott 'Scat' Delaney's.

Note I say 'date'. That is exactly how you must approach the trickier cases of entrapment. Not all honeytraps require such forethought, of course. Ugly men, like Minister de Groot, need cleavage, filthy eyes and the assurance of absolute discretion. Other targets, however – gorgeous, famous ones like Scott Delaney – require the full-out employment of Stanislavski's method of acting.

And so I prepare psychologically for my date – stoke the fire in my belly, pull on some truths, wildly embellish others and get into the zone . . .

Scott Delaney.

A man I have seen on TV and in magazines. His music is as omnipresent in my life as a family member, one it's totally legal to procreate with. I've made love to his music, wept to his velvet voice and pertinent lyrics. His songs have provided a soundtrack to some of the most poignant moments of my existence.

And a bit of me hopes – no, a bit of me must *believe* – that when we meet, Scott Delaney will feel something too.

Because I'm like Cinderella, only a super-confident one with a first in evolutionary biology and a seventy-one per cent success rate at entrapment. And soon I will have my big chance.

Yet here's the coup – I will have only moments to incite within him reciprocal feelings of connectivity.

I *cannot* scare him off.

I *must not* use words to tell him how I ache for him.

I must instead channel my sexual and spiritual hunger entirely via subliminal cues.

How on earth do you do that? you ask.

You use science.

Number one. Pop to Tesco Express and buy ready-made cinnamon rolls. Don't bake them yet. Wait until just before you leave the flat for your date. Allow the aroma to infiltrate your clothes, hair and skin, because cinnamon smells exactly like a woman's sexual pheromone, androstenol.

If baking's not your thing, try a perfume with top notes of cinnamon and bitter orange, a middle note of vanilla and a base note of musk. It's a combination more potent than amyl nitrate.

A useful aside: adjust your choice of aroma according to the cultural background of your target. The Daasanach of Ethiopia, for example, are driven crazy not by cinnamon but by the odour of cows, the scent being associated with fertility and social status. The menfolk wash in cattle urine and moisturise with manure. The womenfolk smother themselves in butter to increase their desirability. I won't knock it; I haven't tried it. In most industrialised societies, however, cinnamon is your best bet.

Number two. Wear clothes that allude to the colour of your private parts. Peach is my top tip. Flattering for most skin tones, it emits a healthy glow and vulnerability, peach being the colour of a pubescent girl's genitals.

No-argument anthropological fact: this is *not* paedophilia. This is called neotony.

Men have evolved to be attracted to baby-like traits in woman. It's not a fault; it's the entire reason why *Homo sapiens* infests the globe. Baby-like features make men want to protect and provide for their women, in the same way they protect and provide for their offspring. It fosters a monogamous society and has enabled the successful propagation of our entire species.

As a consequence, women have retained a childlike appearance.

And in contrast, men have retained their childlike behaviour.

No-argument anthropological fact: this is *not* sexist. This is called neotony.

In particular, men have retained the childlike element of play via risk-taking. As a result, they are fifteen times clumsier than women. They are also more likely to come up with hare-brained ideas like jacking in their job to become an inventor or a ventriloquist. In turn, women nag yet defend them in the exact same way they nag yet defend their offspring; because it fosters a monogamous society and has enabled the successful propagation of our entire species.

I digress.

During a honeytrap, a dress the colour of peachy genitals is a smart choice. Though while we're on the subject, men like other neonate cues too.

Neonate cues that drive a man wild:

1. Lower basal metabolisms (i.e., fleshier women – hips and chest).

2. Baby-like ears.

3. Voices within the soprano vocal range (i.e. C4–C6, where C4 is middle C).

4. Large, vulnerable eyes, no less than one inch apart.

5. Waxed fufus.

Colours to *avoid* wearing during a honeytrap case: red. This includes burgundies and plums, any shade in fact that falls within the wavelength range of 630–740 nm. You might find the avoidance of red at first surprising – is it not the very embodiment of sex, sin, lust, passion and danger? Absolutely yes, and the last thing I should be oozing is danger.

On the contrary, I have to appear to be the safest punt Scott Delaney has ever taken.

I try not to stare.

He sits, eyes shut, in an armchair just ten feet away from mine. A woman pats foundation at his cheeks.

We are in the presidential suite of the Landmark Hotel in Marylebone – eighteen hundred square feet of opulence, swathes of marble, a litter of flat-screen TVs, double bathroom, dressing room, a sitting area the size of a lounge bar. This suite is just stunning.

As is Scott Delaney.

While his eyes are shut, I take a longer look at him. I'll describe him as best I can.

His hair is a sun-kissed brown. Wavy, a length that suggests he's growing it out, yet he's not – every lock has been deliberately groomed to snuggle at his ears and neck. And to now and then fall into his eyes, just like a beautiful girl's hair does when, half naked, she straddles you, her intense stare chock full of agonising erotic promise.

Only Scott is rugged, with stubble and unplucked eyebrows, and he's as heterosexual as an Etruscan gladiator. Yet the hair, the wanton lock that he gently sweeps now and then from his forehead, gives him a hint of androgyny that makes me want to jump him, here and now.

I twist my feet around the legs of my chair.

His teeth don't help either; they're heart-crushing – whitened, of course, but nonetheless his own. The heart-crushing thing about them being: they're ever so slightly bucked at the front. It gives him the most vulnerable air. Personally I can't think of a more aphrodisiacal quirk.

And if that's not enough, he has a forehead that concertinas like corrugated iron when he smiles or looks concerned, furnishing him with ice-cream scoops full of ingenuousness and sincerity. This, an international star, values you and your opinions: his forehead says so. And your lowly position in the world, he digs that too, because those were his roots once upon a time. Oh, this universally acclaimed musician is utterly natural, unassuming; he couldn't do bullshit if he tried.

Scott Delaney fact: he *can* do bullshit. He's been doing bullshit since he was fifteen years old – being exactly who his PR machine wants him to be.

But right now I'd forgive him everything. Because – nail me to the chair, I swear I'm going to faint – when the make-up lady's gone and Scott's eyes reopen, I have to brace my vocal folds to prevent a gasp, because there they are again, eyes of the most fluorescent blue, just like Jesus's.

And now Scott Delaney is saying warmly:

'I'm especially proud of this album – it's a compilation of duets with jazz giants and pop greats.'

He is not saying this to me. He is saying it to Ricky Hart, the show-biz correspondent for the *Daily News*.

Ricky sits in a chair to my left and leans towards Scott as if physically attempting to dangle from every syllable. I want to tell him to grow some dignity – surely he knows Scott will have said the same old shit to every journalist who's entered the room today; there's no need to look so grateful.

But I'd wager my Femidom I'm looking that grateful too – the man inspires the urge to thank him for simply existing.

Maeve arranged this suite as a favour for Scott. She is consummate at keeping A-listers sweet. In return, Ricky Hart will get the exclusive at the end of this interview run.

And my job?

Pick up keys from reception and let Scott into the suite, her email said. *You're like an usher, the type of usher who fucks off out of there as quickly as possible. Any questions, I will deny knowing you.*

What a shame that when some people fall in love it's all about them. Did Maeve never notice I like to wing things?

'Hi, Isabella, event coordinator.'

That's what I told them. All of them. Scott Delaney. The PA, Harvey Cadwalader. The visiting journalists, thirteen in total. Nobody asked who I was coordinating the event for exactly. Journalists are used to being herded. Scott expects people to facilitate his existence. And, to give praise where it's due, I'm inhabiting the role completely. If anything gets back to Maeve, it will be only that the event coordinator displayed professional proficiency bordering on the pathological.

Pathological. I don't growl, although my disappointment in Maeve escalates by the hour.

There have been thirteen back-to-back interviews so far. It's how you might expect a sheikh to speed-date. Each journalist is awarded just seven minutes of Delaney's time. Except for Maeve's minion, Ricky Hart; he got fifteen minutes, forty-three seconds.

I have sat through every single interview, and this is what I've learnt about Scott 'Scat' Delaney so far:

The square root of jack.

And that show-biz journalists possess two attributes: an NCTJ diploma in journalism, and an astonishing ability to pander and fawn.

I got very impatient with them. Why weren't they asking the questions people really want the answers to? Like, have you ever had a threesome? Who's the least attractive person you've shagged? If your mother was about to be murdered – a gruesome, strung-out, tortuous death, which you'd be forced to witness – and the only way you could save her life was by *doing it* with her, would you? It's the uncomfortable questions people are interested in.

Scott might as well have been reading from an autocue.

His answers were identical, regardless of the questions, each interview a regurgitation of his last.

These were the main points covered:

It was 'the greatest honour' working with the likes of Tony Bennett and Robbie Williams. His favourite colour is green. His second favourite colour is orange. His third? White, of course – he is very proud of his roots. But not in an IRA type of way. Delaney loves all religions and creeds and nationalities, is an ardent advocate of world harmony and peace, but naturally has the softest spot for the Gaelic countryside of his youth. His grandfather offered free gardening services to performers who let Scott sing on stage.

You must have another story, I thought.

And the most important thing in his life? The music – it remains the only reason he gets up in the morning and does this crazy, wonderful job.

Yeah, but would you do it *with your mum to save her life if she was getting murdered?*

And the exclusive, just for Maeve and her show-biz subordinate:

When the time is right, yes, Scott would very much like to settle down, get married and start a family. The right girl? He just hasn't met her yet.

Blah.

Nonetheless, I rewarded Delaney's 'exclusive' with a series of sycophantic gasps. I also saw his mock-embarrassed shrug, what with his talking about such a personal issue, because having babies has clear connotations: he is going to have sex with a woman. Or certainly he plans on it in order to facilitate procreation at some point in his future.

Sex sells, so this revelation will make the Sunday supplement's front page.

The most significant truth I've learnt today, however, is that Maeve is a very silly woman. She missed a trick not hiring me as a journalist. I'd have got her an exclusive all right, added the fill, given the piece an angle lesser journalists won't have picked up on. I might not have a City and Guilds in transcribing the banal, but I am an astute observer of truths. Things like, in the flesh, he doesn't come across as remotely agoraphobic. His ability to leak vulnerability via the asymmetry of his teeth is intriguing and requires further scientific consideration. Darwin would definitely palm-clap his social skills, especially his talent for making everyone feel special when, categorically, they are not.

Those other journalists will have come up with none of this.

Nor would they say, *I'd mate with him in a flash*. I would. The whole world would. The man is quite possibly the most exquisite creature I've ever studied in the flesh. In fact, as the day rolls on, it's becoming crucial that, despite the likelihood of my seducing Scott Delaney being approximately nil, he might secretly find me a little pretty and a little captivating.

The interviews are over.

Scott rubs his face roughly. 'I need a sandwich. Is there food?'

Harvey and I look at one another. Which of us he's talking to is anyone's guess. I take a punt. 'Anything you want.'

Scott looks up, nods at us both. 'So let's get room service.'

'OK, but not a sandwich,' Harvey tells him sternly.

'Harvey, man, I'm starving.'

'Two words, Scat – *glycaemic* and *load*.'

Scat. Harvey called him Scat. It feels like I'm part of the team. The rectal quill really starts to flutter – I have properly wheedled myself into the Delaney circle of trust.

Scat. Scat. Scat. Scat. Scat . . .

'Do you have a non-carbs menu?' Harvey asks me.

I'm an events coordinator, not a fucking butler, so I nod at the door. 'Phone's in the hall.'

Delaney still moans. 'I haven't slept properly in weeks. I need carbohydrates. Or a vodka Red Bull. Or a bucket of espresso.'

'OK.' Harvey points his pen, draws an imaginary line under the matter. 'A ham sandwich on wholemeal, no butter.'

'Counting the minutes until you go, Harvey.'

'Try counting sheep – it might help you get some shut-eye. Anyway, you're stuck with me for,' Harvey looks at his watch, 'another twenty-nine hours.'

'How about I just sack you.'

'We both know you'll be lost without me.'

As Harvey goes to the hall to ring for room service, I notice things about the colossal PA.

That he ducks and turns to the side when going through door frames, even when there's plenty of room to spare; that his trousers are slightly too short; that his demeanour is bossy, yes, but benevolent – like the Big Friendly Giant or Louis Armstrong.

Most important of all, I notice that Harvey Cadwalader refuses to suck up to his boss.

I take his lead.

Casually I sit opposite Scott. 'Where's Harvey off to in twenty-nine hours?'

'Guyana, visiting his folks for a month.'

'Wow, what will you do without him?'

He leans towards me conspiratorially. 'Gorge myself on saturated fats.'

I want to giggle like an idiot. Instead I lean forward too. 'How long have you suffered from insomnia?'

Scott engages the right side of his brain – I know this because he's looking that way. 'Twelve years, four months and three days. Give or take.'

'Is it episodic or chronic?'

'Both.'

I shake my head. 'It can't be. Episodic is when it comes and goes, the bouts lasting up to three weeks. Chronic is long-term.'

'Yep, I've got both.' Now I watch him fidget as if he's sitting on gravel. He digs two fingers at his glute. 'The sciatica doesn't help, or the tight iliotibial bands.'

If God existed, I'd grab his ears and kiss Him on the head – there is no sitting duck like a hypochondriac. They don't want useful suggestions, they want unabated pity. And that I can do.

'My gran said that sciatica is more painful than childbirth.'

'It's true,' he nods. 'People don't understand, not unless they've suffered from it properly.'

The silence lasts for no more than ten seconds, yet Scott suddenly looks uncomfortable. He examines the freckles on his arm, for melanoma I assume, then cranes his neck towards the hall and looks for Harvey, like a toddler who's lost sight of his mum.

'Maybe I'll just grab some shut-eye now,' he says.

'No,' I tell him.

'Sorry?'

'Daytime naps exacerbate insomnia.'

'Let them,' he mumbles ungraciously. 'I'm dog tired. Seriously knackered.'

I nod kindly, because I see it in every millimetre of his face – irritation. Not your common or garden irritation. The unhinged variety experienced solely by the sleep-deprived. Forget sciatica, melanoma, childbirth; Scott Delaney and I suffer from the most brutal affliction of all – one prohibited as a torture technique by the European Convention for Human Rights.

'You can die from insomnia,' I say.

He knows this already; all insomniacs know this already – it's a fate we live with daily.

'Fatal familial insomnia,' Scott nods.

Few of us know the medical term, though. I'm impressed. 'Have you read Rechtsschaffen and Bergmann's, *Sleep deprivation in the rat by the disk-over-water method*?'

He laughs – a real laugh, not a stage laugh – and I feel wonderful. 'That one passed me by,' he says.

Yes, I hear his sarcasm. *No*, I have no idea why I say, 'I can get you a copy, if you like.'

'Certainly sounds like it could put me in a coma.'

I giggle coquettishly – an accident; this is only Bump One. Giggling coquettishly is reserved strictly for Bump Two. I'm getting ahead of myself, am certainly smoothing the creases from my skirt too sensually. 'I think you'll find Tolstoy is the ultimate cure for insomnia.'

'I love Tolstoy.' He watches me caress my thighs.

I remember Harvey and lose the sycophancy. 'No you don't.'

'I do.'

'Everybody says they *love* Tolstoy – but only because it sounds clever.' I lean forward, rub at an imaginary mark on my shoe. 'He's boring.'

If all is going to plan, Scott is looking at my décolletage. '*War and Peace* is my favourite book,' he says.

'Now I know you're lying.'

'Not.'

I look up, smile widely. 'In that case, there it is!'

'There's what?' He looks around playfully.

'Your unattractive bit.'

'Go on.'

'*War and Peace*. It's rambling and formless; the man tried to do too much in one novel.' I point earnestly. 'Lev Nikolayevich Tolstoy had an ego the size of Jupiter.'

'He was very spiritual. He influenced great men – Martin Luther King, Gandhi . . .'

I ignore him, because Tolstoy genuinely gets on my nerves.

'I just knew there had to be something wrong with you, *Scat* Delaney,' I rib.

'Well, I'm glad it's just one thing.'

'I'm sure I can find more.'

'Go on then.' He crosses his arms; his smile is huge and thoroughly expectant.

I laugh. Then stop. This is awkward. Nothing comes to mind apart from his agoraphobia and his addiction to video games, which I can't say out loud because it'll give the game away.

'For the moment, Tolstoy is my only bugbear. Then again, I've just watched you do thirteen interviews, and know what, Scott? You're impenetrable.'

'Impenetrable, eh?'

'Yep.'

'As impenetrable as what?'

I don't bloody know. 'Another person's dream?' I cringe a little, whereas Scott's head lolls wistfully to one side.

'Impenetrable as another person's dream. That's beautiful.'

A tingle salsas down my spine – his accent is as melodious as his secret girlfriend's, a mixture of Cork and Los Angeles. His t's sound like d's.

'Beau*d*iful?' I ask.

'Yes,' he says. 'I'm going to write a song called that.'

'What, "Beau*d*iful"?'

'No. "Impenetrable as Another Person's Dream".'

'Really?'

On second thoughts, he shakes his head. 'That's a really long title for a song, but I'm loving the concept.'

I can only apologise and swear on the lives of those I love most that *never,* in my two years of entrapment experience, has this *ever* happened before. But for a split second I feel unbelievably flattered and extremely star-struck.

Who am I kidding: I feel like his muse.

He looks at my face for a moment too long. 'I've totally forgotten your name.'

I hold out a hand. 'Florence,' I say. 'Florence Love.'

Not only do I tell him my whole name, I then give him the Look.

The Look: *n.* (the – *unstressed before a consonant.* look – *luk*) when two people's eyes lock and, for an epiphanic moment, their inner psyches become as tangled as post-coital dogs.

That's a corker of a moment, isn't it? Of all the branches of kinesics, eye contact is the trickiest to master. The Look is certainly the most powerful tool in my armoury.

I'll run through the basics.

First, you must teach yourself acceptance, i.e., to acknowledge everything that's been and everything you are. Then adore yourself for it. Such mental poise usually takes decades of therapy. In this case, however, you don't have to *really* believe it; you just need to *really* delude yourself.

Second, show this delusion via your eyes. Push it all up towards your head and out of your sockets. Useful hint: never do it in an observable way, like you're passing wind. Do it in a super-cool way. Watch the master in action – Steve McQueen in *The Thomas Crown Affair*. Pseudo-assurance spews from his eyes for one hundred and two minutes. It's extraordinarily erotic. Like Steve, you might want to enlist the inferior oblique muscles of your eyes and accompany it with a Duchenne smile (one that contracts both zygomatic major muscle and orbicularis oculi muscle).

Go on, practise it in a mirror now.

Third, without words or gesticulations, make the person opposite feel spellbinding. Look at them like you've suddenly seen their soul and, fuck me sideways, it is wonderful. At least that's what they must believe. Because, Jean-Paul Sartre fact: successful relationships are created not by a person's attraction to another person, but as a consequence of how that person makes them feel.

Be warned, however: much like clutch control, the Look is difficult to master. For those in an emergency situation, take this shortcut; do what my gran did when she met my grandad.

I looked at him like I had a very naughty secret.

They were married for fifty-five years, *such* is the power of eye contact.

'So, you work for Maeve?' Scott has broken free of the Look. In truth, he looks a little shell-shocked; he's now unsure what to focus upon.

'I have to go.' I gather my bag and coat.

I could kid you, tell you I'm being elusive. In reality, I have fucked up; prematurely ejaculated my game plan.

I did the Look.

And before that, I gave him my real name – having previously given him an entirely different one.

My scalp starts to tingle, forewarning of a nervous sweat, its job to dampen my root sheaths and leave my hair unattractively limp. In fact I feel like I could actually burst into tears. During cases of entrapment, *never, ever* burst into tears.

Knitting my brow, I point, matron-like.

'Whatever you do, don't nap. We've not evolved to sleep during the day. Try valerian. It's herbal and smells like arse, actual proper arse, but it also happens to be a half-decent sedative in the right quantities. The packet says thirty drops before bedtime. Take sixty.'

'That works for you?'

'I sleep like a baby,' I say, patting the beginnings of a sweat moustache, omitting crucial information. Like the fact that herbal remedies are placebos, yet occasionally work given the psychosomatic nature of sleeplessness. That my narcotic of choice is not valerian, but Zopiclone – a prescription-only non-benzodiazepine hypnotic agent that causes the tranquillisation of the central nervous system and killed Heath Ledger.

Harvey returns and I hurriedly bid them farewell, wish Scott luck with his new album, tell Harvey to enjoy Guyana. They wish me luck too, for what I'm not sure.

And as I leave the suite, I don't bother imagining I can feel Scott's eyes burning holes in my back.

A regrettable point about the Look:

During cases of entrapment, the Look must only be used in one situation – immediately prior to the money shot. This is because it marks the end of the case. Nobody's fooling themselves any more. This is *all* about sexual attraction. It's too powerful a moment of clarity to unleash during Bump One – it frightens a target off.

Outside the presidential suite, I dab at damp temples and wait for the private lift. I feel utterly empty. It's unlikely I will see Scott Delaney again.

Scat.

I console myself – attraction and entrapment never make harmonious bedfellows. At least I got this far. Nonetheless, I leave something behind. Not a glass slipper, but my purse. First I take out my unlucky coin and dig it safely into a pocket, then I drop the purse on the floor outside his door.

It contains the following:

Fifty-seven pounds: enough money for normal people to filch the contents, but for minted people to return it to its owner.

A card: I've scribbled my name, mobile telephone number and private email address.

A tiny glass phial: L de Lolita Lempicka – an Oriental fragrance with top notes of cinnamon and bitter orange, a middle note of vanilla and a base note of musk.

Stamping on the purse with my heel, I get into the lift.

DABDA

Slowly I make my way to Michael's. It feels like I'm walking against a gale-force wind. I'm not. The July sun scorches the top of my head, yet I don't worry about heatstroke – on the contrary, I welcome it.

I'll be frank. I'm heartbroken.

It's as if I've been through the eight stages of an intense yet doomed relationship in half a day – the honeymoon phase, the discovery stage, the commitment stage . . . I'd explain them in detail but I'm too depressed, what with being stuck rigid in the second D of DABDA, a five-stage model of bereavement also suited to the breakup of a relationship . . . Oh, Wikipedia it.

All this and I've known Scott Delaney for but half a day. I'm not crackers, just terribly honest. Tell me you've never met somebody you unexpectedly want so badly, the need to possess them borders on unhinged.

The Greeks call it *theia mania* – madness from the gods – a passion that arrives suddenly thanks to Eros shooting his metaphorical love darts. Today's love dart got me bang in the eye, which is *the* most powerful place for it to hit. From the eye it travels directly to the heart; the subsequent wound is rarely repairable.

I've felt this only once before, when I met Husband Number One.

Sadness overwhelms me.

Biochemical fact: I'm in no place whatsoever to deal with a surprise visit from my father.

Yet it's Dad who opens the door to Michael's flat on Greek Street and forgets to say hello.

'What in heaven's name were you thinking, Florrie?'

The OAP doppelgänger of Michael, my father is tall and slim, with the broad, flat shoulders of a one-time breaststroke specialist.

'Why, *why* would you tell Michael something like that?'

'Because it's true,' I grumble, then hug him very hard indeed. And he hugs me hard too. Smells my hair. It's a while before we let go of one another.

When we do, I immediately huff up the stairs.

Dad follows me into Michael's living room. Defiantly I sit on a scatter cushion. My father shakes his head, disappointed.

This is the first time Dad's been to London since I've been in the capital. He looks wrong here. In Michael's flat.

His hair is whiter than I remember. There's a hole in the elbow of his crew neck. And he's doing a stress blink – the one where he stands rigid as a robot and takes photos with his eyes.

I watch him walk to the bookcase.

There he fingers Dr Dan's self-help book, *Family: Nature's Masterpiece* – the one with the covert camera inside. For a moment I teeter on the edge of the couch, ready to snatch it from him, but he sees the photo of Mum and loses interest.

'Michael didn't tell me you were planning to visit.' I look out into the hall for my brother.

My father brushes a fingertip across the glass picture frame. 'She was younger than you when this was taken.'

'She'd disappeared off the face of the earth by the time she was my age.'

'Have you seen her?' he asks without looking up from the photo. '*Actually* seen her?'

'No.'

'Then why put those ideas in his head?'

'She sent me a birthday card.'

My dad stops blinking entirely, just stares inert at the photo. For a moment I think he's died. To my relief, the stress blinks resume with gusto. Careful to put the frame back exactly as he found it, he tells me:

'He won't leave the flat. You know he's not slept in two days in case he misses her?'

'Where is he now?'

Dad nods in the direction of the bedroom. 'Asleep. I told him I'd keep an eye out for visitors. Florence, what are you playing at?'

'I got a birthday card from her. Dad, did you not hear that bit?'

'You told Michael that only you can see her. That everyone else has a condition.'

'Tunnel vision. It was metaphorical.'

He tugs at an ear lobe. 'Michael responds so well to the metaphorical.'

'I know, I know, I pitched it wrong . . .'

'Have you been seeing your medical man?'

'Dr Malik?' I squint. 'What's that got to do with anything?'

'Answer me.'

'Yes.'

'Every week?'

'Mostly.'

Suddenly he's on his knees in front of me, rubbing my triceps as if they're made of gold. 'You promised when you came to London that you'd keep up with your therapy, especially now you have Michael to look after.'

'Life coaching.'

He nods, humours me, brimful of pity.

'It *is* life coaching, Dad.'

'Yes, yes, I get all mixed up.'

In Dad's book I'm more perplexing than Michael.

'I'm all right, really.'

Nonetheless he pulls me to him. I sulk like a pubescent, yet hold him so tight back, secretly inhaling the fusty perfume of his sweater.

'I worry about you,' he is whispering. 'I know you're an adult, but you'll always be my little girl.' He holds me away from him, his look one of inestimable love. 'Look at you, the both of you – Michael with his TV commercial; you and your books, the courses, those big words.'

Now is not the time to explain how I decimated Michael's acting career before it got started. Now's the time to bathe in the sanctuary of his bony chest: my father thinks I'm really qualified, with a large vocabulary.

'We are pretty fantastic,' I say, like I'm five.

This makes him smile and I see his bottom teeth. They are stained a Cabernet Sauvignon red. A bottle of wine and a TV meal, that's my dad's routine of an evening. Funny how I find his discoloured teeth a comfort – he has a whole life going on without me, even when I forget to think about him.

'How about I open a bottle of something?' I nod at the kitchen, eager to please.

'Later,' he says, suddenly solemn. 'When are you going to tell Michael?'

'Tell him what?'

'That you made it up.'

'I got a card, Dad. Someone came into my apartment – not to steal anything, just to have a look around.'

He grabs my hands firmly in his. 'Let her go.'

'No.' I pull them free. 'You never talk to us about it. What are you protecting us from?'

I hate the look on his face.

It's the one parents wear to tell you you haven't got a

fucking clue – they made you, and as their personal creation, you will never be as wise as them; are destined instead to remain needy, hapless and deluded as Frankenstein's monster until the day they die.

'Florrie, darling – Mummy has gone.'

Particularly I hate it when he says that. Over the years, including today, he has said it thirty-seven times. Each time it's like he's stomach-whipping me with a sack of netballs.

'We deserve the facts,' I say, flatly.

'Absolutely. The *facts*. Michael can't cope with ambiguity. He hasn't the mental equipment.'

'He's gay, not retarded.'

'Stop that,' he shouts, and I feel instantly ashamed. 'I don't live in the Dark Ages. I've never judged either of you. Neither would I.'

It's true – on paper, he's an exceptional parent.

'I'm begging you, let it go.' With weathered panache, he now draws his trump card: 'For me, Florrie? Let it go for me.'

A plump tear threatens to escape his eye.

Pity floods my chest, because human dads are born with the power to induce compassion so fierce it stings a daughter's heart. Dutifully I pretend he's not a functioning alcoholic. I go to church with him when I'm back in Laurelbridge. Sing the offertory hymn like it's a power ballad. Laugh at his rubbish jokes. One day I'll even pay for a top-notch care worker to change his incontinence pads and say hourly, *A nice cuppa tea, George?* That's how sorry I feel for him.

I exhale loudly and nod, beleaguered.

His relief is palpable. 'It's for the best. We both know what Michael needs.'

'Boxes and neat bows. He's not ill.'

'Just tell him you made it up.'

'Like he'll ever trust me again.'

'Blame it on something – Dr Malik; blame it on your therapist.' He corrects himself. 'Your life coach. Say he's given you some new medication.'

'Why can I feel her, Dad? It's as if she's only around the corner, *every* corner. Why has she never felt dead?'

I know the answer already:

'Closure, Florence, is difficult when there's no body, no grave.'

Want to know all I have?

A memory of a piece of paper stuck to a car window. *Dan8erous. Toxic 8as.*

No corpse, no explanation.

I know, I know, I should plant a tree or build a bench or arrange a stack of stones by an attractive body of water. That's the type of thing the families of the 9/11 victims did. And the astronauts blown up before their rockets reached the stratosphere. It's what the relatives of missing soldiers do. And the loved ones of holidaymakers drowned at sea. Every life coach I've ever seen has suggested a memorial of some sort – but they can fuck right off. A memorial would imply it's over.

13 February 1988.

When I ask people what comes to mind when I say that date, the answer invariably is *zilch*. In my head, however, it conjures a three-dimensional snapshot. A scene frozen in time through which I can actually walk:

A car in a clearing in private woods. A faceless body, male, in the passenger seat. Stickers on the windows. A sharp February breeze that fails to make the naked branches shiver – but it's there, I can feel it; the scene's as frigid as a morgue.

This image isn't real, though. It's nothing I've seen before, not accidentally nor fleetingly. I've constructed it. Yet it's *my* construction, and that makes it as real as my nose.

Know what's missing from this mental snapshot?

My mum – which is exactly the reason why I won't plant a tree or build a bench or arrange a stack of stones by an attractive body of water.

Michael would be furious if I said that out loud. He is vehemently loyal to a mother he's never known. Post-natal depression caused her to end it all. That's his explanation, because that's what Dad told us, and Michael deals excellently in absolutes.

My dad shuffles and taps his feet. Without looking up, he says, 'Can I see it?'

'See what?'

'The card.' His gaze remains rooted on his feet.

My eyes become huge. 'It's at home. My home.'

'Is that far?'

'No, not at all.' I point into the distance. 'The tube and a walk.'

He takes a deep breath and, with peculiar gravitas, says: 'Take me there.'

'What about Michael?'

'Let the boy sleep.'

He pulls on his body armour – a navy padded Barbour, its job today to protect him from London – and leads the way down the stairs and out through the front door directly on to the bustling Soho pavement.

It's afternoon, and people spew on to the streets from bars, restaurants, a tiny art gallery. In this neck of the woods, cars and taxis play second fiddle to the pedestrian. Soho-ians inhabit the road as if it were their front garden. A stickler for road safety, Dad, however, sticks to the pavement, nudging a polite route through the people, apologising to every stroppy suit who doesn't move to one side, which is what people in Laurelbridge would do. But my dad's open-minded like that.

Forgive London, Father, for its lack of common courtesy, for they know not what they do.

At Soho Square we stop briefly at St Patrick's, a slim and elegant Roman Catholic church, so that Dad can do a sign of the cross. I do one too. I also pray that he thinks I chose Michael's flat because of its proximity to God. That would make him very happy indeed.

And I think there's a good possibility he might, because suddenly he says, 'OK, Florence, I'm ready.'

I nod. 'OK, Dad. Let's do this.'

United in thought and purpose, we will now make our way back to my bedsit, where we'll read a card from my dead mother, his dead wife.

It's wonderful to feel a connection with your dad.

Though first he tugs a blue inhaler from his pocket. It evokes such a sharp stab of compassion that for a moment I think I could cry. Two bullish puffs and my dad marches off, in the wrong direction.

I wish I'd known he was coming.

Knickers soak amongst food cartons and dirty cutlery in the sink. My Femidom hangs from the bathroom doorknob. Zanna and Norm are having a domestic and/or copulating thunderously next door.

'There's a picture of a balloon on the front.' I point at the card. 'I liked balloons when I was little.'

Dad has perched himself on a thin edge of table. He looks intently at the card. 'All children like balloons,' he mutters.

'Michael doesn't. They scare him when they pop.' A week ago the balloons felt so conclusive. 'Look at the writing, Dad. See the g's, they look like 8's.'

'That's not her writing.'

'It is!'

'I can see the similarities, but no.'

'Who's it from then?' I demand furiously, like he's a graphologist and can provide a full psychological profile.

My dad shrugs. 'Six billion people in the world.'

'Seven billion. Just look at the g's.'

He doesn't. He gazes blindly at the balloons on the front, then puts the card to one side.

I want to cry.

'When your mother disappeared, I turned the house upside down,' he says. 'I was looking for an explanation. I was hoping to stumble upon a letter.'

This information is new to me.

'Did you find one?' I ask.

'No. I found a poem she had written, though.'

'Mum wrote poetry?'

'It was a silly poem really. A bit childish, rhyming couplets.'

'What was it about?'

'Her faith.'

'And she used rhyming couplets?' I frown.

'I've read it many times, looking for something new . . .'

'Nobody uses rhyming couplets to write about God.'

There was an old man called God,

An enormous, elusive cruel sod . . .

'She's with Him,' he says, using his thumb to anoint himself, tracing a small cross on his head, lips and chest. 'This card, it's not her writing. I'm sorry.'

Now he takes his glasses off to rub the bridge of his nose – a visual cue that translates as *conversation over*.

I am pushing my luck when I say, 'The man in the car, Mum's suicide buddy: she must have known him, you know, before that day.'

Dad's knuckles clench on the side of the table on which he sits. This is a subject he won't budge on. The cruel truth is, the man might have been her lover. The sting's too acute – I see it in his face.

'You have a few facts on him, though? Surely you were curious. Did he have a family, for example?'

'We've been through this before.'

'We haven't. I ask, you clam up. Please, Daddy.'

He shuffles uncomfortably.

Talk! Just talk! my eyes beg.

'I believe he had a family, yes.'

An answer. Never has my dad given me a straight answer before.

'A wife? Children?' I ask quickly.

'Yes.'

'Small like me and Michael?'

'Yes.'

'What was his name? The dead man.'

'I don't recall . . .'

'You do!' I stamp.

'Eric. I believe his name was Eric.'

'Eric?' It's the most information he's ever proffered. 'That's it? Just Eric?'

'His name never appeared in the paper. I heard it from the police.'

This is true – I've been through the archives, every last one of them. The media referred to him as *an unnamed local man*; then the story fizzled out.

'Didn't you dig a bit? Ask questions? Surely you'd want to know who he was?'

The blinking starts up again. 'Some things are better left alone.'

'Like, where did he live?'

'Sandbanks – now that's as much as I know.'

'Sandbanks? Nobody from Sandbanks wants to die. It's the fourth richest place on earth.'

'Depression is a private and complicated illness.'

'You know for a fact he was depressed?'

'No, Florence. I have no idea as to why he wished to end his life.'

'Or why he chose a fume-filled car with my mother, your wife, a woman he had apparently never met before? What about his children, didn't he think of them?'

'Sometimes blood isn't thicker than water.'

What is he saying? 'Yes it is. Always.'

'No, Florrie.' He says it ever so sadly, but I don't understand at all: he's talking in riddles.

'What about Eric? Did he leave a note? A poem, perhaps – rhyming couplets?'

Dad starts to cry.

'Dad, don't.' I frown, passing him some kitchen roll. 'Please don't be upset. It's just I have questions too, so bloody many of them . . .'

'For pity's sake, let me be, child.'

My window of opportunity has closed.

Dad pops each of the buttons on his Barbour shut, tugs at its hem, straightens his collar and says:

'It's time to come home, Florence.'

I'm not twelve, yet I feel like I'm being rude by standing my ground. 'No, you go back to Michael's. I'll see you tomorrow, I promise.'

'Back to Dorset, I mean.'

'Yeah, right.'

'It's not a question.'

'I'm doing a course.'

'Thadodastic systems, I remember.' He kicks at a damp towel. 'The state of this place . . .'

'It's homey.'

'It looks like a squat.'

'I can look after myself.'

He raises his voice. 'Why is it always about *you*? I'm seventy next year. I want to slow down. I've humoured your wanderlust, kept the post office ticking over for you. Let Michael come here to be with you . . .'

'He's a grown man.'

'I've done my very best to protect you both.'

'I know, and I'm grateful, but . . .' I take a step towards him.

But Dad puts a hand up. 'Florence, I'm tired.'

I don't answer back or tell him I'm not ready, that I don't want a bloody post office. Guilt weighs too heavy in my gut. My dad is seventy, and he's tired.

I should accompany him back to Michael's, at the very least call him a cab, but I want to stop this conversation now. I can't make him the promises he needs. Not tonight.

Dad's halfway down the stairs when he huffs lethargically and returns. Pulling a small square card from his pocket, he says: 'I promised I'd give you this.'

I take the business card and frown. It's from Husband Number Two.

'How did you get this?'

'I was in the Royal Oak for Sunday lunch. He was there with his mother. He seemed keen to meet up with you. Wouldn't surprise me if he wanted to reignite things.'

'I'd rather die.'

My dad's face confirms that I'm the world's most disappointing daughter. Because of all my husbands, Dad liked Julian the best. Probably because he looked like a priest – a young, quite clever, half-attractive one. The trendy type with enough social skills and interest in contemporary culture to make people wonder if they've entered the clergy for paedophilic reasons.

That's not true. It was because Julian was a good man.

The card slipped into my pocket, I nod slowly. 'I'll contact him.'

Dad retraces his steps down the stairs.

Inside the flat, I look at that card again.

Julian Doe.

Technically I'm still Mrs Doe. Destined never to escape anonymity. Neatly I fold the card in half, squeeze it into an empty Coke can, give the tin a shake and plop it into the bin.

Husband Number One was gold-standard in the looks department.

A mistake.

Never marry a beautiful man. It puts you on an aesthetic pedestal (in your own head). Should the marriage go tits-up, you're left with an unrealistic visual benchmark, when maybe the good-looking husband just had really shoddy taste in wives.

Luke Birmingham fucked me over. I've stopped being so picky.

I'm moving on thanks to Dad – he prayed a lot, mainly for forgiveness for himself, because by the end of my marriage he loathed Luke with an enthusiasm that made him ill. Our Lord has a soft spot for the repentant, so four years later He bequeathed Dad Julian – ideal son-in-law material.

Look now at Julian's face.

He sleeps on an inflatable mattress on the floor. I'm in the single bed above, my head dangling over its side. A splash of moonlight illuminates his strong nose and chin. I spy on his nostrils as he dreams – utterly content, they scarcely flare and wane. It's as therapeutic as watching fish.

Plus Julian looks infinitely more handsome when he's unconscious; awake he's quite pleasant to look at too, though individually none of his features sing. It doesn't matter: the sum of his parts is greater than the slim lips, slightly under-sized eyes and excessive body hair.

Pros: underneath the fur Julian has an athletic physique. *And* he's six feet one. *And* when he laughs his attractiveness cranks up a good notch or two. *And* above and beyond all of this, his heart is good. I cannot stress how irrelevant it is that you're pretty when your personality is gangrenous – it seeps through your pores, etches spiteful lines into your face.

A cruel case study:

I saw Husband Number One's come-face.

Above him was my best friend, Olivia.

I saw her come-face too.

Julian and I met at a church do. Father John was retiring; I was Dad's plus-one. I hovered friendless at the buffet until Julian started chatting to me. Then his pals joined us. Immediately I liked being part of his gang. A charity shop worker, a phlebotomist, a local watercolour artist and a professional cyclist – that constitutes a super-cool gathering for a church do in Laurelbridge.

More importantly, Dad liked Julian straight away.

'Julian's in retail,' he told me, like we'd won the Euromillions.

I was generous about our new friend too. 'It's very right-on – a specialist butcher's. *Everything's* organic, even the wine, preserves, the trendy cookbooks . . .'

Dad elbowed me hard. 'You like him, right?'

I elbowed him back. 'Not as much as you.'

Three months later, *bam!* I've got a boy on my floor.

Julian does a sharp double-breath. Half a snore later, he's motionless again, dreaming effortlessly.

This is the room in which I grew up, and it's the first time ever I've been allowed to have a non-husband sleep over. I'm extremely grateful for it. At twenty-five, there are things you should know about a man before committing. As it turns out, Julian is excellent in bed, and when I say excellent, I mean he's a silent sleeper.

Of course, in an ideal world our body clocks wouldn't be continents apart. Nonetheless, I find it reassuring, him sleeping peacefully below me. I don't stare at the walls like I have eight thousand times before. Walls that are unchanged since the day my mother disappeared. The lampshades, cushions and bedspread are all the same design as the wallpaper – Californian Buckwheat. The vintage *Little House on the Prairie* look was big in the eighties. My room is a migraine-inducing celebration of a tiny pink weed indigenous to another continent.

Other facts about Julian in the sack:

He nods off quickly, at exactly the time he wants to. He has assured me that if ever he has a late night, that's not a problem. His sleep will adjust itself in intensity, ensuring his batteries are fully charged for the morning.

Insomniac fact: we become embroiled in other people's sleep patterns. We feel tired for them when in truth we're ill-equipped to deal with the extra worry. It's liberating to see that Julian sleeps like he's in a coma.

Unlike me. For fifty thousand hours I have stared at these walls, at night its flowers morphing into colonies of pinhead spiders. Gazed from my attic window at a nocturnal view unchanged since time began – *my* time – a crudely painted backdrop, three horizontal stripes of dark. In the foreground, gun-metal-grey woodland. Mid-distance, battleship-grey pasture. And far in the distance, though I can't see it, an impenetrable perimeter of silver-grey sea. *No. 666 (Grey on Grey),* Mark Rothko might have called it.

For five million night-time minutes, I've thought I might never escape that vista, this room.

But tonight Julian is here and there's a whole new world going on inside my bedroom. I forget the unpeopled view. The decor. This house, a working museum to a dead mother's taste.

I watch Julian instead, and it's nice, because he makes me feel like I'm in rehab. Like we're teenagers again, and Amish, and dating in accordance to strict Amish scripture. Like I can erase the shame of being a divorcee, start again, properly this time.

Other reasons I might keep hold of Julian:

We do things together. Walks in the countryside with his parents, Pete and Pam. We cook recipes out of the Sunday supplements. Play badminton with the gang at a sports centre. Help Dad with the post office books. Let Michael win at Pictionary.

'Julian!' I whisper down at him loudly.

'Huh?' He wakes up immediately. Leans on an elbow. Wide awake, just like that.

I smile. 'Sneak into bed with me.'

His laugh is nice. It's warm and thoughtful and cloggy with sleep. It's also quite final. He'd never be disrespectful in my father's house – disloyalty is not Julian's bag, unlike others I can mention.

Husband Number One and my ex-best friend are married now. They live in Spain. With their children. But the sting of them *will* dilute. My life coach told me so. She said there comes a time when it's prudent on mental health grounds to jettison yesterday's pain and to seize today's happiness instead.

I shake my head free of them. Remember today. My new and clean place, emotionally unsullied, all about longevity and friendship.

I peer down – he's snoozing again already, mouth slightly ajar, silent as a guppy – and I decide that Julian Doe could just be the most sensible decision I've ever made.

Chick Lit

I'm doing the washing-up, smoking a joint, thinking about Scott Delaney.

Pisceans, another up side:

They are hypochondriacs, puppy-like in their need to be liked and deeply insecure. Today I saw that first-hand.

Did I make the slightest imprint on him too, I wonder? Does his heart feel a little less empty what with someone new and intriguing knocking around his temporal lobe? Is he doing a little googling of his own?

I should update Alice as to today's developments. Yet I lack my customary professional zeal; a little disloyal, I know, but I find myself preferring to clean filthy dishes, whilst hoping Alice isn't a Cancerian too.

There's a loud and sudden knock. I jump, drop the glass I'm washing. It smashes into the enamel sink. My joint remains suspended from one fear-dried lip.

I fly round to where the knock came from. The window. The curtains are closed, yet behind them I can hear angry glass rattling in its sash. I stare from the kitchenette, unable to move.

There it is again. A frenetic knock. But I'm seven floors up.

The clattering continues.

Wide-eyed I watch the curtains billow hysterically, as if attempting flight; the books and pamphlets stored on the sill – my local studies section – tumble on to the mattress.

Dear God, make him go away. I stare at the ceiling and ask for favours.

But directly above the ceiling is a roof, a roof upon which any number of ex-targets could now be accumulating – a zip-wire vigilante troop, their sole purpose payback.

A good move would be to fling the curtains apart, open the sash and give my assassin a one-liner like *You're outta lives, bud*, followed by a generous squirt of pepper spray and a hearty backwards shove.

But it's too late. They're on to phase two of their attack. The window is now bombarded with stones – hundreds and hundreds and *hundreds* of them. They've got a fucking pebble gun or something. Sweet Jesus, the vigilante group have spent thousands developing a weapon just to fuck with my head.

Throwing my dishcloth to one side, I fly at the window, jerking the curtain clean off its rail.

It is hail that crashes against the window pane. An irascible, naughty wind jangles the glass. The summer storm is now accompanied by a raucous roar of thunder.

And for a while we laugh together, me and the prankster weather, until I see a figure on the rooftop opposite – a black and unidentifiable person, hands limp at his sides, drenched beneath an oversized hoodie. He is looking straight at me.

I'm downstairs, outside on the street, squinting up into sheet rain illuminated by street lamps that hunch over me like monstrous showerheads.

There is no way to get up on to that roof. Not using the traditional front-of-house method anyway. Because it sits above five floors of very grand Victorian flats, huge London pads, utterly inaccessible to hoi polloi like me.

At ground level, however, there is a pub and two Italian cafés.

It's late. The cafés are shut. So I dash into the Marlborough

Arms, an unfriendly establishment, the staff barely noticing me bypass the bar.

My destination is the toilet.

The cubicle to the far left has a grubby frosted window that opens directly on to a square of concrete. Here the pub and cafés store wheelie bins, cardboard boxes, bicycles and crates. The space also doubles as an assembly point for the metal fire escape ladders that scale the hidden side of the luxury flats; minted residents demand an adequate escape route in the event of arson or lightning strike.

I *hate* ladders. Particularly ones beneath which firemen fail to hold the corners of a jump-blanket. Especially I hate very tall, barely lit ones. But most of all I hate climbing them while bastard clouds shoot water, sharp as raw rice, at my eyes.

I take it slowly, recite the periodic table in my head, concentrate only on chemical elements and the next rung. Pretend I'm in a movie and getting to the top is a matter of life and death. And my legs serve me well – though when I reach the top and heave myself safely on to the roof, they are quick to buckle.

For a bit I inhale a puddle, a cheek and ear flat against the wet floor, the scent of drenched asphalt momentarily pacifying.

From here I survey the space around me.

A jumble of rooftop materials, air vents, chimney stacks, all rimmed by a little wall. No hoodie.

Taking the pepper spray from my jacket pocket, I push myself to my feet and tentatively make my way towards the edge. Not too close. I certainly don't look down into Torrington Place. Instead I stare directly ahead, across the street, at the window of my flat.

It feels strange, like I'm someone else looking back at me objectively. I find I prefer it, prefer observing me to being me. The human condition demands we want what we can't have. We strive to be better, jealousy being key to our domination as a species.

I glance left and right, wipe my dripping face with a soaking hand.

Nobody.

Quietly I follow the side of the building, a three-foot wall separating me from a thirty-metre nose-dive into traffic. As I walk, I scan the ground for debris. It's a saturated trampoline; raindrops bombard it, bounce back up and away like a masochistic tumbling troop.

Maybe this storm has pressure-washed the roof clean. There are no chewing gum wrappers, paper coffee cups or cans of Red Bull. No leaves from the trees; much less bird shit than I'd have imagined.

I examine it more closely.

It looks swept.

I find my voice.

'You bin watchin' me?' The cockney accent is ideal in such situations. The east London glottal stop, the vocalisation of the dark L: they're unrivalled in providing the illusion of murderous intent (watch all episodes of *The Sweeney*).

But I mumble it too timidly. The rain drowns me out.

'Well 'ere I am. Come out, you fuckin' coward.'

I notice something in the far corner of the roof. A heating vent, steam spewing from it excitedly only to be swallowed quickly by the sodden air. I approach it gingerly, because there's a dark nook behind the vent. The closer I get, the sharper my eyesight becomes. A small fabric fishing stool with a rain cover dotted with yellow rosebuds. Under the seat a book has been neatly placed in a sandwich bag and secured with a small twist of white wire to stop it from getting wet.

And to the book's side, a carrier bag, its handles tied in

a double bow. My fingers are inflexible from the wet wind; it takes a while to dig the thing open.

Inside I find the remnants of a meal deal:

One sandwich wrapper – low-fat roasted vegetable wrap. An empty fruit salad carton. The sell-by dates for both tomorrow.

Peach-flavoured water – empty apart from two cigarette butts. I tip it upside down so the cigarette filters sit in a puddle in my palm. I frown down at them. White, extra-long, Silk Cut – not even a proper cigarette. You'd get more of a hit inhaling the air on this rooftop, parasympathomimetic alkaloid fact.

It wasn't what I was expecting.

The Hoodie's not hard-boiled. He's a health nut. Fastidiously neat. Unwilling to get his bottom wet, so much so that he's fashioned a cute rain cover for his stool. He worries about his body mass index, is an uncommitted smoker and cares enough about the workplace to put a broom round now and then, regardless of meteorological conditions.

Raindrops aquaplane the length of my nose.

An educated guess: the Hoodie's not a young man.

Now I take the book, pull it free of its sandwich bag. Stop breathing entirely. It's a novel I also own – *PS, I Love You*, by Cecelia Ahern.

And when things are a little slow, he catches up on his chick lit.

A more educated guess: the Hoodie is not a man of any sort.

I make my way back down the metal ladder. More quickly this time, sure-footedly.

The Hoodie is a middle-aged woman with a penchant for cleanliness.

Bambi.

By six I knew the difference between *Clostridium botulinum* and *E. coli*: how they liked to live, dine and reproduce inside the human body; how to them our internal organs were the equivalent of a six-star Petri dish. Just like Michael, our mother was a stickler for domestic order.

At the bottom of the ladder I scavenge through water-logged wheelie bins. Discover two more carrier bags, each identical to the bag on the roof – the same meal deal, two cigarette butts in the empty peach water bottle.

She's been watching me for a while.

I lift dank hair from my cheeks, look to the rooftop again, wonder if she can see me from wherever she's hiding up there, or whether she's long gone.

PS, I Love You.

A book about a loved one coming back from the dead, sending clues and letters and stuff.

I take the stairs two at a time. Fumble for my keys. Think about my birthday card – its balloons *were* a clue.

Throwing open the door to my apartment, I head straight for my books. They teeter in Jenga-like piles, but I know where every one of them is; I use a derivation of the Dewey Decimal System. I have a copy of this book too, thanks to my brother. He hadn't read it, he told me on my twenty-seventh birthday, so didn't have a clue what it was about. Nonetheless, he thought the title was just perfect.

And it was.

More than anything, I wish I'd read it. I intend to right now. But *The Blind Assassin* leans against *The Wolves of Willoughby Chase* – there is a gap. I know where *all* my books are.

I inhale sharply.

She took my copy when she broke into my apartment.

Kneeling on my mattress, I gaze at the empty rooftop across the road. When my mobile screen jerks and flashes angrily, I put it blindly to my ear.

Answer vacantly. 'Yes?'

It's Maeve, and she's very pissed off. 'What the fucking *fuck* have you done?'

I speak flatly. 'Maeve, can we do this another time?'

'You asked me to facilitate, and I quote you directly, *the briefest of bumps*. Christ, I was complicit in locking Scott in a room with a lunatic . . .'

I quickly sit down on the mattress, my back flat against the cool wall.

'What's happened?' I demand. Please God, don't let Scott have got wind.

'You were supposed to have a quick chat with him and go – that was the deal . . .'

'Did I upset anyone? Have there been complaints?'

'No.'

I'm safe, but not elated. I look at my watch. The shops are long shut, but I need a copy of *PS, I Love You*. The library – I could break in.

'I hung around for a bit. Made sure things ran smoothly. What do you want?' I ask impatiently.

'I am not happy, Florence.'

The joint from earlier is on the floor. I relight it and exhale quickly. 'Living a lie is hard.'

'With you, Florence. I am not happy *with you*—'

I cut her short. 'Did Scott say anything about me?'

'Why would he?'

A heavy disappointment returns. It was too big an ask. I should be pleased he hasn't worked out I'm a fake – I gave the man two different names *and* the Look.

Dense blue smoke streams from my lips.

I take my frustration out on her.

'That Ricky Hart guy, where did you get him? I mean, seriously, is there a journalist alive who thinks outside the box? Answer me this, Maeve: if your mother was about to be murdered – a bad murder, you know, strung out and totally excruciating – and you've got to watch, but you could save her by *doing it* with her, would you?'

'For fuck's sake.'

'It's a good question. Hold on. Your mum's a horrible homophobe. Probably best you let her croak.'

I relax my shoulder, the phone drops free and I press *Call End*.

But the bitch calls back.

'Scott phoned me this evening to thank me for the suite.'

'I'll whittle you a medal.'

'He said you dropped your purse.'

Instantly motionless, my voice softens. 'I've been wondering where that was.'

'Yeah, right.'

'I have.'

'He referred to you as Florence. You gave him your real name?'

Scat using my real name out loud makes me overwhelmingly happy.

Maeve's sigh is lengthy. Fed up with this game, she asks me straight, 'What's this all about? Are you setting him up?'

'I am *not* setting him up.'

'What then? Please, Florence.' I've not heard this tone in almost a year – it's half amicable.

'It's Michael,' I lie.

'Is he OK?' She asks this quickly. She's not met him, but she always showed concern. In hindsight, that was kind. Who am I kidding: even at the time, her compassion was appreciated.

'No, Maeve, he's not good. Not good at all.'

The resurrection of our mother is, however, none of her business. I scan the rooftop opposite, its dark corners, but the sheet rain and dancing steam plays tricks with my eyes – her aura might as well still inhabit it.

I sigh heavily. 'Michael worships Scott. I was hoping to set up a surprise meeting, backstage passes . . . oh, I don't know. I was chancing my fucking luck. I didn't get the opportunity. Scat was too busy. *Far* too important, if you know what I mean.'

'*Scat*, eh?'

'Yes, Maeve. Scat.'

'Right,' she says slowly.

'Perhaps you could tell him there are forwarding details in the purse?'

'How about I don't,' she says flatly. 'I told him I don't know you. That you're agency.'

Welcome back, the old Maeve Rivers. I can't see her face, but I know I'd want to punch it quite hard.

My smile is thin and sad. 'I think we're done here. You're off the hook. Goodbye, Maeve.'

I hang up quickly. Farewells are brutal. I hate them. Tonight, however, bigger shit has happened.

First Mum.

Now Scat.

Maeve has nothing more to worry about – she'll not be seeing me again.

I put *PS, I Love You* on my mental urgent-things-to-do list, and log straight on to Hotmail, refreshing every thirty seconds, composing an email to Alice.

Marital case
Saturday 5/7/14 11.09 p.m.
From: <u>info@londonpiservices.uk.net</u>
To: <u>asc345@hotmail.com</u>

Alice!

OMG, you'll never guess what. He only wants to contact me. Scott fucking Delaney. Or Scat, as I now like to call him. I've not even heard *you* call him that before! One thousand smackeroonies says I'll decimate your marriage in less than seventy-two hours!

LOL & FPC (fast palm-clap)

FL xx

Naturally I redraft it several times; try to erase elation, replace it with the requisite amount of solemnity, remember who my friends are.

This is what Alice will actually receive:

Marital case
Saturday 5/7/14 11.39 p.m.
From: <u>info@londonpiservices.uk.net</u>
To: <u>asc345@hotmail.com</u>

Hello Alice,

I hope Tuscany continues to treat you well. Along with being considered the globe's largest repository of art, the region also boasts an outstanding literary tradition. May I suggest a little poolside reading – poetry, something by Petrarch or Alighieri perhaps?

I have news. Following my conversation with Scott today in the Landmark Hotel, Marylebone, I have been apprised of his desire to make contact with me. I currently await an email. Don't be alarmed by this development. I dropped my purse; I'm sure he simply wishes to return this, along with telling me face-to-face about my professionalism.

I will now contrive to arrange a further meeting during which I will attempt to take our liaison beyond that which is morally acceptable.

I will contact you as soon as I have news regarding subsequent arrangements.

Much love,

FL

I thought about adding a kiss, but professionalism prevailed.

Refresh . . .

Refresh . . .

Refresh . . .

I don't feel alone tonight.

My mum.

Scat Delaney.

Tonight I choose to imagine I left quite an impression on Mr Delaney. That he's puzzled as to why I keep popping uninvited into his head. That against his better judgement he finds he wants to see me again.

Refresh . . .

It's less that he finds me irresistible and everything to do with the fact that I titillate his brain – the right ventral tegmental area, to be precise. Because my ability to orally massage, tease and possess this part of a man's anatomy is quite a knack. Of course he wants to come back for more. Two point four million years of evolution tell him so. Dopamine rushes don't happen every day.

Refresh . . .

The glossy page from *Architectural Digest* is still stuffed into the pocket of my cagoule. I pull it free.

Delaney's lounge . . .

I look at it, imagine him all alone in there with its *clean lines and allegiance to soul, light and order.*

Yet I know more than most.

The backing track to this Zen-inspired space will be all wrong. Scott won't be playing dharma pop or ambient garage or some New Age shit by Enya. He'll be playing Red Dead Redemption – a computerised re-enactment of death in the Wild West, with its bolt-action rifles, and lassos, and the pained, unvarying yelps of the butchered. Yes, Scott Delaney will be whiling away another evening alone, cowboys and murder taking his mind from the long and fitful night that lies ahead.

Difference is, tonight he knows it doesn't have to be like this – he just needs the right excuse to contact me.

And clever old Florence gave it to him in spades – the purse, my professional proficiency, the medical knowledge of a qualified sleep therapist.

When you're ready, Scott.

Refresh . . .

Refresh . . .

Refresh . . .

When you're ready.

LIFE COACH

Sunday. Day Seven: Operation Delaney.

8.12 a.m.

Dr Malik's office – I wouldn't say it's typically Ayurvedic. Walls the colour of tired mushrooms (Portobello). Carpet tiles (algae green). Two chairs (retirement-home orange) at a cosy angle, as though a TV sits in the corner. It doesn't. A bin does – one just big enough for a few tear-soaked tissues, assuming you bring your own, because the tissues on the windowsill are more suited to the redistribution of snot than absorbency. Definitely you could grease a baking tin with them.

These tissues remind me of the toilet paper we had at school, which is maybe the point – they're here as a prop to evoke memories and encourage regression. And good grief, they do it every time – sweep me back to a time when, having just learnt to wipe my own bottom, the nuns upped the ante, provided us with an adapted type of tracing paper for the purpose; it was the equivalent of using a plasterer's trowel to remove our excretions. Penance for our original sin.

Dr Malik smiles at me widely, his teeth blazing an unpolluted white.

Truth be told, I'd fancy the dhoti off him were it not for his insatiable need to lighten the mood.

I'll describe him for you.

Imran Khan, the cricketer, when he was young, who interestingly looks a lot like a Pakistani Richard Gere, Richard Gere being my first celebrity crush ever, who interestingly had slightly buck teeth just like Scott.

'It's good to see you, Florence,' he says warmly. 'It's been a while.'

'Three weeks.'

'Two months.'

I see Dr Malik because sometimes it gets lonely here in London. When you live life in the shadows, it's good to offload. It's not unlike having a boyfriend for whom you're never an irritant. Naturally you pay for the privilege. Dr Malik nods, listens and occasionally comes up with some scientifically sound advice. Naturally he doesn't put out, but on all other levels he is excellent company. Plus I think I fascinate him a bit, which is just the tonic for those of a solitary disposition.

'I don't normally see clients on a Sunday. You said it was urgent. Is everything all right?'

I hand him a slip of paper.

It says: *I, Dr Ekram Malik, confirm that Florence Maria Love attended her life coaching session today.*

'It's for my dad,' I explain. 'He worries. If you could sign and date here.'

He obliges as if this is the most natural thing in the world. His empathetic look is consummate. I certainly intend on using it when I'm profiling psychopaths in Manchester.

'You must really want to please your father,' he says kindly.

I fill him in. 'Dad wants me to leave London and go back to Laurelbridge. I'm appeasing my own guilt.'

'You don't want to go?'

'No.'

'So don't go.'

'Dad's almost seventy. He's tired. He's been ready to hand over the family business for a while.'

'Do you want it – the family business?'

'Christ, no.'

He doesn't see the issue.

I stare perplexed. 'It was a present. He'd be devastated.'

'Devastated for whom?'

I give this some thought. The answer is 'himself'; nevertheless, I defend my father. 'He worries about me and Michael all the time.'

'A condition of having children.'

'Well it makes me feel bad.'

'Here is another condition of having children – you must allow your offspring to make their own choices and live their own lives.'

I shake my head. 'Michael and I are all he's got.'

'Could that assumption be a little self-important?' wonders Dr Malik.

'Nope. It's a statement of fact.'

'So when your father is back in Dorset, he sits in a chair all day twiddling his thumbs, bemoaning how lonely he is.'

I nod sadly, because most of the time, in my head, that's exactly what he does.

Dr Malik leans forward and drops his head to the left.

'He doesn't, Florence. He exists just as successfully and self-sufficiently as you do. Sometimes he's sad. Sometimes he's happy. Sometimes he'll go a whole hour without giving you or Michael a single thought.'

'You don't know him.'

'I have a father. I *am* a father. We are not emotional invalids. If you disobey us, we won't have a nervous breakdown.'

'My dad's not as ontological as you.'

That apparently is no excuse. 'Sometimes we need to remind our parents of truths: that we are as valid a human being as they are. Your father can function perfectly well without you kowtowing to his every insecurity. And deep down, he knows it perfectly well too.'

Dr Malik looks at me very wisely.

How I wish I could live next door to him in La La Land.

Sitting back heavily, I look at him for a while. 'My mother has contacted me,' I tell him flatly.

'Your . . . Excuse me?'

'She sent me a birthday card.'

'Forgive me, your birth mother?'

'It had balloons on it. And somebody broke into my flat – a very domesticated woman. She spies on me from the roof opposite.'

'I'm sorry, Florence. I thought your mother had passed.'

'Me too.' I rub my face.

'How much marijuana are you smoking?' asks Dr Malik. This irritates me. 'I told you I quit.'

'It can precipitate paranoia and delusions.'

'And moments of intense lucidity.' But the Catholic in me takes over. Dr Malik's saintly poise has the same effect as a truth serum. 'I had one joint last night.'

Dr Malik drops his head, this time to the right side, looks at me silently and waits for me to beg forgiveness for my narcotics blip.

I shan't. There are worse vices. Consuming fifteen tins of wife-beater of an evening, for example. Or snorting bath salts. Or injecting diacetylmorphine (interestingly the opioid analgesic synthesised originally by Alder Wright back in 1874 as a non-addictive alternative to morphine); today it's better known as black dirt, tar, diesel or heroin.

Marijuana fact: one joint *never* killed anyone (apart from those who are susceptible to cannabis toxicity, which is by and large fatal).

Never meet a dealer face to face, though. Go on the darknet; order a bag of weed from a site that's as efficient as Amazon though a lot less licensed. Goods are sent first-class delivery via Royal Mail. You pay via Bits and provide no personal details whatsoever, other than an address. Twenty-four hours later there's a Jiffy bag on the front-door mat.

Important note: in the eyes of the law, this is very wrong.

The law would also agree, I'm sure, that it's extremely convenient and a much safer way for lone women to score.

I don't tell this to Dr Malik. I've come here simply to get my chitty signed, to make my dad happy again.

'Thanks for this.' I take it from his lap. 'Do you have any literature for me?'

Dr Malik's been caught on the hop, yet he pulls a leaflet from his leather document folder. It's called *The Art of Living: Better Food; Better Mood.*

I flick through it. I chose Dr Malik because he said he was a proponent of self-help therapies. I assumed he'd do more than provide me with fucking leaflets, then tell me to go off and help myself.

Before I go, I ask if he's read *PS, I Love You*. No, he says, delighted, but he has seen the film. I shake my head, because that's no good – the plot might have been bastardised, the nuances lost. I need to read the original work.

I take the number 24 home.

On the filthy tartan seat beside me sits a pair of Harry Potter glasses – black plastic children's ones. A heavy sadness fills my chest and I've no idea why. I pick them up, decide to give them to the bus driver in case the child's mother calls the bus company.

And I totally intend to.

But when the bus stops at Waterstones, I forget, get straight off, sit outside the shop because it's Sunday and it doesn't open until midday.

In the meantime, I check my emails . . .

Nothing.

Reluctantly I call Michael. When he answers, however, he sounds chirpy. I'm infinitely relieved. He even invites me to lunch to celebrate Dad's visit to London.

I tell him nothing of the last two days.

At twelve o'clock, I push past the assistant who opens the doors and go straight to the contemporary fiction section. Whilst waiting to pay for the novel, I read the back cover.

Life is for living, it says. *But it always helps if there's an angel looking over you.*

Sébastien

Michael's flat is small but perfectly formed. Not quite big enough for two people, its ideal occupancy is probably one and a half. Which perhaps explains his attraction to Sébastien – he's a convenient size.

My dad, Michael, Sébastien and I sit knee to knee in the living room. It feels quite tight, like we're sitting opposite one another on the train and trying not to touch feet.

But spacewise you get what you pay for in Soho, and Michael's paying by the square inch. (When I say Michael, I mean Dad and me.) Though he does get this place at a discount. The gallery owner downstairs fancies him. As do most of Soho, I'm sure. Which is why – apart from his dimensions – I've no clue what the pull is with Sébastien.

Sébastien . . .

He sits in the armchair opposite me looking small and frail. The chair's billowing arms give the impression he's being propped up, like a baby. Michael sits beside him on a matching footstool. Dad's beside me on the couch, gulping his way enthusiastically through a bottle of wine, for which I'm delighted – his mood is altogether merrier than yesterday.

Then there's Bambi: mystified, she looks out at us from her photo frame. I wonder which of us concerns her the most.

I give her a secret wink.

'So, Sébastien,' Dad says, jubilantly. 'What is it you do for a living?'

I lean forward, excited. I've not really heard him talk out

loud before, not properly. Maybe I'll like him better when he enunciates.

'Mr Love, thank you for asking. I'm an osteopath.'

I want to laugh. Sébastien's voice is childish and American – a mixture of Andy Warhol and Michael Jackson and Janet Jackson and Thumper. Utterly sinister. The man smacks of arch-villain.

My father slaps his thigh. 'What are the chances? I've got a bad back.'

'You have tight glutes,' I tell him, because he has; I looked it up.

Dad ignores me. 'I've had it for years. In my lower back and hips. It affects everything. Watch this.'

Michael forgets to watch Dad and goes to get nibbles. I make up for his social clumsiness by giving our father my entire attention.

Standing up unsteadily, Dad dangles his long arms at his sides. For a moment he looks a hundred years old, anthropoid, achingly vulnerable – the sadness takes me by surprise; my dad has marched too quickly through his life. He leans gently to the left, then even more gently to the right.

'There is a difference,' I tell Sébastien.

'Yes,' Sébastien says in an evil genius voice. And that's it. Now if that was me – if I was a bona fide osteopath – I'd get up, go over to said dinner guest and have a poke around their sore bits:

1. Because that's my job and doing osteopathy spontaneously and without charge shows great willing.

2. Because I'd want to show off – diagnose and cure them whilst appearing to be the fountain of all physiologic knowledge.

3. Because everybody likes to be touched, especially by a stranger. It makes your coccyx tingle.

Sébastien, however, remains seated. I conclude he's either very selfish or a fantasist.

'Do you work for a firm?' I cross-examine him.

'No.'

'Do you have any clients?'

'Yes.'

'Here or in America?'

'I'm Canadian.'

'Oh.' I rather like the Canucks.

'Osteopathy is an excellent profession.' My dad provides Sébastien with a list of advantages. 'It's very stable. People will always get backache. Osteopaths are quite academic – they're failed doctors, you know.'

'That's a bit rude,' I tell Sébastien.

'How much do you make?' Dad asks.

'That's ruder.'

'It's OK,' mouths Sébastien – his voice, I notice, is beginning to fail.

'No, Sébastien. Don't answer that.' I can't help it, though: I giggle at Dad. 'Honestly, what are you like?'

'Last year I made—'

'I said don't.' I put a no-nonsense finger in the air.

'You're on a good wedge, though, eh?' says Dad mischievously, refilling his own glass.

Wrong as it is, I love my dad best when he's leathered.

Sébastien hedges his bets. 'It pays the bills.'

I test him.

'Have you read *Non-pharmacological therapies for acute and chronic low back pain: A review of the evidence for the American College of Physicians*?'

He shakes his head, blows through pursed lips then speaks

resolutely to his knees. 'Miss Love, I *am* an osteopath.'

'No, *I'm* an osteopath.' Dad punches the air.

'No, *I'm* an osteopath.' I punch it too.

'No, *I'm* an osteopath,' says Michael, arriving with a platter of hors d'oeuvres.

We laugh like teenagers, apart from Sébastien.

Sébastien is taking a moment. He closes his eyes, swallows slowly and starts again.

'Sir, your daughter could be right in her diagnosis. The gluteus maximus and gluteus medius are the two most common causes of lower back pain. The gluteus medius muscle attaches along the ilium, between the anterior and posterior gluteal lines. Distally, it is attached to the lateral surface of the femur . . .'

His explanation is painfully slow and, some might say, extremely self-indulgent. If he had turned out to be American I'd have put his attention-seeking down to his nationality. Americans are innately histrionic. European biochemists are actually doing tests to see if they have a unique gene.

I shit you . . . slightly.

He must have a splash of the Yank, I decide. Look how he's still monopolising the conversation, all that deep breathing he's doing, like he's on the verge of a panic attack.

'The anterior fibres rotate and assist in the flexion of the joint.' (Inhale, exhale.) 'The posterior fibres laterally rotate and may assist in extension.' (Inhale, exhale.) 'Sir, may I have your email address? I'll forward you some stretches. If the problem persists, then I'd be honoured to treat you, either in my clinic or at your home.' (Inhale, exhale.) 'For free, of course.'

What an arse. 'He does live in Dorset,' I say.

Sébastien avoids my gaze, looks only at my dad. 'As I said, I'd be honoured.'

Michael offers me a nibble from his platter. I shake my head and tell my dad proudly, 'I only eat rajasic now.'

'Who's he?' says Dad, deadpan.

'It's the perfect nutritional path for energy, action and creativity.' Michael states it exactly as I told it to him.

I give him a little clap.

'Ayurvedic cuisine,' adds Sébastien, ignoring the fact that I'm addressing only blood relatives.

'Actually, Dad, I've been busy since I saw you yesterday. I think you'll be happy. I went to see my life coach this morning. Look what I got you.' I pass him the signed chitty. 'I'll be getting him to sign one every week from now on.'

My brother sits himself beside Sébastien on the chair arm. Sébastien looks like his ventriloquist's dummy.

'This is Seb's first dinner party ever.' Michael interrupts my story.

'Why?' I ask. 'How old is he?'

'Twenty-five,' says Michael.

'So he can speak for himself.'

Michael speaks conspiratorially with Sébastien, then says out loud: 'Somebody's got the painters in.'

Sébastien either laughs or has cramp in his mouth.

Hurt, a hand floats to my chest. For a moment, I don't know what to say. My brother just ganged up on me.

'Seb's got a stammer,' Michael explains. 'He's making brilliant progress.'

Thankfully Dad steals the spotlight. 'At least you're with f-f-f-friends,' he says.

'Dad!' I try to redeem myself; to make my brother love me the most again. 'That is so out of order.'

'Just trying to lighten the mood, Florrie.'

Michael pats Dad's knee.

So I say quickly: 'Have you seen *The King's S-S-S-Speech*?'

Sexist fact: pretty women should never attempt satire. It does not translate as clever or dry. When you're good-looking and female, the audience assume all humour emanates from the part of the brain responsible for smug malevolence. Old men in a navy Barbour, however, must *always* do satire, because when they do it, it lightens the mood.

'I need to talk to you, Michael.' I change the subject.

Michael's eyes instantly grow large. He knows from my tone that I want to talk about Mum. So does my dad who, without looking away from me, fills his glass and takes a good slug.

'Maybe we should take it to the kitchen,' I say.

Dad nods, starts to manoeuvre himself to his feet, but I shake my head and point at Sébastien.

'You look after our special guest, Dad,' I tell him maturely. 'I can handle this on my own.'

Despite Michael being in the middle of preparing a three-course meal, his tiny pristine kitchen looks as if it's been airlifted directly from the Ideal Home Exhibition.

'I'm going to be truthful with you, Michael,' I say, gently. 'More than anybody in the whole world you deserve that. What I told you the other day, about Mum – I didn't mean it how it came out.'

'You didn't lie,' he states unswervingly. 'Whatever Dad says, I know you didn't lie.'

'What did Dad say?'

'That you have an active imagination.'

I smile. 'I've never pretended otherwise.'

'So active that sometimes it takes the place of reality.'

My nod is philosophical.

'A vivid imagination is the gift of the great. Artists, writers, film directors, inventors – they don't just think outside the box, they *live* outside it for walloping hunks of their life. A vivid imagination is an essential prerequisite to being a pioneer. Oh Michael, don't ever be like *them*.' I point at the wall, at Middle England. 'Insipid, narrow-minded, uninspired, mistaking the imaginative for being pathological liars or deluded. Look at Aristotle, Jimi Hendrix, Steve Jobs – their imaginations were astonishing.'

'Madonna.'

'Well . . .'

'Sherlock Holmes.'

I don't tell him Sherlock Holmes was not real, just clasp his hands between mine. 'I do know one thing for absolute certain, though. I love you more than anything in the whole world.'

His sigh is long-suffering. 'That you do.'

'Partners for ever, eh, you and me?' Encouragingly I back-fist his abs, but he doesn't say it back.

He never says it back.

'Best you leave this job to me, because I *will* find out once and for all if Mum's alive. If she isn't, I'll never stop making it up to you, I swear. I'll admit I'm as mad as a box of frogs – to you, to Dad, to the whole bloody world. But if she's alive . . .' I flare my nostrils, 'I will find her.'

'At least we'll know, one way or the other,' he says.

'You got it.' I want to squeeze him hard. Swing him round in circles by the hands. Instead I cup his cheeks. They fill my palms. 'So – what's going on with this Sébastien, then?'

The smile that inhabits his face is entirely carefree. And now I thank the Lord for his madness. It's his saving grace. Bambi who? He's forgotten whether she's dead or alive.

He giggles like a toddler and I feel a piercing stab of happiness for him.

'Looks to me, Michael Love, like you've got yourself an admirer.' I rub my hands together and demand answers. 'OK, what are the four basic stages for successful entrapment?'

Like the class swot, he points and says: 'Surveillance, Bump One, Bump Two and the money shot.'

My heart fills like the Basilica Cistern. See how important I am to him. 'And what if you want to see him again?'

'You can't. Ever.'

'But what if you did, hypothetically, want to take it to the next level? I don't know, maybe you're not on an entrapment case. Maybe you like someone a lot and want to start a relationship.'

Michael's stymied. I haven't taught him this bit before.

'You can stop kissing him for just five seconds,' I say. 'Maybe try ten seconds the next time. Then fifteen.' I nod towards the front room; flap a hand in the direction of the ventriloquist's dummy.

Now Michael gets it. 'But what if he doesn't like me that way?' he whispers.

'He has a speech impediment, Michael. You are leagues better-looking than him. Truth be told, everybody is better-looking than him. Plus, look at the clues – he's at his first dinner party *ever*. He's meeting your family. It's physiologically impossible for him to get his head any further up Dad's arse.' I even make fun of myself a little: 'For fuck's sake, he's sitting through a whole evening with me.'

'True.' He nods earnestly.

'Do one thing for me, though, Michael. Stop hanging out for Mum to turn up. She's not going to come here. She would never unsettle you like that. She loved you far too much. She tickled your ears, remember?' I kiss his hand as if he's a maiden I intend to rescue. 'I will sort this, sweetheart. One way or the other, I'll make things right.'

For a self-centred second I wish he'd bear-hug me back, reassure me. For a lonely second, I wish I had someone to promise me a resolution or two.

Entrapment 101 Tip #5: Surveillance is a gross violation of human rights

For this reason there are just two surveillance rules.

Surveillance rule #1: Never get caught. Then no harm's done.

Practice here is key. Follow people you know – the family you've extricated yourself from, perhaps. Warning: that's outré but necessary, like training for a marathon and doing hill runs. They're chest-screamingly painful. You wonder why you're doing it to yourself. Then you slow to your usual pace and it's a piece of piss. Just as civilian surveillance will be if you practise like you're a member of the Special Forces on your heartbroken folks.

Surveillance rule #2: Eye contact means game over, you are off the case.

Which puts the target at an advantage. Always be on the lookout yourself. Should you suspect you're being followed, join in the game; enlist countersurveillance:

- Finger your salt-water and chilli pistol.

- Walk casually around the block, ending up back where you started.

- If they're still following, turn and give them the finger.

• Take a bloody photo.

• Look them firmly in the eye and shout, 'Bad luck, you're out!'

The two rules of surveillance are pithy. They're also as cut-and-dried as paintballing.

Bump Two

I left Michael's place shortly afterwards. I needed air. I wanted to start my book.

But I don't want to go home.

Maida Vale seems as good a place as any to go for a walk. There are a lot of blue plaques.

Alan Turing, a codebreaker, lived at number 2 Warrington Crescent, Maida Vale. The man who shot the world's first movie film did so at his home, 136 Maida Vale. Ambrose Fleming (9 Clifton Gardens) got his plaque for writing *The Evidence of Things Not Seen*. And *Electric Lamps and Electric Lighting: A Course of Four Lectures on Electric Illumination*.

Scott Delaney doesn't have a commemorative plaque yet.

He does, however, have electric lighting. And even though it's gone eleven, it's still on. A tender glow emanates from the penumbra of his bedroom curtain. Standing on the opposite bank of Regent's Canal, I speak under my breath.

No point lying there staring at the ceiling, Scott. Get up. Do something soporific. Read a book. Better still, send an email. I gave you enough excuses to contact me. They don't even have to be lost-purse-related.

Telepathically I transmit email suggestions.

Hey there!
Monday 7/7/14 12.23 a.m.
From: ScatDelaney@ScatDelaney.com
To: florencemarialove@hotmail.com

Hey Florence,

Hope you don't mind me emailing unannounced. But you mentioned when we met that you had a copy of Rechtsschaffen and Bergmann's *Sleep deprivation in the rat by the disk-over-water method*. Be great to meet and chat about this and more recent neurological experiments on sleep deprivation, subsequent cognitive dysfunction and death amongst laboratory animals.

Very best wishes,

Scat

Girls are so much better at this sort of thing than boys. In case Scott didn't like the sound of that one, I suggest an alternative:

A business proposition

Monday 7/7/14 12.24 a.m.

From: ScatDelaney@ScatDelaney.com

To: florencemarialove@hotmail.com

Cc: maeve.rivers@thedailynews.com

Dear Ms Love,

It was great to meet you at the Landmark Hotel. I was frankly bowled over by your proficiency, medical knowledge and refusal to boot-lick, regardless of my celebrity status. I would therefore like to offer you temporary employment as my PA, whilst Harvey Cadwalader visits his parents in South America. Rest assured, I am prepared to pay some way over the going rate given the exemplary service exhibited during your time as my event organiser.

Best wishes,

Scott Delaney (Scat)

Failing that:

Purse
Monday 7/7/14 12.25 a.m.
From: <u>ScatDelaney@ScatDelaney.com</u>
To: <u>florencemarialove@hotmail.com</u>

Hi,
   You dropped your purse. Let me know how you'd
like me to return it to you.
   Mr Delaney

'Come on, Scat,' I mutter and look to the right.

A man stands five feet away from me. Like me, he's
squinting across at Scott's house.

My eyes become huge. My legs malfunction entirely. I should
bolt, at the very least wave my pepper spray at him, because
the man whose profile I'm currently scrutinising is the Poet.

He's also the motorcyclist – the blond guy on the Triumph
Scrambler who followed Michael and me on the night of
the de Groot case.

Catatonic, I stare.

This close he has the doomed air of a lovelorn medieval
knight. His image could adorn the Pre-Raphaelite postcards
they sell in museum shops. Tristan, out of *Tristan and Isolde*,
only the Poet is wearing a one-piece tailored cowhide motorcycle suit in liquorice. Plus his nose, cheeks and forehead
are a blush of beige freckles. The dense stubble on his chin
is dappled saffron, as are his eyelashes. This gives him an
unusual pallor, like multicoloured sand. The nervous type
who grinds, his teeth belong to an infant – their mesiodistal
crown length is far too short. And to top it off, he dons a
loneliness that is disconcertingly contagious.

I shiver. The Poet is not that good-looking up close.

Suddenly he's finished looking at Scott's house. Putting his helmet on, he walks slowly back to his bike. Tucked into the back of his motorcycle jeans I spot a book. The one he was reading whilst standing on the narrowboat's stern? Maybe, but it's not pulp poetry. Neither is it *PS, I Love you*. It's an A–Z London street map.

'Who are you?' I shout weakly after him.

He mounts the Triumph Scrambler. I wait for him to roar off menacingly, mysteriously. To at least pull free a pistol and shoot me dead. He doesn't. He lifts his visor so that I can look at those angry eyes again. And I wish he hadn't, because they're mesmeric, but not in a good way. His hair is sure to have woken up inside his helmet, the hateful white snakes trying to slither free, to spit and strangle me.

A take a step back.

The Poet grows impatient. Snaps his visor shut. Fires up the bike.

It growls angrily, off and away.

I bend over the canal railings, inhale the stagnant water's aroma, my heart thrashing about in its cavity, confused.

Wasn't there a serial killer called the Poet, who made the deaths look like suicides, leaving Edgar Allan Poe quotes at the scene of the crime?

Looking at the spot in which he previously stood, I suddenly spot it.

A little white card. It balances on the canal railings.

I pigeon-step towards it, snatch at it – a business card.

Noah Steensen, it says.

Nothing else, not a phone number or address, not even an email.

Steensen is a Nordic name. I've read Scandinavian thrillers. This is the card of a man with assassination in mind.

The Poet is following me.

Me.

For a peculiar second, I feel both fear and excitement, each completely indistinguishable from the other. I don't know whether to choreograph a celebratory dance move or call the police, because I have an actual stalker.

My laugh is abrupt and extremely troubled. I beseech answers of Scott – stare at his bedroom window – but as is best in this job, he ignores me entirely. In fact he turns his light off.

I feel achingly alone.

I try to gather my resolve; I'm a little rooted to the ground. I'll get the tube, I decide. The Poet won't be able to get his motorcycle down the escalators, plus there's CCTV. I'm gearing up to my jog to the underground station when I spot a movement in Scott Delaney's drive.

I squint, because I'm a good thirty metres away.

The security lighting hasn't come on, yet I can make out the outline of a person. Skirting the perimeter of the gravelled drive, tiptoeing through soil borders to avoid the light's activation beam.

The intruder is a man.

But he isn't breaking into Scott's house; he's breaking out.

Avoiding the electric gates, he scales a wall, jumps into the neighbour's front garden and from here wanders on to the road via their driveway.

Under the amber hue of an old-school street lamp, I study the man's gait, height, his 59Fifty LA baseball cap.

I try not to gasp, yet my heart does a hell of a fist-pump. Scott Delaney has a secret after all.

I look at my watch: 11.39 p.m.

'Scat, Scat, Scat,' I tut. 'What are you doing out? It is *way* past your bedtime.'

Scott walks briskly, keeping his head down, the cap's peak hiding his face.

Remaining on the other side of the canal, I follow. Exactly ten metres behind him, the regulation distance for on-foot surveillance.

I yank a beanie from my bag, push every last strand of my hair into it. Pull free a pair of glasses – the Harry Potter ones from the bus. Without binoculars Scott can't see they're plastic and, technically, a children's toy. They'll provide an extra layer of camouflage. Though I promise myself solemnly that the next time I pass a bus depot, I will hand them in.

I also fall in line with Scott's footsteps. *Always* do this. It hides your own gentle thuds. Tonight it will have to cancel out the tip-tap of my kitten heels.

Also pretend to text. Should the target glance back in your direction, you'll look uninterested.

Scott won't glance anywhere, however. He's an A-lister who doesn't want to be clocked. The last thing he intends to do is establish eye contact.

Which means that tonight I have lucked right out. Usually surveillance is impossible if you're the only one doing it. In the end you get spotted.

Surveillance suggestion: thinking about following someone? Hire a team. The bigger the better. In an ideal world, push for a small military unit. If you're an oligarch, you might think about static surveillance, whereby you plop operatives all over an entire city and they just *stay put*. The target moves from one zone to another, while the team never reveals itself. The online tutor for my diploma in private investigation course said, *It's like playing a zone defence in basketball*, and it totally is.

Scott approaches the end of Blomfield Road. Café Laville, my lunchtime haunt, is in sight. Immediately behind it, the Edgware Road.

On the one hand, this is excellent. It's a major road. A busy one. Shadowing him will be easier. The angry traffic, bumper to nose, rude reds and oranges, brake lights and street lamps, voluble pedestrians; I can melt into it.

However, if he jumps in a cab or catches a lift, it's over.

The likelihood of me then grabbing a taxi instantly is small. Plus it's awkward jumping in and shouting, *Follow that car*. Especially when you've got no money.

Always have fifty quid (in small denominations) secreted about yourself when on a case.

But I hadn't meant to be on a case. I haven't got a bean.

Scott continues left on to the main road. Uninterested in taxis, he marches head down past an estate agent, an American nail bar, the Islamic Clothing Boutique, a Topps Tiles, restaurants from the hottest edges of the world, more than one clinic that deals in exfoliation.

He sees none of it.

He's hell-bent on getting somewhere fast and unnoticed.

A familiar gripe arrives – it skips from one side of my stomach to the other. Nerves. Excitement.

Do not have a woman on the side, I tell Scott telepathically. *Be loyal to Alice.*

God sees right through that one: *What if it were you on the side? You've never wanted a man more!*

But He forgets I'm a professional. That I have a golden rule, mantras, the lot.

Arguing with God puts me off – I almost miss it when Scott scoots into a small twenty-four-hour petrol station.

Do not buy condoms, I warn him. He has to be perfect husband material. For Alice. Of course for Alice.

You can't blame a girl for window-shopping, though.

The store's front is as luminous as a theatre stage. I hide in the hushed black of its forecourt and watch.

Scott smiles widely at the assistant – an Asian guy; they know one another well. He pushes the peak of his cap up, leans amiably against the counter. They banter for a while.

Then Scott does a quick shop. Pepsi Max, Snickers, Monster Munch, Oreos.

That's it. No prophylactics whatsoever.

Paying in cash, he salutes the sales assistant cheerio, pulls his cap back down and strides towards the automatic doors.

It's time to think on my feet.

Pulling my hair free of the beanie, I ensure that it tumbles wantonly around my shoulders. I grab house keys from my bag. Looking doggedly at my feet, I rush at Scott.

Bump Two . . .

The collision knocks the wind clean out of me.

'Oh my God . . .' I look up at him, too angrily, because I can't remember the last time I received a blunt trauma to the solar plexus, and it's really unpleasant.

'Florence?'

Oh, sweet choir of angels. He didn't have to think about my name – it tripped instantly off his tongue. I try very hard to smile winningly, but my bastard diaphragm is in spasm and, regardless of Scat Delaney's presence, it plans on recovering at its leisure.

'Are you OK?' he's saying.

I put a finger in the air. *Give me thirty seconds and I'll get straight back on with entrapping you.*

'Can I do anything?'

Stop talking to me. I smile. Nod at his snacks. 'Midnight feast?'

He makes a show of hiding his booty under his jacket. 'This is our secret, right?'

I tap my nose.

He's more excited to see me than I'd expected. 'What are you doing here?' he asks.

I shake my house keys at him, nod at the forecourt. 'Just filled up.'

For a while we look at the two cars sitting at the pumps.

One is a Smart car, the other a Fiesta. Neither is a boy-magnet, which is just as well. Scott might have asked questions had my motor been a Lamborghini or a Range Rover Sport. The truth is, I can't drive.

'You live close by?' he asks.

'Not far.' The pain is starting to dissipate; I'm able to stand up a bit. 'On my way home from a party – my little brother's.'

'Fancy dress?' he smiles.

Evidently I look a bit confused. Scott taps my specs.

Oh, fuck. I take the plastic glasses off. 'There were kids there.'

'You're a pleaser, that's cute.' He's amused – with the glasses, with me, with my innate need to humour small children.

Fully upright, I'm able at last to give him a disarming grin.

'Wow. Getting winded is like childbirth,' I tell him. 'When it's done, it's done. No pain, just a memory of something you'd rather not repeat.'

He grins back too. 'Like towel-whipping a testicle.'

'That's funny,' I smile.

'It feckin' isn't. You've got kids?'

'No, free as a bird. I'll have to tell my brother I bumped into you – he'll be stoked, seriously, he's such a fan. I'm not even joking.' I'm being a bit screechy. Scott may remember that it's approaching midnight and he's an A-lister. Outside. Alone. With an events coordinator who's turning out to be a gushing, slightly vacuous groupie.

Forgive me, Father, for what I'm about to say.

'My brother, Michael, has a condition.'

'Ah, Florence. I'm sorry about that.'

'I've got his back,' I tell him earnestly, because I bloody well do.

'Will he be OK?'

I shake my head – there's no cure for autism.

The compassion in Scott's eyes makes me feel ashamed. Michael's condition is our business, mine and Dad's. I just used it for evil. Yet the hand he places on my shoulder is so tender I want to purr.

'Is there anything I can do?' he asks.

Carry out studies on the causes of Asperger's – the ones not tied to genetic etiology. Find out if having a sister who begrudged his existence for the first three years of his life had a lasting impact.

'I'm afraid not.' To displace my own guilt, I point at his snacks. 'There's sixty-nine milligrams of caffeine in a tin of Pepsi Max. That's more than a normal Pepsi.'

He shakes his head. 'The formulation's different in the UK. About forty-two point six milligrams.'

'Is it?'

'Yep, and it's also got ginseng in it. That's good for cancer, heart disease and high blood pressure.'

It's not a competition, but I feel obliged to point out the obvious. 'Ginseng is a stimulant, Scat.' It's also excellent for erectile dysfunction. During a honeytrap, however, avoid mentioning penis problems. It puts negative scenarios in a man's head. They'll lose their bottle.

'Ah, well, when the cat's away.'

Is he referring to Harvey, or Alice? Who cares: Scat Delaney has a naughty streak.

I am beyond disappointed when he says:

'Well, I'd better let you pay for your petrol.'

'Right. Thanks.'

Though he does put a sombre palm to his chest. 'Say happy birthday to your brother for me. I hope the little guy's OK.'

I didn't say it was his birthday party, yet I don't put him

right or tell him that the little guy's six-feet-one and twenty-nine next March. What's the point? Even I can hear my disappointment.

'Will do. 'Bye.'

Riveted, I watch him walk away. His pace, however, is too slow – several miles an hour shy of his earlier tempo.

Scott is thinking of other things to say.

I should walk away too. But I don't actually have a car. Neither do I need anything from the shop.

The truth: more than anything, I want to sit on the kerb with Scott, share his Coke and Monster Munch, and have a natter. Nothing calculated. Just a friendly chat that culminates in us falling in love under the twinkly tube lighting of an Esso forecourt.

'Oh! Your purse!' he shouts back at me.

'Do you have it?' I say, too quickly. 'I was so worried – it has all my personal details in it—'

He cuts me off. 'Give me a lift home? I'm round the corner, literally. I can run in and drop it out to you.'

I gasp. I am *brilliant* at this.

Once there, I'll wheedle a way into his pad. *I will!* Alice said I'm not allowed, but it doesn't count if we chat in the porch. Yes, we'll sit on the stoop like teenagers. Or in the potting shed. I don't technically have to go into the house.

Essential issues to overcome first:

Stealing the Smart car. (The Fiesta's gone.) Then working out how to use the gears, pedals and steering wheel.

Devastated, I say: 'I'm in a hell of a rush. Can I pick it up another time? Any other time. My email and phone number are in the purse.'

'Maybe I'll courier it.'

But I can't give him my address.

He's patting his pockets. 'I don't have a pen or my phone. I'll remember it. Your address? Shoot.'

I waver. A lot. A very lot indeed.

'Email me,' I say with finality, spotting the owner of the Smart car emerging from the shop, about to drive off with my wheels. I point at her. 'Looks like we're ready to get off.'

'Oh, sorry, I didn't realise.'

'Great to see you, Scat.'

It takes me by complete surprise when he sings his farewell, *properly* sings it, in a jazz voice:

'You too, *Flo-Lo*.'

And although I don't recognise the notes – they're astonishingly highbrow – I have to stop myself from singing something back; which would be an awful idea because I have a very non-musical ear, but I do *think* about it, because I sway delirious on the velvety hammock of his vocal cords.

When he pulls his cap back down and says, 'You look nice, by the way,' I even do a little twirl, then pop the glasses back on to my nose, like I'm fifteen years old and cute as a button.

He laughs loudly, his eyes disappearing amongst a generous hug of eyelid and cheek.

Stunning.

Doffing his baseball cap, he drops his head and strides back towards Blomfield Road.

My head scream is wild – for a lot of different reasons, but mostly because I'm a professional, and this is a honeytrap, and falling for the target is a *dreadful* mistake.

The Butcher

Re: Marital case
Monday 7/7/14 07.39 a.m.
From: asc345@hotmail.com
To: info@londonpiservices.uk.net

Just three days left and I am beginning to doubt your
abilities, Ms Love. I can only reiterate how important
this is to me. We will be going public on Thursday.
I'm pinning my entire future on your promise to allay
my fears. Assuming you have been honest with me
regarding the likelihood of you meeting my partner
again, and your boasts regarding your professional
proficiency.

No *Dear Florence*.
No *Lots of love, Alice*.
No kisses.
It's as though Alice has slapped me; physically slapped me.
I am gutted. I thought we were sort of friends.

Immediately I respond to her. Assure her of my entrapment success rate. Remind her that I adhere to the strictest
moral codes and highest standards of professionalism with
clients and targets alike. In fact this very evening, I facilitated
Bump Two. Should she be concerned with regards to my
proficiency, she has only to ask Scott.

Or Colin – my old boss, the one who recommended me
to her – yes, ask him . . .

I rub my face. How the hell did they meet? But I'm not currently in a position to demand answers, what with her thinking that I am, by and large, incompetent.

So many people are unhappy with me.

Noah Steensen.

Is he the Hoodie? I suddenly wonder.

Of course not. He doesn't do low-calorie meal deals; he does protein shakes. The leathers preclude the need for a floral stool. His cigarette of choice is most likely a Woodbine, lots of them.

The door buzzer jerks me from my thoughts. I answer the intercom quickly. 'Hello?'

'Clean your teeth, Florrie, and open the door.'

'Dad?'

'Chop-chop.' He issues commands via the porch seven floors down. 'You've got a visitor.'

He is gratingly chirpy for a man who downed two bottles of wine less than eight hours ago.

I've neither the time nor the inclination to do as I'm told. I don't brush my teeth, let alone shower, straighten my hair and get dressed. I press the 'release door' button with my forehead and stay there for a good minute and a half.

Two sets of footsteps fade up into earshot.

I open the door to face my father and one other.

'Oh, for fuck's sake,' I complain loudly.

'Florence,' Dad says sharply.

I point at his companion. 'Did you invite him here?'

Husband Number Two's voice is as measured and considered as ever.

'I was in London,' says Julian. 'I heard you were in the capital too. I thought we could catch up before I travelled back.'

'You *heard* I was in London?' I scowl at Dad – sometimes

he has the familial loyalty of a cannibalistic wolf spider. 'Honestly. You can't take a crap around here. The birds have fucking binoculars . . .'

'Florence.' Dad's warning has the tone of finality.

'Well . . .' I flatten my hair. Brush at eye cack. Imagine what I look like; then wish I hadn't. This is mortifying. In an ideal world I'd have a secret spy suicide tooth – one I could loosen with my tongue and suck the cyanide from before welcoming the sweet tendrils of death.

'I take it this isn't a social visit?'

'It might be,' says Dad hopefully.

If nothing else, get this:

Julian Doe, Husband Numero Dos, does not want me back. And I sure as hell don't want him back. He was that painfully slow rumba, devoid of the tease-and-run theme, sexual tension or any rhythmic prowess whatsoever. Which is not to say I wouldn't prefer it if he'd hankered a bit since we split. But he hasn't. It's completely humiliating.

'Perhaps we can chat in private,' suggests Julian.

'No problemo.' My dad sits on the top step in the hall, pulls a *Metro* from his Barbour, waves us both inside as if we're sex-starved lovebirds reunited after a war.

Note: I am *very* angry with my father. This officially constitutes one of the few moments I do not feel sorry for him. He brought Julian here – a man who no longer loves his daughter – with no heads-up. I could have half coped with the situation were I looking exquisite.

'Are you well?' Julian surveys the bedsit.

'Are you still a butcher?'

He shakes his head. 'I went back to university.'

'You have to have been there before to *go back*.'

'Ah well, I've moved on a bit now.' His smile is thin and modest.

'Don't tell me – a senior meat quality controller.'

'An archivist.'

I laugh. Perfect. 'Let's skip the social bullshit, shall we? What do you want?'

'A divorce,' he says, pleasantly.

'Why?'

'I've not seen you in two years.'

'You left me, Jules.'

I call him Jules to solicit a reaction. He is not a Jules. I am more of a Jules. Zanna next door is more of a Jules. Aphrodite, goddess of love, is more of a Jules.

Julian is unequivocally a Julian.

'Yes, I left, Flo. Shortly after you told me to. Please don't pretend your world fell apart.' He's right. It didn't. 'I'm now engaged to a very nice lady,' he explains.

'*A very nice lady.* How erotic. That's bigamy, you know.'

His frown is full of pity. 'Let me go, Florence.'

My knuckles turn white. How fucking dare he. Acting like he's Don Juan Demarco and I'm hanging on to his trouser hem in some desperate attempt to reignite the least fervid marriage in which I've ever been incarcerated. Yes, he was kind and predictable. But within a year of marriage, his eating noise was making me murderous. His cock started to look like a skinny banana. I couldn't put it near my mouth without dry-heaving.

I point.

'You're the one knocking on *my* door. One sniff that I'm within a fifty-metre radius and you're here. Look at you, like a mentalist or something. I bet you've been watching me from roofs and stuff. I should get a restraining order.'

Julian has not been watching me from roofs and stuff. Julian doesn't do planes, sit on the top deck of buses, walk in undulating terrain or cycle across flyovers. Like me he suffers concern around heights. It was one of the few things we had in common.

'How about you just sign these papers?' He pulls an envelope from his jacket pocket.

Snatching them, I flick through the sheets without reading. I know what they say. I've been here before with Husband Number One. I refold them. Throw them on to my table.

'So, who is she?' I ask.

'Her name's Gloria.'

I put a hand in the air: *Say no more. I can picture her already.*

I can't.

Gloria.

The type who totters around Bournemouth of an evening – pencil skirt, flab-boobs, needs saving, hot sex low on her agenda, being a thoroughly affable wife right at the top. The image I create is incongruous. Why the hell can't I picture her?

I find the answer. '*Nobody* is called Gloria any more?'

'Well,' he smiles, a little too lost in the romance of whatever private thought he's having, 'I have physical proof.'

Oh my God, I spot a look, a *sexual* look on his face. I've not seen him do that before. And it's being evoked by the thought of someone else's name.

'And what does this Gloria do?' I ask, too angrily.

'A senior archivist.'

I don't laugh. 'Lots to talk about, then.'

Oh, the PI in me wants to ask a million questions:

Where did you meet?

How long have you been together?

Do you go at the same tempo in the bedroom?

Is she prettier than me?

Are you in love properly this time?

Am I, Florence Love, now officially considered a 'mistake' in the potted history of your comfortable little life?

Christ, I am close to tears. I pat the table proactively. 'Right, if that's all, I'll take a look over these later.'

His nod is infuriatingly compassionate. 'Shall I pop by your dad's tomorrow evening? Pick them up then?'

'My dad's?'

'He said you're travelling back with him today.'

'I am not,' I protest, and concoct a love life. 'I have a date.'

With acceptance and not an iota of jealousy, Julian nods and offers me a business card.

Reminder to myself: never buckle; remain elusive; always act the bitch, then you have them for life.

'Anyway, love to chat, Jules, but places to go, people to see. I'll be in touch.'

I retire to the bathroom. Lean on the sink. Inhale deeply.

It's absurd my being so angry with Julian. His only crime was to agree with me when I suggested our marriage was boring. Which it was, terribly boring. Yet I took it to heart – I was allowed to say it, he was not.

Freudian fact: the ego makes us horrible hypocrites.

And I am a human woman bound by the shortcomings of my species. It doesn't make me proud that secretly I wanted Julian to be mortified. That I hoped his reaction would be primeval and animalistic – that he'd beat his chest and shout things like *I will fight for my wo-man*. Failing that, he might have suggested counselling or swinging, anything that could inject passion, hope, some hint that he adored me enough to try everything to retain ownership of me.

He didn't, so I threw him out on his ear.

I examine my face in the murky mirror. It's a stark ivory; smudged make-up from the previous night completes my living-dead mien.

I hear the front door close behind Husband Number Two.

My dad has let himself back into my bedsit.

'Well?' he shouts expectantly from outside the bathroom door.

'St Julian has met an archivist called Gloria and wants a divorce,' I shout back. 'Now I'm going to shower, though some might argue that's like closing the gate after the horse has bolted.'

'I wondered who she was,' I hear him mutter, confused. 'But you're still married?'

I don't scream: *Horse shit, it's all horse shit – commitment, love, they're as transient as a sneeze. Get with the programme, old man.*

I shout: 'Gloria's downstairs?'

After a moment's silence, Dad cuts to the chase. 'I'm back down to Dorset today.'

I brush my teeth unnecessarily hard.

'How about I pack a few bits for you? A break will do you good. You can see how the post office is doing. They miss you, you know, Graeme and Suzy-Anne.'

Graeme and Suzy-Anne – technically my employees – couldn't give a shit if I was dead or alive. Receipt of their wages on a Friday forms the outer periphery of their earthly concerns.

Dr Malik's eyes pop into my head, hypnotic as spinning tops:

Tell him now: I don't want the post office; especially I don't want your life. He won't collapse into a cheerless heap and demand a lifetime's supply of uppers. And if he does, he'll be thinking only of himself.

'I'd love to,' I shout back, a mouth full of froth. 'But I've got commitments this week. Another time definitely.'

'You have commitments in Dorset,' he says sternly.

'Here too, Dad.'

'Like what?'

'A date. Come on, my husband's engaged to another woman. I'm in pieces. A date's just the tonic.'

'Who's it with?' he tests me.

It's the only name that springs to mind, other than Scott 'Scat' Delaney's, and I can't say that.

'Noah. That's very religious, isn't it?'

'Noah who?'

'Steensen.' I only borrow his name. 'Three E's. It's Nordic.'

The ensuing silence is lengthy.

Dropping my toothbrush into the sink, I wipe my mouth with the back of my hand and peak around the bathroom door.

Dad is grey as cremated bone.

'Are you OK?'

'You self-centred little . . . Leave it alone, I said . . .'

'Leave what alone?'

He skulks towards me, his finger now less than a foot from my nose. 'How you became so manipulative, I will never know.'

I take a step back.

Quietly I ask: 'Is this about the post office?'

His glare is utterly exasperated: of course it's not. It's much, *much* bigger than that.

'I have had enough of this, Florence. Of you. The mind games . . .' He yanks his Barbour down over his thighs.

Apparently I've hopped, skipped and jumped across a line without even realising. Dad has never said anything this hurtful to me before; neither has it been accompanied by the broken look he's doing now.

'Your mother would be turning in her grave.'

Stunned, I take a step back. 'What have I said?'

'Hard as I try – and believe me, I try – I can't seem to get a grasp on the workings of your logic.' He looks at me, baffled. 'Tell me, where, where *exactly*, does your moral compass lie?'

'Wow,' I say, because that's a monster of a question, and secretly I've been hoping – no, praying – that he might like who I am by now. That after thirty-three years he's grown fond of me at least.

A hush-hush truth: for a little while now I've thought I've dawned on him. That he's grasped that my methods might not be his, yet our hearts occupy a similar angle on morality's compass.

I've been trying to show him – by being an excellent sister to Michael.

Which I totally fucked up.

'Am I a burden to you?' It's a ridiculous question, but I need to know.

'Stop being so dramatic,' he tells me, firmly.

'Do you pray for my soul?'

'There you go again, ridiculing me and my faith.'

'I'm not!' And I'm not. I want to know how fucked-up he thinks I am. Whether I'm a regular in his prayers.

Equally confounded, we look at one another.

Finally I ask: 'Who's Noah Steensen?'

But my father's sigh is exasperated. He decides to storm from the bedsit without a backwards glance. I call after him: far more than he deserves. Quite a lot more, actually. Nonetheless, he slams the door behind him.

For a good thirty seconds I stare dumbfounded at the wall.

I jump when Dad shouts back in through the peephole, 'And please get somebody in to look at the tap in your bathroom. And tidy up a bit, it smells musty.'

I sniff the air.

'I'll text you when I arrive at Christchurch.'

'Elephant juice,' I shout angrily.

It's secret code, so he doesn't tell me he loves me back.

I listen to the soft thump of his Hush Puppies as he walks away, along the hall and down the stairs.

Then I frown, because I just hit *the* cervical plexus of nerves.

Familial Alcoholism

Dad's reaction spurs me on.

It was out of character – I've broached the Mum topic many times before, but his reaction has never been like this. Never as irritated.

I'm not a fool.

The name Noah Steensen has resonance with him. Is the Poet a hit man? Am I getting too nosy, sniffing out an awful truth?

More than ever, I'm sure there *is* something to find out.

First of all, I do a psychological profile of my mother. Task number one being *PS, I Love You.*

Throwing on combats, a vest top and Birkenstocks, I make my way to Gordon Square Gardens, a short walk from my mansion block. I sit on scorched grass and cigarette butts, defended by clusters of undergraduates, shaded by silver birch, London plane, sweet chestnut. Behind me a stone plaque states how a woman called Emily Kent-Smyth, beloved mother and wife, loved this Victorian garden square before she was taken.

This place feels right.

I read the novel from cover to cover. And to those yet to read it, I can verify the following:

It is a cruel, cruel book.

I sobbed, properly sobbed, because it's not a book about someone coming back to life. It's very much a book about a deceased husband counselling his wife via a series of notes he wrote prior to his popping off. And thanks to her late husband (who can never return because he has irrefutably croaked), his wife moves on, learns how to love again, skips off into the fucking sunset.

Where's the hope in that? I blow my nose loudly.

The dead husband is left looking like a mug. Nobody's world has fallen apart because he no longer inhabits it. The poor guy battled brain cancer, expired, putrefied and perished into dust. That's awful.

A mockery of love and death, the novel is exactly what I did not want to read.

On the bus to Michael's, I weep a little more, because that's the very thing Mum would have adored about the book. Like her son, she liked things simple, neat, clean. According to my dad, she wrote a poem about God in rhyming couplets.

Move on, the book decreed.

I press Michael's front door bell. He bounds down the stairs; I can hear him. The door flies open. His welcome is jubilant. I can't help grabbing his cheek and kissing it hard.

He scrubs it clean as if I have oral thrush, then tells me conspiratorially, 'Upstairs, now.'

Without a sound, he ascends the stairs. Instinctively I follow suit, try to avoid the squeaky boards. At the door to his flat, he stops me dead.

Clasping his hands prayer-like, he now enunciates slowly. 'I have a surprise for you.'

'What is it?' I whisper.

'It's a who.'

I slouch. 'Not Sébastien?'

Michael puts a hand on his hip. 'We are in love, you know.'

'That's disgusting,' I say, because he might as well have peppered my heart with machine-gun fire.

What about me? You've never said you love me.

'Love is a big word, Michael,' I tell him with serious eyes. 'Is Sébastien here or not?'

Yes, I'm being mean, but Michael having a boyfriend is a lot to absorb. Plus I've had a nerve-rattling twenty-four hours. And at the best of times there's nothing more irritating than sharing the company of new lovers. They foist their rapture on you at every opportunity – a rapture that is independent of you in every way.

Rapture fact: public displays of affection are thoughtless and smug. Your joy does not rub off on other people. It makes us want to spit at you.

'It's not Sébastien,' says Michael.

'Who is it then?'

'If you could see *anybody* in the whole world right now, who would it be?'

But I'm not allowed to go there. I daren't even say her name aloud. I'm supposed to be protecting him from all this.

Bambi. Bambi. Bambi!

'You know who,' I whisper uncomfortably.

'Yes, I do,' he says, his expression as empathetic as I've ever seen it. It takes me aback. My eyes become coin-slot thin.

His nod is slow and heartfelt.

Both hands float to my head. 'No?' I say.

'Yes,' he says, taking my hands gently in his.

I thought I was all cried out, but tears plunge down my face. Fat tears, the type I cry in dreams. Cathartic gobbets that come from a place deep inside me. I don't know the name of this place, but it's somewhere between my bowel and my soul.

It unnerves Michael.

'Stop it,' he demands, searching his pockets for a tissue or a tranquilliser gun. 'Just stop crying.'

But I can't stop.

So he starts to sob too.

For a while we're inconsolable.

Then I take charge, just as Mum would expect me to, because otherwise Michael might never stop. Grabbing his hand, I squeeze it hard and smile a tight smile.

'Deep breaths,' I tell him.

He teeters on the edge of delirium, yet does as he's told. A minute or so later he nods bravely. It is he who leads me to the door.

Hand in hand we walk into the living room.

Scott Delaney is in glycaemic heaven. Perched on Michael's sofa, he devours a brie and cranberry toastie as though it's a Michelin-starred signature dish.

Until he sees us.

Concerned, he flies to his feet. The plate tumbles to the carpet.

'Fuck!' shouts Scott, ignoring the spilled food, staring at us both. 'What's happened?'

Before I've time to blow my nose, he has grabbed my shoulders.

'What is it? Tell me.'

I open my mouth. But nothing comes to mind. I gulp a lot of air and wish I could wipe my top lip, but Scott has a strong grasp of me. Without letting go, he glances around the room, looks urgently at the land phone, finally decides on a course of action. He gives instructions to my brother, who is currently on all fours picking up globs of pink pickle.

'Micky, get her a whisky,' he says, handing me a tissue, pulling me into a sitting position on the sofa beside him to look into my face.

His cerulean eyes say: *I am Scott Delaney. Jazz phenomenon. King of scat. Rich. Handsome. Your best friend. Very probably your fantasy. It goes without saying I expect a comprehensive explanation.*

I hold the tissue to my nose. It smells of Olbas Oil.

Mentholated ointments don't help the situation at all: my mum used to put it on our chests when we had a cold. I start to sob again. This is ridiculous. I can't stop.

So Scott soothes me, places my head on his soft chest and strokes my hair.

'Hush now, girl. That's it, hush. Just try and start from the beginning.'

I can't say: *I thought you were my mum.*

He's a target. *The* sodding target.

Neither can I say: *What the bloody hell are you doing in Michael's flat? I'm so unprepared I'm wearing orthopaedic footwear and a vest top I sometimes sleep in. How am I going to annihilate your relationship after this humiliatingly snotty performance?*

Especially it would be disastrous to say: *Sod it. I like it here. Nestling into your expensively perfumed neck. Your tanned and manicured hands caressing my cranium like you made me yourself.*

Truths are the best foundations from which to build colossal lies.

'I've just been with my dad,' I tell Scott's chest, sniffing his shirt. It's new, straight from the packet; it smells of nothing, not of Summer Breeze or Passion Flower and Ylang Ylang; maybe just the sweetest hint of cardboard.

Men only ever put on new clothes for two reasons:

1. There's nothing clean/ironed.

2. They want to impress.

It's the latter, I hope.

'I didn't exactly say goodbye to my dad,' I admit, noticing the dry skin on my heels, wishing I'd pumiced and creamed.

'You had a row?' he asks.

I sit up. 'He's an alcoholic, Scott.'

Michael looks alarmed. 'Who, Dad?'

I nod sadly.

'Familial alcoholism.' Scott's sigh is fatalistic. 'A disease that affects the whole clan.'

'The children are the biggest victims,' I say quietly.

He nods. 'They lack support and love, miss being cherished – every child deserves to be cherished.'

'But how can you feel cherished, Scott, when your life is an anarchic roller-coaster of inconsistencies?'

'That's beau*d*iful,' he says.

'You should name a song after it.' I turn to my brother and explain, 'Scott is from Ireland. His family will have been through the same as us.'

'Been through what?' asks Michael.

I try not to sound racist. 'Certain nationalities are genetically prone to addictions.'

This amuses Scott.

'I'm a musician first and foremost, Mick, and your sister's right. I've watched my friends destroy themselves and their families with excesses – booze, drugs. Talented men and women. Liver disease, jaundice, alcoholic hepatitis, suicide, premature wrinkles . . .'

Michael stares, alarmed, while I decide that Scott Delaney is wonderful.

His sermon is hackneyed, yes. He fails to mention Wernicke-Korsakoff Syndrome (aka wet brain), or the cessation of the menstrual cycle, or cardiovascular disorders. Yet it matters not a jot. Right now I'd pre-order his self-help book and give it to everyone for Christmas. The man is a born entertainer.

'Dad's a good dad,' Michael tells us.

Scott points wisely at us. 'Do as I do – never take a drug that doesn't come with a leaflet.'

Confused, Michael nods, while I want to give Scott a standing ovation.

'God, sorry for the tears.' I take a cathartic breath. 'We're just worried. We're probably too protective. I wasn't expecting company; I'd never have let myself get like that if I'd known. Look at the state of me.'

Scott waves an entirely forgiving hand. 'You look good enough to eat.'

I giggle.

Michael frowns. 'How much is he drinking?'

Scott even picks an eyelash from my cheek. 'Go freshen up,' he says, no argument. 'Then we can all start again.'

I gape at my reflection.

What on earth is he doing here? Answers fail to present themselves.

Hastily I apply some make-up in the bathroom mirror – just enough to make it look like I'm not wearing any at all.

There are always cosmetics in Michael's medicine cabinet – it's my touch-up stash. This flat is where I come to carry out the money shot. And Scott Delaney is sitting slap-bang in the target area.

Many an entrapment case has been closed on that sofa.

In Michael's bedroom I check to see that the cameras are running. They are. Clever boy. Though he's not clever enough to pop out of the living room to proffer an explanation as to how Scott came to be here.

I hang around the bedroom for a bit, hoping he might.

And whilst there, I watch Scott on the computer from two different angles.

One view is from above – via the camera in the ceiling-mounted smoke alarm. The other is straight-on – via the self-help hardback and its tiny hole in the dot of the 'i'.

This is bizarre yet wonderful. If there was an entrapment award, I'd be up for it!

I keep the client in the loop; email Alice on my smart-phone:

Contact established. Money shot scheduled for tonight. Will email later with full report.

Then I give her an affable middle finger – and with three whole days to spare, O ye of little faith.

Before I get this show on the road, however, I make a phone call.

'No way,' says Husband Number Two.

'Wrong answer,' I tell the phone.

'Do you know how illegal that is, Florence?'

'Err, yes.'

It would not be politic at this juncture to tell Julian facts about his job:

Archivists are secretaries with a very controlling nature. It's best all round that society puts them in a room and leaves them to their own organisational devices. Dress it up all you like, *Jules*: you and your contemporaries are not high-brow; you are administrators with an obsessive compulsive disorder.

I sit on Michael's bed and watch Scott on the computer screen in front of me. My brother is saying something to him. Now they laugh together. Scott has got up, is patting my brother's back. He looks ready to split.

'Don't go,' I say out loud.

'I have to,' says Julian quietly. 'I've moved on.'

I remember Julian's Coca Cola-stained business card. It stated that his office is in the Nuffield Industrial Park in Poole – a secure facility for the independent storage of data. I know the type of place. Local government, businesses, schools, law firms, doctors' practices, even the police contract out their filing, it being a very tedious job.

'The answer's no, Florence. I'll be struck off.'

I exhale gratefully – Scott has sat back down. He's going nowhere. 'Struck off from what?'

'The Society of Archivists.'

'That's not even real.'

'Never mind losing my job; I'm a lecturer at the university.'

Sceptically I look at the phone. 'What university?'

'Plymouth.'

'Where you lecture in what?'

'Archival science.'

'Ah well.' Using a tissue and some spit, I clean a smudge from the PC screen. 'Fingers crossed you can get a job at a proper university. In the meantime, be a doll and get me his name.'

'No.'

'Eric. That's all I know. He's the man who died in Mum's car. Mullett's Farm, thirteenth February 1988, carbon monoxide poisoning – you know the story. I need his full name. That's all. There must be a way. Coroner's reports, medical reports, police files . . .'

'I don't deal in that type of information.'

'But you'll have archivist friends. And you've got Gloria. What about contacts at the Society of Archivists? All that networking, the breakfast meetings, isn't that how the fast-paced world of filing works?'

'No.'

'Julian, don't you want the truth about what happened to your mother-in-law?'

His voice oozes compassion. 'No.'

'Get me the details of the man who died in Mum's car and I will sign the divorce papers.'

'I'm sorry for you, Flo, really I am. But I can't.'

'Very well, Julian. I'll see you in court, where I shall tell everybody how desperately I want to give our marriage a second go, despite your adulterous affair.'

'Florence, we've been separated for too long.'

'So it'll be extra annoying. The time, the money . . .'

'When did you become such a bitch?' he mumbles.

I give this some serious thought. 'It's actually quite hard to put a date on.'

Julian delivers a beaut. 'I used to love you, you know.'

Fact: I *never* used to love him. That doesn't mean I entered into marriage with less anticipation than other wives. Wholeheartedly I hoped to make an indelible impact on his life.

The silence becomes awkward.

Listen carefully and you'll hear only the caustic hum of apathy, so embedded he hasn't asked one solitary question about my new life – not this morning, not now.

His last words before he hangs up: 'See you in court.'

Not if I see you first.

On the computer screen ahead, Scott Delaney and Michael laugh like old friends. I rub my hands together, stand up, smooth every crinkle from the duvet.

Rohypnol

My walk from the bedroom along the hall and back into the lounge is excellent. Not quite as out-there as my slink – that is best reserved for flirting with doormen and middle-aged clients who need it spelling out. This walk is classy, sensuous, with a good pinch of unattainability, exactly as is needed when seducing an icon. It doesn't matter if you're wearing Alexander McQueen, oversized combats or an ironing board cover, you simply have to *own it*.

It's just a walk, you might say.

And I would counter: you could not be further from the truth.

Walking is classic primeval foreplay. Hip sway, for example, exaggerates the feminine silhouette – and it's as effective as wearing eighteenth-century panniers. You ooze the ability to procreate.

That's assuming you get it right.

There are thirty-six varieties of walk, or bipedal gate. The mince, the stride, the dart are just a few. Today I enlist a complicated hybrid – it's a mixture of the glide and the wiggle.

The gliggle, if you like.

The wiggle enlists both hips and breasts – it's super-erotic but loose-moralled. The glide, on the other hand, is impossibly elegant – you appear barely to move at all, only to hover ethereally. Geisha girls have nailed that walk.

In truth it was Michael who taught me the gliggle.

It's like salsa. You lead with the pelvis and glide like you're a shop dummy on a conveyor belt. Then do hip juts. Not too much, though, just like this . . .

Like you're doing the hip jut in secret, slowly, I nodded.

No, Flo, or otherwise there's no point.

I knew what I meant. And I made him show me over and over, because he was awesome at it.

I'm a conscientious student. Look at me now. See how I re-enter the living room with action-stopping grace.

'That's better,' I declare, waiting to be admired.

Neither Michael nor Scott looks up from the television.

They have forgotten the earlier incident – my hysteria, the familial alcoholism, the fact that my life has been an anarchic roller-coaster of inconsistencies. All ancient history now that they have plastic controllers in their hands.

Michael and Scott are immersed in a PlayStation game.

'What you playing?' I ask.

'Batman: Arkham Asylum,' smiles Scott.

'Batman's a comic-book character,' my brother explains. 'His real name is Bruce Wayne.'

'I know who Batman is, Michael.'

Scott joins in. 'Arguably *the* best comic-book game, eh, Mick? The voice-acting, stunning visuals . . .'

'The bat-gadgets.'

'The bat-gadgets.'

'Scott brought it for me.'

Scott is talking to me, I presume, because he tips his cheek in my direction. 'Can I get a drink?'

I sound too wanton: 'What's your tipple, Scat?'

'Vodka lemonade.'

No please or thank you. No mention of liver disease, jaundice, alcoholic hepatitis, suicide and premature wrinkles.

'Make that two,' says Michael. 'And some Doritos.'

'Doritos!' Scott shouts. 'Micky, you're a ledge.'

'I'll have to do half an hour extra at the gym tomorrow, though,' moans Michael.

'You and me both, my friend,' says Scott.

I frown down at them.

Scott Delaney is behaving like a teenager whose parents are out of town. Michael copies his behaviour. It's either the best acting I've seen him do ever, or he's forgotten the job in hand.

Whilst they cultivate a bromance, I linger on the outskirts like a mum.

'Your PA's gone to Guyana, right?' I ask.

Eyes fixed on the TV, Scott smiles. 'Selfish so-and-so. Oh, and painkillers, I'll need some of them. I might get a headache later.'

Because of the simple carbohydrates? Because he's allergic to admitting he's in perfectly good health?

'Leave it with me.'

This whole scenario requires a change of tact. I stop acting French. It's old hat to him anyway, what with Alice and her Gallic heritage.

'Two vodka lemonades, sugary carbs and a shedload of analgesics coming right up.'

When I say analgesics, I mean Rohypnol – a date rape drug also known as roofies, roach, rope, Mexican Valium and (its pharmaceutical name) flunitrazepam.

Rohypnol facts:

It is a solid white pill with a melting point of between 166 and 167°C, and a molecular weight of 313.3. Like Valium, it's a benzodiazepine, only ten times stronger. Its medical use is as a pre-operation anaesthetic. Its recreational use is as a sedative that causes amnesia and unconsciousness – colourless, tasteless and soluble in ethanol, it's ideal for spiking drinks undetected. More often than not, therefore, the person using Rohypnol recreationally is unaware of the fact.

This is very wrong indeed.

A PI non-negotiable definite no-no: never drug a target – unless it's a truth serum, which is terribly tricky to get on prescription. Not that your average private eye administers hypnotic medications too often – the practice of intravenous narcosynthesis is nigh-on impossible to do secretly. In entrapment cases especially, rendering a target unconscious defeats the objective entirely. He isn't straying of his own free will. It wouldn't stand up in court.

Plus my ego would never allow it – I want to be all the incentive he needs to destroy his marriage.

I plop half a Rohypnol into Michael's vodka lemonade.

That and the alcohol is enough to have my brother snoring into his games console within an hour. It's perfectly safe. I've practised on myself when I've run short of sleepers.

Please note: I didn't purchase these tablets personally. I stole them from a Premiership footballer who had a penchant for his teammates. I was on a case for Maeve, my brief to follow the left-back on a night out.

In Mayfair's Playboy Club he plopped a roofie into the centre-forward's drink.

Rape is below the belt, so I intervened. Knocked the centre-forward's drink to the floor. And the next three. Oblivious to the pill-plopping left-back with designs on his arse, the centre-forward started getting yappy with me. I thought it safest all round to steal the drugs and be gone.

Today Michael has forgotten that Scott is the target. He acts as if he's got a new friend to play with. I know my brother – he might never go away.

So I stir his drink. Run the spoon under the tap and put it in the dishwasher. Then I take the vodka lemonades into the lounge.

I hand one vodka (quadruple/undrugged) to Scott, one drink (single/mildly drugged) to Michael, and sip one drink (quadruple/undrugged) myself.

'Down in one,' I tell them, like I'm one of the boys.

They're as excited as teenagers at a house party

Less than twenty minutes later, Michael is sparko in an armchair.

'Is it because of his condition?' whispers Scott.

I nod. 'It has a narcoleptic element.'

Truth is, Michael snoring in the corner has put a downer on things. Scott has no one to play Batman with.

'He's a great guy,' says Scott. 'Very upbeat, considering.'

I wonder what he thinks is wrong with my brother.

'It means the world to him, you coming here, Scott.'

He leans towards me and mouths, 'I thought he was younger. I bought him a video game. That's not cool.'

'No, no. It was an excellent idea,' I tell him. 'People like Michael like video games.' *People like Michael.* 'He's not mental or anything,' I clarify. 'He's alternative. Psychologically.'

'Aren't we all?' Scott states this without a whiff of irony.

The pause in conversation is small, yet immediately he examines his fingers for ailments. It's the look he did at the Landmark when Harvey left the room to phone for food.

'I think I'm getting a whitlow,' he tells me.

'Herpetic or melanotic?'

'Both.'

'You can't have both. One is a cold sore on your hand. The other's fatal.' I take his perfectly healthy, soft and handsome finger, examine it and nod resolutely. 'Herpetic. In the absence of a topical acyclovir treatment, I have exactly the cure.'

I fetch the vodka bottle from the kitchen.

'It breaks open harmful bacterial cells, killing them and sterilising the wound.'

He half laughs, half baulks. 'That's got to sting, right?'

'God, yes. It's best all round that we drink it instead.

'Thank God.'

'How are you sleeping?' I refill his glass.

'Argh, you know . . .'

'No harm in a little sedation, then.' I wink. 'When was the last time you kicked back with friends?'

'Harvey's been away,' he explains.

'I mean anyone not in your employ?'

He narrows his eyes, as if I've just declared war. I'm certainly being a bit bolshie. Slowly he screws the top firmly back on the vodka bottle. Places it on the carpet between us and gives it a spin.

'Oh, I can kick back, baby.'

I clap.

But the bottle rotates barely half a turn. Its neck points towards Michael. On medical grounds he can't play; it would be almost impossible to wake him. Scott re-spins the bottle properly. This time its neck points at me.

'Who was the first person you ever snogged?' he asks quickly, like we're fourteen.

And I wonder if he's ever been out in his life.

Though it does make me beam. It is *so* rare when a target shows an interest in you.

I tell a porky – technically I was six and Uncle Fergus was the culprit, but that's way too much information.

Entrapment fact: when playing Spin the Bottle with a target, never be candid.

I go straight to Snog Number Two:

'The boy in the *Miami Vice* jacket. He had the whole Don Johnson look going on. We kissed how grown-ups kissed on TV in the eighties. Do you remember? Closed eyes, closed lips, cocked head, gently moving in a horizontal figure of eight.'

'I remember!'

We laugh, and remind ourselves of the action on the back of our own hands. I don't know about him, but I'm pretending my metacarpophalangeal joint is Scott's lips. It's absolutely hysterical. Afterwards we laugh for a good three and a half minutes.

He spins the bottle again.

Again the neck points at me.

'What the fuck?' I put my hands on my hips, loving the attention.

Scott cocks his head. 'Who was the second person you kissed?'

Further entrapment fact: when playing Spin the Bottle with a target, never let them see your vulnerable side.

'I can tell you the fifth.' My voice becomes too small. 'He ran off with my best friend.' I wave a flippant hand. 'Ancient history.'

'Flo-Lo, that's harsh. How old were you?'

'Twenty-one.' A tremble threatens my bottom lip. 'Their affair was the first time my inconsequentiality dawned on me.'

Hastily I turn the bottle's neck so it points at Scott. 'Your turn.'

He slaps his forehead like he never saw this coming. 'Flo-Lo, what have I let myself in for?'

I cross my arms and contemplate excellent questions:

Have you ever had a threesome?

Who's the least attractive person you've shagged?

If your mother was about to be murdered – a gruesome, strung-out, tortuous death, which you'd be forced to witness – and the only way you could save her life was by *doing it* with her, would you?

For the moment, however, I have one way more pertinent question.

'What *exactly* is it you're doing here, Scott?'

Scott Delaney goes on to tell a lot of lies . . .

Maeve Rivers contacted him to ensure his day at the Landmark had gone smoothly.

Lie: Maeve told me it was Scott who had contacted her.

He told Maeve the day had been a roaring success, thanks largely to the events coordinator, i.e. me.

Fact: I was consummate at my job.

During the telephone conversation, Maeve mentioned that my brother was a huge fan, that his birthday was coming up and that it would be a lovely idea for him to pop by and surprise Michael – by way of a thank-you for my events-coordinating skills.

Lie: Maeve can only have mentioned this in a subsequent conversation, and *extremely* reluctantly. A conversation entirely instigated again by Scott, probably this very morning. Because as far as possible, Maeve would want to distance herself from me.

Then he bumped into me at the petrol station. Call him a superstitious fool, but he saw it as a sign that he should honour his fans more often, give a little back. So he decided to turn up today and make Michael's day.

HUGE lie: Scott is borderline agoraphobic. He does not wander out without his PA to thank the people who fawn. They frighten him.

He got Michael's address from Maeve.

Fact: when Maeve's husband Harry was home, she and I would liaise at my brother's flat and make out on the money-shot couch.

Scott consequently turned up half an hour before me. Michael and he hit it off instantly. They played Call of Duty: Modern Warfare 3 and Michael made him three varieties of cheese sandwich.

Oh, and he almost forgot . . . He gives me my purse.

'And I'm very grateful for it,' I say sincerely.

Because not only is Scott wearing a shirt fresh out of the cellophane, he's making up stories as to how he turned up announced.

Anybody would think he liked me.

Intimate Behaviour

Scott Delaney is a rubbish drunk and a God-awful sport.

Cross-legged, we sit opposite one another on the carpet. He wears a vest, pants and socks. The rest of his clothes – jeans, shirt, shoes and watch – are in a heap to his left.

I, on the other hand, am fully clothed.

This is because, unbeknownst to him, I am a grand master at Shithead.

Shithead: a card game of astonishing visualisation and analytical skill, popular amongst twenty-something travellers. The object of the contest is to lose all of your cards. The last player to do so is considered a TOTAL shithead and is subject to a forfeit of the winner's choice. In our case, removing an item of clothing.

I would have gone gentle on Scott had he not made a fundamental mistake – he boasted that he'd win.

Trouble is, I worship a gauntlet.

Scott flings his remaining cards on to the floor between us.

'Are you card-counting or something?' Half-naked, he glances around suspiciously. 'That or you've got cameras in here.'

I clap, overexcited. 'Left sock off! Left sock off!'

One foot disrobed, he drunkenly throws the sock at the sofa and demands answers in a thick Killarney lilt. 'I need to know your Shithead secrets.'

I'm half-cut too. When I shuffle the deck, most of them tumble to the carpet. 'I've studied my sport, Delaney.'

'You're a hustler?'

'Let's say I'm a bit of a name in Shithead circles.'

He laughs loudly, his eyes doing that adorable squinty thing.

Wow.

Now he slaps his bare thighs. They are hairy and undefined. No matter, his face is exquisite. The physique of an underwear model would be overgilding the lily. He'd look too unattainable – his management wouldn't like that.

'Know who you remind me of?' he is asking.

I stare at his teeth. 'Beatrice Dalle? When she was younger.'

'No, no, Flo-Lo, *much* better than that,' he says.

'Wow. Really?'

I decide I like his teeth so much because my first boyfriend, Trevor Tuesday, had slightly buck teeth. As did Nick Heyward, lead singer of the eighties band Haircut 100. Come to think of it, Uncle Fergus had buck teeth too – not that I was remotely attracted to him, what with him being a grown-up, a blood relative and a paedophile. Nonetheless, my uncle's buck teeth, and Trevor Tuesday's buck teeth, and Nick Heywood out of Haircut 100's buck teeth all serve to create a medley of remembered dental anatomies from childhood. And childhood is such a safe place – so written in stone, so done and dusted.

'What about Pocahontas?' I ask Scott's central incisors. 'Someone called me that once.'

'You remind me of my girl.'

I gasp. 'You have a child?'

'My girlfriend, you ditz.'

Instantly I shut up. I'd forgotten about her entirely.

Alice St Croix is an eight out of ten, tops, and very nice in a cup-of-tea-and-scones type of way. I, on the other hand, am not. I can't be. I have to be the fantasy. Alice warned me about this, that I had to be physically viable. It is imperative I'm everything that his girlfriend isn't, because strange is erotic and that's the law.

'Your girlfriend?'

He addresses his whitlow. 'She's the only woman I've ever, you know, properly *loved*.' He whispers it, as if it's a huge secret. 'Sounds sad, man, but she makes me feel real. That's good. It *is*. It keeps me on the straight and narrow.'

Totally unlike me, then. Look at us now – pissed, playing Strip Shithead – we're so fly, one of our gang is drugged in the corner.

'Wow. Your girlfriend.' No wonder he's not allowed to drink in public. Talk about loose lips. 'I didn't know you had a girlfriend.'

Resting his elbows on the sofa behind him, he looks me directly in the eye.

'Ah, but beauty's a subjective thing. Sometimes I look at her and I don't feel worthy, you know?'

Nope, I do not know.

Alice is not simply in a different league to Scott; she inhabits a different taxonomic rank. But if there's one thing I've learnt over the years, it's that facial attraction is particularised and completely narcissistic. We have an inherent need to replicate our genes. We can't help how we look and cannot, therefore, help who we're attracted to. This is why we pair off with people from whom we could have been separated at birth.

Yet Alice and Scott could not be less alike.

Whereas Scott and I are *much* closer physically. He has slightly buck teeth, like my uncle (who is a blood relative). His hair is dark, like mine (who is actually me). His left foot, I now notice, over-pronates, like Michael's (who is another blood relative).

He's still talking . . .

'Then sometimes you meet someone, someone who's everything you're not. You can't think why, but they are *magnetic*. I'm not talking about the superficial things like a tiny nose and big titties. I'm talking about an amazing brain. Women like that are more addictive than heroin, crack cocaine or methamphetamine, MDMA, marijuana.'

I think of drugs too. 'Psilocybin mushrooms, phencyclidine, temazepam . . .'

'Know why, Florence?'

'High-maintenance?'

'Because loving them isn't enough. I want them to love me back. But that's the challenge. The LA clones, sycophantic journalists, groupies with not a grain of self-respect – they'd lie in nettles for it. Why? Because I'm on a feckin' stage. That's the long and short.'

'That's depressing,' I agree.

'Know who *I* want to love me?'

I do: 'The woman with the amazing brain.'

'*She*, Florence, is my creative fodder.' He takes a large gulp of vodka.

It was quite a speech.

If he wasn't talking about Alice, who frankly is getting on my nerves, I'd struggle to my feet and give him a round of applause. I would also suggest he drinks more often – the heartfelt quality of his sermon has increased exponentially from the alcohol-themed one earlier. I don't give him a standing ovation, however; my face is more symmetrical than Alice's – somatic fact – and that makes me prettier than her, medically.

It's no wonder I'm unprepared when Scott leans towards me and uses the crown of his head – like a bear cub – to deliver a hard nudge to my right shoulder.

Falling backwards, I knock my head on the coffee table and ashtray consecutively.

Body language fact: play-fighting is a surefire sign of attraction. A primary school move, boys revert to it when they fancy you and are flummoxed as to how to verbalise it successfully.

His speech, that heartfelt sermon: Scott Delaney was talking about me.

I copy his violence, deliver an excellent knife-hand strike to his knee.

Physical mirroring is essential when your aim is to fall in love a little. It builds rapport and initiates an easy ambience whereby you both feel comfortable, understood and protected.

He massages his meniscal cartilage and grins like a teen. 'I'll get you back for that.'

Then I go all serious, because suddenly I feel as sober and compelling as the high priestess of the entire solar system.

'Sing for me, Scat.' I hear myself saying.

I am totally taken aback by my unashamed lasciviousness. Yet I remain one million per cent certain I have never sounded sexier.

He smiles. 'That'll be a personal request?'

Sing for me, Scat. If only I could bottle it. I even tell him what to sing.

A jazz standard. '"My Funny Valentine".'

'Interesting choice. Written by the great Richard Rodgers and Lorenz Hart,' he nods. 'Did you have a version in mind?'

None whatsoever.

'The original.' I kind of pout it.

This is highly amusing. 'Mitzi Green?'

He shuffles closer until our toes touch. An electrical current makes us both twitch.

'Let's wander off-piste,' he suggests with sudden poise, as though he's being broadcast live. 'Will the Scat Delaney version do you?'

He knows my response already, is commencing the steamy jazz ballad before I've stopped double-fast palm-clapping.

At first I struggle to maintain eye contact as faithfully as he. He's too accomplished. Yet his voice envelops me like Egyptian cotton on a balmy New Orleans night; his pitch is as pure as pinged crystal; he has an outlandishly extensive range, his low notes sending tiny tremors to my genitals; tones of caramel carry me to a meditative place.

Until finally I find myself able to behold his eyes.

There are technically sixty-two shades of blue, and every single one of them lives in Scott Delaney's irises. Cobalt, periwinkle, ultramarine, zaffre, indigo, Tiffany blue; his eyes are intricately dappled, like mystical marbles, and the deeper I look into them, the more entranced I become.

Then something curious happens.

His life flashes before him – just I'm the only one who can see it.

A parochial hamlet in south-west Ireland. Country lad with an astonishing gift. Wins a talent contest. Hits the big time aged fourteen. No need to go to university, not with a voice like his. Hence he fails to sow his oats, get stoned, discuss politics and cosmology until sunrise, sleep all day, miss lectures, go on a boys' holiday to Benidorm, get off with a lady-boy. His pubes haven't reached double figures, yet there's an entourage and a fan base. For this particular boy it's too much. His comfort blanket? A girl he dated when he was a child; a spurious anchor to the real world, a world of which he's no longer a part. Thirty-one now, he can give a good talk – he's been well groomed by his captors. Yes, captors: Scott Delaney is as worldly-wise as a kidnap victim, one who's spent their entire adult life living in a purpose-built box in the cellar.

Turns out Scott's major malady isn't hypochondria or insomnia or immaturity or acute creativity – it's Stockholm Syndrome.

One third of kidnap victims exhibit symptoms of it – positive feelings towards their captors, to the point of defending them and depending upon them. At awards ceremonies, A-listers always thank their management. See their warped view of those who keep them imprisoned.

Scott 'Scat' Delaney has become little more than a luxuriously penned cash cow.

But what mostly falls into place as I gaze at his perfectly arched hairline and into his bewilderingly blue eyes, whilst he sings to *me*, whilst he bestows upon *me* a performance as improper as a lap dance and as deliciously intimate, is this:

Scott Delaney has never strayed in his life.

Neither will he stray. Not unless he's told it is perfectly OK to do so.

Scott finishes the song. We sit in dazed silence.

It's almost eleven. Time is running short. I remember his schedule at home:

10.55 p.m. Scott turns the light in his front reception room off.

10.56 p.m. Scott turns the light in the upstairs hall on.

10.59 p.m. Scott turns the light in the upstairs hall off.

11.00 p.m. Scott tries (fruitlessly) to sleep.

I shuffle on my knees to the bookshelf.

There I waver. Of course I fucking waver. Personal gratification verses the decimation of a relationship. Alice, a woman I like, a woman to whom I have something to prove. I remember her plum-sized purse, ready to spend her savings searching for some sign that she *can* live the soulmate dream. Genuinely I want her to have her dream. It's one of the reasons I do this job.

Yet when I reach up, I ignore *Family: Nature's Masterpiece* – its pinhole camera remains pointed steadfastly at the couch. Instead I locate the carriage clock, turning it around so we can no longer see its face.

Tonight, you will have a slightly later night. It's a special occasion. Two new friends – me and the snoozer over there: what's not to celebrate?

I don't tell Scott this out loud. Knowing a late night is imminent is hellish for an insomniac. Nights on the razz have to take you by surprise.

And so I find myself ready to close Case 0135/Operation Delaney.

Warning: the money shot it is not for the soppy-hearted. It requires a ruthless and single-minded professionalism. Please refer to the merciless tactics I utilised when entrapping Pieter de Groot, the Dutch Minister for Security and Justice. There is no room whatsoever for personal emotion, however vulnerable, however beautiful a target.

Those who are easily offended, turn away now.

'You have ear lobes.' I tell him this for no reason I can rationalise. 'Ear lobes don't have a single function, biologically speaking.'

'An erogenous zone?'

I go bashful. 'Apart from that.'

He leans forwards. 'May I?'

Without waiting for a response, he fondles my ear. That electric current again. We feel it, both of us. Now he tips my chin up. My face, I can feel, is a broiling magenta.

'I can't do this,' I hear myself tell him.

So Scott Delaney does the gentlemanly thing. He kisses me first; takes the onus entirely off of me, cements the destruction of his own relationship.

His lips are astonishing.

His breath is astonishing.

His tongue is astonishing.

I barely know where I am – it's little wonder I forget entirely to count to five.

Entrapment 101 Tip #6: Your objective is the unmitigated truth

It will be your redeeming feature. Private investigators don't have many.

What are you otherwise?

1. An unprincipled hermit.

2. A two-bob shamus.

3. A conman.

Answer: Yes.

Truth is a unique selling point in a profession populated by scoundrels and recluses. Make yourself a luminary in your field, the protagonist of your own secret production, a hero to the client in your search for nothing but the undiluted truth. To this end, *never* lie to your client about the results of a case. *Ever.*

Remember your motivation: nobody should be duped into living a lie, whatever that lie may be.

Letter Bomb

Tuesday. Day Nine: Operation Delaney.

11 a.m.

I sit crossed-legged, unseeing, petting my own ear.

Last night I closed this case.

More than anything I wish I hadn't.

Not because I reneged on my professional code, but because I can never see Scott Delaney again. The depth of my dismay is overwhelming.

Alice will be frantic, desperate to know the outcome of my attempts to seduce her soulmate. Yet I don't check my emails. Neither do I answer Michael's calls, even though he's been ringing since nine.

Instead I relive my evening with Scott, again and again. The most suffocating waves of euphoria and disappointment submerge me. It's relentless; at times I struggle to catch my breath.

Oh, deep down I knew I'd fall for him. I fell for him the first time I heard his voice on the radio, years ago, before I'd ever seen his face. And now I've become his friend, the type of friend that peers into his eyes and sees his fucking soul.

Neither of us have many friends like that.

More crucially, I've kissed his lips and, sure as shite, there is no way back from that.

I suddenly wish I had a BFF to call up, to tell all, a girl, someone like Alice. The shame arrives. What the fuck have I done to her?

What Olivia did to me.

With gusto I push my face into the mattress, making sure its dust-clogged tufting buttons dig into my forehead and cheeks. Still I can't erase the memory of my betrayal.

I returned to my bedsit in the early hours. Once inside, I quickly popped a sleeping pill. Not that I needed it – euphoria releases endorphins and endorphins increase happiness and happiness helps insomnia. But I was wired. My brain was doing star-jumps and insisting on reliving the evening over and over in rapid succession.

I wish I could phone Scott and see how he's slept . . .

My face deeper in the mattress, I try for a good twelve seconds to smother myself to death. Because when we hugged goodbye at 2 a.m. this morning, I knew the score. Scott would return to his old life in a cruel and relentless spotlight. And I would turn my cameras off, saving the video footage to a secret folder I'm not sure I'll ever revisit.

How can this feel anything other than insanely raw?

At some point today, I will contact Alice St Croix. My feedback will be invention.

Florence Maria Love fact: I have never lied on a case. Not until now.

Nothing happened, I will tell her. Zilch, nada, not a sausage. My, what a faithful man you've bagged!

What a damaged man.

I could fix him. I know I could.

But I'm fifteen years too late: Alice got there first.

For now I need a moment to grieve.

Never have I felt this disconsolate about a man. I think back, double-check: excluding family, how many people have I *properly* loved? Just four spring to mind.

1. The boy in the *Miami Vice* jacket.

2. Husband Number One.

3. Husband Number Two (a *very* tenuous inclusion).

4. Maeve (though I am not a lesbian).

Listlessly I recall how you categorise love, because veracity is my comfort blanket.

There are three distinct but not exclusive states. This is not *Cosmopolitan* magazine pseudo-psychology. This is biology. For each romantic state, humans have a specific neural circuitry – neurotransmitter fact.

You have the lust stage – a basic desire to mate. It produces testosterone and oestrogen. Duration: 1–3 months.

Then there's the attraction stage – a desire for commitment. It produces pheromones, dopamine and norepinephrine. Duration: 1–3.5 years.

Finally the attachment stage – the desire to bond based on children, marriage or shared interests. It produces oxytocin and vasopressin. Duration: many years, often decades, sometimes a lifetime.

The boy in the *Miami Vice* jacket . . .

Lust. Definitely lust. I was seven-ish. At a guess, he was too. His name was Junior. His outfit is etched in my hippocampus. Jeans, a salmon-pink T-shirt and a cream casual suit jacket with rolled-up sleeves, like Don Johnson, the height of fashion back then. Now and then he'd throw his head back, adeptly flicking his eighties fringe without involving his hands. I met him a few times, at church fetes and children's parties, inevitably spending every second fantasising about kissing him. When finally he tried to hold my hand, I called him a pervert, because although I worshipped him, I was achingly prissy.

I did kiss him in the end. Just once.

Husband Number One . . .

Both lust and attraction. And when he proposed, I was

grateful – he was gorgeous, spontaneous, irresponsible, impassioned about whatever new idea he'd thought up that week. He was also shouldered with the inability to see anything through. Yes, Luke was everything my dad was not. At nineteen, we were married. From that day forward I swore to be a subservient wife. At twenty-one, I caught him doing a bucking bronco with my maid of honour.

Husband Number Two . . .

Never ever any lust. Maybe a soupçon of attachment. We were married. We enjoyed pub walks, which is a shared interest. Blah.

Maeve . . .

Attachment. When she laughed at me, she held her belly, because she got me, enjoyed my brain. It made me feel validated. And my feelings for her were equally cerebral. We shared what the ancient Greeks called philia – a love of one another's mind. Yet for me it wasn't sexual. Though her cunnilingus was bewildering – like a classic sonata, four movements, each with distinctive characteristics. She also did that thing where you imagine the love-nut is a Polo mint and concentrate only on the solid bit.

Maeve Rivers should have been my friend for ever.

I wish I hadn't started on this train of thought, because it solidifies a realisation. I had never met an individual who fulfilled all three expressions of love – lust *and* attraction *and* attachment. Testosterone and oestrogen. Pheromones, dopamine and norepinephrine. Oxytocin and vasopressin.

Then last night I met someone with whom I felt a primal need to experience all those neurological states.

Only he has a secret girlfriend – secret until Thursday, when he'll be introducing Miss St Croix to his distraught public.

They are *not* suited, Scott and Alice. His public will see it immediately.

But that is no longer anything to do with me. *Me*, a lying, manipulative entrapper of men.

Scott Delaney will move forward with his life.

Then again, *Love is to be delighted by the happiness of another.* Gottfried Wilhelm von Leibniz said that, a philosopher who is German and therefore probably on the right track. Nonetheless, at this moment in my life I have one word for Gottfried and his altruistic psychobabble.

Bullshit.

And a few more words too:

I am not delighted. *My* dejection at watching him stroll into the sunset with another woman is as subterranean as a woman's dejection can get.

Look at me now.

Standing cruciform at my window in bra and knickers, beseeching that the Poet or the motorcyclist or Noah Steensen or whoever my stalker is finishes me off. A single bullet to the heart, I plead of him.

Better still: Mum, come out of your corner on the rooftop. Rush up to my bedsit and into my arms.

I've long forgotten her voice. Sure I could describe it to you, sort of. But I can't actually hear it any more. I know what she'd say, though.

It'll be all right, Piccolina. Mamma's here.

Half-naked, arms outstretched, I stand in front of a window for no one to see.

Histrionics overtake me. I press my nose and my breasts against the cool window pane. For a childish moment I pretend I can fly away, like Bambi.

Winchester University halls of residence, 2001.

Olivia's room. Motionless I stand outside, a cold metal doorknob in my hand.

It sounds like quite the jamboree is going on inside.

Vocal reed on vocal reed. Box spring on box spring. Headboard on plasterboard. At an educated guess (ref: *Sexual Psychophysiology in Primates*), Olivia is currently at the plateau stage, also known as the second stage of orgasm.

The first is the arousal stage, but I've missed that bit. I can attest, however, that for all his faults, my husband would not have rushed that phase. Marijuana has its pros – Luke's full and personal investment in a woman's pleasure being one.

It's the cruellest timing. I've arrived for the crescendo. The last two stages of a primate's orgasm – the orgasm proper, and resolution – are the most intensely private thing.

Get this absolutely straight.

I don't want to see this. Nobody in their right mind would want to see it. So perhaps someone can explain why I can't fucking well stop turning the door handle.

It's not as though I don't already have all the evidence I need. A love note in his wallet signed with a nom de plume: *Betty B*. Lying like spoons in my single bed, Luke and I have looked at that film poster each night of our marriage. It provided an insight into my head, I told him. He knew *Betty Blue* was my cute, deluded secret. Yet all the time we looked at her, he saw only his mistress.

Conjecture is pointless – I'll never be privy to the whole truth – but I can guess they chose her alias together. What a giggle they must have had – Florence and her ridiculous belief that she could ever be a femme fatale.

You're my heroin, 'Betty B' had written in that note.

How edgy.

Deep down, I recognised the handwriting, but the truth wasn't an option. How could it be? So I checked Luke's phone for a Betty. There was an Elizabeth. Her mobile telephone number was Olivia's mobile telephone number too.

I know the password for Luke's Hotmail account. It's *saintsFC* – Luke's wedding gift to me because he had nothing to hide. That's clever, declaring an artlessness from the start.

I scoured a lot of folders. But he'd been diligent. Mostly. Eventually I discovered a neat trick – assign your lover's emails to the junk box, just in case. It was there I found one email, months old, arranging a *liaison dangereuse* between him and my best friend.

But Olivia?

She'd spent my entire marriage scooping shit from my eyes. Luke Birmingham was baggage-ridden, worryingly immature and a twat, she said – no sugar coating, no cotton wool, no nothing. I should get rid, full stop.

And I let her say all that stuff because she was right.

Luke told me what to wear. It was Luke's decision that we marry within six months of our first kiss. He failed to suggest contributing to the rent on my digs, so lived on campus buckshee. Dusting or changing the sheets never occurred to him, though now and then he'd put his spliff down to sneak into lectures to see who I was sitting next to. Or that's what I thought at the time. In truth my stalker boyfriend was watching his own back, ensuring it was safe to philander.

But Olivia?

Verbatim she said: 'Luke treats you like a possession. It's *so* wrong. Darling, this is going one place only – arse-up.'

Slowly I open her door. The noises increase. A bedhead butts the wall ferociously. She faces away from me. There's a body beneath her. Two pairs of feet.

My heart is not in my mouth – that vital organ dropped free of my arse half an hour ago, when I found her email. I left it where it fell – a mound of damp sand, adorned with the remnants of my dignity, sprinkled with the fantasy of friendship and fidelity.

But Olivia?

She sent me a postcard with a quote on the front: *When you find people who not only tolerate your quirks but celebrate them with glad cries of 'Me, too!' be sure to cherish them — because those weirdos are your tribe.*

She was my tribe.

I've done it a hundred times before, poked my head around her door. Today I don't shout *Coo-ee*. My timing is too brutal.

They're at the orgasm proper phase. Luke's toes are clenched in preparation.

Impotent I stand. Forgetting entirely to fly at them both, missing the opportunity to stab her to death with the vibrator I spot fitting on the floor.

Unbreathing and paralysed, I stare, because it is absolutely *revolting*.

Luke's last upward thrust is decisive.

I watch the final nail in my marriage's coffin.

They breathe heavily, unaware of me, Olivia on top, her cheek against my husband's sated chest. Her splayed arse, his deflated balls — they point directly at my face.

The resolution stage complete, I puke on her rug.

Alice can wait — she'll get her happily-ever-after, I will make sure of it.

For the moment, however, I decide to ride the tube. To nowhere in particular. I need me-time.

Slamming the apartment door behind me, I stamp down every stair. Kick at a spray of letters on the front-door mat. Bang the heavy black door, its toughened glass refusing to shatter into as many pieces as my heart.

Outside.

The sky is a baked blue.

Pedestrians exude an infuriatingly sedate air. Shopowners have left the cold tinkle of tills to lean against warm windows.

Chins aloft, eyes shut like lazy cats, they allow the sun to pet their temples, cheeks, necks. Its analgesic heat plays games with their cynicism, dumbs it down, leaves them gullible.

I scowl at them all. And at the bastard sun – it blows indolence at a day that deserves anything but.

There's a short cut to Goodge Street tube station. An alley, shaded and scented by slow-cooked rubbish. I welcome the dank air; the change in atmosphere is as rude as a decontamination shower.

Fact: I'm not ready for one-to-one combat.

I fail to assume the uchi hachiji-dachi stance when, just a few steps into the shortcut, I'm grabbed from behind. An arm is twisted behind my back faster than I can say: *Shorinji Kempo is a Buddhist-inspired martial art. It hurts a lot. Want a demonstration? Then by all means attack. Be warned, however, I will elbow-strike you to death.*

'What the fuck!'

'Be quiet,' a woman's voice snarls into my neck. 'Now you listen to me good.'

She sounds like a West Country primary school teacher doing Clint Eastwood. Her s's whistle. Bent over, I see only her shoes. They're very unfashionable, yet I do as I'm told – the woman has the upper body strength of a mountain gorilla.

'You have not seen me,' she says. 'You will never see me again. You do not know who I am.'

'Get the fuck off!' My shoulder ligaments feel close to rupture.

'I said shut it, all right!'

Between clenched teeth: 'What do you want?'

'I want you to get out of our hair and to never return. And if you do return, because you've got family commitments and stuff, which I totally understand, you just stay right out of our hair. Got it?'

'Whose hair? Never return to where? To London?' They're valid questions.

She pushes my arm further back and up. I wince. 'There's an envelope on your front doormat. It's addressed to Mr Tumnus.'

I don't ask why, just nod quickly at those awful shoes – buckled, with a small Cuban heel; like tap shoes only uglier.

'Take the letter,' she continues. 'Do not open it until you're back inside your flat.' Her face is so close to my cheek, I can smell medicated soap. 'I hope for your sake you are a woman of your word, Florence Doe.'

Florence Doe?

Nobody's called me that in years.

'And remember this, the most important thing of all . . .'

I grimace and nod.

'This is our secret. Nobody on the planet knows about it. Just you and me. Oh, I may burn in hell for this, but should you blab, I will deny it until the day I die.'

With that, the insanely strong woman is gone.

Shell-shocked, I rub my shoulder.

My phone tinkles politely in my pocket. 'I'll phone you back,' I tell Michael quickly, then I hang up and hurry out of the alley and back towards the mansion flats.

Sifting through the post on the hall carpet, I find a large Jiffy envelope with *MR TUMNUS* typed in capitals on the front. That's all. Unlike the rest of the mail, it's been posted by hand. Its seal has been secured by several strips of Sellotape.

Tentatively I pick up the package, hold it out in front of me and carry it unopened up the stairs.

'Coming through,' I warn Chinchilla Guy, who approaches in the opposite direction. His girlfriend is nowhere to be seen, so he shoots unctuously to one side, performs a bow and ushers me past.

By way of a thank-you, I do a half-grin. It's perfunctory, yet says: I could have you in a flash.

You've got to respect his gall – he mirrors my body language. His half-grin says: I could do you in a flash.

And that he could. I've timed him. From the onslaught of squealing bedsprings to his rodent-death-song finale, Chinchilla Guy rarely lasts a minute. I put a spanner in the works: wiggle my arse as I shimmy on past. I'll time how long he lasts tonight. Guaranteed he'll be imagining it's my booty he's nailing at supersonic speed. Forty seconds top, I reckon. Or maybe forty minutes – why rush perfection?

See what a little fear and stalkery does to me. It's all wrong, but I feel sought after.

Door closed behind me, I place the letter in the middle of my table, swivel a chair, sit astride it, my elbows on its top rail, and look at the package.

A possible realisation makes my heart clatter. Is the strong woman the Hoodie? The healthy meal deals, the low-fat cigarettes, the camping stool.

But why steal the book?

Relieved, I quickly realise it cannot be her. My assailant didn't smoke. She smelt sanitised as a children's ward. Then I remember the rooftop – that was pretty sanitised too.

Using just my fingernails, I slide the envelope towards me.

I recognised her accent, though. She's from Cornwall. Truro, at a guess. I can't think of anyone from Truro who wants to kill me. Still I put an ear to the package and recall a post office team meeting we once had about letter bombs.

The training guy from head office had given us a leaflet: *Be Alert About Terrorism*.

The main characteristic of an incendiary device is excessive postage and a thoroughly correct address – this stops it being singled out at the post office. My letter was hand-delivered to a character out of *The Lion, the Witch and the Wardrobe*. Letter bombs also have an uneven weight distribution, are rigid or oddly shaped, display yellow stains and possess the aroma of marzipan. My neat A4 envelope smells of hotel soap.

A little bit of me would like to go out with a bang.

Roughly I yank at the Sellotape, pull the Jiffy bag's lip up and away. There's nothing inside. Turning the envelope upside down, I shake it vigorously, dig a finger inside, a fist and much of an elbow. Finally a small square of paper flutters free. Just two words are written on it:

Eric Steensen.

Dead man Eric.

Things take a while to sink in.

Things like:

The Poet's name is Noah Steensen. Dad said he knew only that the dead man in the car was called Eric, yet he recognised Noah's name – Eric's son perhaps? My father knows more than he's letting on.

My dad is a liar.

That's the best news I've had today, because he has said *Florrie, darling – Mummy is dead* too many times to remember, and the evidence now suggests I shouldn't trust a thing he says.

The Paradox of Probability

Gloria was my Cornish assailant. A senior archivist prepared to fight for her man.

And I am a woman of my word. Dropping the signed divorce papers into the Jiffy envelope, I scrub out *Mr Tumnus* and write:

Julian Doe, Archive Lecturer, Plymouth University, Plymouth.

No postcode. Postcodes make the post office lazy. It'll get there. I also put the stamp on wonky, to show my displeasure at being replaced by a less fashionable model.

Be clear I *will* get the bitch back; my arm hurts like mad. And yes, Julian remains as spineless as an annelid, yet I give him his dues: Wife Number Two is my type of girl.

Envelope in hand, I run down the mansion block stairs, hop over the spray of letters on the front mat, slam the heavy black door behind me. Its toughened glass doesn't shatter. I weave through students, cyclists, pedestrians and their sedated air, ignore the shopowners, lazy like cats, avoid shortcuts, take the less direct route to Goodge Street tube.

There's a post box on Tottenham Court Road. On my way past, I push the divorce papers at its mouth.

Then I go to the office.

The office. Aka the public records library.

Technically it's not *my* office, but a communal facility manned by widows and boys with beards. I frequent it to find people – debtors, missing relatives, rapists, my mother – individuals who avoid the electoral roll, Facebook, Experian. Here I look for the extra-sneaky ones.

I search for new babies or other family members. Especially I look for secret marriages, because people, however devious, will at some point fall in love.

Anthropological fact: love is our universal downfall. It leaves a paper trail.

The plan today is simple: did a man called Eric Steensen have a son called Noah Steensen? Had he given me a card with contact details, I might have phoned my stalker directly. It's prudent, however, to first check that Noah Steensen is who I think he is.

Greedily I inhale the office's air, the smell of old paper as consoling as ever. Row after row of identical volumes – births, marriages, deaths – the lists inside them multiplying, abandoned as streptococcus. Millions upon millions of entries, and somewhere amongst them, one line that could lead me to Noah Steensen to Eric Steensen and eventually to Bambi.

I spot Zanna.

She's in the black corner, leaning on an impractically tall study table, a magnifying glass to her eye. Intently she studies the departed, making notes in a pad, genning-up on the welcome party that awaits her on the other side.

Creeping up beside, I look over her shoulder. 'Wotcher.' Her head shoots up and round.

'How nice,' she says loudly. 'I thought you were dead.'

I smile fondly. 'Why?'

She roots in her carpet bag and pulls free what looks like a baby's bootie. Ice-white, crocheted and enormous, it's big enough to swaddle a melon.

'For when you're on a job,' she winks.

A balaclava for an Inuk! I give her a long hug, cradle her ear in my cleavage, promise that the next time I have a case in a circumpolar region, I'll wear it constantly. And I really will, because her kindness makes me feel a little less alone.

'Why on earth would you think I was dead?' I ask.

'Norm saw a stranger coming out of your flat in the early hours.' She confides in me as though I'm not the object of her gossip.

I put a hand to my mouth. 'And you thought I'd been murdered?'

Her eyes are animated. 'Norm said it didn't look right.'

'Norm? What was he doing in the hall?'

'On his way home.'

'What time?' I ask. Last night I was out until gone two.

'Four-ish.' She elbows me mischievously. 'It's all right, it wasn't a school night.'

His poor unsuspecting wife. Hold on one moment. I point. 'Fuck-buddy Norm?'

Zanna cranes a little ear in my direction. 'Sorry, dear?'

'The brave prisoner of war who escaped Fritz with a bullet in his head then joined the French bloody Resistance and lived in a coffin for, what, four years? *That* Norm didn't think to knock to see if I was all right? What with a suspicious man escaping my home?'

With not a morsel of compassion and a considerable hunk of defiance, Zanna says, 'It was a woman, and we don't like to interfere, dear.'

'What did she look like?' I ask quickly.

'Young.'

'How young?'

'Younger than me.'

'So anywhere between what and what?' I hold her hands in mine. 'Think hard, Zanna. Could she have been sixty-three?'

Zanna hasn't a clue. Pulls her hands free. 'I wasn't actually there, dear.'

I do a skip. Without reasonable doubt she cannot say the intruder was not sixty-three.

'I have a top-secret job for you, Zanna.'

I want to get back to my flat to assess angles and submergence levels. Zanna, apart from a shabby affair, has nothing going on.

'I need the answer to one question. Did a man called Eric Steensen give birth to a son called Noah Steensen?'

Reluctantly she picks up her pad and turns to a fresh page.

'I need you to confirm that Noah's surname is not a coincidence. The paradox of probability theory says that dreadful or uncanny coincidences are not unusual. Eric was local to Poole – the papers said so. Dad said so too. Then again, Dad's a liar.' My mobile rings. It's Michael. I cut him off for the umpteenth time today. 'Let's just say, if Noah Steensen was born in England, I'll find him.'

She looks baffled.

I speak slowly. 'Did *an* Eric Steensen, *any* Eric Steensen, have a son called Noah between 1975 and 1985? I'll come by tonight for the findings. And tell Norm, thanks a million.'

I'm striding free of Goodge Street tube station. Jogging, out of breath, almost home.

'What?' I shout at my phone.

'I have got *the* worse hangover ever,' Michael says back.

'Don't drink, then.'

'Sorry about last night, Flo, I don't know what happened.'

'You zonked out is what happened.'

Glancing left and right, I cross Tottenham Court Road, whilst Michael tries to redeem himself.

Eagerly he is telling me: 'Alice has been and gone. Everything is sorted. Case closed.'

This statement takes a while to permeate.

I stop dead on a traffic island in the centre of four lanes of London traffic. Vehicles whizz either side of me.

'Did you say Alice?'

'Yes.'

'As in Alice St Croix?'

'Soon to be Alice Delaney.'

In the Atari game of my childhood, the cars don't swerve to avoid the chicken. They knock it dead then carry on blithely with their day. Blindly I wander to the opposite pavement. Traffic circumnavigates me, beeps and screeches against a back-beat of *fuck you*s and *stupid cow*s.

'Why has Alice been and gone, Michael?'

He thinks I'm being pedantic, humours me nonetheless – he's the one who got drunk on a case and passed out.

Patiently he says: 'She came this morning, just like you said.'

'I didn't say she was coming to you this morning.'

'You did.'

'No I didn't.'

'You did. You texted me.'

'When?'

'Four o'clock this morning. I didn't pick the text up until she arrived, though.'

'Until who arrived?'

'Alice.'

There he goes again, saying *Alice*.

'She's not back from Tuscany until tomorrow.'

'She is. I saw her.'

I stop outside a furniture store. Stare urgently at its window display, searching for a semblance of rationality. 'Let me get this straight. Alice St Croix turned up this morning at your flat?'

'Yes.'

'And I sent you a text from my phone at four this morning to tell you she was coming?'

'Yes.'

'Michael, she doesn't know where you live.'

'You sent her a text too. With my address.'

'No I didn't.'

'She showed me.'

PI facts: Philip Marlow never texted. Miss Marple never texted. Neither Holmes nor Magnum PI ever texted.

Nor did any of them share the addresses of close family members, because giving a client any detail too personal yields a quagmire of shit.

Taking the smartphone from my ear, I check my sent box. Indeed there are two texts. Two texts I categorically did not write.

One was sent to Alice. It reads: *Footage ready for collection. 8C Greek Street, W1D. 9 a.m. sharp. A pleasure doing business with you. FL*

A second text was sent to Michael: *Alice coming at 0900 hours to pick up DVD. Super-important that footage is ready. Chop chop xx*

Both were sent in the early hours of this morning – at 4.12 and 4.15 a.m. respectively, when I was very much asleep. When Yellow-Belly Norm saw an intruder leave my flat.

'I didn't write those,' I tell the shop window, then put the phone back to my ear. 'I did not send those texts, Michael.'

I inspect my bedsit. Nothing has moved. There is no evidence of an intruder.

I cast my mind back – was my phone in a different position when I woke up this morning?

I haven't the foggiest. My eye was off the ball. I was wallowing in the afterglow of last night. For much of the morning I stood disconsolate at a window in my underwear.

One thing's for sure – I glance at the door: last night when I returned, I forgot to rim-latch, deadlock, barrel-bolt or tower-bolt.

There's one explanation only:

Mum has keys.

Who am I kidding? Mum doesn't have keys.

With a disconsolate swipe of my forearm, I clear the kitchen surface of its microwave cartons, coffee cups, cutlery. Livid, they clatter at the floorboards.

Alice St Croix has keys.

Michael stands mortified in a corner.

I haven't told him to stand there. This is a historical response to very bad situations. He's been doing it since he could crawl. Today, however, I refuse to console him.

'But you couldn't find the footage, could you?' I tell him sternly. 'You told Alice to come back later.'

Michael speaks conspiratorially to his stomach. 'It was in a folder called Flo's Stuff.' Quieter still: 'She helped me find it.'

'For fuck's sake, Michael, that's a *private* folder . . .' I squash my nose against the grimy window pane. Look down on to the street below, at the rooftop opposite.

Alice played me at my own game. She watched me as closely as I watched her boyfriend.

Peering down at the pub opposite, I wonder:

Is she sitting outside the Marlborough Arms now, a cigarette holder in one hand, a gin and tonic in the other, extravagantly wrapped in mink, wearing whore-red lipstick and a savvy smile because she, Alice St Croix, outsmarted me?

'I told her I couldn't find the VT at first, because I couldn't.' Michael is busy explaining things to his abdomen. 'I made her sit in the living room and wait while I looked.'

'You left her alone?'

'She just sat sad-looking and smoked. I watched her on the camera.'

He fumbles for his notebook and tries to make amends:

'She was wearing jeans – size ten, bootleg, Next or M and S. A vest top – khaki, Primark, a hundred per cent polyester, size eight to ten. It had seen at least fifteen washes. Slingbacks, flat, size five. Her hair was tied back in a ponytail; it looked different from when we saw her at the hotel.'

'Different how?'

'Not as tidy. She probably hadn't slept all night.'

Sometimes my brother is an utter fool. 'Frenchwomen, even sleep-deprived ones, have kempt hair and quality vest tops, Michael. What about her cigarettes?'

'She smoked half of one.'

'Make?'

'Silk Cut, low-tar, duty-free.'

'Long white filters?'

He nods. I bang my thigh.

'I did good?' he asks, ready to vacate the dunce's corner. I shake my head at the rooftop opposite. 'She's been watching me.'

'She was nice,' he says, confused. 'She said we had the same nose.'

'You and her?'

'Me and you.'

'She knew we were related?'

'Other stuff too.' His voice peters out a little. He readdresses his midriff. 'That we lived in Laurelbridge, that Mum is dead . . .'

'You what?'

'Alice said her dad was dead too and it made her sad every day. I thought you told her stuff, and if you told her stuff, she had to be nice.'

'What time did she leave your place?'

He looks at his notepad. 'Ten-seventeen.'

'Did you watch any of it together – the footage?'

'She wanted to watch it alone.'

'Somebody broke into my apartment a couple of weeks back. Someone with keys. I'd assumed it was . . .'

'Who?' he asks quickly.

I don't tell him Bambi: 'A dyke-in-denial. We met on the tube.'

Then it falls into place.

Pickpocketing fact: there are two chief methods. Distraction is only one of them; the other is compassion.

At the Charing Cross Hotel I held Alice's hand as she passed to leave. *Chances are we'll discover what an admirable and faithful man you've bagged*, I said. And she bent down to give me a hug that lasted too long. *And that, Ms Love, is a special platform on which to build a future together.* At the time I patted her back, puzzled, but feeling needed and excited about the job she'd proposed.

In reality she was robbing my bloody keys.

But why would she want to break into my apartment? I was in her employ. I was trying to help her.

Because it's exactly what I'd have done in her situation?

Chances are I'd be as fatuous as the groupies from whom she's tried to keep her famous boyfriend. It was imperative she keep a close eye on me. Asking someone to seduce a man as beautiful and naïve as Scott Delaney is fraught with risk. The heart is bound to get involved, however principled an entrapper you are.

Most embarrassingly, I gave the woman all the bugging advice she needed – shared best-practice tips with her. I, for example, would have planted a recording device in their home. That would enable me to overhear telephone conversations and tête-à-têtes, I said, a recording device being key to an efficient and cost-effective surveillance operation.

The bugs should be hidden in two places, I explained, providing her with too much detail. But I'm a surveillance anorak and you should never knock passion. Though I might have been too excitable. What with the target being Scott Delaney. What with me forgetting I was preparing to raze a love story – *her* love story – and replace it momentarily with mine.

First I'll tap his landline via a telephone transmitter. You so have to get one of these, I gushed as normal women chit-chat about Hermès bags. *A fabulous bit of kit. It's disguised as a common dual modular adaptor – one of those little contraptions you use when plugging a telephone and a modem into the same telephone socket. His telephone conversations can be transmitted up to a quarter of a mile away. We listen in using an FM transmitter and headphones.*

Most clients jump at this. It's James Bondesque and exactly the service they hoped to receive from a real-life PI.

But Alice was uninterested in boys' toys.

Not in his home, she said. *You do not set one foot near it.*

Deep down she knew the outcome, perhaps – so she drew lines in the sand.

They only cost fifty quid. Google 'telephone bugging'. There's a gazillion online spy equipment shops.

I tried to help, even told her how to purchase one and perhaps put it in herself.

I look around my bedsit. I don't have a landline, so Alice didn't break in here to plant a telephone bug.

Lucky for Alice, I went on to tell her about an even better tapping device. Arguably the best ever invented – because *nobody* has ever noticed one.

This bit of kit is even niftier than the phone tap. A thirteen-amp fully working three-pin double-outlet plug adaptor, hidden behind the television, into which we plug Scott's PlayStation and Sky box. Guys don't fiddle with the plug adaptors coordinating their entire home entertainment system.

I held the plug socket up as if it were a premier cru.

This model uses the latest quad-band GSM technology: thirty-two GB; that'll give you almost six hundred hours' recording time.

Voice-activated. It uses a SIM card to transmit to anywhere in the world with a cellular network.

Thinking back, Alice did well not to laugh out loud, hold her belly and point at me delighted as if I'd just arrived on earth.

I slowly fall to my knees and pull the crate beside my bed away from the wall. The dust balls are the size of tumbleweed. Tugging the three-pin adaptor plug from the socket, I remove the plugs for my laptop and iPhone charger.

Quietly I examine the adaptor's casing.

The cheeky cow hasn't even gone to the bother of spending six hundred quid (RRP online, incl. VAT) on this bit of kit. She has used mine.

My surveillance vanity case sits as ever on top of the wardrobe. Inside I find a three-pin double adaptor all right. Not the £600 one; a £6.99 one from B&Q. Categorically this version does not record conversations. It just enables you to plug more than one electrical item into the wall socket.

She swapped them.

There's a screwdriver in the vanity case. I use it to open the spy adaptor plug. Alice has inserted her own SIM card. This enables her to phone my plug socket from anywhere in the whole world.

Tuscany, for example.

I pick the SIM free. Place it on the floor. Stab it nosily with the screwdriver.

Cellular network fact: Italy definitely has one.

Jabbing the screwdriver in Michael's direction, I demand answers.

'Did Alice have a tan?'

'Yes,' he says, disconcerted, splaying his limbs as if I'm an insatiable screwdriver-thrower.

'*As* orange or *more* orange than Sebastien's?'

'Satsuma orange.' Michael squints, then drops his hands, puts them on his waist. Things seem to have fallen into place for him too 'Double-dip, definitely.'

'That's a spray tan, right?'

'God, yes,' he complains. 'Two level fours. She still had the stains on her hands.'

I stare across at the jagged rooftop opposite. Why would she waste the cash – go all the way to Tuscany when there's a perfectly good playground for insane secret girlfriends just across the street?

Star Wars

Blomfield House.

I've not stood this close to Scott's home before. Trembling, I peek in through the wrought-iron gates, like an infatuated groupie. It's a sumptuously gilded enclosure, along with his other enclosures of course in Cork, Tuscany and Bel Air. Obediently he pops from one cage to the other via private jet.

There's a buzzer built into the wall by the gates. A deep breath, then I poke it apprehensively. There's no answer. Second time round I press more resolutely, relieved that he might not be in, impatient to see him again.

A woman says: 'Hello?'

It's not Alice. The woman's voice is pitchy and too cheerful. She has not had her life recently shattered. This is the voice of someone whose present is going swimmingly and whose future – as far as she is aware – is exactly as planned.

'Hi.' I'm terrified but equally upbeat. 'Is Scott about?'

'Who is it, please?' she asks.

Fair enough. I could be a fan chancing my luck, or a stalker, or an entrapment specialist desperate to update him before his secret girlfriend bowls in, mad as a premenstrual Artemis, waving the unabridged DVD of our love story and telling him wicked truths about me.

'My name is Florence Love,' I tell the entry system. 'I'm an events coordinator, a colleague of Maeve Rivers. I've been helping Scott since Harvey went to Guyana. I have paperwork that needs signing – he is expecting me.'

'Come in, come in,' says the woman cheerily, and I smile

professionally into a camera I've just spotted set into the wall.

The bars of Scott's cage electronically release.

And so I find myself on the gravel drive – on the inside, somewhere I have been forbidden to go. But my bowels do not prickle excitedly. Nobody in their right mind would be enthused at what I am about to do.

Currently number one on my wish list is to turn on my tail, squeeze an exit through the closing gates and escape Scott's impound. Failing that, I want a sense of self-righteousness because I am doing the right thing – forewarning him, telling him the truth, and in the process seeing him one last time. And as someone once said (I forget who), *When it comes to true love, profound revelation reveals the whole.*

Who am I kidding. Andrew Cohen said it – a spiritual guru, author and musician responsible for creating a path of spiritual transformation called evolutionary enlighten-ment. He is also American, so most likely hysterical. Nonetheless, at this juncture in my life I have one word for his cult-like pseudo-spiritual Yankee bollocks:

I'll-give-it-a-bloody-good-go.

And a few more words too:

It will not work. When it comes to love – truly profound love – revelation may expose the whole, but the whole is always uglier than your carefully edited best bits.

More so when it comes to entrapment.

Targets never see it from the private investigator's point of view. They err on the side of feeling hard done by and violated and, often, vengeful. They join the Death to Entrapment Specialists Facebook group. Sometimes they even feel a little heartbroken because they've lived that magic moment; the moment authors and artists and screen-writers bang on about – that make-believe instant when you felt cherished by someone who didn't have to feel a thing but just really, really did, because they had experienced the transcendent meeting of minds.

Nevertheless, I choose the American guru route. I choose cloud cuckoo land.

It's Scott's sister who opens the door.

Elle Delaney.

Resplendent in nude. Nude skinny jeans, nude shoes, nude cashmere jumper, nude lipstick, an American manicure (colour: nude), nude(ish) highlights. The woman is as breathtaking as her brother, and boy, can I see the familial resemblance.

Her once slightly buck teeth are now slightly less so, thanks to veneers moulded to simulate a toned-down, more fluorescent version of the original.

Her smiley eyes are Jesus-blue.

They share the same pheromones, so she smells just like Scott.

And when she moistens her full lips, I see her tongue is as pink and spotless as her brother's. At a guess, it's velvet soft as a baby's. Oh, imagining her tongue in my mouth makes my heart sink horribly – the most unsoiled night of my life is to morph into something sordid and wrong.

'Scott's out at the moment,' Elle tells me pleasantly. 'He'll be back shortly.'

Unlike Scott, her Irish accent has become diluted; it's as Londonised as mine. It's her one shortcoming. I forgive it instantly. In another life, she'd be my sister-in-law.

'Would you like to wait?' she asks.

'I would indeed,' I say, slightly leprechaun-like. I was going for jolly and cheery, not racist. I'm so nervy, I struggle to contain it.

Smoothing my skirt self-consciously, I follow her into the living room, where I take a seat on the vast white sofa.

Scott sits on this couch. Secretly I stroke its fabric. The

room is just like the magazine article, only more beautiful, what with Scott's sister standing in it.

'Well, do excuse me, I'm in the middle of cooking a roast,' she declares, and leaves so graciously I want to applaud her bit-part in my day.

Waiting for Scott, I fill time looking for plug sockets. I shouldn't have. It leads to my discovery of a mortifying fact:

The stinking rich don't have plug sockets. Visible wires, electrical points, any clue as to how a gadget works is all a bit middle-class. There aren't even light switches. Voice-activated, I imagine.

Alice must have been pissing her pants.

A 13 amp fully working three-pin double-outlet plug adaptor is the best ever invented, because nobody *has ever noticed one* . . .

Oh, they'd be noticed all right in this room. I feel as conspicuous as a liver spot. It's the embodiment of elegance. Even the photographs are at one with the theme. Their frames are ebony. The prints are black and white. I tiptoe closer to have a better look. They provide the most artistic foliage.

But I don't smile at them.

I squint perplexed and gasp loudly.

Not in his home, Alice said. *You do not set one foot near it*.

Now I understand why.

I have to get out.

Regimented as an android, I walk out of the front room. In the hall, I don't shout *See ya!* to Elle, which is terribly rude, but I've made a catastrophic mistake.

Easing myself through the front door, shutting it soundlessly behind me, I tiptoe across the gravel of the drive.

On the inside wall to the left of the electric gates is another aluminium button. I jab at it a lot of times.

Please God open, please God open . . .

Once more the gates float deferentially apart whilst making the exact same noise as a light sabre.

Thank you God, thank you God . . .

Yes, they make an electric-light-sabre *juuuuu w*hen they open and an equally electric-light-sabre *juuuuu w*hen they clink shut behind me.

If I weren't so horrified, I'd have a little titter about that, what with light-sabre sounds being so extremely poignant; anything remotely *Star Warsy* is delightfully ironic.

Because Luke Skywalker was shagging his biological sister too.

Breathless from jogging, I rest my back and head against cool brick, then look left and right as if I'm being pursued by the police.

Think, think, I have to think . . .

The photograph in the living room:

Scott lies on a deserted beach, starfish in the surf, bestridden by a woman. Playfully she holds his hands above his shoulders. My, they're absorbed in an intimate moment. A moment I'm especially familiar with. The Look. Photographers, like entrapment specialists, strive for this moment. The resultant print is as illuminating as an auto-biography; indeed, this is what I instantly gathered:

The couple know each other quite well. Later they'll enjoy dinner at a seafood restaurant, a carafe of wine and comfort-able banter. They will return to their room to make peaceful love. Lying beneath his armpit, its aroma as comforting as a lavender drawer cushion, she will then sleep soundly. Because this is a man with whom she's experienced lust and attraction; they're certainly close to the attachment phase. Her neurological system will have released testosterone and oestrogen, followed by pheromones, dopamine and norep-inephrine, followed by oxytocin and vasopressin – in the exact, organic, unhurried order that the courtship takes.

Yet the woman in the photograph is not Alice.

Not the Alice who claimed that Scott would be introducing her to the world at an awards ceremony on Thursday.

The girl in the photograph, her bikini-clad breast enlargements hovering contentedly at Scott Delaney's collarbone, is Elle. A ten out of ten. A woman designed for him by evolution. Physically they could be siblings. Even their biological perfumes have mingled, evolved into something new and indistinguishable, and that is intense, when your pheromones become one.

Elle isn't his sister. Elle is his real-life girlfriend. And it's serious between them, because Piscean men don't have pictures of any old woman in their living rooms; especially not ones who cook them roasts of a Tuesday.

Which begs the question:

Who the fuck is Alice?

Alice St Croix

A warning about social networking sites: never join one. And avoid people who do. Chances are they'll broadcast your life via their non-existent one. Admittedly sometimes you *have* to be friendly with people who poke and tweet (i.e. blood relatives and work colleagues); just never let them point a mobile phone at you.

Cyber-psychological facts:

1. Social networkers have wildly increased levels of narcissistic, depressive and pathological tendencies.

2. The sites to which they belong reinforce gender-related stereotypes not seen since before the third-wave feminism of the 1980s.

3. Interacting with a PC means people feel less empathy and stop pretending to be nice, a behaviourism that separates us from other species, thus making social networking a serious evolutionary arrière.

Plus point about social networking sites: PIs, local authorities and paedophiles love, love, love them.

My number one tip when snooping using social networks is this – take the twisty route. Today I travel via a man called Gerald O'Rourke, an ex-classmate of both Scott Delaney and Alice St Croix.

Here is a quick rundown on Gerald O'Rourke, according to his profile:

He's single. Into clubbing. Has 433 'friends' and a publicly accessible photo album. The latter two facts translate as follows: Gerald O'Rourke is a social networker incapable of being social or networking in the real world. His uploaded photographs prove my hypothesis. Five hundred shots of Gerald (taken by himself using his mobile phone), all of which exhibit him having a blast – pint in hand, draped around a nonplussed, cosmetics-laden girl who doesn't know him from Adam.

Thankfully for me, one of these albums gives a more historical insight into Gerard O'Rourke.

'School Dayz', it's called.

These photographs showcase Gerald at a different juncture in his life – the one at which he donned a head brace and Eric Morecambe specs.

At least he stands out. It takes longer to spot any other familiar faces amongst the schoolchildren organised into rows according to their height and the availability of gym benches.

There! Finally I spot Scott Delaney.

He's just thirteen years old, yet my stomach performs the warmest lurch at the sight of him. Without doubt those Jesus-blue eyes will have gone down a storm at Our Blessed Mother Mary Lady of Perpetual Help Roman Catholic School. Because Scott is a doppelgänger for the Son of God, regardless of the unkempt hair and his top button being undone.

The tip of my finger touches the grinning face of a child destined for world fame and professional incarceration. For this moment in time, however, he is entirely free.

And Alice.

She's especially tricky to find, even though Gerald O'Rourke has painstakingly written the name of his class-mates in the correct order in an associated photo-tag.

In my defence, she's changed an awful lot.

And Scott Delaney was absolutely right – Alice was utterly, *utterly* beautiful. Hornet-stung lips. A nose delicately sculpted from the tiny shell of a marine mollusc. Indian Ocean eyes, fifty shades of green. Her hair very much darker – blue-whale black. And her skin a sumptuous mahogany.

Yes, back in 1993, Alice St Croix distinctly erred towards Mauritian.

Furious, I drop Michael a text: *Come back to mine ASAP.*

Michael phones me within ten seconds to double-check: 'That text – it was definitely from you, right?'

I don't reward his prudence. 'Alice isn't Scott's girlfriend. Alice isn't even Alice. Get over here now.'

Michael is back in his corner. This time he has three fingers in his mouth.

'The photographs in his front room weren't of Scott and Alice?'

'No they were not,' I tell him, as if it's entirely his fault.

'Who were they of then?'

'Scott and Elle.'

Michael's brain looks set to detonate. 'But they are *brother and sister*, Flo. That is illegal.'

'Yes,' says Sébastien, prim as the school swat, sitting erect in *my* chair at *my* table. 'Marriage between siblings is frowned upon universally.'

I take an especially exasperated look at Sébastien, the product of inbreeding if ever I saw it.

'Yep, even primates avoid incest,' I say, because it seems not to have crossed Sébastien's mind to fuck off and leave Michael and me to our private work-related chat. There's a café outside, and a pub, and a newsagent's, and a clinic that specialises in aesthetic treatments.

'Sorry, what are you doing here?' I ask him.

'I was visiting my boyfriend,' he says in that voice of his.

It makes me quiver. More so when he issues Michael with what I assume is the look of love. 'I came along with him because it's dark out.'

'He's almost thirty.'

Sébastien continues: 'Sweden and the Netherlands have a more tolerant view of that sort of thing.'

'What sort of thing?'

'Incest.'

I decide to address only Michael. 'The woman I met in the Charing Cross Hotel is not Scott Delaney's girlfriend. She's an impostor. Let's call her Fake Alice.'

'No way,' gasps Michael.

'Way,' I say.

'So if Fake Alice isn't his girlfriend, who is?'

'Elle.'

'His sister?'

'No, Michael, not his sister. Fake Alice led us to believe Elle was his sister. But Elle is not his sister. Elle is his *actual* secret girlfriend.'

'Not for much longer,' says Sébastien. 'Fake Alice plans to show Elle the footage.'

'How do you know?' I frown.

'Otherwise what was the point? Fake Alice didn't want you to go into the house to plant recording devices, right?'

Michael puts his hands on his hips. 'That should have given the game away.'

My consolation is slim. 'I bet Fake Alice thought Scott had visible electrical sockets too. She couldn't have got me into the house if she'd wanted to.'

'It wasn't her house?' gasps Michael.

'No, Michael! What with her being an impostor.'

'I said it all along, didn't I?' Sébastien tells Michael. 'That Fake Alice was weird. The information she provided was as informative as his Wikipedia page.'

'She probably actually got the information *from* his Wikipedia page,' says Michael. 'That's why she called him Scott, not Scat.'

I remember Alice's paltry list of facts about Scott. When describing his album, she used the same clichéd shit as the newspapers and magazines. *It's a compilation of duets with jazz greats and pop giants.* She was very precise, unimaginatively precise.

'She wasn't pretty enough either.' Sébastien holds a small hand to his pigeon chest. 'The man is a god.'

I am in total agreement.

My shoulders bomb, sadness leaking from its box in my chest. Regret tickles my limpid system into action; I brush at rogue tears.

'It does seem obvious now – her being a phoney,' says Sébastien. 'If it quacks like a duck, swims like a duck, looks like a duck, what is it?'

He and Michael nod unequivocally. 'A duck.'

Sever my arm and beat me to death with it, why don't you!

'The paradox of probability theory says that coincidences are not unusual,' I tell Michael, holding back furious tears. Then I point at Sébastien: 'What's happened to your stutter?'

'It's not so bad when I'm re-re-relaxed . . .'

Michael interjects. 'But why would Fake Alice want you to entrap a man who isn't her boyfriend? Does she even know him?'

'An obsessed fan who wants to wreck his relationship?' I try to take back control. 'With Elle out of the picture, she thinks she can make romantic inroads.'

'Alice is a fantasist,' Sébastien says darkly.

'Definitely,' Michael whispers back.

Admittedly, stamping a foot is childish, but seriously, Sébastien is doing my head in.

Why oh *why* when people become a couple do they

automatically sit in on everything that's bugger all to do with them? And on the rare occasions when they're absent, why oh *why* must everything get reported back to them like it's an ancient relationship by-law or something:

No friend or family member of said couple is entitled to any degree of privacy ever again. Past and future confidential conversations now belong equally to both members of the partnership.

'This is a work meeting,' I tell Sébastien.

'I know. And thank you. I'd love to do what you do, Florence. You're a legend.'

'She is amazing,' Michael tells Sébastien, stony-faced.

Michael and Sébastien then perform a synchronised palm-clap – it's as if their mental assimilation is complete.

In my whole life I've not received a more depressing, camp and less deserved round of applause. Without appreciation or dignity I watch them reduce my existence to light entertainment. The fact that I've screwed up a potential soulmate's life is such fabulous fun – a man already attempting to live some semblance of a life in a cage the size of an old-fashioned TV set. A man who has a stunning woman with whom he has been on an romantic holiday, with whom he has shared the Look, with whom he's experienced a morsel of normality away from a cruel and mercenary media machine.

I, Florence Maria Love, have single-handedly robbed him of that.

Case closed.

The rap on my door is impolite. It's Zanna. Time is marching on and she and Norm have plans.

'I can't hang around for ever,' she complains, then proffers a small sheet of paper.

It is full of spidery writing.

First Love

This is my favourite view of London.

I come here when I need cheering up. Take a tube to Southwark, walk six hundred metres to the Tate Modern, make your way to the top floor and swing a left for the bar. Then stand at a tall table by the giant windows and smile.

St Paul's Cathedral.

Its dome is a lid, installed so that God can lift the top off and sneak a peek at his laboratory ants. And when he puts the lid back on – usually quite quickly, because they're up to the same sycophantic shit as the last time he looked – the dome makes a bored clatter, just like a silver chafing dish.

The Millennium Bridge.

A river crossing that suffers from positive feedback for all the wrong reasons. The natural sway motion of people walking across it causes the bridge to rock from side to side. When they first opened it, people were hanging on to the sides as if it was an unravelling rope bridge. Children screamed. Mothers hugged their pushchairs. You'd think the walkway was building up to a three-sixty-degree flip.

I've never laughed so hard in my life.

Today, however, I don't see the humour in any of it. Today I swirl a meagre drib of 2009 Grüner that cost me the best part of a tenner around my wine glass, and wonder what the fuck is going on.

I look at my watch anxiously.

Noah Steensen is seven minutes late. When I phoned him, he said I wasn't to move, that he'd be here in twenty.

I'm regretting my decision to meet him.

So you have smiled at the cathedral's lid. Grinned at a kamikaze bridge. Now look left, have a giggle in the direction of Maida Vale.

Here Fake Alice could be turning up at a superstar's stucco mansion, waving an incriminating DVD, because a halfwit private investigator didn't know the client was a fraud, and to further compound things, contrived to fall in love with the target.

I am in love with Scott 'Scat' Delaney.

It's preposterous.

Did Fake Alice do it for money? Scott will be good for blackmail. But my client had bundles of cash. Even at the beginning of the case, when I was getting nowhere fast, payment was never an issue. She hurled the readies at me.

Forget it! I tell myself. *All is dandy in W9. Scott would have contacted me had anything unexpected happened.*

Yeah, right. As if the entrapped make contact with the bitches who've fucked them over. As if they don't spend the rest of their lives despising the very bones of you.

Suddenly I want my dad. London doesn't look fun, not even from here. It looks eerie and malevolent. I want Scott to turn up and sing to me, proper jazz, unrecognisable notes making the warmest of phrases.

'Misty', 'There'll Never Be Another You', 'What a Difference a Day Makes' . . .

I rub my eyes hard. The stimulation conjures a rich nebula on the inside of my eyelids, but its lifespan is short-lived. When I reopen my eyes, the stars clear, and Noah comes into focus.

'Fuck!' I jump.

He presses his back against the window and surveys the bar. His voice rumbles like an underground train. A Scottish one. 'Safety in numbers, huh?'

'You don't frighten me.'

Not seeing Scott Delaney for the rest of my days. That frightens me. Christ, I need another drink, I wave my purse at a bartender.

'What's with the accent?' I ask him. 'It's not like you're a proper Jock.'

He ignores my question. 'How did you get my number?'

'An illegal subscription to Equifax. Past addresses, telephone number, all PIs get themselves one of those. You know I'm a PI, right?' He fails even to look at me. 'Sorry, am I a voice in your head?'

Quite openly I scrutinise him.

Converse All Stars pumps and a skinny vintage suit – trendy garb, perfect for this place. He's made an effort, yet he doesn't fit in. Not one bit. Standing with his back to the view, to the capital, to all the bloody Sassenachs, he is angry, friendless and self-sufficient.

I decide I don't like him one bit.

'OK, I'll go first.' I drop my purse on the table. Place my fingertips together as if in prayer. Remember precisely what I deciphered from Zanna's notes.

'You were born in Dorset in 1979. Your sister, Hannah, came three years later. Your middle name is the same as your dad's – Eric. Your mum is called Elaine.'

'That all you got?' he says.

'On thirteenth February 1988, Eric died. The district of his death was also Dorset. It was the same day my mum disappeared, leaving a body in her Datsun Sunny 1200. His name was Eric. The evidence suggests the dead man was your father.'

'You don't know who I am, do you?'

'You're Eric's son. What do you want me to say? What I think happened? OK, I think they were having an affair – your dad and my mum. There was a suicide pact. My mum bottled out.' I wave my empty glass urgently at somebody, anybody. 'Are you actually all right, Noah – you know, in the head?'

I am apparently absurd. 'From the one with mental health issues.'

'Excuse me?'

'You know your dad used to let me sit on his lap and steer his car?'

Whoa there!

I put a cautionary finger in the air. *Dad let you steer the car? Dad didn't let me steer the car.*

'He let me do that a lot, drive his car. I suppose he felt bad.' Noah turns to scrutinise the view, but he doesn't stare at London. He looks far beyond it, past the horizon and all the way to Laurelbridge in Dorset. And as he ponders the distant past, I watch him throw his jaw aloft and to the left. Deftly his hair flicks itself up and away from his forehead.

The manoeuvre is as unique as a fingerprint, but for a moment I can't place it.

'Always did think you were better than me.'

'I'm sure I didn't.' I squint. 'Sorry, how do you know my dad?'

'They were friends. Our mums and dads.'

'No they weren't. I'd have remembered.'

'My dad didn't die in that car.'

'He did. There's a death certificate.' I embellish the truth. 'I've seen it.'

He shakes his blond head, each strand as fat as bear's fur. 'You saw *a* death certificate. My dad was alive and kicking until four months ago.'

'Are you sure?' I whisper.

'I married in March. He passed away one week later.'

What type of stalker is he? 'You're married? Does your wife know?'

'That he's dead?'

'That you're stalking me?'

He squints. 'Git tae fuck, I'm not stalking you.' Irritated, he pushes the sleeves of his suit up to the elbows. His forearms are the same sandy hue as his face.

Hold on . . .

I swallow a gasp.

You wore jeans, a salmon-pink T-shirt and a cream suit jacket with rolled-up sleeves.

He's still complaining. 'You and that superior fuckin' air.'

I squint at him. The boy in the *Miami Vice* jacket? This isn't at all how I remember you.

Your name was Junior.

'It's not possible,' I argue with him. 'My dad said Eric was the dead man. The coroner's report said he was the dead man. Dad wouldn't lie about that.'

Proven fact: Dad is a liar.

Noah blindly pushes my purse around the table. 'Sometimes, I guess, blood isn't thicker than water, huh?'

My dad said that – exactly that.

'It is, it *always* is!'

This is too much. I grab my purse from him, place a finger back in the air.

'I do not remember you.'

Because I assumed I'd be getting this information on my terms. It *has* to be on my terms. And I'm not ready. I wave him off, stare rigidly at Maida Vale.

He looks baffled, as if he assumed I'd be begging for the opportunity to have this conversation.

'We share a history neither of us understands,' he tells me urgently. I'm not looking at him, but I hear it – Noah Steensen needs answers as badly as I do. 'Mum, Dad, Hannah and me, we left for Scotland after the . . . you know.'

'No?'

'The *incident*.'

Oh, he tries to tempt me with facts, but I refuse to look at his face. It'll give me clues. I'll see answers in his expression. And I will discover whether my mother is dead or alive in my own time, thank you very much, without his opinions either way. I've only been waiting twenty-five years; what's another quarter-of-a-hundred.

'If our parents were such good friends, I'd remember you.'

I remember a boy I kissed in a pattern of eight, but he didn't look like you. He was between seven and nine. You're much, much older than that.

I see the delicate changes in the contours of Noah's face. The buccinator muscle contracts, as do the modiolus and the occipitofrontalis – I have wounded him and I'm ashamed. But this is *way* too much.

I stare at his pumps.

'Just like your dad. Balls all beef.'

'What did you just fucking say?'

But the boy in the *Miami Vice* jacket has had enough. He walks away forsaken.

I try to stare livid at his retreating back. But solitude hangs from him like a sodden cloak. I feel sorry for him, though I've no need – the pint-sized woman, the one who likes to sucker herself to his arm on canal boats, is suddenly beside him. She must have been waiting at the bar. Vigorously she rubs his forearm, and in response, Noah pats her small, slim hand rather tenderly. Her wedding ring shimmers under the bar's halogen lighting; that ring has not yet seen its first anniversary.

He really does have a wife.

I think back, try and remember how often I met the boy in the *Miami Vice* jacket. Junior. Everyone called him Junior; because he was a mini-me of a man who didn't die in my mum's car? We certainly only kissed the once – it was a one-afternoon stand – I know this because I was desperately disappointed. Back then, I'd have relocated to Xanadu if he'd asked me to. I was besotted.

Not now, though.

That's disappointing and unsettling. Isn't childhood the uninhibited truth? I think of my mum. Of her depression – the illness I don't remember seeing any evidence of. Ever. But Noah, the bastard, makes me rethink things; thoughts, truths, photographs, dreams, they get tangled over time. I'm becoming a less and less reliable witness.

No.

I put Noah – my first love – out of my mind. Vehemently I refuse to revisit what happened to Bambi, because *no way* – I did not sepia-tint her.

Mum's new car is called Sunny.

'It's been a total lifesaver,' she says.

And I think so too, because when she drops me at infants, I worry that she's being sad all day. Michael's conversation is not mature or hilarious like mine. And school is very hard work; sometimes I get too busy to think about her.

It worries me when I forget to think about her, because she might stop existing.

My teacher says I'm talking nonsense.

This is a Jesus fact: He looks after mums after they've dropped their children off. He knows how we kids feel because he's got a mum too. She's called the Virgin Mary. Jesus and the Virgin Mary are dead in heaven, which is exactly the same as being on earth only cloudier. And instead of a king and queen, you have God, Jesus and the Holy Spirit, who's also a Holy Ghost but a not scary one.

That's relieving news.

But to be on the safe side, I'm most happy about Sunny because it has magic powers.

This is what happens after my mum drops me at school and we've waved goodbye:

'Piccolina, I chug off down the road, left into Church Manor Way, my little car clattering and clinking, and I think, oh no, not the gasket. If the gasket goes, Datsun Sunny's a goner. Then, quite out of the blue, there's a flash. For one unsettling, terrifying moment I'm *blind*, Piccolina. Totally *blind*.'

She covers her face with her hands to show me what being blind looks like.

'Ever so slowly the darkness clears, and ahead . . . I see nothing but blue sky.'

I gasp. She does too.

'My, it's so beautiful. I look down, to my sides, above my head, and guess what I see?'

'Nothing,' I whisper dramatically, because she's told me this story fifty-hundred times before.

She nods, her eyes as big as ping-pong balls. '*Niente*. No car. Just fresh air beneath my feet, and sky all around. Oh, it smells fresh up there.'

'Can you see me on the ground?'

'You're small as a freckle.'

'How high are you?'

'A mile.'

'That's high. Why doesn't Michael get scared?'

'Florence, that's the strangest thing! He laughs and laughs like it's the best fun ever.'

This I'm not so happy about. 'How comes he gets to go with you when Sunny gets invisible?'

She thinks hard about this. I can see she's deciding whether to tell me something grown-up or not. 'OK,' she nods. 'Remember Austin, my first car?'

'No, I do not.' I shake my head.

'When you were a little girl, we'd go on missions all the

time. Austin was an older version of Sunny, but you work with the vehicles you're given . . .'

'I don't remember,' I tell her, definitely.

'And neither will Michael when he gets to five like you. Five is the age your memory gets wiped.'

I ask it maturely. 'Are you an alien?'

'Don't be a donkey,' she giggles. 'I'm a Libran.' She waves: I'm not to worry about that. 'It's something you're going to have to learn to live with.'

But I have a lot of questions. Where's Libra, for a start. 'Will I ever remember our missions?'

'Nope,' she says, no argument.

'What if I pray?'

Mum does her serious face. 'Please, Piccolina, the Lord has far more important things to deal with.'

I sulk because God would have definitely helped. 'Is your plane like Wonder Woman's?'

'Identical.' Now she leans in front of me and gives me strict instructions. 'It keeps me very busy during the days, which means you don't have to worry about me when you're at school. Not at all. Not ever.'

Get this straight. I am not silly. My teacher has gone and spoken to her. *Never* trust a teacher. *Never.* Not unless you've bumped your head or stapled your thumb.

Mum's still saying stuff.

'Sometimes I forget to think about you, I'm so busy. There's the odd moment I can't even remember your name.'

'Is it *totally* invisible, though? Because Wonder Woman's plane isn't. On the TV, you can see its invisibleness.'

With serious eyes she says, 'I got the newest edition.' And with that she hurries me up the stairs and into the bathroom.

'Now get in and wash all your nooks. I put the grown-up stuff in – bath salts and soothing muscle soak. Don't forget behind the ears.'

No-nonsense, she leaves the bathroom. End of conversation.

'What about candles?' I joke, like Dad does.

She doesn't laugh.

I count her footsteps. Just six. Not enough to get her anywhere.

I worry when she doesn't laugh at my jokes.

So I spy on her through the door crack. She is sitting on the top step of the stairs, all hunched up, her shoulders going up and down, which is what happens when you cry.

I shout in my cheekiest voice:

'If it's *totally* invisible, though, how can you see the steering wheel?'

Nothing.

It's her Latin temperament, and I hope I don't get one, because it makes you deaf. I know exactly what to do, though. I wash my nooks really fast and dry the front of me on a towel. I'm still damp on my back, but I don't tell her – she'll get worried about fungal infections.

Now I squeeze in next to her on the step and do my best not to shiver.

'Tell me about Auntie Carina Campanella from Monte San Savino in Italy,' I say strictly, pushing up her sleeve, tickling her arm with the tips of my short nails. Because that's what you have to do with people like Mum – keep them talking until your daddy gets home.

'I'll get myself a fucking drink, shall I?'

I jump out of my skin. Maeve stands in front of me. Dropping a black portfolio at my feet, she clicks the air for attention.

'What are you doing here?' I demand, looking around the bar.

'You're not answering your phone.'

'Err, because I don't want to talk to you. We're done, remember?'

'I popped by yours. Michael was there.'

'You met Michael? He didn't tell you where I was.'

'No, his dwarf did.'

Sébastien. Furious, I nod at the leather folder discarded on the floor. My voice is flat: 'You submitting something to the Tate?' Absently I kick the folder. 'I seem to remember you have an excellent line in doodles. *Maeve Loves Florence TLF*, that sort of thing.'

'Should I hate or pity you?'

'Either/or.' I take a large gulp of air from my empty glass.

I don't look out of the window, seven storeys down on to the pavement, to see the direction in which Noah Steensen walks. It's only been twenty-five years since Bambi disappeared – suddenly it's too soon for truths.

'A glass of what she's drinking,' Maeve tells a waiter. 'Her tab.'

I frown.

She scowls back. 'I find myself in a predicament. A man turned up at my flat this evening.'

'Anyone I know?'

'Intimately, I imagine. He had a pulse.'

I laugh through my nose. This is what I liked the most about Maeve. When we were sleeping together, she tried hard to belittle me. Trouble was, I could make her feel smaller. Not because I was cleverer – but because she loved me more.

When your heart gets involved, it puts you at a disadvantage. I warned her at the time.

A waiter arrives with her drink. She downs it in one.

'Another,' she calls after him.

This surprises me. Maeve's not a big drinker.

'The man who came to my apartment spoke very little

English. He simply passed me a folder. That one.' She nods at the floor. 'Then he left.'

I look at the folder properly.

'Oh, he attempted to string a sentence together,' she continues. 'Told me something about Callaghan and his employer being good friends. I got the gist. Not much else.'

'Callaghan? As in your boss, Callaghan?'

'As in Toby Callaghan, yes.'

My heart doubles its pace.

Toby Callaghan: founder, chairman and CEO of the Daily Newspaper Corporation. A rich and insanely powerful man. In my whole life, I have not spoken to him once. Not ever.

'Don't pretend this is news to you.'

'It is,' I say unequivocally.

Maeve doesn't believe me.

'My predicament is this, Florence. Your man at my door handed me a scoop – a bloody marvellous scoop, probably the best of my career. Any newspaper in the world would jump all over it. But they can't have it. It has been gifted exclusively to me. *Me*, Florence. How fortunate. And for that it appears I have to thank you.'

'I don't know what you're talking about.'

But I can guess.

Oh fuck, I can guess.

'This scoop will secure my paper even more firmly as the UK market leader. I will be hated and lauded by the public in equal measure. Toby Callaghan will give me a bonus.' She rubs her face roughly. A clump of mascara is left on the apex of her left cheek.

'You don't want to run it?' My voice is small, hopeful.

'No, I fucking do not want to run it.'

'So don't,' I beg.

She's confused. 'You went to Toby Callaghan personally.

Callaghan didn't want the story to leak. He sent the foreigner and his photos directly to me.'

'Maeve, this is nothing to do with me.'

'Right. So you don't know the guy at my door?' She scoffs. 'Probably sensible employing a non-English-speaker – he doesn't have to listen to your incessant bullshit. You do know that when I told you to find yourself a celebrity and take a shedload of photos, I was being facetious? Or are you actually autistic?'

It's a low blow, but I don't react. Instead I look down at the black portfolio. I should pick it up, but there's no need.

In less than ten hours, the photographs of Scott and me have winged their way to the chief executive and editor of the second-biggest-selling newspaper on the planet.

I plead. 'Don't run it.'

Maeve looks at me, baffled. 'This is your revenge. I wouldn't give you a column. You've got yourself in the papers off your own steam – and for a lot longer than fifteen minutes.' She downs her second glass. 'Congratulations. Florence Love, as recognisable as the Pope. As infamous as Myra fucking Hindley.'

'Myra Hindley killed *children*.'

'Why is everything a power struggle with you?' She bangs the table hard. 'You've been back in my life for two minutes and already I'm exhausted.'

This is as close as I've seen Maeve Rivers come to tears. Not that she actually has tears in her eyes; they're not even moist. But that clump of mascara, it looks like a Pierrot tear.

I put a hand on hers. 'Has it upset you, seeing me with someone else?'

'No!' she shrieks. The bar goes quiet. 'He's a friend, Florence.'

'Who?'

'Scott.'

I shake my head. 'His friends call him Scat.'

'Like you, you mean?' Maeve's look implies I'm ridiculous. 'Elle is a nice woman.'

'You know his girlfriend?'

'*Of* her, yes.' She comes clean: 'In the vast fabric of things, I barely know Scott, but I've met a lot of people in this business. There are some people who just don't deserve this.'

'Who don't deserve *what*? An exposé?' My laugh is a little hysterical. 'You mean, the hell you let loose on other perfectly nice people of a Sunday morning?'

'Don't go all Mother Teresa; you've played your part in the past.'

She's right. I have. But that's not the point.

'I didn't know you knew him, a bit,' I say.

'Why would you?'

Jealousy is wholly inappropriate. 'Anybody would think you were in love with him or something.'

'No, I am not in love with him. What is wrong with you?' She actually does an impression of me. 'Sane person fact: people sometimes meet other people they really respect and don't want to fuck over.'

My laugh is sad.

Nobody gets me.

'Who was the man at my door?' she demands. 'The man who gave me this folder?'

'I don't know.' I smile thinly at the other punters. 'Scott really was different, you know.'

'Like I was different?'

'Never once did I say you were different.' That sounded bad.

'Do you take photographs of everybody you sleep with?' The patrons are rapt.

'I didn't take photos of you and me,' I say between gritted teeth and a fake smile.

'You said you did.'

'I know what I said. I lied. I never would. Yes, because we were different.' This time I mean it. 'Nobody paid me a bean to kiss you with tongues for five seconds. I did that and a host of other sexual activities through choice.'

'You blackmailed me, Flo. You blackmailed *me*?' She looks so vulnerable, it takes ten years off her. I can't hide the shame I suddenly feel.

But I thought you didn't care.

Grabbing her hands hard, I hold them firmly in mine. Quietly and urgently, I speak:

'Somebody's been watching me, Maeve. I told you when I visited that my place had been broken into, remember? Then someone – a woman – employed me to entrap Scott Delaney. It was his girlfriend.'

'Elle?'

'Yes. Only it wasn't Elle. It was a woman called Alice.' My explanation is feeble. 'A very clever woman out to make a few quid.'

Maeve shakes her head. I'm wrong. 'We've been given the scoop for free. Did you meet her – the very clever woman?'

I nod.

'Did she look like Elle?'

'We were advised that Elle was Scott's sister.'

'What?'

'Let's just say Michael fucked up. Suffice to say, Scott and I became friends. Like you and Scott.' I squeeze her fingers earnestly. 'Me and Scott had stuff in common. Yes, we shared a moment – just like you and I shared a moment – but I never intended for anybody to know about it.' I look at Maida Vale. 'It belonged to us.'

'It belongs to Toby Callaghan now.'

'Make it go away.'

'If I don't print it, someone else will – the *Sun, USA Today, China Daily*.'

'Burn the folder.'

'Because we don't live in the technological age? This isn't the movies; it'll be on somebody's hard drive. I'll lose my job. It's too big a scoop.' Agitated, she continues, 'I'm not allowed to have friends, you see. I have so few fucking friends. That's what happens when you sell your soul to light entertainment.'

'We were friends, you and me,' I tell her.

Her response is monotone; her fingers become limp in mine. 'Friendship and sex don't mix.'

That's what I told her when I was breaking it off. When she was grappling for excuses to stop me from vanishing from her life.

Let's be fuck-buddies. No? Platonic friends, then. OK, none of the above. Just take this cheque.

Yes, I was the catalyst for a brilliant woman's foolish behaviour. Yet right now I don't feel sorry, not for her. Right now I think about Scott. My regret is reserved solely for him.

I finally nod. 'The foreign guy who approached Callaghan, who gave you the folder – did he leave a name, a contact number?'

She nods at my feet.

For a while I look down at the leather file. Then I pull it on to the bar top and flick through the photos.

There are twenty stills. Each has been taken from the DVD Michael handed to Fake Alice. Some shots are from above. Some are from the side. They are grainy, but clear enough for purpose. And they read beautifully – like a storyboard for a screenplay about a sordid affair.

In the last cellophane wallet I see a card. I read and reread the name, number and office address through the transparent plastic.

Then I snap the folder shut.

Maeve is right. I know the man who knocked at her door all right. In fact I know an astonishing amount about him.

His full name is Gustav Aart Nijstad. He is an extraordinarily dedicated employee of the Netherlands government, and particularly of Minister Pieter de Groot. A bullet-saver who would triple-jump into hot oil rather than allow anyone to compromise his blubbery boss.

And his blubbery boss – I know him especially intimately.

Entrapment 101 Tip #7: Become fluent in the silent language

Kinetics is now your mother tongue. Refer to the case study below. Note how plainly the minister told me he wanted sex.

Case 0134/Operation de Groot

8.25 p.m. Minister de Groot turned his knees to face me, indicating that tonight was a goer. He stated that he'd returned from a day's coarse fishing in Horsmonden. I said I preferred to fly-fish, having taken it upon myself to read *A Complete Guide to Fly Fishing*. His response was: *That is unusual.* I lied: *I grew up in Scotland, it was on the school curriculum.* He did not ask me to do the accent. Just as well: I have a non-musical ear. The target then stated that he collected vintage fishing tackle, his latest purchase being a Coxon Aerial reel. Fully apprised of this fact, I gasped: *That's extremely rare.* He smiled, nodded and partook in subconscious erotic touching, i.e. swept the hair from his forehead, stroked his bottom lip.

20.49 p.m. I stated I'd once played at a golf course in Spijk. This was a green-light statement – the target flung golfing facts like confetti, his final statement being *I have a handicap of twelve.* I sat with a mischievous look on my face. Shutting one eye, he asked for mine. *Eighteen*, I lied. He clapped, relieved, then undertook symbolic stripping, i.e. undid the top button of his shirt, loosened his tie, pulled up his sleeves.

21.15 p.m. The target is soon to visit Vilnius, in Lithuania. *I own half the city*, he boasted, rubbing a thigh. *Like real-life Lithuanian Monopoly,* I said, placing a flirtatious hand on his arm. Accurately I counted to three in my head. He reciprocated within the statutory ten minutes.

Other ways the minister told how he craved me:

1. A slight nostril flare each time he took a peek at my chest.

2. A tilted head when I spoke.

3. The triangulation of eye contact (i.e. three seconds of direct eye contact, followed by a lingering gaze at the nose, lips and chin consecutively. It is very sexy indeed. When undertaken by someone hot).

Disappointing fact: entrapping attractive men for money rarely happens. If it's a steamy, meaningless and slightly life-threatening encounter you're after, get on Tinder. Entrapment is your day job. End of.

Gedogen

Pieter de Groot, the Dutch Minister for Security and Justice, has quite a talent for retribution.

I imagine Gustav as a grovelling golem:

But how, sire, do we kill an entrapment specialist?

And Minister de Groot, Jabba-the-Hutt-like, his voice more subterranean than the mesosphere:

We put her face on every front page of every newspaper in the entire world.

If I was a better sport, I'd applaud Minister de Groot's hubris, certainly his ability to avenge so inventively. But the ruined are rarely dignified in defeat.

And all he had to do was hire one of my own kind. Alice pointed directions to the edge of the cliff. Like a lemming, I pootled towards my professional and personal nosedive.

The worst thing: the bastard taught me a valuable lesson about the Dutch. Namely their ability to think outside the box. *Gedogen*, they call it. It has no direct translation in the modern world, it being a mindset exclusive entirely to the Dutch. It's all very existential, but put plainly, finishing me off would have been very un-Dutch indeed. They prefer to accommodate tricky conduct, work with it, tolerate it; in essence they *permit* it. Doesn't mean they can't have a little laugh at your expense, though – especially when they're the Minister for Security and Justice.

It was Pieter de Groot who hired Alice. Alice (or whatever her real name is) had inside information on Scott and his secret girlfriend, who knows how – like me she's a private investigator; she'll have sources, illicit methods, tabloid connections. She and her client then played me at my own game, meting out the ultimate wrist-slap.

What a hoot. It is the most infuriatingly cool and ironic revenge ever.

I should walk away. Nod wryly at de Groot's chutzpah. Concede: *This time I got beat at my own game and, in the process, was imparted an interesting socio-cultural lesson.*

Trouble is, Minister de Groot's revenge is not at all English.

My dad will see me kissing a man with tongues. And English dads must never see that. They are very anal and cannot cope with the thought of their daughters getting up to rudies, even with their husbands. Catholic dads are worse. And then you have dads from Laurelbridge. Add to this the fact that some dads (i.e. mine) have a climbing-wall of newspapers and gossip magazines for sale in their post office. The people of east Dorset will be queuing around the block, the morning paper rush akin to the Boxing Day sale at Harrods.

I can see Dad now, shoulders slumped in his glass booth, the seemingly friendly queue as innocuous as a gathering of bull sharks.

Here is a list of people who will pore over the practical demonstration of what I, Florence Love, do for a living:

1. My dad.

2. The residents of Laurelbridge.

3. The residents of the south-west of England.

4. The residents of the entire United Kingdom.

5. The European Union.

6. The United Nations.

7. The rest of modern civilisation.

8. God.

Every man I've ever entrapped will perform a joyous Mexican wave. Except Scott Delaney; he'll sit out that celebration. Return to his fortified box. Tell the facilitators of his cottage industry never to let him out again.

Maybe my mum will see me in action too.

My heart clatters south.

The Dutch should be envied. *Gedogen* is a formidable tool.

And so I am alone at last.

Kneeling as if in genuflection on my mattress, my elbows and chin on the windowsill, I look across at the rooftop where Alice camped out. She gleaned my routine, listened in on my conversations and wrote reports to Minister de Groot apprising him of my most private moments.

Today Florence is showering . . . reading . . . practising flirtatious banter with an imaginary Scott Delaney . . . working on her cockney accent with its glottal stops and double negatives . . . taking class Bs . . . talking to the little dead Gran that lives on her shoulder . . . singing . . . crying . . . masturbating.

The ill-mannered bitch even read my most cherished chick lit. *I* don't even read my most cherished chick lit.

Neither does my mum.

I punch a hole clean through the window pane.

On returning from the Tate Modern earlier, I filled in Michael and Sébastien. They left with varying expressions of disbelief on their faces. From this windowsill I watched them walk quickly from the building in hearty conference, hand-in-hand like father and son, or owner and chimpanzee, or my beautiful brother and an Addams Family pet.

There was a time when my brother would have chosen to stay with me.

I have three choices.

Choice Number One: kill myself forthwith. This idea is scratched almost instantly. There's a very good reason atheists never cross the road, there being no such thing as the other side – which is not a joke, but a dreadful truth.

I inspect my bruised knuckles. My choku-zuki was a corker: the skin has not split.

Choice Number Two: disappear to Manchester. Change my name via deed poll to Anne Bland. Dye my hair ginger. Stop wearing make-up from the earthy and coral palettes; replace it with rosy and violet tones. Affect a limp. Wear polo necks and A-line skirts. Become a (slightly) less attractive forensic psychologist. Giggle whenever anybody says *Know who you remind me of?* Admit they're not the first to say it. Then mutter things ever so wistfully: *If only I had shared a moment with Scott Delaney; I'd have never let go.*

Looking into the street below, I'm pleased to see people going about their business without injury or laceration.

Choice Number Three: man up, take it on the chin and do the right thing by all those involved.

But most especially, do the right thing for Scott.

'Morning, Harry.' I nod at Maeve's husband when he answers the door, then walk straight past him into their flat. I glance at rooms.

'She's at work,' he shouts after me.

Harry's American. I never knew that. Then again, Maeve avoided conversations about her nearest and dearest.

'Anything I can help you with?' he asks.

'It's seven in the morning,' I tell him.

His tone is extremely good-natured considering I've gate-crashed his breakfast. 'Thanks for the update.'

'So where is she?'

'In meetings, I guess.'

'She's not answering her phone.'

'Something to do with the meetings?'

I've forgotten my manners. I put a hand on my chest. 'I'm Florence.'

'I guessed.'

I look Harry up and down.

Unfazed, he smiles back. Reading glasses perched on the end of his nose, a tumbler of fresh orange juice in his large tanned hand, stripy dressing gown, slippers ribbed like corduroy – Harry Rivers looks thoroughly minted.

'She's at the office then?' I ask.

'Florence,' he says. 'Leave a message on her cell. I'm sure she'll get back to you when she can.'

This is the first time we've ever chatted, and I find I don't mind Harry at all. His breath smells of porridge and he seems unflappable in a thoroughly dependable type of way. He's older than Maeve – fifty-three at a guess – but broad-shouldered and macho. I can see the attraction, if you like that all-American Marlboro Man sort.

'It's urgent,' I tell him.

'I'll be sure to tell her you called by.'

'Right.'

I leave. Halfway along the communal corridor, I realise I didn't hear the front door shut behind me. I look back. Harry stands in the hall. A shoulder against the wall, he sips his juice, watches me leave.

'Everything OK?' I frown.

'Oh sure. I'm just seeing.'

'Just seeing what?'

'What the fuss is about.'

I shake my head, because I don't understand.

He continues: 'Dutch ministers, Scott Delaney, my wife . . . You're a fine-looking woman, but I was imagining more of a *siren*.'

Heat sweeps up my neck and into my cheeks. Loyal as St Peter, I scoff and shake my head. Harry's mistaken.

'Oh, don't go and spoil it,' he pleads. 'Do not tell me she made you up to titillate me. The escapades in her car, your brother's flat, my bed, the kitchen table, the alley behind Smithfield Bar and Grill. She is my wife.'

Putting his hands in the air, he pretends he's treading on eggshells. He's not. He's being a bitch.

'That's what husbands and wives do – fulfil each other's fantasies. She does a lot of that extracurricular stuff for me. Name me one man who doesn't get off on hearing the juicy details afterwards. She's allowed only women, mind you. That's the golden rule.'

'You're sick.'

'Oh, I think I'm a pretty healthy red-blooded male.'

'Well unfortunately for you, Harry, she fell in love with one of her extracurricular activities.'

His smile is delightful. 'You gals do love to involve the mind. But the mind is just an erogenous zone. As fickle and easily manipulated as the neck or the small of your back or your toes or the nipples . . .'

When he turns to go back inside, I see Harry Rivers from the side. He has a hard-on beneath his dressing gown. He doesn't try to hide it or rearrange it, just wears it as matter-of-factly as a pregnant lady wears her bump.

Before quietly shutting the door, he clarifies: 'She paid you, right? Five thousand. For services rendered. That's a whole lotta love.'

'It was a *bribe*, you mug, to get me to stay.'

I waste my breath. He's gone back in.

'We were fuck-buddies,' I tell an imaginary Harry whilst marching towards Regent's Park tube station.

I imagine his response:

Don't try and sex it up. We're swingers, Maeve and me. You were our plaything.

'It was private. We were friends with benefits. She fell for me. I did the honourable thing. I finished it because I didn't want to lead her on.'

You took our money.

On the underground train I mutter other things. Things like:

'She played you like a fool, Harry Rivers.'

And:

'The Poet is Noah Steensen, who is also the boy in the *Miami Vice* jacket!'

I don't say it loudly enough for anyone to hear, just enough for the camera to see my lips move – the camera I imagine is attached to the external chasse of the tube train, its lens staring in at me through the filthy window like a daredevil voyeur. They can add my voiceover later. For the moment I work my medium-close-up.

The *Daily News* building is in Thomas More Square in the East End. There I slink to the main desk and tell a security guard that Maeve Rivers is expecting me and, therefore, *will* be seeing me.

The man, however, is a unicorn. He issues instructions perfunctorily. Anyone would think there's not an alluring woman in the vicinity.

'Take a seat. I'll let her know you're here.'

Obediently I move to an arrangement of circular pouffes. They make exactly the same shape as bacteria in the streptococcus genus. My mum would have hated it. I sit in one of the seats and instantly sink towards the floor.

Feet perpendicular to my thighs, I put an elbow on the pouffe closest to my head. It would appear to passers-by that I am simply chillaxing on a chaise longue.

No worries. I won't be here for long.

For an hour and ten minutes I watch the electric doors slide open and shut from the streptococcus pouffes.

A lot of people come and go. The Unicorn points most of them straight to the lift. As they pass me, they do not look – I'm ensconced in soft furnishings, plus they haven't the foggiest idea who I am.

It's disconcerting that, for the briefest second, I smile bitterly at their ignorance.

Not yet, you don't know me.

Not yet . . .

Because I was sure I was above the celebrity-obsessed culture. Yes, a fast slice of excitement is the birthright of every twenty-first-century *Homo sapien*, but that does not entail getting our tits out for the lads, appearing on reality shows, or bragging how we snogged a footballer or *the* most kind and harmless jazz singer ever to be afflicted with Stockholm Syndrome.

See what I've become?

I glance at my watch. Come on, Maeve. Why haven't I been ushered up to her office?

One million per cent fact: Maeve did love me once.

Two million per cent fact: any relationship is only ever your personal interpretation of it. That interpretation is not two-dimensional or four-dimensional, let alone the eleven dimensions espoused by string theorists. Normal people in normal relationships don't see the world from many angles, like Picasso, or Harry the Husband.

Maybe I misread Maeve.

I imagined she spent her evenings pining for me, reminiscing secretly and ever so romantically about our private liaisons. Yes, she reminisced all right – just out loud and for the benefit of the fucking Marlboro Man.

By the time the Unicorn issues me with directions to the top floor, my smile is as cold as his.

Not yet, you don't know me, mister. Not yet.

The Scoop

Maeve sits on the edge of her desk, her arms folded defensively.

'Toby Callaghan's like a man with two dicks. The story runs this Sunday whether we like it or not.'

'Good,' I say, folding my arms too. 'Let's turn the perspective of the piece on its head.'

She juts her chin belligerently. 'Go on.'

'How about I sell you my story? You've got the photos for free. Fuck it, I can give you more where they came from. But throw this into the mix: my exclusive. I'll tell you – the *Daily News* – everything. There is one condition only. It has to be in *my* words. Nobody can argue with me. If they do, we will sue the arse off of them. I was there. I have the VT. Make Callaghan's day, publish those photos de Groot's bullet-saver dropped off. Let's just rewrite the speech bubbles.'

Maeve squints.

'Those photos,' I point dismissively at her desk – at the twenty prints of me and Scott. 'OK, at first glance they tell the obvious story, the one your readership has heard a thousand times before. That's a shame – what with the real story being *so* much better.'

'Go on,' says Maeve.

The real story.

I, Florence Love, a specialist in entrapment and other generic private investigation duties, was duped by an impostor. The impostor was a PI hired by an ex-target who wanted revenge. On the instructions of said impostor, I pursued a successful musician – watched him, followed him, sneaked a route into his glamorous world and made myself a regular. Finally I attempted to decimate his up-and-coming marriage by kissing him for five seconds with tongues.

'Bored,' sings Maeve – but she's not, I can tell.

He kissed *me*. Why? Because I got him drunk, manipulated him, broke him down, then made him feel safe. He sang to me and I saw his soul. Seeing someone's soul is big shit. Especially when it's benevolent. It made me shy. Too shy to make the first move myself.

'That has never happened to me before,' I tell Maeve with serious eyes. 'I am a professional when it comes to seduction.'

'You're certainly something else.'

'Thank you.' I nod graciously and continue.

We played Strip Shithead. Not because he wanted to at first, but because I hustled him – wore some puppy-pug eyes and made out I was shite at parlour games. He is man. Man must go war. Not for a moment did he think he'd lose. Ending the evening in his pants was simply not a possibility.

He ended the evening in his pants.

And if you look closely at one photo, you'll see my brother's knee. *That's* how innocent it was. I had a blood relative in the room.

'Yardy ya,' she says, but her eyes are smiling.

Scott and I kissed. That photo cannot be explained away. Our smooch lasted for longer than the obligatory five seconds. It did involve tongues. Unfortunately it came to an abrupt end less than twenty seconds in.

'Why?' asks Maeve.

'Because Scott giggled and accidentally blew snot out of his nose.'

She laughs, unfolds her arms and leans forward.

'He also said, *This feels really weird, doesn't it?*'

'Did it?'

'To me it was as perfect as a kiss can get.'

Can we stop doing this now? Scott asked.

I was ashamed. Like I was a teacher seducing a GCSE student. But I realised soon enough that Scott didn't see it like that at all. Mainly he was mortified that he might have offended me. But truth is, he was too in love with his girl-friend. That's exactly what he said. That he knew now for definite he was never going to stray. He tried hard to make me feel special. I was the One, he said. The One who had enabled him to come to a wonderful conclusion – he was a one-woman-only man.

His exact words:

I'm so glad we kissed, Flo-Lo. Imagine spending a lifetime with someone, but always wondering – is there someone comparable?

There was a compliment there. I was trying to find it when he asked me to tell him about big words I knew.

I taught him the meaning of *withershins* (anticlockwise), *incunabula* (any book published before 1500) and *pusillanimous* (being a complete pussy).

Like me, he decided he was going to read the dictionary whilst doing a number two. The medical journals sounded like hard work, though, and whilst he respected my desire to self-educate, he'd give them a miss. That made us belly-laugh for a good twelve minutes.

The evening drew to a close.

We knew our friendship was in its winter. But it was as real as any other friendship either of us had had before. He'd write a song about me, he said; a song as poignant as 'Ben' by Michael Jackson. *That's a song about a rat*, he said, *but you know what I mean.*

I did.

Emotions ran high. Scott wanted to leave. We knew we would never see one another again. So I dug in my pocket, pulling free my unlucky twopenny coin.

I knelt before him.

Like Dad had done twenty-five years before, I held that coin between reverent finger and thumb, like a priest proffering communion bread. Scott didn't say *Amen* and stick out his tongue, although for the tiniest moment I think he wondered if that was the correct response.

Then I explained in a voice deserving of choral accompaniment:

It is extremely rare, Scott. A collector's item. Like a four-leaf clover. Or a Kabbalistic amulet.

'Then what happened?' she asks, uninterested in the backstory of my coin.

He listened to me, bitch. I told him a very private story. And he listened.

Her indifference smarts.

I folded his fingers around the twopence piece. *Take it,* I told him. Because I wanted to give him a little piece of me. And a little piece of that night – the night he realised he worshipped his girlfriend and would never play away because no one, not even I, was comparable.

And for me, giving him that coin represented a fresh start, new beginnings.

'How much do you want for your story?' Maeve teetered on the edge of her desk, one eye shut.

'I don't want money.'

'What, then?' she demands.

'A job for Michael – on the TV. An advert. Whatever you can swing. But not any old shit. Something with a storyline. Like the Oxo family.'

We shake hands on it.

'And what about you?' she asks before I leave.

'What about me?'

Maeve assumes it's rhetorical.

Do Lay Me, Scat!

Scott Delaney, jazz superstar, has been the subject of a sensational honeytrap. Florence Love, a former post office worker from east Dorset, attempted to seduce the global icon at the request of a crazed female fan. Yet Love's charms fell short and Scott failed to Scat-ter his seed, instead declaring his love for percussionist and current squeeze Elle Mueller.

Photographs taken during the honeytrap show the pop star, a notoriously private man, drunk and in a state of undress. Harvey Cadwalader, spokesperson for Mr Delaney, stated, 'Miss Love led Scat to believe she was his friend. He is deeply hurt, disappointed and embarrassed for his partner and family.'

Speaking exclusively to the *Daily News*, the duplicitous double-divorcee, 34-28-35, tells the story of her hapless attempts to bag a global pop sensation (pages 6–11).

On Sunday 27 July, my face appeared on the front page of a major tabloid.

By the end of August, I was global.

The world was kinder to me than I deserved. This I put down to two factors. One, everyone loves Jessica Rabbit – the range of cheesy one-liners and an endearing splodge of self-effacement. Two, under no circumstances did I let my brain loose on them – my glial cells were kept tightly under wraps. There are enough deep women in the world, Maeve told me; let the ugly ones appear on *Newsnight*.

The paparazzi arrived on the rooftop opposite for a while. A few crazy fans played knock-down ginger on my door buzzer.

The deal was that I would play the game for four weeks only.

Maeve agreed. One month was more than enough time for the media to fine-tune my caricature.

Then the story died down.

Of course I was offered TV interviews, a book deal, a column in a lads' mag, a spot on *Celebrity Big Brother*. I refused them all. They didn't want truths. They wanted wank-fodder. How ironic: they asked the questions people actually wanted the answers to . . .

Have you ever had a threesome? Who's the least attractive person you've shagged? If your mother was about to be murdered – a gruesome, strung-out, tortuous death, which you'd be forced to witness – and the only way you could save her life was by *doing it* with her, would you?

Nonetheless, I rubbed Maeve's face in my potential, journalistically speaking.

Diary of a Honeytrapper. A PI blog. I am so current, Maevie. Now do you understand what I was offering you? We live in a biological world. Humans are programmed to value one function above all others. Sex. It figures there will always be a market for women like me.

Women like me.

Regarding the details of the scoop itself, Maeve and I arrived at an understanding. One that soothed her conscience. One that soothed mine. And in so doing, it created a new respect between us.

Still we regard one another with lifted chins, squinty eyes and karate hands at the ready. People as pathological as Maeve struggle to emerge from a relationship like ours with dignity intact.

The Marlboro Man can shove it up his arse. His wife still adores me.

I didn't go to Manchester – though I intend to one day, watch me.

I went back home to Laurelbridge for a while and told my dad everything. My job. Scott Delaney. Pieter de Groot. It went down like a nail bomb.

A wander around the village when the story broke and I saw he'd get over it quick enough. The village women awarded me the status of celebrity. It made Dad a little bit famous too. The women saw beyond the unexplained disappearance of his wife. His daughter was home-grown Dorset talent. A girl they'd always known was destined for something. They didn't know what, mind you. Certainly they had no idea it was to kiss Scott Delaney for less than twenty seconds with tongues. And now they wanted a piece of me too.

Then you had the Sunday supplements.

They gushed about what an honest man Scott Delaney was. An old-fashioned icon, easily led, but hopelessly in love with his secret girlfriend. My exposé did his reputation the world of good. I imagine his captors thought about letting him out more often.

Loaded magazine and *Cosmo* sexed up 1980s articles on *Can a man and woman ever be friends?*

Err, I'd like to think *yes*.

I never heard from Scott Delaney again.

He and Elle appeared to weather the storm. The girlfriend nobody knew about got the sympathy vote. He never went to the Urban Music Awards – it transpired it wasn't his sort of gig. And they never got engaged, Scott and Elle. Not when women worshipped the almost-unfaithful pop icon more than ever, because what's not to love about a man who's a squidge left of fallible. Or maybe he was unable to commit, what with me haunting a painfully romantic cranny in his brain.

Pieter de Groot.

I didn't name him as the international politician who set me up. I entrapped him, he outed me, my career for the moment was over. We are quits. However, should the DVD materialise on the internet or any further dirt on me arise, I will name him – tell the world about our evening together. Maeve forwarded him that warning via Gustav the bullet-saver.

The minister and I reached a truce.

And my mother . . .

She stayed characteristically quiet. No *Con8ratulations* cards were slipped under the door. For a while I wondered if the birthday card – the one that said *Thinkin8 of you* – had been a bonus rabbit punch from Minister de Groot. But fake cards from dead mothers is piss-poor form, *gedogen*-speaking.

And so for a while, I put my mother and Eric Steensen to one side; and Noah, especially Noah. There's only so much even I can deal with at once.

A Death

'Hiya, sexy. Fancy entrapping me today?'

Chinchilla Guy has become impossible, though the spineless moron still ignores me when his girlfriend's around. In fact, when the girlfriend's around, she's the one who does the smiling. Because we're friends, it would seem – now that she's read about me in the paper. To her family and colleagues, we're probably besties, though we've only ever exchanged a few words.

And to Chinchilla Guy – as long as she is nowhere in the building – I am fair game.

'Go fuck yourself,' I tell him.

'Why would I when I've got you next door?' He watches me Chubb-lock my front door and disappear down the stairs.

I don't slink. I do an ugly stomp.

Still he calls after me: 'I'm game, whenever you are. You can trap my honey for free!'

Like I paid *them* for the pleasure. Fuckwit.

Today's plan of action: to get out of the flat and visit the office.

I haven't been there for a couple of months. Haven't been anywhere much for a bit; have kept myself to myself.

I'm nervous at first. But the bearded boys at the front desk are kind, uninterested or have been quarantined in a lunar receiving lab for the last forty days – if they recognise me, they don't let on. The old people are equally impassive. Researching the dead *and* noticing a globally renowned private investigator is, for them, an unrealistic ask – neurodegenerative fact.

It feels just like the old days.

I breathe in the air, the smell of old paper as consoling as ever. I'm safe here.

I see Zanna and shoulder-barge her fondly. 'Wazzup?'

As soon as she faces me, I see her grief. Her eyes are milky blue, like she's got cataracts; her face is ashen.

'What's happened?' I demand.

'It's Norman.' She doesn't have to say anything else.

I feel unexpectedly distraught. In fact I actually have to stop myself from weeping. I hardly knew the man at all. Truth be told, he was one of my least favourite old people. Not because he wasn't delightful – which he wasn't – but because he was an adulterer who loved the sound of his own voice.

'What did he die of?' I ask.

A hand on mine, she addresses me as if I'm liable to faint. 'A broken heart.'

Christ. I hold on to the table. 'His wife, the French one – she died?'

Zanna nods.

'When?'

'Nineteen ninety-three.'

I stand up straight. 'That was over twenty years ago.'

Her voice is small, desolate. 'Norm never got over it.'

The guilt arrives.

I should have shown more interest in his stories. He wasn't a philanderer. He was a prisoner of war who escaped Fritz twice, once with half a leg, the other time with a bullet in his skull. He joined the French Resistance, lived in a coffin, fell in love with a French farmer's daughter whom he brought back to England, married and impregnated. They had a girl because he was virile and only virile men have girls.

'His life was like something out of a movie, only real,' I tell Zanna. 'If only he hadn't repeated his stories a trillion times. The drama of the piece waned.'

Zanna pulls her small crocheted cardigan tight around her heart, all-seeing of the past, looking blindly into a corner. She thinks I'm puerile, I can tell.

Yet her eyes ask a final favour of me: 'The funeral – it's this Friday.'

Sash window open, I inhale an autumn breeze from my top-floor flat. It smells of hot pastries, hot petrol and the imminent promise of cold, sunny mornings.

I hear the hee-haw of police cars, squeaky bus brakes, the unfailing whoosh of traffic, angry voices on the street below, ethnic diversity homogenised by the universal language of *fuck you*.

'Fuck you!' 'No, fuck you!' 'No, fuck you!'

The venom used to serve as a genial cattle prod – it reminded me I was not alone. Today the noise is vapid, like it's happening for somebody else's benefit.

This used to be my film set. I was the star of the show.

Nobody spies from the rooftop facing me – a pointless eyesore now: powerful men don't use it as a platform from which to seek a brutal revenge. My days as Isabella Purdy-Valentine are over. I'm somebody else now, available for public consumption. People don't want to harm me. They want to be my friend but without actually being my friend.

I know which I find most depressing.

A computer trill; an email.

Re: My freind missing
Wednesday 24/9/14 13.38 p.m.
From: tarikma68@yahoo.co.uk
To: info@londonpiservices.uk.net

Dear Sir,
    My freind leef Brazil. He in Italy and join Mafiosa.
I wonder if you do cheep deel to find person that join
Mafiosa?
    Yours sincerly
    Tarik Mohammad Amazigh

The man is incorrigible, yet never fails to raise a smile. I
am about to write a response when there's a knock at the
door. I pull out my pepper spray. I'm not scared, just aware
that Chinchilla Guy is the civil-servant type nobody ever
suspected capable of raping and murdering his next-door
neighbour.

Looking through the peephole, I can't see a soul.

'Who is it?' I call.

Sébastien takes a step back, tilts his head up and shakes
a carrier bag. 'Got you some shopping,' he shouts through
the hole meant for eyes.

Door open, he walks straight past me and puts food in
my cupboards.

Since the Scott Delaney exposé, Sébastien has ensured
I'm eating properly. I have no idea why. Twice a week he
turns up, articulating clearly as if I'm hard of hearing. He
also does the washing-up and picks my undies up off the
floor. It's like I've won a Canadian boy scout – a sinister
one, who most likely spends his days off working as the
harbinger of evil.

'There's no need,' I tell him.

'It passes the time,' he says.

His stutter has disappeared entirely. A miracle he attributes
entirely to my brother and his ability to see the core beauty
within others.

It makes me want to puke too.

The food he buys me is all wrong – an irreverent mish-mash of rajasic, satvic and tamasic foodstuffs. Dr Malik would have a fit. Yet I haven't put Sébastien right. It's tasty stuff, plus I haven't seen my life coach in a while. Let's say I've parked the Ayurveda for a bit. Sometimes it's extremely therapeutic to live life by the seat of your Agent Provocateurs.

Sébastien picks up a large pair of knickers – comfortable ones, the type you wear when you're having a period. Brushing out the creases, he places them neatly over a radiator.

I wish he'd hurry up.

Before he gatecrashed, this was the grand plan – take a few Zopiclone and go back to bed until Friday, because apart from Norm's funeral, I've nothing else on.

'How about we all go out for dinner tonight? You, me and Michael?' suggests Sébastien.

'No,' I say. 'How is my brother?'

He holds eight fingertips to his chest. 'Busy and fulfilled.'

I hope he's talking about Michael's career, which is certainly on the up. So far he's appeared in an ad for a sunflower spread, and a corporate video for a chain of gyms. In both he played a guy on a treadmill. He's not worried about getting typecast, though – not now he has a day booked working as an extra on the *Coronation Street* Christmas special.

My dad is beside himself.

Sébastien sits on the edge of my mattress.

'Any thoughts about going back to work?'

'Nope.' I decide to roll a fresh joint for when he's gone. Marijuana sprinkles into a cigarette paper like fresh thyme leaves into a hotpot. 'Financially I am tickety-boo.'

And I am.

I'm on a retainer from the *Daily News*. I didn't want to be, but their lawyers were insistent. This way I get paid a basic monthly salary and as a consequence am the legal property of the Daily News Corporation. It is illegal for me to go elsewhere with any future exposés, thoughts, reflections. I am the intellectual, physical and spiritual property of Toby Callaghan, a man I have never met.

I don't have the energy to dissent.

'Well, if there's anything I can do.' Sébastien gets up and collects tea towels, to take home and wash, I assume.

'Actually,' I point a roach at him and smile, 'do you have a car?'

Anatomy fact: yes, Sébastien has grown-up hands, but they're action-figure-sized. Plastic-looking too, like he's had them Botoxed (along with everything above the clavicle). The chances of him being able to operate man-sized machinery are remote.

'I do,' he nods.

'Really?' I squeak.

'It's a truck.'

Hysterical. 'Like Action Man's?'

'No. A Ford F-Series twelfth generation. Would you like to borrow it?'

'I'm kind of in-between licences at the moment. I could do with a lift, though, Seb.'

I've never called him Seb before. His smile is absurdly wide. 'Now?'

'Friday.'

'OK.'

'Wear black. We're going to a wake.'

He's halfway to the door when I call after him. 'Why are you doing all this for me?'

Sébastien's shoulders slump. He turns and looks at me as if I'm adorable. 'Michael's worried about you. He thinks you're depressed.'

'He's frightened I'll top myself, like Mum.'

'Yes.'

'Well I won't.'

And that is the truth.

Most of my days and all of my Zopiclone nights are absolutely bearable. Plus killing myself would defeat every objective I've ever held dear – nobody palm-claps a suicide victim. And I'm an atheist – give me the name of one atheist who *wants* to die. Because even in the *remote* case that there's a higher being and He/She is, say, a scientist, and we're one of many planets upon which He/She carries out empirical observations, He/She is hardly going to have the time to create an even more pretend reality for when we croak – a thanks-for-everything reality, a recompense-for-the-shittiness-of-laboratory-life reality.

'Good,' says Sébastien. 'But Michael can't be here for you as much as he used to be, so I will.'

'Why will you?'

'Because I *love* him, silly.'

I laugh loudly, because he's wrong. *I'm* the one who loves Michael.

He mistakes my scorn for delight. 'Which puts you and me on exactly the same team.' Now he examines his knees, swallows hard and says, as if he's been practising really hard: 'I *really* love him, Flo.'

The joint was supposed to be for later. I whip it between my lips and hold an ashtray under my chin. 'Well just don't get married, do you hear me?'

Like we're the tightest of pals, he makes a solemn promise. 'Cross my heart.'

'Adopt one of those dogs you can keep in your pocket or something.' Without taking my eyes off him, I light my joint. 'Friday, nine a.m. Don't be late.'

The Beginning

Cremation fact: up until 1966, the Catholic Church was opposed to incineration after death. Incineration *prior* to death was OK – as long as you were a witch or guilty of heresy. After death, however: that was considered irrational. God would have no body to resurrect in the afterlife.

Protestants, on the other hand, were more trusting of Our Lord's preternatural abilities, their rationale being: 'He can resurrect a bowl of ashes just as conveniently as he can resurrect a bowl of dust.' And so the Prods plumped for the burning, vaporisation and oxidation route.

A bizarre thing: I wasn't born before 1966, yet I have genetically inherited an antiquated Roman Catholic belief. That cremation is *really* wrong. Not for the dead person, but for those forced to bear witness.

Look now. I attend the funeral of someone I barely knew. Still I'm inclined to fling open the purple curtains, hug the coffin and roar, *Nooooooo!* It's an insanely barbaric ritual. I hold myself together, however. Remember the reasons I'm here – to listen, one final time, to Norm's signature story:

An incredibly brave prisoner of war . . . escaped Fritz . . . bullet in head . . . joined French Resistance . . . lived in coffin . . . fell in love with beautiful foreigner . . .

I nod at the ceiling – to show Norm's spirit that it *is* a bloody good yarn.

The vicar finishes his speech by mentioning the loss of Norman's wife in 1993, though he says, categorically, that we must not be sad; for now they will be reunited in the kingdom of heaven in everlasting peace, for ever and ever, Amen.

It would be wrong to put my hand up and ask how he knows this for sure.

Then the service is over. Zanna, Sébastien and I solemnly join the procession from the chapel, accompanied by Bette Midler's 'Wind Beneath My Wings', which is lyrically powerful shit.

And as we pass the closed curtains, heads bowed, I know one thing for certain: only one person chose the soundtrack to his death – the one woman who would never have the soundtrack to his life. Zanna chose this, the suzerain of all funeral ballads, for Norm.

Outside in the concrete courtyard, I watch her standing lost, like a thousand-year-old toddler. She digs at her coat pocket, pulls free a hankie; guests jostle past her, keen to inspect a splattering of budget wreaths.

The crematorium's gardens, I notice, are surprisingly vibrant – given that winter approaches, given that the soil is ninety per cent skeleton. Blindly I gaze at flower beds, their dirt dusted white – the exact same colour of ghosts – and think about Norm.

This is what I conclude:

What a soul-destroying waste. His irreversibly broken heart, I mean. A waste because the bond between humans is little more than a cruel trick. Norm's love for his wife was not super-romantic; it was an extraordinarily efficacious propagationary tool. Just like the love a mother feels for her offspring. You simply have to look at other species – yes, motherly love manifests itself in disparate ways, but it has exactly the same function. The survival of the young.

Look at octopuses.

The females protect their eggs so devotedly, they refuse even to hunt. If they become hungry, they eat their own arms. Shortly after her offspring hatch, the mother will die emaciated, limbless, but happy, job done.

Look at Bambi.

Perhaps she disappeared for our sake – mine and Michael's. The survival of her young.

I rub my shoulder tenderly with a finger.

Look at Gran, another first-rate example of maternal devotion. Uncle Fergus was a terrible son. Reliable as summer snow, he flitted in and out of her life, borrowed money, never paid it back, slept with people's wives, kissed small girls, forgot his mother's birthday, failed even to turn up at her deathbed or funeral. Yet in life, she refused to hear a word against her youngest son.

Uncle Fergus.

When did I see him last?

The day he locked his lips against mine, pillaging my kissing virginity. Maybe a couple of fleeting times after, although never on my own.

Then, zip.

'Sébastien!' I'm suddenly shouting. 'Take me home.' Because my synapses have finally fired into action, and something feels very off beam.

Uncle Fergus has been trying to whisper stuff to me all day. There's a present in his car, but it's our secret. I don't know why. It's Granny's birthday, not mine. I don't even want one. Not because I wouldn't like a present – I am six – but because he's the huggy type who holds on for too long and puts his hands too close to uncomfortable places.

So I hang around Mum, but she's putting snacks into the oven and taking other snacks out, so she shoos me off like a naughty puppy. In the end I go to my bedroom to play with my Twirly Curls Barbie.

My Twirly Curls Barbie is not a normal blonde one. It's

the Hispanic type. Auntie Carina Campanella sent it from Monte San Savino in Italy. That's my mum's sister, who I've never met but who loves me very much. This is because Auntie Carina knows Mummy inside out, so knows me inside out too.

Hispanic Twirly Curls Barbie is my total twin, according to Auntie Carina Campanella.

She's not.

She's the total twin of Isabella Purdy-Valentine, who is the most prettiest girl in my whole school. It's so unfair. Her teeth line up. Mine are growing in all the wrong directions. And I have gaps. I don't care what anyone says, gaps are not lucky. I've not had one boyfriend ever.

I do, though, more than anything, wish I had a slinky pink dress like Hispanic Twirly Curls Barbie. It ties up around her neck. But I don't have the figure and Mum would never let me wear it even if I was *twelve*. Unlike Isabella Purdy-Valentine's mum, who gave her daughter a film star's name. I was named after a town, which is *concrete*.

I jump a mile when Uncle Fergus catches me hiding cross-legged in the gap between my bed and the wall, having a grumble with my doll.

I look up at him, guilty.

My dad's brother is tall and podgy. Without asking, he squeezes on to the floor next to me. The bed moves backwards, making a noise like a squealing pig.

It's very squashed and I want to get out. But Uncle Fergus's fat knees are up by his chin, and he blocks me in. He's also got that present, and he presses it into my lap.

'I popped back to the Capri to get it.'

It's not Christmas but it's wrapped in reindeer paper. I'm a little bit excited and it turns out to be a brilliant present. A vanity case just like Mum's, only not beige. My one's pink, and it has a plastic comb (rounded teeth), a mirror with a plastic handle (pretend glass) and a plastic perfume bottle (empty but with a hole for *actual* perfume).

As soon as I can get out of this gap, I'm going to borrow Mum's Charlie. Pour it into my pink plastic bottle, then water it down a bit so it looks properly full up.

'This is our secret,' Uncle Fergus is saying, looking at the ends of my hair like they're pretty. I flinch, which is an accident, but Uncle Fergus doesn't take it to heart.

'I didn't get your little brother anything.'

I wave a never-mind hand, because all I can think about is scarpering — up and out and away.

'Hey, you were here first, why shouldn't your uncle treat you now and then?'

For what happens next, I do take some blame, because I like that present, but I *so* want him to go. Plus I've already flinched once, which isn't godly or grateful.

I say exactly what I hope he wants to hear.

'My lips are sealed.'

'Good. We don't want to upset your mummy or daddy.'

'Should I hide it?' I ask maturely.

'Absolutely, babe. They won't approve. We both know who their favourite is.'

I frown. That is not a nice thing to say. *I* think it sometimes, but for an adult to say it out loud sort of makes it official. In fact I feel so hard done by, I want to slap his old, saggy face, which is suddenly too close — I can smell his moustache; it's smoky like cigarettes.

'Go on, give old Uncle Fergus a thank-you kiss.'

He taps the vanity case in my lap and pushes a fat cheek at my lips.

As fast as I can, I peck it. But he's *supersonic* fast, swinging around, planting a smacker straight on my mouth.

'Fergus?' Suddenly I hear my dad — he sort of screeches it and it's very relieving.

Grabbing the vanity case, I swivel round, prise myself free of the gap, hop on to the bed.

Dad's standing in the doorway, and straight away I can tell from his face that one of us is in a lot of trouble. I don't even bother trying to hide the present.

Oldest child fact: you never get a break.

Guiltily, I hold the vanity case out to him.

Front door barely shut behind me, I use a forearm to sweep papers, ready-meal cartons and back editions of *New Scientist* from my table. Then I fling open my laptop. It takes a while to whirr into action. I haven't used it much recently. Not for work purposes, anyway – private investigation is impossible when you have one of the most recognisable faces on the planet.

I retrieve a half-smoked joint from the ashtray.

Google eventually arrives, enabling me to log on to one of the most extensive and powerful personal databases in the United Kingdom: my illegally acquired credit company subscription.

It's criminal really, using this resource. *Really* criminal.

Immoral advice for the budding PI: when wangling yourself a subscription with a credit agency, you must do two things.

First, get on the Data Protection Register. (Piece of piss – visit website, fill out form, send cheque, job done.)

Second, tell the credit agency some lies. Use mine if you like.

Yes, hi there, I'm an employee verification specialist employed by private and public companies to carry out human resource functions on their behalf . . .

Yes, they outsource to me . . .

My main function? To carry out pre-employment screening . . .

Naturally I adhere strictly to British vetting standards . . .

Yes, regularly audited . . .

BS 7858:2006, BS 7499, BS 8507–1:2008 and BS 8470:2006 . . .

The last British Standard ensures the secure shredding of sensitive data. You've not heard of it? Ah well, you need to be on top of the DP legislation in my game . . .

Yes, I am officially on the Data Protection Register . . .

My Data Protection Number? Of course, it's . . .

Bingo.

I type in 'Fergus Love'. Link him with my Gran, 'Martha Love'.

Usually lists galore pop up – financial details, addresses, telephone numbers, aliases, associates, directorships, a delectable menu of the most confidential data – but not for Uncle Fergus.

According to these records, Fergus lived with my gran in Plymouth until he was twenty-five, then in a few bachelor pads. Thereafter, he flitted free of the radar, became Lord-Lucan-enigmatic.

Just like with my mum's entry, the last year of any significant banking or official activity was 1988.

I push the laptop away.

The sensation I feel is akin to being hit in the pectoral girdle with a coal shovel. And it solicits a curious reaction. I laugh. Not a normal laugh, or any laugh I've ever done before. I'm not even sure there's any scientific purpose to my ability to make this noise; I'm probably the only human capable of it. Freud, I imagine, would say its peculiarities mirror an insufferable disharmony of emotions. Whatever, the truth swells in front of my eyes until it's as manifest as the sky.

I don't investigate the exact date in 1988 on which Uncle Fergus disappeared. Deep down, I know already.

The business card is beneath my bedside crate. *Noah Steensen.* I've scribbled his number next to it.

It rings just once before he picks up.

'Noah? Florence Love. What do you know about the stiff in Mum's car?'

His voice is as tortured and Scottish as ever. 'I'm fine, thanks for asking.'

'The dead man?' I demand.

'It wasn't my dad.'

'I got that bit. Just tell me who it was.'

Cars hooting, loud talking, an ambulance – Noah's not indoors, yet he speaks precisely, gravely, as though he has all the time in the world, and he intends on using every last second of it.

'They said a business deal had gone wrong, that dangerous men were after my father. That's why they said it was him in the car. We fled overnight. I don't know who the dead guy really was.'

'The Jock accent?' I demand.

'Inverness.' He gives this information gingerly, as though he's not sure he can trust me yet. 'We lived there for a long time.'

'Why was your dad so scared?'

'That's not information you give your kids. They'd throw us a bone now and then.'

Just like my dad did.

'My dad was a venture capitalist. You know what kids are like – we decided he owed a lot of money to the Triads or the Russian mafia. That if he didn't pay up, he'd be counting worms. Dad had no choice. He had to pretend he'd topped himself. Hence our new secret life north of the border.'

'You've had twenty-five years to tell me this, Noah. Why were you following me around? Why now?'

'They're gone,' he says brusquely.

'Who've gone?'

'Mum and Dad.'

I knew about his dad, but his mum too? I gasp. 'Were they murdered?'

'Just dead. My sister, Hannah, she's married and abroad.'

I bow my head. 'I'm so sorry for your loss.'

Noah ignores me. 'Leaving me free to delve all I want. Nothing can hurt them now.'

'But why not just knock on my door—'

He cuts in. 'I *had* to be sure about you, that I could trust you. I have a wife, a bairn; somebody may want revenge. All I know is there was a corpse in a car and my parents were implicated. I could be in the firing line too.'

'You're not,' I tell him firmly.

'My family have been hiding for *twenty years*,' he reminds me.

'You're safe.'

'How do you know?'

'Because the man in the car was my uncle, Noah. His name was Fergus Love.'

Silence.

I check my handset: I've not lost connection. Noah's still there.

Empathy is ideal in these situations, so I take my tone down an octave.

'Noah, did you know him?'

'He was a friend of Mum's.'

I jump to conclusions. 'She was an air hostess or an under-wear model, right?'

'No, it was nothing like that.'

'Obviously you didn't know Fergus very well.' I disparage his mother. I don't deserve to be privy to the next snippet of information.

'No, Florence, but my little sister knew him intimately.'

'Oh no,' I say feebly. Tetris-like, facts fall into place. 'Where are you now?'

334

'Not far.'

'How far?'

'Just arriving.'

I sidestep to the window. Instinctively look at the rooftop opposite – of course there's no one there, so I lean gingerly out of the window and peer down.

Noah issues a weighty salute up at me. His stride is long and urgent; beside him he pushes his Triumph Scrambler.

'You *are* a stalker.'

'And so she starts . . .' He doesn't have to shout back; his rumbling bass glides through seven storeys of air.

'Oh my God, you so are.'

'From the crazy lady.'

'From the bloody bona fide stalker.' I bang the sill with an open palm, then hang over the edge, watch him below.

Throwing a boot at his bike's side-stand, he peers up at me, nudging his chin back as far as it will go. Legs astride; a royal-blue jumper tied around his neck – it flaps behind him like a superhero's cape.

'You were much happier as a child,' I shout down at him.

'You fuckin' weren't,' he replies.

I sit on the windowsill, my arms tightly crossed.

'Uncle Fergus kissed me on the mouth when I was six.' I say it flippantly, because a bit of me still feels responsible. It was creepy and wrong, yes, but I really liked that vanity case. I don't deserve Noah's pity.

He doesn't proffer any. 'Sounds like you got off lightly.'

'Why?' I ask this too eagerly. 'Did he do something to you?'

His frown is quickly bottomless. 'What the fuck do you want to know for?'

'I don't.' I squirm. 'I was just asking.'

But I *do* want to know – I'm ready to know everything. Noah tells me far too much:

335

'I think your concern should be what he did to Michael.'

Horror fucks with my sense of balance. My head becomes heavy as a bag of ballast – it threatens to topple me backwards out of my open window into a seven-story free-fall. I stab a hand in front of me. Steady myself on the curtain. Yank it free of its tracks.

'Michael was three,' I mutter.

'And before that he was two, and one. I guess we'll never know.' Noah folds his arms, puts a line under the matter.

But I can't.

I won't.

I think back. When I asked Michael if he remembered Uncle Fergus, he said he did, but only vaguely. Was it Fergus who sent my brother's brain slightly off-piste?

Hindsight fact: if they hadn't have killed Fergus, I sure as fuck would have.

I don't need to be shouting quite this loudly, but suddenly I'm emphatic. 'Did they knock him off? Our parents?'

Noah Steensen sort of smiles as something clicks for him; and at long last I recognise him.

Of course, I've known him for ever.

The boy in the *Miami Vice* jacket.

Suddenly excited, like I'm attending a school reunion, I build a scene . . .

'They went their separate ways, that's obvious. Your dad, my mum, they were the sacrificial lambs. But how, *how* did they do it? The murder, I mean. Fuck, because it *was* murder. Our parents *murdered* Fergus. To cover their tracks they made it look like your dad had gassed himself in the car. Maybe your dad had to disappear anyway, for business reasons.'

'What about the police, identification of the body?' Noah holds his fringe away from his face, stares at me unblinkingly. 'One of them identified the body. Who was his next of kin?'

'No, he wouldn't have.' I say it feebly, because I have firm proof – my dad is a big fat liar.

For a while we gawp blindly at one another, eyes locked yet unseeing, comfortable as old friends.

Then I ask the gazillion-dollar question – because Noah's opinion is the only one that now counts.

Yes, I am ready. Today I am ready for truths.

'Do you think my mum killed herself?' I half shout.

I'm unsure whether he's humouring me, but I'm wholly grateful for what he says next.

'Your mum's Spanish, right?'

'Italian.'

He uncrosses his arms, pats his thighs slowly, as if it's all falling into place. 'The Eyeties love a bit of self-sacrifice. One thing I know for sure about the Papes – suicide is a *big* no-no.'

'It's totally banned.' I nod fast. 'God says we are his property and life is a gift so to destroy it is to assert dominion over what is God's and that's really disrespectful.'

'But you like a bit of contrition, eh?'

'We love it.'

'Know what I'd do if I was a paid-up member of your gang?'

'What?' I ask greedily. I know the answer already.

'I'd starve myself, do that penance shite, whip myself, go to confession – all that Catholic stuff.'

'Me too,' I tell him back.

'Know where I'd do it?'

'Where?' Tell me, tell me, even though it's plain as day.

'I'd get as close to the Big Boss as possible, so he sees how sorry I am.'

'And the Big Boss isn't silly.' I point at the sky, at my just and practically minded God. 'He knows there's no cure for paedophilia.'

'Best to cull them.'

'Just as long as you do it quietly, then repent a lot after.'

'Aye.' He bangs the table on which he sits and his blue jumper cape faints, falling to the ground like a Victorian lady.

'How's marriage?' I suddenly ask, politely.

'It's been the making of me.' His nod is sincere.

He's too taupe for me, so I don't feel remotely aggrieved that he's moved on romantically.

'All right for some,' I smile. 'What is it you actually do?'

'A courier,' he nods. 'Moved to London last June.'

'Definitely not a stalker, then?'

The man has anger-management issues. His eyes taper.

'No, no, it's just you look like one,' I tell him encouragingly. 'And you totally sound like one.'

He examines his cuticles. 'In a good way?'

'In an alpha-male way.' I examine his cuticles too. Perfect half-moons. I like that in a man. Half-moon cuticles.

'I'm picking up Gaby from work this afternoon.' He's suddenly telling me about his domestic arrangements and heading towards the door. 'We'll talk again.'

'Yes, yes, of course.'

'Two heads and all that . . .'

But I'm ignoring him already, because repeatedly, triumphantly I need to bang my windowsill hard. Grit becomes embedded in my palm, the mortification of flesh being a sign that I have discovered the truth. Bambi knew everything there is to know about murder – she watched all the programmes. Was she complicit in planning the perfect one, killing a paedophile then returning home to repent in the sight of the successor of St Peter, in front of the Holy See?

The door is barely closed behind Noah when I start searching litter-laden surfaces for my phone. It's low on juice. Quickly I press *Phone*, *Favourites*, *Dad*.

Come on, come on, I hurry him along.

'Hello, George speaking.' I don't take it personally: he always answers like that – he can't see his phone.

'You lied,' I tell him triumphantly.

'About what?'

'You know what.'

'Not again. Come on, child, how many more times.' But he's less mulish than usual. Reticent and uncomfortable, yes, but a smidge interested. Then again, he now knows what I do here in London – what I *did*. My capabilities must have dawned on him; given the information I can discover, our family secrets are suddenly on rocky ground.

My soliloquy starts off extremely measured.

'Bambi needed to disappear, quickly. I'm right, aren't I? Because she would *never* kill herself – she may have had issues, but she was strong. I saw it. Even when she was low, she had mechanisms just like other normal people do. Like *me*, because I'm a real person too, by the way – which is big shit for dads, I get it, but you're going to have to accept it one day. So fuck it, how about today? Dad, I am as valid an individual as you!'

If he tells me off for swearing, I don't hear it. I'm too outraged.

'Years and years of this bull. I'm thirty-three, *thirty-three*. That's an excellent age to be allowed truths. Categorically I can cope with it. So here's the new deal: you *will not* let me feel like I'm mad or clutching at straws any more, not if there's a smidge of truth in what I feel *here*.' He can't see me, but I pat my gut hard. 'Not if you love me, properly love me. Do you actually love me?'

Apart from an electric purr, the telephone line is silent. Most likely he's collapsed into a cheerless heap. Or had a heart attack. At the very least, his stress-blinks will be breakneck.

However, when finally he speaks, I'm taken aback.

He's stopped sounding seventy years old and tired. I barely recognise his new tone. My father has acquired the determined throat-polyp growl of a freedom fighter.

'Florence. Listen to me very carefully indeed. You're dabbling in events that are extremely dangerous. You must *not* get involved.' The gravitas in his new voice unnerves me – he speaks to me as if I'm an equal, and it's totally disconcerting. 'Do not look for her. I cannot help you or talk to you about this again.'

I look at my phone, at a picture of my dad grinning inanely back at me. 'She is actually alive?' I whisper at his photo.

I hear him reiterate his earlier point.

'Do not look for her. I cannot help you or talk to you about it.'

Instinctively I fall into a sitting position on the kitchenette floor. Cross-legged on vinyl, impotent as a toddler, I experience something I can only describe as a possession. The clunk of Bambi arriving back in my life leaves my heart winded; the whole building sways beneath my bottom. I think I might fall off the floor.

'Florence!'

I put the phone back to my ear.

'Where is she?' he demands.

I say it a bit blindly:

'It's best to confess our sins to those to whom the dispensation of God's mysteries is entrusted before the saints, but only if you're Catholic – Basil the Great said that.'

'Florence, cut the baloney. Do you know where she is?'

I take quite a breath.

'Daddy, I think she's in Italy, with God.'

My name is Florence Love and I became a private investigator for all the right reasons.

I am extraordinarily nosy. On paper, it sounds super-glamorous. When I tell people, they beam and do that fast palm-clap – and I do too, because being enthralling never wears thin. Particularly I find their facial expression a joy. For one uninhibited, bullshit-free moment, they want to be me.

Yet I don't tell Tarik Mohammad Amazigh any of this.

PI fact: keep your identity closely under wraps. Clients can be a lot left of hinged. I for one don't want them adding me to their Christmas card list.

Simply tell them what they want to hear:

Re: My freind missing
Friday 26/9/14 18.38 p.m.
From: info@londonpiservices.uk.net
To: tarikma68@yahoo.co.uk

Dear Tarik,
    Your friend is in Italy. This is a region I know well. From antiquity to modern day, Italy is synonymous with art, music, fashion and iconic food.
    Let's meet to discuss your requirements. Please note, we have a 98% success rate at finding missing people and can assure you of our strictest moral codes and highest standards of professionalism with clients and targets alike.
    Yours sincerely
    The London PI Services Team

Other things I don't tell him: mnemonic rule of thumb – 'i' before 'e' except after 'c'.

My mobile phone rings, but it's not Dad. Our conversation ended abruptly. I wanted to tell him what I knew, what

I'd discovered, but he forbade it. *You're mistaken,* he kept telling me, whilst refusing to elucidate how exactly. I liked his new voice, though. For the first time ever, I understood something: murdering your brother has repercussions. Nobody wants to admit that to their progeny, however deserved the execution may have been.

From here on in, I will leave my dad be.

The phone call is from Michael.

My baby brother.

The sadness I feel seeing his name is immediate and excruciating – I can only guess what a blood relative may or may not have done to his little body and brain. Thankfully when I answer the phone Michael sounds like he's ingested helium. His joy appeases my guilt for not protecting him well enough when he was three.

'Guess what?' he squeaks.

'You're going to be the next James Bond.'

'No.'

'You've bought a chihuahua.'

'No.'

'Give up.' I smile.

'I've proposed!'

'To who?'

'Sébastien, silly.'

It comes out as a roar: 'Why?'

'And guess what he said?'

'Given the fact you sound like you've inhaled a balloon?'

'He said yes! We've set a date and everything.'

'Oh no, Michael, I'm not sure I'm going to be able to make that day.'

'You don't know when it is yet.'

'When is it?'

'June the sixth!'

'Oh crap. Yep, I'm busy.'

And now for the speech. The one my father never gave me. The one at which I would have laughed heartily, asked him what the hell he knew about love, then flounced away self-importantly.

'You do know marriage is seriously overrated, Michael? If I were you, I'd keep the spark that legal agreements destroy in a matter of days. Yes, *days*. I mean, what is marriage really?'

Michael sees this as a lovely test. 'It's a very serious commitment, Flo.'

'It's a piece of paper. A piece of paper that makes it awkward when you want to go your separate ways – which you will one day. Oh, I know that doesn't feel possible now, but time is a cruel magician. And I wouldn't be your sister if I didn't present you with all sides of the argument.'

'I'll need a certain *someone* to walk me down the aisle,' he sings.

'A sister who has been there doggedly for the whole of your *entire* existence. A sister who may have failed you – through no fault of her own – but who has nonetheless taken her role as protector and pedagogue very seriously indeed.'

'I know. You are fab. Isn't she fab, Seb?'

Christ, he's there. Of course he's there.

'Then you won't mind me telling you that marriage is the fucking kiss of death. I cannot give you my blessing. In fact you will marry that man over my dead body, do you hear me? I forbid it. So I'm very sorry and all that, but the wedding is off.'

'You're not really busy on the sixth, are you?' he says, as if I'm the funniest thing. Sébastien giggles in the background too.

Watch the delicate changes in the contours of my face. The contraction of the buccinator muscle, the modiolus and the occipitofrontalis.

343

I have lost him.

'Trouble is, Michael, I'm thinking of going away for a while.'

'Where?'

Very important note on forethought: when you feel alone – so agonisingly alone you might as well observe your own autopsy – never speak. Speaking is a selfish biological mechanism undertaken simply to make you feel better. In my defence, sadness often wrings the brain free of logic.

Bollocks.

There is no defence for what I say next.

'It's Mum. I'm not a hundred per cent sure on the minutiae, but chances are she's living a secret life in Rome, so I'm going to check it out. Plus I've got a job over there – a Haji friend of mine, his pal's gone and joined the Mafia. Thought I'd kill two birds.'

The silence lasts for some time. It's only temporary, however. My darling Michael works up to a wail; I hear it evolving in his head.

My phone dies, leaving me to point weakly at fresh air. 'You have Sébastien now.'

I will not cry, no way. But my bastard nostrils let the side down, with viscous snot-tears. Roughly I rub my nose with the back of my hand, throw the phone aside, snatch at the computer.

Do not look for her. I cannot help you or talk to you about it.

No worries, Pater, I'll sort it myself, because if ever a statement could tease a private eye out of retirement, that's the one.

First things first. I book a one-way ticket to Leonardo da Vinci International Airport.

Entrapment 101 Tip #8: If your cover gets blown, diversify

Remember your PI website, that extensive list of specialities: paternity tests, lie detection, child recovery, corporate espionage, bounty-hunting. None of them is as satisfying as nailing a Lothario, but let's talk turkey: it's inestimably better than, say, working in a post office.

Further reading material:

Child Recovery 101

Bounty Hunting 101

Bigamy and Polygamy 101

Serial Killers 101

Finding Bambi 101 (available for pre-order)

Final advice – possibly the most important you'll be given:

1. Try never to kill anyone deliberately.

2. See *every* case through to the end, however far from your comfort zone it takes you.

3. Whatever it is you decide to do, be bloody brilliant at it.

ACKNOWLEDGEMENTS

Now and then you meet someone whose faith and generosity changes the direction of your life – my sincerest thanks go to Toby Litt, who read and re-read and edited and nagged and refused to let Florence Love remain a pipe dream.

To the gorgeous Jo Unwin – the best agent in the business (*total* fact) – and to my publisher Mari Evans and her lovely team at Headline – their guidance and vision have been right on the money.

My workshop buddies, *Friday Night Writes*, you know who you are – *do not* read this book with a red pen in your hand; a glass of wine, however, is obligatory. You too, Julia Bell – an extraordinary teacher and mentor.

Tom Bilsborough – your support has been unfailing and I'm forever grateful.

Lastly, to my family. Thank you. All of you.

So what happens next?

Read on for an exclusive preview of
Florence's next exploit

(Total fact: it'd be rude not to . . .)

The End

The gun in my mouth belongs to Father Massimo Satori. Its barrel reflects the amber and gold of a stained glass window to my left; I strain my eyes towards it. The Fourth Station of the Cross — Jesus heaving his crucifix to Golgotha and encountering his Blessed Mother, Mary. Me dying beneath this particular one is God's little joke.

The ache in my jaw is excruciating — it leaks into my eyeballs and down into my shoulder blades. Plus Father Massimo keeps digging the piece at my tonsils and it's making me gag. That and the saccharine smell of incense.

Sage advice: never puke on an assassin's gun, it irritates them no end.

I've no option but to enlist Transcendental Meditation.

An excellent mechanism in stressful situations, skilled practitioners can efficiently hop into their happy place at will. I could tell you how to do it but that's bad form, spiritually. You have to have been trained by a resurrected yogi. Plus I'm hopeless at alternative therapies — about to be murdered and I fail to remember my mantra.

Instead I attempt deep-breathing. In through the nose, out through the nose. The air is 100 degrees, I might as well inhale a hairdryer.

The blood drains from my face. It was only a matter of time. My old foe arrives; Panic is her name, and the bitch jabs a bony elbow at my adrenal glands.

Basic field survival techniques – I remember some of them . . .

When confronted with a life-threatening situation present an appeasing stance . . .

I am cross-legged in a pool of my own piss. Check.

Maintain thoroughly friendly eye contact throughout . . .

This is tricky. My mouth is full of Colt 45. The gun's cylinder obscures his face. Desperately I tilt my head to the left, show him my eyes, make them wide, beseech that he examine my irises. Because irises are a precise indicator of character, and mine contain densely packed crypts: people with densely packed crypts talk far too much, but they're loyal and valiant.

But Father Massimo's not your usual priest. He's uninterested in whether or not I have a nice personality.

Honour your enemy's personal space . . .

Panic reminds me that, once upon a time, this priest's workmates gave him an unambiguous nickname. The Eradicator, they called him, with no affection whatsoever.

I lose complete control of the situation.

Whipping my head away from the gun, I shuffle frantically backwards, my bare heels scraping angrily at the flagstones. I gasp at hot oxygen, a final treat before my goodnight slug in the head. Because it is coming, oh boy, it's coming. Eyes squeezed shut, I wait for wrap-up.

Total fact: I knew this would happen one day. Death, I mean.

Aged eight, I discovered I was mortal. The hush of night. Listening to the heartbeat in my temples, an ancient clock clunking in the hall downstairs – my chest, its chest, producing an interminable beat that marched me in one dreadful direction. Death. The night frights didn't give an arse that I was too immature for the subject matter – they still laid the gaff:

Florence Love, you are not special. You will die. Nobody

avoids it. Not even Jesus who is *actually* God avoided it. Expiration is a devastating blip in the big guy's masterpiece.

Eight is too young to have a light bulb moment about death. I've wasted too much life anticipating it.

Father Massimo cocks the trigger. I hear it clicking. Two metal snaps, quick as an old clock dying. Yet it seems to last an hour or so.

To be fair, I had suspected my death would be sooner than most. What I'd not anticipated was the abject disappointment. The anticlimax of expiration. The appalling realisation that I, Florence Love, didn't have a big enough role.

That awful possibility had never crossed my mind.

The bullet itself takes a day or two to arrive. Its journey is so long and so silent, I begin to wonder if I have actually passed over. Eventually I allow one eye to relax into the smallest slit.

Father Massimo's head is tilted to the left. He studies me from behind the gun then, quite suddenly, loses the will to kill. I watch him clean the gun's nozzle on his cassock. Polish my bile from its tip.

'It's blasphemous getting killed in a church,' I mumble, in case he speaks English. Then firmly, 'I'm not ready to die. I'm only twenty-nine.'

In truth I'm thirty-three, but that is none of his business. Things I still have to do . . .

Write a book, star in the film of my life, have an Indian head massage, swim with dolphins, come to a definitive conclusion about an awful lot of things.

I certainly cannot die before finding my mum.

'Chiudi quel cazzo di bocca.' The priest suggests I put a cork in it.

Secretly I give him The Death Stare even though you can't actually give it in secret – it's too powerful a weapon. And by God I wish I hadn't started it. I clock his irises – they are alive, every shade of black squirming within.

This is a very bad omen indeed. The genes responsible for the eye's development play a critical role in the formation of the frontal lobe thus providing scientific proof that our eyes are the windows of the soul. Father Massimo has the contraction furrows of a sociopath.

Other things about the priest:

He looks nothing like the photo Rocco gave to me; in that photo the priest is thirty-five with a mop of black hair and a cracking set of teeth. Now he's rising seventy and has let himself go. Marlboro-ecru dentures. Bald as a balloon. He's swapped his Marines' battledress for a cassock, one that smells of yeast infections and communion wine. His long nails are packed firm with filth, very possibly with other people's DNA. And his wrinkles – they're likely to have been etched into his forehead and cheeks with a machete, each furrow a nod to a man's expiration.

He takes a step back. Waves the gun at me. Gesticulates that I'm to sit on the front pew. I stumble to my knees. Pull myself up on to the wooden bench. But the priest becomes agitated once more – urgently he points the gun at my knees.

I look down at them. Back up at him. At the altar ahead.

A life-sized Virgin Mary gazes back, her blue stone head confusedly cocked . . .

You were brought up a Catholic, my child. You know the rules.

'Si, si!' I understand.

Standing back up, I drop on to a knee with gravitas. Then I cross myself solemnly. I mean it more than I've ever meant a genuflection before.

Catholic etiquette:

Never sit in a church's pew without genuflecting. Do not enter a church without genuflecting. When in a church, genuflect as often as you might check your mirrors when taking your driving test, just to be on the safe side. Overkill is impossible when it comes to adoring God.

Father Massimo nods, satisfied, does his own lacklustre sign of the cross, then sits too close to me.

Our hips touch.

Silently we stare at the stained glass ahead.

I'm very bad with silences. I was born with the need to fill them. Sincerely I wish I wasn't, because within minutes I'm nodding up at a stained glass window and explaining, in pigeon English, the Fourth Station of the Cross to a man of the cloth.

'Jesus – he on way to get crucified. The people spit and shout. They are angry and hate him. He feels sad. He looks for his mother. She can't stop his pain. She can't do a thing to save Jesus. But just to *see* her – he knows she understands, that she cares. He's not alone – that helps Jesus a very lot.'

Father Massimo thinks I'm insane, I can tell.

I address the Mother Mary instead. A more sympathetic counsellor, her wet marble eyes don't bother with my face; they scrutinise the cartilaginous pockets and folds of my soul.

I tell Her quietly, 'I'm looking for my Mum too.'

For the smallest second, I think I've been rescued, because I hear an educated man. His Italo-American accent is exquisite; its cadence, hypnotic and wise.

'When people disappear,' the priest says, 'it is better they stay that way.'

Quickly I turn to face him. He is a snarl of pockmarks, scars and furrows, yet I hold his stare. 'Father, it is not.'

'Sometimes it is,' he grumbles.

'She's my mother.'

'So?'

Oedipus issues are extremely bad news in an aggressor. 'She has responsibilities,' I explain empathy to him. 'Not just to me – to her son; to our father.'

'You coming here – that won't help your family. The opposite.'

But I don't understand.

Rocco said this priest would help me. When alluding to the ex-Marine's past, he'd made The Eradicator sound like a benevolent Rambo. A grandfatherly renegade. Henry Fonda in *On Golden Pond*. Most of the cast of *Cocoon*.

I watch the pistol teeter on his bony knee. The Colt 45 was first issued to US Marines in 1986. I shiver: a hundred serrations dint its steel.

'My search for my mother has hit a dead end. I met a guy up north – a friend – he said you could help me.'

He squints. 'What guy?'

'His name is Rocco.'

The gun clatters to the floor. Instantly I yank my legs up and on to the pew. But his pistol doesn't spin in circles and shoot repeatedly at my shins. Neither does Father Massimo stoop to retrieve it.

Open-mouthed, he stares at me.

'Rocco?'

'He said you were a friend of a friend.'

'Rocco, who?'

'Rocco Bellini.'

There's always a small room off the church alter – a holy Green room where priests nap between services. Father Massimo picks up the gun and wanders blindly towards it.

It's my chance to escape.

This is the plan:

Sprint from this pew to the wooden doors of the stone church – it's a distance of twenty-two metres. On a good day I'd do that in four seconds. On a day fuelled by abject terror, I'd knock half a second off. Next, I'll run down the hill path, swinging SSW into bracken and olive trees, dodging a route over boulders and goat shit, I'll sustain a fracture or two, but adrenalin will keep me anaesthetised. When eventually I tumble free into the village below, I'll steal a bike then cycle full-pelt for 800 kilometres, back to Ronchi dei Legionari, back to Rocco bloody Bellini to ask why the fuck he suggested I pay a surprise visit to a sociopath.

I'll have to do all this whilst outrunning a bullet, of course. The one as focused as a cruise missile at my head. Because if there's one thing The Eradicator can do, it's murder a moving target. In 1987, he recorded a kill from a distance of one and a half kilometres using a sniper rifle. The bullet would have taken two seconds to hit. When Rocco told me this story he'd put such a romantic slant on it.

The priest returns from the Green room with a bottle of Fairtrade communion wine. He gulps from its neck, patting his lips with a musty sleeve.

'Tell me about Rocco Bellini,' he says. 'Everything. I want the tiny details. Eye colour, hair, height. Are you his wife?'

'No,' I say sternly, because although Rocco is a genuine keeper – or at least I thought so up until twenty minutes ago – our connection was utterly platonic.

I tell the priest:

'He saved my life. It's the only thing I'm sure of.'

'The beginning. We'll start there.' He sits on the steps to the altar. 'Tell me how Rocco saved your life. Then we can discuss why he sent you to me, to your death.'

And so I talk at length. While blethering I retain a bit-part in this mortal coil. Naturally I keep a peripheral eye on handguns, but mostly I expose the unmitigated truth; give Father Massimo the director's cut, because Rocco doesn't know this priest from Adam. My friend has stitched me up.

My *friend*.

I wouldn't mind, but I've not had too many of them.

To find out more about Florence Love and keep up with her latest news head over to her Facebook page

www.facebook.com/FlorenceLovePI